DATE DUE	
DEC 0 5 '98	OCT 14 '99	
JAN 25 '99	JUL 0 5 '011	
FEB 27 '99	July 19	
MAR 15 '99	for Beth W.	
MAR 30 '99	MAR 2 4 '03	
MAY 10 '99	FEB 1 9 '08	
	MAY 2 6 '08	
JUN 17 '99	JUN 1 7 '08	
JUL 1 2 '99	MAR 63I1	
JAN 2 2 '011	OCT 3 0 2012	

MIDWIVES

Also by Chris Bohjalian

Water Witches
Past the Bleachers
Hangman
A Killing in the Real World

MIDWIVES

A Novel

By

CHRIS BOHJALIAN

Harmony Books
New York

Published by Harmony Books, a division of Crown Publishers, Inc., 201
East 50th Street, New York, New York 10022. Member of the Crown
Publishing Group.

Random House, Inc. New York, Toronto, London, Sydney, Auckland

http://www.randomhouse.com/

Harmony and colophon are trademarks of Crown Publishers, Inc.

Design by June Bennett-Tantillo

Printed in the United States of America

Library of Congress Cataloging-in-Publication Data
Bohjalian, Christopher A.
    Midwives : a novel / by Chris Bohjalian.
       p.   cm.
    I. Title.
PS3552.0495M5   1997
813'.54—dc20   96-22953
                                 CIP

ISBN 0-517-70396-3

10 9 8 7 6 5 4 3 2 1

First Edition

For Victoria,
the woman whose labors have beautified my whole life
And for our little girl,
Grace

In memory of my mother,
Annalee Nelson Bohjalian (1930–1995)

For the Lord will not
cast off for ever:
But though he cause grief,
yet will he have compassion
according to the multitude of his mercies.
For he doth not afflict willingly,
nor grieve the children of men.

LAMENTATIONS 3:31–33

We are each of us responsible for the evil we
may have prevented.

JAMES MARTINEAU

MIDWIVES
PROLOGUE

THROUGHOUT THE LONG SUMMER BEFORE MY MOTHER'S TRIAL BEGAN, AND then during those crisp days in the fall when her life was paraded publicly before the county—her character lynched, her wisdom impugned—I overheard much more than my parents realized, and I understood more than they would have liked.

Through the register in the floor of my bedroom I could listen to the discussions my parents would have with my mother's attorney in the den late at night, after the adults had assumed I'd been sleeping for hours. If the three of them happened to be in the suite off the kitchen my mother used as her office and examining room, perhaps searching for an old document in her records or a patient's prenatal history, I would lie on the bathroom floor above them and listen as their words traveled up to me through the holes that had been cut for the water pipes to the sink. And while I never went so far as to lift the receiver of an upstairs telephone when I heard my mother speaking on the kitchen extension, often I stepped silently down the stairs until I could hear every word that she said. I must have listened to dozens of phone conversations this way—standing completely still on the bottom step, invisible from the kitchen because the phone cord stretched barely six feet—and by the time the trial began, I believe I could have reconstructed almost exactly what the lawyer, friend, or midwife was saying at the other end of the line.

I was always an avid parent watcher, but in those months surrounding the trial I became especially fanatic. I monitored their fights, and noted how the arguments grew nasty fast under pressure; I listened to them apologize, one of them often sobbing, and then I'd wait for the more muffled (but still decipherable) sounds they would make when they would climb into bed and make love. I caught the gist of their debates with doctors and lawyers, I understood why some witnesses would be more damning than others, I learned to hate people I'd never met and whose faces I'd never seen. The state's medical examiner. The state's attorney. An apparently expert midwife from Washington, D.C.

The morning the judge gave the jury its instructions and sent them away to decide my mother's fate, I overheard her attorney explain to my parents what he said was one of the great myths in litigation: You can tell what a jury has decided the moment they reenter the courtroom after their deliberations, by the way they look at the defendant. Or refuse to look at him. But don't believe it, he told them. It's just a myth.

I was fourteen years old that fall, however, and it sounded like more than a myth to me. It had that ring of truth to it that I heard in many wives'—and midwives'—tales, a core of common sense hardened firm by centuries of observation. Babies come when the moon is full. If the boiled potatoes burn, it'll rain before dark. A bushy caterpillar's a sign of a cold winter. Don't ever sugar till the river runs free.

My mother's attorney may not have believed the myth that he shared with my parents, but I sure did. It made sense to me. I had heard much over the past six months. I'd learned well which myths to take to my heart and which ones to discard.

And so when the jury filed into the courtroom, an apostolic procession of twelve, I studied their eyes. I watched to see whether they would look at my mother or whether they would look away. Sitting beside my father in the first row, sitting directly behind my mother and her attorney as I had every day for two weeks, I began to pray to myself, *Please don't look at your shoes, please don't look at the judge. Don't look down or up or out the window. Please, please, look at me, look at my mother. Look at us, look here, look here, look here.*

I'd watched the jurors for days, I'd seen them watch me. I'd counted beards, I'd noted wrinkles, I'd stared beyond reason and courtesy at the way the fellow who would become the foreman had sat with his arms folded across his chest, hiding the hand disfigured years earlier by a chain saw. He had a thumb but no fingers.

They walked in from the room adjacent to their twelve chairs and found their seats. Some of the women crossed their legs at their knees, one of the men rubbed his eyes and rocked his chair back for a brief second on its rear legs. Some scanned the far wall of the courtroom, some looked toward the exit sign above the front door as if they realized their ordeal was almost over and emancipation was at hand.

One, the elderly woman with white hair and a closet full of absolutely beautiful red flowered dresses, the woman who I was sure was a Lipponcott from Craftsbury, looked toward the table behind which the state's attorney and his deputy were sitting.

And that's when I broke down. I tried not to, but I could feel my eyes fill with tears, I could feel my shoulders beginning to quiver. I blinked, but a fourteen-year-old girl's eyelids are no match for the lament I had welling inside me. My cries were quiet at first, the sound of a mournful whisper, but they gathered fury fast. I have been told that I howled.

And while I am not proud of whatever hysteria I succumbed to that day in the courtroom, I am not ashamed of it either. If anyone should feel shame for whatever occurred that moment in a small courthouse in northeastern Vermont, in my mind it is the jury: Amidst my sobs and wails, people have said that I pleaded aloud, "Look at us! Oh, God, please, please look at us!" and still not one of the jurors would even glance in my mother's or my direction.

MIDWIVES
PART ONE

ONE

I USED THE WORD *VULVA* AS A CHILD THE WAY SOME KIDS SAID BUTT OR PENIS or puke. It wasn't a swear exactly, but I knew it had an edge to it that could stop adults cold in their tracks. *Vulva* was one of those words that in every household but ours conveyed emotion and sentiments at the same time that it suggested a simple part of the basic human anatomy for one sex or an act—like vomiting—that was a pretty basic bodily function.

I remember playing one afternoon at Rollie McKenna's, while her mother had a friend of hers visiting from Montpelier. It was one of those rare summer days in Vermont when the sky is so blue it looks almost neon—the sort of blue we get often in January on those days when the temperature won't climb above zero and the smoke from your neighbor's woodstove looks as if it will freeze when it first appears just above the tip of the chimney, but rarely in June or July.

Like Mrs. McKenna, her friend worked for the state education department. As the two adults sat around a wrought-iron table on the McKennas' brick terrace (a terrace that seemed inappropriately elegant to me even then), sipping iced tea with mint leaves from my own mother's garden, I proceeded to tell them about Cynthia Charbonneau's delivery in all the detail I could muster.

"Mrs. Charbonneau's baby was nine pounds, two ounces, but my mom was able to massage the vagina and stretch the muscles so the perineum didn't tear. Most women who have babies that are around nine pounds have to have episiotomies—that's where you cut the perineum from a lady's vagina to her anus—but not Mrs. Charbonneau. Her vulva's fine. And the placenta came right behind Norman—that's what they named the baby—by, like, two minutes. My mom says the placenta was big, too, and it's buried right now by this maple tree Mr. Charbonneau planted in their front yard. My dad says he hopes their dog doesn't dig it up, but he might. The dog, that is."

I was probably nine at the time, which meant that the McKennas had lived in Vermont for a little over a year, since they had arrived in our town from a Westchester suburb of New York City on my eighth birthday—literally, right on the day. When the moving van started chugging up the small hill in front of our house, I told my dad I expected it would turn left into our driveway and unload my presents.

My dad smiled and shook his head and said I might just as well expect the moon to drop out of the sky onto our rooftop.

I had never been to Westchester, but I had an immediate sense that the McKennas were from a town more mannered than Reddington: The terrace was a dead giveaway, but they were also a lot more stiff than those of us who had put in any time in Vermont—especially my parents' friends from the days when they hung out with the folks from the Liberation News Service and viewed love beads as a profound political statement. I liked the McKennas, but on some level I suspected from the moment Rollie introduced me to her mother that the family wasn't going to last long in our part of Vermont. They might do okay in Burlington, the state's biggest city, but not in a little village like Reddington.

I was wrong about that. The McKennas did all right here, especially Rollie. And while there were actually parents in town who would not allow their little girls to play at my house—some merely fearing their daughter would wind up at a birth if my mother was unable to find a baby-sitter, others believing that among the strange herbs and tinctures that were my mother's idea of medical intervention were marijuana, hashish, and hallucinogenic mushrooms—the McKennas didn't seem to mind that my mother was a midwife.

Telling Mrs. McKenna and her friend about Norman Charbonneau's passage through his mother's vaginal canal was as natural for me at nine as telling my parents about a test at school on which I'd done well, or how much fun I might have had on any given day in December sliding down the hill behind Sadie Demerest's house.

By the time I was fourteen and my mother was on trial, I had begun to grow tired of shocking adults with my clinical knowledge of natural delivery or my astonishing stories of home births. But I also understood that words like *vulva* were less endearing from a fourteen-year-old than from a younger girl.

Moreover, by the time I was fourteen and my own body was far along in its transformation from a child's to a teenager's—I had started to wear a training bra in the summer between fifth and sixth grade and begun menstruating almost a year before the county courthouse would become my second home—the whole idea of a nine-pound, two-ounce anything pushing its way through the ludicrously small opening between my legs made me queasy.

"I just don't see how anything that big will ever get through something that small!" I'd insist, after which my father would sometimes remark, shaking his head, "Bad design, isn't it?"

If my mother was present she would invariably contradict him: "It is not!" she would say. "It's a magnificent and beautiful design. It's perfect."

Because she was a midwife, I think my mother was bound to think this way. I'm not. Moreover, I'm thirty years old now, and I still cannot begin to fathom how anything as big as a baby will someday snake or wiggle or bash its way through what still looks to me like an awfully thin tunnel.

Although my mother would never have taken one of my little friends to a birth, just before I turned eight I began to accompany her to deliveries if a baby decided to arrive on a day or night when my father was out of town and her stable of sitters was busy on such short notice. I don't know what she did before then, but she must have always found someone when necessary, because the first birth I remember—the first time I heard my mother murmur, "She's crowning," which to this day makes me envision a baby emerging from the birth canal with a party hat on—occurred on a night when there was a tremendous thunderstorm and I was in the second grade. It was late in the school year, perhaps as close to the commencement of summer as the first or second week in June.

My mother believed babies were more likely to arrive when the sky was filled with rain clouds than when it was clear, because the barometric pressure was lower. And so when the clouds began rolling in that evening while the two of us were eating dinner on our porch, she said that when the dishes were done she might see who was available to baby-sit tonight, if it came to that. My father was on the New York side of Lake Champlain that evening, because builders were going to break ground the next day for a new math and science building he had helped to design for a college there. It wasn't his project solely—this was still three years before he would open his own firm—but my father could take credit for figuring out the details involved with building the structure into the side of a hill and making sure it didn't look like offices for the North American Strategic Air Command.

The first infant I saw delivered at home was Emily Joy Pine. E.J., as she would come to be called, was an easy birth, but it didn't look that way to me a month short of my eighth birthday. I slept through the phone call David Pine made to our house about ten in the evening, probably because my mother was still awake and answered promptly. And so Emily's birth began for me with my mother's lips kissing my forehead, and then the image of the curtains in the window near my bed billowing in toward the two of us in the breeze. The air was charged, but it had not yet begun to rain.

When we arrived, Lori Pine was sitting on the side of her bed with a light cotton blanket draped over her shoulders, but most of the other bedding—blankets and bedspread and sheets—had been removed and piled in a small mountain on the floor. There were some fat pillows at the head of the bed that looked as if they came from an old couch. The mattress was covered with a sheet with the sort of pattern that might have looked appropriate on a big, ugly shower curtain: lots of psychedelic sunflowers with teardrop-shaped petals, and suns radiating heat and light.

That sheet, I would overhear, had been baked in a brown paper grocery bag for over an hour in the couple's kitchen oven. It may have been tasteless, but it was sterile.

When my mother and I arrived, the woman who was her apprentice back then was already there. Probably twenty-four or twenty-five years old at the time, Heather Reed had already helped my mother deliver close to forty babies at home; when we walked into the bedroom, she was calmly telling Lori to imagine the view her baby had of the uterus at that moment.

My mother was nothing if not hygienic, and after she had said hello she went straight to the Pines' bathroom to wash up. She would probably spend ten full minutes scrubbing her hands and soaping her arms before she would place her palms softly upon a woman's stomach, or pull on a pair of thin rubber gloves and explore a laboring mother's cervix with her fingers.

When she emerged from the bathroom, she asked Lori to lie back so she could see how she was doing. Lori and David's two small sons had already been taken up the road to their uncle's house, while their aunt—Lori's sister—was here, rubbing Lori's shoulders through the blanket. David had just returned from the kitchen, where he had been preparing tea made from an herb called blue cohosh, which my mother believed helped to stimulate labor.

Lori lay back on the bed, and as she did her blanket fell away and I saw she was naked underneath it. I had assumed she wouldn't be sleeping in pajamas with pants like me, but it hadn't crossed my mind as I stood in the bedroom that she wouldn't be wearing a nightgown like my mother, or perhaps a big T-shirt of the sort my mother and I both slept in on hot summer nights.

Nope, not Lori Pine. Buck naked. And huge.

Lori Pine had always been a big woman in my eyes. She towered over me more than most moms when we would find ourselves standing together at the front register of the Reddington General Store, or in the crowded vestibule before or after church. Her boys were younger than I, one by two years and one by four, so I had no contact with her at school. But I did seem to find her standing near me often, and I had this fear at the time that if I ever needed to get past her in an emergency, she would plug up the entire doorway, an ample, spreading, broad-bottomed plug of a woman.

In a real emergency, I now imagine, Lori Pine would actually have used her size to whisk me up and out of danger, tossing me through an exit or doorway with the same ease with which I throw my cats outside the house in the morning.

But what struck me most when I saw Lori Pine naked on her bed was simply her pregnant belly. That's what I saw, that's what I remember: a massive fleshy pear that sat on her lap and protruded as high as her bent knees, with a small nub in the middle that reminded me of those buttons that pop from the breasts of fully cooked chickens or turkeys. I didn't know then that a pregnant belly was a pretty solid affair, and so I expected it to flatten and slip to her sides like a dollop of mayonnaise when she lay back; when it didn't, when it rose from the bed like a mountain, I stared with such wonder in my eyes that Lori rolled her face toward me and panted what I have since come to believe was the word "Condoms."

I've never figured out whether the word was meant for me as a piece of advice that I should take to heart, as in "Demand that your man always wear a condom so you don't end up trying to push a pickle through a straw," or as a warning against that particular form of contraception: "This is all the fault of a condom. There are better forms of birth control out there, and if I'd had any sense at all, I'd have used one."

Whether Lori Pine really did say the word *condoms* or something else or merely my name when she saw me standing there—my name is Constance, but at a young age I learned to prefer Connie—I'll never know. I like to believe she said *condoms;* so many other beliefs shatter when we grow up, I want to keep this one intact.

In any case, whatever she said made everyone in the room aware of the fact that I was there, leaning against the wall.

"Do you mind if she stays, Lori?" my mother asked, nodding slightly in my direction. "Tell me honestly."

Lori's husband took her hand and stroked it, adding, "She could join the boys at their uncle's, you know. I'm sure Heather wouldn't mind driving her up there."

But Lori Pine was as generous and uninhibited as she was large, and she said she didn't mind having me there at all. "What's one more pair of eyes, Sibyl?" she said to my mother, before starting to wince from a contraction, her head snapping toward me as if she'd been slapped.

And so I stayed, and got to see Lori Pine's labor and E.J. Pine's birth. My mother and I had arrived about ten-thirty in the evening, and I stayed awake through much of the night and into the next morning. I did doze in the bedding that had been tossed onto the floor, especially when the thunder that had rolled east across the Champlain Valley and the Green Mountains passed over us into New Hampshire, but they were short naps and I was awake at quarter to six in the morning when my mother had Lori begin to push, and again at seven thirty-five when E.J. ducked under the pubic bone for the last time, my mother pressing her fingers against the infant's skull to slow her down and give her mother's perineum an extra few seconds to yawn.

E.J. was born at seven thirty-seven—like the airplane. Labor was about nine and a half hours, and it was in the opinion of everyone present a breeze. Everyone but me. When I dozed, it was probably because I could no longer bear to watch Lori Pine in such pain and had shut my eyes—not solely because I was tired and my eyes had drooped shut on their own.

The room was dim, lit only by a pair of Christmas candles with red bulbs David had pulled from the attic for the event just after my mother and I had arrived. Had it not been such a windy night, they would have used real candles, but Lori wanted to labor with the windows open, and David had recommended sacrificing authenticity for safety.

Lori had started to express her disappointment when she saw David reappear with the plastic sconces instead of wax candles, but then another contraction ripped through her body and she grabbed my mother's arms with both hands and screamed through clenched teeth: a sound like a small engine with a bad starter trying to turn over.

"Breathe, Lori, breathe," my mother reminded her placidly, "breathe in deep and slow," but by the way Lori's eyes had rolled back in her head, my mother might just as well have told her to march outside and hang a new garage door, and that was the last any of us heard that night from Lori Pine about candles.

I hadn't really seen an adult in pain until then. I had seen children cry out, occasionally in what must have been agony—when Jimmy Cousino broke his collarbone when we were in the first grade, for example. Jimmy howled like a colicky baby with a six-year-old size set of lungs for speakers, and he howled without stopping until he was taken by a teacher from the playground to the hospital.

It was a whole other experience, however, to see an adult sob. My mother was great with Lori, endlessly smiling and reassuring her that she and her baby were fine, but for the life of me I couldn't understand why my mother didn't just get her the adult equivalent of the orange-flavored baby aspirin she gave me when I didn't feel well. The stuff worked miracles.

Instead my mother suggested that Lori walk around the house, especially in those first hours after we got there. My mother had her stroll through her two boys' bedrooms; she recommended that Lori take a warm shower. She asked Lori's sister to give the woman gentle backrubs and massage her shoulders. At one point, my mother had Lori and David looking at snapshots together in a photo album of the home births of their two sons—pictures that had been taken in that very bedroom.

And while I don't believe witnessing Lori Pine's pain frightened me in a way that scarred me, to this day I do remember some specific sounds and images very, very well: My mother cooing to Lori about bloody show, and the blood that I glimpsed on the old washcloth my mother had used to wipe the sheet. Lori's panting, and the way her husband and her sister would lean over and pant beside her, a trio of adults who seemed to be hyperventilating together. Lori Pine slamming the back of her hand into the headboard of her bed, the knuckles pounding against it as if her elbow were a spring triggered by pain, and the noise of the bone against cherry wood—it sounded to me like a bird crashing into clapboards. The desperate panic in Lori's voice when she said she couldn't do it, she couldn't do it, not this time, something was wrong, it had never, ever hurt like this before, and my mother's serene reminder that indeed it had. Twice. The times late in the labor when Lori crawled from her bed and was helped by my mother and Heather to the bathroom, her arms draped over their shoulders as if she were the sort of wounded soldier I'd seen in the movies who was helped from the battlefield by medics, good buddies, or fellows who hadn't previously been friends. The image of my mother's gloved fingers disappearing periodically inside Lori Pine's vagina, and the delighted sweetness in her voice when she'd say—words spoken in a hush barely above a whisper— "Oh my, you're doing fine. No, not fine, terrific. Your baby will be here by breakfast!"

And it was. At quarter to six in the morning when Lori Pine started to push, the sky was light although covered with clouds, but the rain had long passed to the east. No one had bothered to unplug the plastic Christmas candles, so I did: Even in 1975, even just shy of eight, I was an environmentalist concerned with renewable resources. Either that or a cheap Yankee conditioned to turn off the lights when they weren't needed.

T W O

*The books say conception occurs when a sperm penetrates a
female egg, and they all use that word—penetration. Every
single one of them! It's as if life begins as a battle: "Let's storm
the egg!" Or, maybe, as an infiltration of spies or saboteurs:
"We'll sneak up on the egg, and then we'll crawl in through
the kitchen window when she's asleep!" I just don't get it, I
don't see why they always have to say penetrate. What's wrong
with meet, or merge, or just groove together?*

—from the notebooks of SIBYL DANFORTH, MIDWIFE

WHEN THINGS GO WRONG IN OBSTETRICS, THEY GO WRONG FAST. THEY FALL
off a cliff. One minute mom and fetus are happily savoring the view
from the top, and the next they're tumbling over the edge and free-
falling onto the rocks and trees far below.

I would hear physicians use those sorts of analogies all the time
when I was growing up. And of course virtually every ob-gyn the State
paraded before the jury when my mother was on trial had his or her
personalized version of the labor-as-aerial-act speech.

"Most of the time, labor is like going for a drive in the country.
Nothing unusual will occur. But sometimes—sometimes—you'll hit that
patch of black ice and skid off the road, or a dump truck will lose control
and skid into you."

"The vast, vast majority of the time, labor doesn't demand any
medical intervention. It's a natural process that women have been han-

17

dling since, well, since the beginning of time. But we've lost our collec-
tive memory of the fact that although labor is natural, it's dangerous.
Let's face it, there was a time when women and babies died all the time
in labor."

Their point was always the same: Women should not have their
babies at home with my mother. They should have them in hospitals
with physicians.

"A hospital is like an infant car seat: If something unexpected
should occur and there's some kind of collision, we have the tools to pull
the baby out of the oven," one doctor insisted, mixing metaphors and
mistaking a uterus for a kitchen appliance from Sears.

In the late 1970s and early '80s, my mother was one of a dozen
independent or "lay" midwives in Vermont who delivered babies at
home. Virtually no doctors did. The cost of malpractice insurance for
home birth was prohibitive, and most ob-gyns really believed it was safer
to bring children from womb to world in a hospital.

My mother disagreed, and she and different doctors often waged
their battles with statistics. As a little girl I would hear phrases and
numbers rallied back and forth like birdies on badminton courts, and I
was fascinated by the grimness behind the very clean, clinical-sounding
words. Maternal morbidities. Neonatal mortalities. Intrapartum fatalities.

The word *stillborn* fascinated me. Still born. At nine or ten, I
assumed it conveyed a purgatory-like labor, a delivery that went on
forever.

"Is he still being born?"

"Indeed, he is. Horrible, isn't it? They're now in their third year of
labor . . ."

My mother believed that home birth was safe at least in part
because she refused to deliver any high-risk pregnancies at home.
Women with very high blood pressure, for example. Diabetes. Twins.
She insisted on hospital birth for those women, even when they pleaded
with her to help them have their babies at home.

And she never hesitated to transfer a laboring mother in her care
to the hospital, if something was—as she once described the feeling to
me—making her heart beat a little faster than she liked. Sometimes it
would be due to my mother's sense that the labor hadn't progressed in
hours, and her patient was exhausted. Sometimes my mother might
recommend a transfer because she feared a more dangerous turn was

imminent, one of those things the medical community euphemistically describes as an "unforeseen occurrence": the placenta separating from the uterine wall before the baby has arrived or such signs of fetal distress as a falling heartbeat.

In all of the years that my mother practiced, the records would reveal, just about four percent of the time she took her laboring women and went to the hospital.

There's no question in my mind that my mother and the medical community disliked each other. But she would never have let their conflicts jeopardize the health of one of her patients. That's a fact.

I could begin my mother's story with Charlotte Fugett Bedford's death, but that would mean I'd chosen to open her life with what was for her the beginning of the end. It would suggest that all that mattered in her life was the crucible that made my family a part of one tragic little footnote to history.

So I won't.

Besides, I view this as my story, too, and why I believe babies became my calling as well.

And I am convinced that our stories began in the early spring of 1980, a full eighteen months before my mother would watch her life unravel in a crowded courtroom in northern Vermont, and at least a full month before the Bedfords would even arrive in our state.

Here's what I recall: I recall that the mud was a nightmare that year, but the sugaring was amazing. That's often the case. If the mud is bad, the maple will be good, because mud and maple are meteorological cousins of a sort. The kind of weather that turns dirt roads in Vermont into quicksand in March—a frigid, snowy winter, followed by a spring with warm days and cold, cold nights—also inspires maple trees to produce sap that is sweet and plentiful and runs like the rivers swollen by melted snow and ice.

My mother's and father's families no longer sugared, and so my memories of that March revolve more around mud than maple syrup: For me, that month was largely an endless stream of brown muck. It covered my boots to my shins in the time it would take to trudge fifty yards from the edge of our once-dirt driveway to the small cubbyhole of a room between the side door and the kitchen, which earned its name as a mudroom in those days: The floors and walls would be caked with the stuff. When the mud was wet, it was the dark, rich color of tobacco; when it dried, the color grew light and resembled the powder we used then to make chocolate milk.

But wet or dry, the mud was everywhere for two weeks in the March of 1980. The dirt roads became sponges into which automobiles were constantly sinking and becoming stuck, sometimes sinking so deep that the drivers would be unable to open their doors to escape and would have to climb through the car windows to get out. Yards became bogs that slowed running dogs to a walk. Virtually every family in our town had laid down at least a few long planks or wide pieces of plywood to span the puddles of mud on their lawns or to try and link the spot of driveway on which they parked their cars with their front porches.

My mother parked her station wagon just off the paved road at the end of our driveway, as she did often in the winter and early spring, to ensure that she could get to her patients in a timely fashion. Nevertheless, there were still those occasional births when even my determined mother was unable to get there in time. The section of our old house she used as her office had one whole wall filled with photos of the newborn babies she'd delivered with their parents, and one of those snapshots features a baby crowning while the mother is attended by her sister. The sister is pressing a telephone against her ear with her shoulder while she prepares to catch the child. My mother is at the other end of that telephone, talking the sister through the delivery since a snowstorm had prevented either her or the town rescue squad from getting to the laboring woman before the baby decided it was time to arrive.

That spring, even a city with nothing but paved streets and solid sidewalks like Montpelier—the state capital—somehow developed sleek coats of mud on its miles and miles of asphalt and cement.

But the sugaring was good and the syrup crop huge. My best friend Rollie McKenna had a horse, and although the two of us were never supposed to ride her at the same time, we did often, and that March we rode up to the Brennans' sugarhouse after school at least three or four times so we could smell the sweet fog that enveloped the place as Gilbert and Doris slowly boiled the sap into syrup.

Of course, there were other reasons for riding into the hills where the Brennans had hung hundreds and hundreds of buckets on maple trees. We also rode there because the roads we took to the sugarhouse would lead us past the town ball field where Tom Corts and his friends would smoke cigarettes.

At twelve (and fast approaching thirteen), I would ride or run or walk miles out of my way to watch Tom Corts—two years older than I and therefore in the ninth grade—smoke cigarettes. I probably would have gone miles out of my way to watch Tom Corts stack wood or paint clapboards. He wore turtlenecks all the time, usually black or navy blue, and they always made him look a little dangerous. But his hair was a very light blond and his eyes a shade of green that was almost girlish, and that made the aura of delicious delinquency that surrounded him almost poetic. Tom was the first of many sensitive smokers with whom I would fall deeply in love, and while I have never taken up that habit myself, I know well the taste of smoke on my tongue.

Tom Corts smoked Marlboros from the crushproof box, and he held his cigarettes like tough-guy criminals in movies: with his thumb and forefinger. (A few years later when I, too, was in high school, one of Tom's younger disciples, a boy in my grade, would teach me to hold a joint in that fashion.) He didn't inhale much, probably no more than necessary to light the cigarette and then keep it burning; most of the time, the cigarettes just slowly disappeared between his fingers, leaving ashes on the dirt or mud of the ball field, the sidewalk, or the street.

Tom had a reputation for driving adults wild, although rarely in ways they thought they should—or could—discipline. I remember the first hunting season when he was given a gun and taken into the deep woods with the older males in his clan, he shot one of the largest bucks brought down that year in the county. The men's pride in their young kin must have shriveled, however, when they saw how Tom mugged for the camera in the picture the owner of the general store took of the boy and the buck for his annual wall of fame. Tom wrapped one arm around the dead deer's neck and pretended to sob, and with his other hand held aloft a sign on which he'd named the deer, "Innocence."

It was also widely believed in town that Tom was the ringleader behind the group that somehow acquired cans of the sizzling yellow paint the road crews used to line highways, and one Halloween coated the front wall of the new town clerk's office with the stuff. The building, a squat little eyesore that not even the selectmen could stand, was a mistake the whole town regretted, and neither the constable nor the state police worked very hard to find the vandals.

On any given day, Tom was as likely to be seen somewhere reading a paperback book of Greek mythology—unassigned in school—as a magazine on snowmobiling; he was the sort of wild card who would skip a class trip to the planetarium in St. Johnsbury, but then write an essay on black holes that would astonish the teacher.

Initially, my father disliked Tom, but not so much that he ever discouraged me from trying to get the boy's attention, or suggested that it might be a bad idea for Rollie and me to try and ingratiate ourselves into his circle. I think my father—the sort of orderly architect who would stack his change by size every single night of his adult life, so that on any given morning I could find atop his bureau small skyscrapers of quarters and nickels and dimes—thought Tom ran a little too wild. My father came from a family of achievers—a line of farmers who actually prospered in Vermont's rocky soil, followed by two generations of successful small-business men—and he thought Tom's bad pedigree might be a problem. Although he knew Tom was very smart, he still feared the boy might end up like most of the Cortses in Reddington: working by day at the messy automotive garage that looked like a rusted-out auto graveyard, while trying to buy Budweiser with food stamps at night. It probably wasn't a bad life if you kept your tetanus shots current, but it wasn't the life my father wanted for his only child.

My mother understood why I found Tom cute, but she, too, had her reservations. "There are probably worse mushrooms in this world than a boy like Tom Corts," she once warned, "but I still want you to be careful around him. Keep your head."

They had both underestimated Tom, as they'd see the next year. He was always there for me when I needed him most.

In the mud season of 1980, Rollie's horse, Witch Grass, was twenty years old, and while her best years were well behind her, she was a good horse for us. Patient. Undemanding. And slow to accelerate. This last character trait meant a lot to us (and, I have to assume, to our parents), because we had given up our formal lessons a year earlier, tired of being told to sit up straight, post, and canter.

Witch Grass could carry both Rollie and me for long stretches on her chestnut back, although we tried to minimize the amount of time we dropped one hundred and ninety pounds onto her aging spine. One of us would sometimes walk beside her.

It was probably during the third week in March that I first let Tom kiss me.

Make no mistake, this wasn't one of those passionate, "we kissed" sort of moments: I was decidedly passive during my first kiss, and although Tom initiated the buss (and I was indeed a willing participant), he broke it off fast, and we were too young—and the ground too muddy—for our small part of the earth to move.

Rollie and I planned, as we had the day before, to take turns riding Witch Grass up Gove Hill, the only spot in Reddington her mother could think of where the ground was not either asphalt or deep mud. When the horse had had a chance to stretch her legs, we would ride together across the street and past the general store to the ball field, stealing a glimpse of Tom Corts and his vaguely truant friends. We might then continue up to the Brennans' sugarhouse, since even in the center of town we could see its steam winding up from the trees like the trail of a small but hyperactive geyser.

So Rollie took off on Witch Grass first, and I climbed over the electric fencing into the field by the barn where the horse grazed when Rollie was in school, and began shoveling the big clumps of horse turds into what Rollie and I secretly referred to as the Shit Barrow. Witch Grass wasn't my horse, but I spent so much time riding her that I tried to help with her care and feeding—which meant mostly midafternoon shoveling.

I hadn't been at it long when I heard my mother's station wagon churning up the street toward me, with its motor's characteristically ineffectual-sounding sputter. The wagon was a giant blue woody from the late sixties, and while my parents had considered trading it in during the oil crisis in 1973—a discussion driven as much by guilt over the way the animal guzzled gasoline and oil as it was by the cost of pumping dead dinosaurs into its belly to keep it moving—my mother was unable to part with it. She had had the wagon almost as long as she had had me, it had gotten her safely to over five hundred births, and she couldn't bear to put this particular partner out to pasture.

The field was beside one of Reddington's busier roads, the street that wound its way to Route 15—the road west to Morrisville and east to St. Johnsbury. That meant that my mother could have been on her way to practically anywhere: the grocery, the bank, a laboring mother.

She slowed down when she saw me, came to a stop in the middle of her half of the road (she didn't dare pull off into the mud beside it), and rolled down her window. I crossed the street with the McKennas' shovel still in my hands and balanced both feet on the yellow lines in the middle of the pavement, pretending the stripes were twin tightropes.

"Wanda Purinton's baby's coming," she said, smiling serenely the way she did whenever one of her mothers' labors had commenced.

"Is she far along?" I asked.

"Don't know. The contractions sound close. We'll see."

"You won't be home for dinner, will you." I tried to hide my disappointment; I tried to present this realization as a simple fact that needed confirmation, but it didn't come out that way.

She shook her head. "No, sweetheart. You and Daddy are on your own. Do you mind making dinner?"

"No." But I did. And of course my mother knew it.

"I took some chopped meat out of the freezer. Make hamburgers."

"Uh-huh." Hamburgers were about the extent of my culinary oeuvre when I was twelve. Hamburgers and grilled cheese. As a matter of fact, until I took a two-week cooking class as a January lark in my junior year of college, they were all I was ever able to cook.

"Maybe it will be a short labor. Wanda's a Burnham, and Burnhams usually arrive pretty quickly."

"And maybe you'll be there all night."

She raised an eyebrow. "Maybe. In which case, we'll have a big breakfast together." She leaned her head partway out the car window. "A kiss, please?"

I obeyed, a perfunctory peck on the cheek, and then watched her put the wagon in gear and head off. I wasn't exactly angry with her as much as I was frustrated: Her job and Wanda Purinton's baby meant I'd have to be home earlier than I'd planned. It wasn't that a dinner of hamburgers and canned peas took so long to prepare, but I always felt a moral obligation of sorts when my mother was gone to be home when my father returned from work. I don't know if the idea was drummed into my head by the situation comedies I watched for hours on our snowy, static-filled television, or if it was a result of my sense of how my friends' mothers behaved—women as different from each other as Mrs. McKenna from Westchester and native Vermonter Fran Hurly—but as far as I knew, with the exception of midwives, mothers were supposed to be in the house when fathers came home from wherever they worked.

I stalked back to the field and shoveled halfheartedly for a few minutes, knowing there wouldn't be time for me to both take a ride up Gove Hill and find a pretext with the horse to watch Tom Corts smoke cigarettes. And so I perched the shovel atop a good-sized dry rock, tucked the cuffs of my jeans further into my high black boots, and decided to stroll by the ball field alone. I told myself I was actually going by the general store for chewing gum, but even that had a conspiratorial agenda: better breath if Tom or I . . . better breath.

Tom was sitting with two older boys when I wandered by, teenagers old enough to have already decided they didn't need to finish high school to wash dishes at any of the restaurants that ringed Powder Peak, the ski resort to the south, or become journeyman carpenters, and therefore had dropped out of school. I recognized that one was an O'Gorman, but he had four years on me and I didn't know which one he was, and the other was Billy Metcalf, the sort of boy whose stubble had become strangely menacing as he had grown lanky and tall.

Had Tom been alone, I might have found the courage for a detour to the bleachers across the muck that in a month or two might become grass, but he wasn't, so I trudged straight ahead to the store. The gums and mints sat in a wire rack directly across from the wooden counter behind which John Dahrman sat day in and day out, a quiet widower with white hair and eyes as deep as Abraham Lincoln's ghostly sockets in the portraits that filled the Civil War chapter in my history textbook. Although his hair was white and his eyes exhausted, his skin was smooth and I imagined at the time that he was much younger than one might have initially suspected. He'd owned the store for at least as long as I'd been alive and aware of such things as commerce and chewing gum, assisted at the register by a seemingly endless stream of nieces and nephews as they grew up and learned how to count.

As I was paying for my gum, disappointed that I hadn't been able to get within thirty yards of the slightly wild object of my infatuation, I heard the bell on the store's front door jingle. The O'Gorman brother and Billy Metcalf were strolling toward the refrigerator case at the back of the store in which Mr. Dahrman kept the beer. They were too young to buy any, but I'd seen them stand around and stare at the six-packs behind the glass before, discussing loudly how much they could drink and which brands they would buy when they were old enough. Eventually Mr. Dahrman would either kick them out or herd them toward the aisles with beef jerky and artificial cheese puffs, products they found almost as interesting as beer and were legally allowed to purchase.

I expected Tom Corts to wander in behind them, but he didn't. I assumed this meant he had gone home, but I still held out the dim hope that he was alone at the ball field, and if I walked quickly, I might have a moment with him before O'Gorman and Metcalf returned with their cache of Slim Jims and Jax. What I would actually do with that moment was beyond my imagination, since the majority of Tom's and my exchanges up till that point had consisted of garbled hellos into our hands as we gave each other small waves.

It turned out not to matter, because Tom was gone. The bleachers on the first- and third-base sides of the infield were empty, and the only life in sight was the Cousinos' idiot golden retriever, a dog so dumb it would bark for hours at tree stumps and well caps. It was barking now at the stone barbecue pit between the right-field foul line and the river that ran beside the field. I tried to lose my disappointment in the satisfaction of well-blown bubbles and the sweet taste of the gum when I pressed it hard against the back of my teeth with my tongue, and marched back to the field I'd been shoveling. I didn't wonder where Tom had taken his scowl and his cigarettes, I just accepted the fact that he had disappeared and I'd have to wait another day to see him.

I stretched my legs over the electric wire and picked up the shovel from the rock on which I'd laid it. Leaning against the wall of the barn no more than twenty yards away was Tom Corts. He pulled his cigarette from his mouth and started toward me, oblivious—or uncaring—of the fact that with each step his sneakers sunk deep into either horse turd or mud.

I stood still, waiting with my heart in my head. When he had gotten so close I could smell the cigarettes on his breath, he stopped and asked, "They pay you for this?"

I paused, thinking, This? Then I realized: the shoveling. "No."

"Then why do you do it?"

"Because Rollie's my friend."

He nodded. "And 'cause you ride the horse."

"That, too."

He jammed the one hand he didn't need for his cigarette deep into the pocket of his blue jean jacket. "It's going to be a cold one tonight. Cold as hell for the animals. Their instincts are telling them spring is here and a cold like January is behind them. But then tonight it'll go down to twenty degrees, and 'cause they aren't expecting it, it'll feel like ten below zero to them."

I had no idea if Tom's theory had any validity, but it sounded wise that afternoon. And compassionate. It suggested to me that this boy had a soul as mysterious as his eyes were gentle.

"Your family have animals?" I asked. I knew the Cortses hadn't farmed in years, but I felt I had to ask something. "Cows or horses?"

"My grandparents—all of them—used to. Granddaddy Corts had a fifty-head herd for years, which used to be considered big. And they had some horses, too. Morgans."

"Do you ride?"

He shook his head. "Nope. Just snowmobiles. And motorcycles."

I'd seen Tom ride snowmobiles, often when my father and I would go cross-country skiing up on the natural turnpike and logging trails in North Reddington. We'd probably pulled off the trail on our skis a dozen times for Tom and his older friends and cousins. But I had a feeling he was lying about the motorcycles, and somehow that endeared him to me as much as his wisdom about animals did.

"I've never ridden a snowmobile."

"I'll take you, if you like. Maybe even this year. We'll get more snow, you know."

"Oh, I know."

"I've seen you ski. With your dad and mom."

"Just my dad. My mom doesn't like to ski."

"She's smart. Snowmobiling's more fun. You go faster, and you get plenty of exercise. More than most people realize."

"I don't think she likes to snowmobile either."

He flicked his cigarette toward his feet and ground it deep into the mud.

"You have Mrs. Purta for French, right?"

"Right."

"Like her?"

"I do. Sure."

He nodded, taking this fact in and turning it over in his mind for meaning. A signal. Confirmation, perhaps, of my maturity. Then he said something that might have been threatening to me had I not heard three of those words from my mother only a short while before, a coincidence

that suggested to me a cosmic rightness. Moreover, his voice was suddenly filled with an unease that mirrored my own.

"A kiss before I go, please?" he asked, and there was a quiver in
his words that transformed "please" into a two-syllable request. I stood
still before him, which was about as close to an affirmation as I could
offer at twelve, and after a second long enough for goose bumps to grow
along my arms and dance along the skin under the sleeves of my shirt
and my sweater, he leaned toward me and pressed his lips against mine.
We both opened our mouths a sliver and tasted each other's breath.

It was only after he stood up straight and our bodies parted that I
realized he hadn't put his tongue into my mouth. I was glad, but mostly
because I wouldn't have known how to juggle Tom Corts's tongue with
the large piece of bubble gum hiding somewhere at that moment in my
cheek.

It would be a good eight months before Tom and I would become
boyfriend and girlfriend, and a full year and a half before I would look
to the back of a courtroom in Newport and see him standing there,
watching. It would be a full year and a half before I would find myself
crying at night in his arms.

THREE

Zygote isn't a bad word, but it's far from perfect. On the one hand, I love the word's origin—the Greek word for "joining together." That feels right to me, because that's about what has occurred. An egg and a sperm have joined together, and they're on this cool little pilgrimage to the uterus.

On the other hand, I don't like the way the word sounds when you say it out loud: Zygote! It always sounds like it needs an exclamation point. It always sounds like a curse from some angry mad scientist. Zygote! The beaker is cracked! Zygote! There's radium all over the lab!

—*from the notebooks of* SIBYL DANFORTH, MIDWIFE

MY MOTHER WAS NAMED SIBYL AFTER HER GRANDMOTHER ON HER MOTHER'S side. Her grandmother was born in a small village in eastern Mexico, the daughter of missionaries from Massachusetts. Those missionaries—my mother's great-grandparents—spent ten years in a little coastal town called Santiago, a decade in which they founded a Catholic church, became very good friends with a village healer named Sibella, and had two children. One of those children lived—my mother's grandmother—and one didn't.

The one who didn't was a boy they named Paul, and it was his death by drowning that destroyed that family's faith and sent them packing back to the United States. I was told Paul drowned in shallow water, which for years in my mind conjured an image of choppy Gulf surf near the beach, and a three-year-old child bobbing for moments in waves before he was pulled under for the last time. Eventually my mother told me this wasn't what she believed happened at all. The family tradition—myth or reality, who knows—is that he died in the bathtub.

When those missionaries and their daughter returned to the United States, they almost resettled as they had planned in central Massachusetts, but in their attempt to rebuild their lives they decided to start fresh in a new place, and just kept heading north until they were beyond Massachusetts and New Hampshire, in Vermont. In Reddington.

I think most people my age assume that children died so frequently in the nineteenth century that people didn't grieve as profoundly or as long as we do today. I don't believe that. The woman for whom my mother was named was born in 1889, and that woman's brother in 1891. He died in 1894: There's one marker for the boy in the Reddington cemetery, another one in that family's plot in a cemetery in the town of Worcester, Massachusetts, and a third tombstone marking the body's actual remains in a graveyard in Santiago.

No one knows who was responsible for bathing Paul when he died. That detail is lost in our family history.

In any case, when those missionaries who had once had the zeal to move to Mexico to spread God's word and build a church—literally, help construct the sandstone structure under the searing sun with their pale New England hands—finally settled in Reddington, they rarely set foot in any church, Catholic or Protestant, again.

My mother was a full-fledged, honest-to-God, no-holds-barred, Liberation News Service, peace-love-and-tie-dye hippie. This was no small accomplishment, since she grew up in a small village in northern Vermont. Villages like Reddington are buffered from cultural change by high mountains, harsh weather, bad television reception, and low population density (which might explain why she never actually tried to escape to places like San Francisco, the East Village, or Woodstock), so it probably took a certain amount of attentiveness, research, and spine to find the revolution—or even a decent peasant skirt.

Although Sibyl never actually moved into a school bus or commune, the photographs of her taken during the second half of the 1960s show a woman who apparently lived in bell-bottoms and shawls, love beads and medallions and sandals. Those photos reveal a woman with round blue eyes and spiraling dirty blond hair, characteristics I've inherited, although my hair is flatter by far than hers ever was.

She went to Mount Holyoke for two years, but met a slightly older man while waitressing on Cape Cod the summer between her sophomore and junior years and decided to drop out and spend the winter in a cottage with him on the ocean. It didn't last long. By Thanksgiving she was settled in Jamaica Plain in Boston, helping the Black Panthers start a breakfast program for the poor, while answering telephones for an alternative newspaper. By the spring she had had enough—not because she had grown tired of the movement with a capital M, but because she longed for the country. For Vermont. She wanted to go home, and finally she did.

She returned just before her twentieth birthday, telling her parents she'd stay through the summer and then resume her studies in the fall. My grandmother always insisted that my mother had dropped out with very good grades, all A's and B's, and Mount Holyoke would have been happy to take her back.

But I don't think returning to college was ever very likely. She had already developed what was then a popular distaste for most traditional or institutional authority, and somehow Mount Holyoke had become suspect in her eyes. Besides, by July she had fallen in with a group of self-proclaimed artists in the hills northeast of Montpelier, an assemblage of singers and painters and writers that included an illustrator who would eventually decide to become an architect instead of an album cover designer—my father. The men in the group remained in college so they wouldn't lose their draft deferments, but the women dropped out and threw pots, hooked rugs, wrote songs.

My mother became pregnant with me soon after that, and she and my father always reassured me that there was never any discussion of finding an expert in Boston or Montreal who would know how to make me go away.

Knowing my parents, I indeed believe the idea of aborting me never crossed my mother's mind, but I'm sure the thought occurred to my father. I'm positive. I have never doubted his love, and I believe he's very glad I'm here, but he has always been a tidy man, and unplanned pregnancies are usually pretty messy affairs. My conception postponed indefinitely, and then forever, any discussion of Sibyl's returning to college.

That's one of the main reasons that my mother became a lay midwife instead of a medically trained nurse midwife or perhaps even an obstetrician-gynecologist: no college degree and—over time—the conclusion that she didn't need one.

Of course, she also believed with a passion that in most cases women should have their babies at home. She thought it was healthier for both the mother and the newborn. Women, in her mind, labored most efficiently in the environment they knew best and that made them the most comfortable; likewise, it was important to greet a baby as it emerged into the world in a room that was warm, and to catch it with hands that were kind. The whole idea of salad server–like forceps and abdominal transducers irritated my mother, and—eventually, this would prove to be the cruelest irony of all—she would give a laboring woman every chance in the world to deliver vaginally. In some cases, she waited for days, always patiently, before she would take the woman to a hospital where a doctor would anesthetize her, then cut through her abdominal and uterine walls and lift the startled child into the fluorescent lights of an operating room.

My mother knew home birth wasn't for everyone, but she wanted it to remain a viable option for those who were interested. And if she had ever become a doctor or nurse-midwife, the state's Board of Medical Practice would have tried to force her to practice in a hospital.

That was how the regulations worked then; that's how they work now. If doctors and nurse-midwives deliver babies at home, they do so without malpractice insurance or state sanction. So from my mother's perspective, there was no reason to get any sort of medical degree. She knew what she was doing.

Did Sibyl Danforth dislike hospitals and what her prosecutors would describe as the medical establishment? For a time, I think she did. Was she, as they called her, a renegade? You bet. (Although when accused of being a renegade in court, she smiled and said, "I prefer to think of myself as a pioneer." Whenever I come across that exchange in the piles of court papers I've amassed, I grin.)

There was a certain humor to her anti–ob-gyn bias that never came out at the trial. In one photo of her taken in 1969, she's leaning against the back of a VW Beetle, and there by her knees are two bumper stickers: QUESTION AUTHORITY! and ONLY DUCKS SHOULD BE QUACKS. The same misgivings that she had for what she perceived to be the entrenched power of professors and college presidents, she had for physicians and hospital administrators as well.

And while she largely got over her distrust of doctors—while she never dawdled when she decided a woman needed medical intervention, while she certainly took me to pediatricians when I wasn't feeling well as a child—most doctors never learned to trust her.

Mine was not the first birth at which my mother was present. Mine was the third.

In the year and a half between her return from Boston and my arrival in Vermont, two other women in that circle of friends northeast of Montpelier had children, and my mother was present at the first birth by accident, and the second by choice. Appropriately, the first of those births was in a bedroom in a drafty old Vermont farmhouse, not a sterile delivery room in a hospital.

The first of those births—and my mother's baptism to midwifery— was Abigail Joy Wakefield's.

The little girl was supposed to have been born in a hospital, but she arrived two weeks early. The six adults who were present the night her mother's labor began, including the two people who would become my own parents, feared they were too stoned to try and drive any of the cars that were parked willy-nilly by the old house as though an earthquake had hit. Consequently, in a reversion to sex roles that in my opinion was part instinct, part socialized, the men agreed to run the three and a half miles up the road to the pay phone at the general store, where they could call an ambulance, and the women took the laboring mother upstairs to make her as comfortable as possible—and deliver the baby, if it came to that.

Why all three men went, including my father, has become another one of those almost mythic stories that were told and retold among my parents' friends for years. My father insisted that it was a spontaneous decision triggered by the fact that all of the men had dropped acid and simply failed to think the decision through properly. My mother and her female friends always teased him, however, that each guy had been a typical male who had wanted to get as far away from a woman in labor as humanly possible. Indeed, after traveling well over three miles in the dark, the men decided to wait by the main road for the ambulance, so they could be sure it found its way to the house.

Fortunately, neither my mother nor Abigail Joy's mother, Alexis Bell Wakefield, were tripping. That evening they'd merely been smoking pot.

Initially, my mother and Alexis were joined in the bedroom by Luna Raskin. Unlike the other two women, Luna did have all sorts of synthetic chemicals in her body, and every time Alexis sobbed, "Oh, God, it hurts, it hurts so much!" Luna would grab my mother's shirt and wail, "They're killing her, they're killing her!"

For a moment my mother assumed Luna meant Alexis's contractions. But when she elaborated, my mother realized with a combination of horror and astonishment that Luna was referring to President Lyndon Johnson and Secretary of State Dean Rusk, whose photograph had been on the front page of the newspaper that day.

At that point my mother threw Luna out of the bedroom and delivered the baby herself.

My mother wasn't sure what delivery tools she would need, and made one of those decisions that suggested she was indeed called to be a midwife: She concluded that women had been having babies for a long, long time before someone invented delivery tools, whatever they were. She imagined the female body had a pretty good idea of what it was supposed to do, if she could simply keep Alexis calm.

Nevertheless, she did round up all of the washcloths and towels she could find, and she filled a huge lobster pot with boiling hot water. She had no idea what one should expect from a placenta, she had no comprehension of what it meant to push, and (in hindsight this probably was for the best) she had never even heard a term like cephalo-pelvic disproportion—an infant head a couple of hat sizes too big for mom's pelvis.

She turned off the overhead light in the bedroom, assuming Alexis would be more comfortable if she wasn't staring straight up into a bright light; the lamp in the corner shed just enough light for Sibyl to see clearly all of the things she didn't understand.

Fortunately, Alexis's own mother had insisted that her daughter visit an ob-gyn, and Alexis had done some reading on her own. The woman was also blessed with a very short labor and a small—but healthy—baby. Yet no labor is easy, and while my mother never lost her belief that the process she was watching was incredibly beautiful, as the pain Alexis was feeling grew worse, Sibyl grew fearful that something was wrong. She would rub Alexis's legs and massage her back, and purr that she thought Alexis was merely experiencing what almost every woman since creation had felt. But inside, my mother had her doubts.

When the better part of an hour had passed and neither the men nor an ambulance had returned, those fears led her to wash her hands once again, this time with a thoroughness that would have impressed a heart surgeon. She took off her silver bracelets and the three different rings she wore on her fingers, including the one my father had given her after a rock concert near Walden Pond, and scrubbed her wrists and her arms up to her elbows.

When her hands were as clean as she believed possible, she placed a finger as far inside Alexis's vagina as she could, hoping to discover whether the baby was about to emerge.

"Am I dilated?" Alexis groaned, rolling her head back and forth on the pillow as if the spine in her neck were made of Jell-O.

At that point in Sibyl's life, the word *dilation* had always been used in the context of pupils and drugs. She had no idea that Alexis was referring to her cervix. And so my mother looked up from between Alexis's legs to scan her friend's face, but the woman had shut her eyes.

"I think so," my mother answered; although she couldn't see Alexis's pupils, she assumed that anyone who had spent as much time with her mouth around a bong as Alexis had must have eyes that were dilated.

"How far?"

"Shhhhhhh," my mother the emergency midwife said. She wiggled the tip of her forefinger inside Alexis and grazed something hard that she understood instantly was a skull. The baby's head. Briefly she rolled her finger across it, astonished by how much of it she could feel.

"Can you feel the head?" Alexis asked.

"I can feel the head," Sibyl answered, mesmerized, and slowly withdrew her finger.

♦   ♦   ♦

Just a few minutes later Alexis screamed that she had to push, and she did.

"Go for it," my mother said. "You're doing great."

Without thinking about the logic behind her idea but assured on some primitive level that it was the right thing to do, she leaned Alexis up against the headboard of the bed and surrounded her with pillows. My mother thought if Alexis sat up, gravity would help the baby fall out.

She then kneeled on the bed between Alexis's legs and watched for a few minutes as the woman pushed and groaned and gritted her teeth, and absolutely nothing seemed to happen. The lips of her vagina may have grown more damp, but certainly no head had begun to protrude from between them.

"Relax for a minute. I think you just made a ton of progress," my mother lied. She wrapped her hands under each of the woman's knees and lifted her legs up and out, hoping to widen the opening for the baby. "Ready?" she asked Alexis, and Alexis nodded.

For the next thirty minutes Alexis would push and rest, push and rest. All the while my mother kept cheering Alexis on, telling her over and over and over that she could do this, she could push for another second, one more second, the baby was about to pop like a cork if she pushed, pushed, pushed, pushed.

A little before one in the morning my mother nearly fell back off the bed when all of that pushing suddenly worked, and the dark swatch of hair that had been teasing her behind the labial lips for what had seemed forever suddenly punched its way out, and she was staring down into a baby forehead, baby eyes, a baby nose, and a baby mouth. Lips shaped like a rose, so small they might have belonged to a doll. She cupped the head in her hands, planning to pillow its fall into the world, when a shoulder slipped out, then another, and then all of Abigail Joy and her umbilical cord. The baby was pink, and when she opened her eyes she started to howl, a long baby cry that caused Alexis to sob and smile at once, a howl so impressive that had my mother at the time had the slightest idea what an Apgar score was, she would have given the child a perfect ten.

As she was studying the two spots where the umbilical cord met mother and daughter, assuming she should snip it while wondering how, my mother heard sirens racing up the hill to the farmhouse, and she knew an ambulance was about to arrive. She was at once relieved and disappointed. She had been scared, no doubt about it, but something about the pressure of the moment had given her a high that made her giddy. This was life force she was witnessing, the miracle that is a mother's energy and body—a body that physically transforms itself before a person's very eyes—and the miracle that is the baby, a soul in a physical vessel that is tiny but strong, capable of pushing itself into the world and almost instantly breathing and squirming and crying on its own.

When Sibyl's friend Donna went into labor a few months later, she asked my mother to be with her in the hospital. I wasn't with my mother when she delivered Abigail Joy, but I was there at the second birth that she saw. I calculate I was six weeks old, perhaps as much as half an inch long, with a skeleton of cartilage and the start of a skull that would be mercifully thick. Unlike my skin.

FOUR

Doctors use the word contraction *and a lot of midwives use the word* rush. *I've never really liked either one:* Contraction *is too functional and* rush *is too vague. One is too biologic and one is too . . . out there. At least for me.*

I'm not sure when I started using the expression aura surge, *or in the midst of delivery, simply the word* surge. *Rand believes it was while delivering Nancy Deaver's first son, Casey, the day after we'd all stood around the statehouse in Montpelier, cheering for McGovern. Rand wasn't at the birth, of course, but Casey was born in the afternoon and it was at dinner that night that Rand noticed my using the words* surge *and* aura surge.

Maybe he's right. I might have made some connection between the way all of us in Montpelier were tripping when McGovern spoke one day, most of us without any chemical help, and the way Nancy and I were tripping the next. I felt really good about the planet and the future both afternoons. When we were all on the statehouse lawn listening to the man, it was freezing outside, and while my cheeks were so cold my skin was stinging, I could see people's breath when they spoke and it looked like they were sharing their auras in this incredibly spiritual and meaningful and perhaps just plain healthy sort of way.

And while I've always understood the biologic rationale for the medical establishment's use of the word contraction,

based both on Connie's birth and all of the births I've attended,
the idea of a surge reflects both the baby's desire for progress
and the mother's unbelievable power. Surge *may also be more*
spiritually accurate, especially if it's called an aura surge.

—from the notebooks of SIBYL DANFORTH, MIDWIFE

AS LATE AS THE FALL OF 1981—THE AUTUMN OF MY MOTHER'S TRIAL—MY father, Rand, was still wearing sideburns. They didn't crawl across his face to the corners of his mouth the way they had in the late 1960s and early '70s, but I remember looking up at his cheeks as we sat together in the courtroom and noting how his sideburns fell like horseshoes around his ears, descending to just below each lobe.

When the testimony was especially damaging to my mother, or when my mother was being cross-examined by the state's attorney, I watched my father pull nervously at the dark hair he allowed to grow beside his ears.

STATE'S ATTORNEY WILLIAM TANNER: So you asked Reverend Bedford to bring you a knife?

SIBYL DANFORTH: Yes.

TANNER: You didn't just ask for any knife. You asked for a sharp knife, didn't you?

DANFORTH: Probably. I don't think I would have asked for a dull one.

TANNER: Both Reverend Bedford and your apprentice recall you requested "the sharpest knife in the house." Were those your words?

DANFORTH: Those might have been my words.

TANNER: Is the reason you needed "the sharpest knife in the house" because you don't carry a scalpel?

DANFORTH: Do you mean to births?

TANNER: That's exactly what I mean.

DANFORTH: No, of course I don't. I've never met a midwife who does.

TANNER: You've never met a midwife who carries a scalpel?

DANFORTH: Right.

TANNER: Is that because a midwife is not a surgeon?

DANFORTH: Yes.

TANNER: Do you believe surgeons possess a special expertise that you as a midwife do not?

DANFORTH: Good Lord, don't you think so?

TANNER: Mrs. Danforth?

DANFORTH: Yes, surgeons know things I don't. So do airline pilots and kindergarten teachers.

TANNER: Are you referring to their training?

DANFORTH: I've never said I was a surgeon.

TANNER: Is a cesarean section a surgical procedure?

DANFORTH: Obviously.

TANNER: Do you think you're qualified to perform this surgery?

DANFORTH: In even my worst nightmares, I never imagined I'd have to.

TANNER: I'll repeat my question. Do you think you're qualified to perform this surgery?

DANFORTH: No, and I've never said that I thought I was.

TANNER: And yet you did. With a kitchen knife, on a living woman, you—

DANFORTH: I would never endanger the mother to save the fetus—

TANNER: You didn't endanger the mother, you killed—

HASTINGS: Objection!

Perhaps I should have been surprised that by the end of the trial my father had any hair left at all. In photographs taken the following winter, his hair looks as if it has begun to gray, but the sideburns are as prominent as ever.

My mother's calling—to her it was never a job or even a career—meant that my father was much more involved with me as a child than the fathers of most of my friends were with them. There was always a long list of baby-sitters pressed against the refrigerator door with a magnet, and occasionally I did indeed wind up with my mother at somebody's delivery, but birth is as unpredictable as it is time-consuming, and my father often filled the Connie-care breach. After all, I was an only child and my mother would have to disappear for twelve hours, or a day, or a day and a half at a time.

My father wasn't much of a playmate when it came to dressing dolls or banging plastic pots and skillets around my toy kitchen (actually, he wasn't very good with regular cast-iron or metal ones either), but he was creative when I needed new voices for trolls, and extremely handy when it came to building a permanent playhouse from wood, or a temporary one from card tables and bed sheets. He would usually endure whatever program I wanted to watch on television, even if it meant an irritating struggle adjusting the rabbit ears atop the television set for a full fifteen minutes before my show began. (Reception in our part of Vermont then was laughably poor. I remember a day one spring—when the baseball season had begun and the basketball and hockey seasons were in the midst of their endless play-offs—when my father was watching a basketball game through so much screen snow and fuzz that my mother sat down on the couch beside him, thumbed through a magazine for five or ten minutes, then looked up and inquired, "What sport is this?")

My father and I also spent a fair amount of time together driving around northern Vermont in his Jeep: Often he was chauffeuring Rollie and me to the bookstore or the toy shop in distant Montpelier, the tack shop in St. Johnsbury, or to some third friend's home in Hardwick or Greensboro or Craftsbury. One September and October, it seemed, he was driving us somewhere every single day, and then working at the dining-room table in our home all night to try and keep up with the work he was missing nine to five at his office: There had been a notable baby boom in the county that fall, roughly nine months after the coldest, harshest winter in years, and my mother was busy.

And although my father was unfailingly patient with me, and always at least feigned contentment at the prospect of another Saturday afternoon or Wednesday evening with only an eight- or a nine-year-old child for company, I know the demands of my mother's calling strained their marriage. When they fought, and I remember them fighting most when I was in elementary school and at that age when I was at once young enough to need virtually constant supervision by someone and old enough to understand on some level the dynamics of what was occurring, their arguments would filter up through the registers in the ceilings of the rooms on the first floor of our house.

"She needs a mother, dammit!" my father would snap, or "You're never here for her!" or "I can't do this alone!" Against all experience, he continued to believe he could use me as a trump card to convince my mother to stay home. It never worked, which usually compelled him to change his tactics from guilt to threats:

"I didn't marry you to live in this house all alone!"

"A marriage demands two people's attention, Sibyl."

"I *will* have a wife in this world, Sibyl. That's a fact."

At the beginning of these fights, my mother always sounded more perplexed and hurt than angry, but underneath that initial sadness in her tone was a stubbornness as unyielding as Vermont granite. She could no sooner stop delivering babies than people could stop having them.

But I also believe that my father deserves high marks for simply enduring all that he did: The husbands of most midwives don't put up with their spouses' hours for long, especially once they are fathers themselves, and most of my mother's midwife friends had been divorced at least once.

Usually my parents' arguments ended in silence, often because my father was incredulous:

"Wait a minute. Didn't the baby arrive at six in the evening?" I might hear my father asking.

"Yup. Julia. Such a pretty girl."

"It's past nine o'clock! What the hell have you been doing for the last three hours?"

"Folding baby clothes. You know I love folding baby clothes."

"You were folding baby clothes for three hours? I suppose the parents own a store that sells baby clothes?"

"Oh, for God's sake, Rand. You know I didn't stay there just to fold baby clothes. I wanted to make sure everyone was okay. It *is* their first child, you know."

"So how long did you spend—"

"Thirty minutes, Rand. I probably spent thirty minutes actually folding Onesies and Julia's tiny little turtlenecks."

"But you did hang around for three hours—"

"Yes, I did. I made sure Julia was nursing, and Julia's mom was up and around. I made sure the family had plenty of food in the refrigerator, and the neighbors were planning to bring by casseroles for the next few days."

"And you made sure the baby's clothes were folded."

"You bet," my mother might say, and I could see in my mind my father shaking his head in quiet astonishment. A moment later I would hear him leave the kitchen, where they might have been bickering, and go upstairs alone to their bedroom. Sometimes, later, I'd hear them make love as they made up: To this day, I remember the noise their bed made as among the most reassuring sounds I've ever heard.

Unfortunately, there were also those fights that would escalate and become ugly, sometimes because my father had been drinking. He might have been drunk when my mother returned, and she might have been tired and cranky. This was a combustible mix. And while my mother would never drink to catch up—her sense of responsibility as a midwife prevented her from drinking or smoking pot whenever she was on call—when she was hurt she could lash out with a fury that was both articulate and verbally violent. I never heard my parents slap or hit each other, but powered by bad scotch and exhaustion, they'd say things as wounding as a fist. Maybe even more so. I'd hear expressions and exchanges I didn't understand at the time but that frightened me nonetheless because I knew someday I would.

I never told Rollie the details of my parents' fights, but I told her enough that one day she gave me some advice that served me well: Every so often, replace an inch or so of the Clan MacGregor with an inch or so of tap water. Be judicious if the bottle is low, and always mark in your mind the exact spot on the label the fluid had reached—the hem of the bagpiper's kilt or the bagpipe itself, for example, or the bottom of the letters that spelled the scotch's brand name.

She had been doing this with her own parents for years, she said, and look at how well their marriage worked.

On those nights my father chose to smother his frustrations with scotch, my parents' fights were like powerful three A.M. thunderstorms: loud and scary, sometimes taking an agonizingly long time to blow over, but causing little apparent damage. When I would scan our yard in the morning after even an especially fierce and frightening August storm, the sunshine usually revealed only minor damage. Some of the white, late-summer blossoms from the hydrangea might be on the ground; a sickly maple might have lost a few leaves; behind our house, there might even have been a small branch from a tree in the woods, blown onto the lawn by the wind.

But the sunshine always reassured me that the storms were never as bad as they'd sounded, and usually I felt that way after my parents' fights when we'd all have breakfast together the next day. I know my parents never stopped loving each other—passionately, madly, chaotically—and one or the other of them was always there for me.

Given the amount of time I spent being transported places by my father when I was growing up, it shouldn't surprise me that my first exposure to the Bedfords was with him. But of course it was through my mother that our families' fates were linked: Mrs. Bedford was one of my mother's patients and the center of the very public tragedies our two families faced.

Mrs. Bedford—Charlotte Fugett Bedford, I would learn later in the newspapers—was from Mobile, Alabama. (It's tempting to refer to her as "one of the Mobile Fugetts," but that would imply a lineage more impressive than the generations of sharecroppers and bootleggers and petty thieves that I know were in fact her ancestry.) Her husband, the Reverend Asa Bedford, was from a tiny Alabama town, farther in from the coast, called Blood Brook. Years later, when I decided to visit the area, I stared at the small dot that marked it on an auto club map of the state for hours at a time before finally venturing there. When I arrived, I was at once frightened and surprised by the accuracy of my imagination. It was a dirt crossroad of shanties, the air thick with mosquitoes and flies, and a heat that would wilt Vermont gardens in minutes.

In my mind there was no school in Blood Brook, and indeed there was not. I had always envisioned a church there to inspire Asa, and indeed there was. White paint peeled off its clapboards like rotting skin, and spiked grass grew tall in the cracks of its front walk: With the end of the world imminent, there was little reason to paint or weed.

That geographic background noted and my own cattiness revealed, I should also note that I liked the Bedfords very much when I met them. Most people did: They were apocalyptic eccentrics, but she was sweet and he was kind. I know they had followers and I assume they had friends.

When they came to Vermont, the Bedfords lived thirty minutes north of us in Lawson, and Reverend Bedford's small parish was another twenty or thirty minutes north of that, in Fallsburg. His church—a renovated Quaker meetinghouse ten miles northwest of Newport, on a two-lane state highway with nothing around it but trees—was an easy morning walk to the Canadian border. At its peak, Bedford's congregation consisted of roughly five dozen parishioners from Vermont and Quebec's Eastern Townships who believed with all their hearts that the Second Coming would occur in their lifetime.

When the Bedfords arrived in the Green Mountains, convinced that Vermont's rural Northeast Kingdom was ripe for revival, they had one child, a seven-year-old boy they named Jared, but whom Mrs. Bedford always called Foogie—a diminutive, of sorts, for her own family's name.

Even if my mother had not been a midwife, I would have met the Bedfords, although I don't imagine I would have gotten to know them as well as I did, or that today our families' two names would be linked in so many people's minds. And although the first link between us was byzantine, it was as natural, cohesive, and inextricable as an umbilical cord. Foogie was schooled at home by his parents, which meant that my friend Rollie's mother visited the family periodically as an examiner for the state education department. It was Mrs. McKenna's responsibility to make sure that the family was adhering to the basics of the required curriculum. Perhaps because the Bedfords were new to Vermont, perhaps because Mrs. McKenna wanted to be sure that young Foogie had as much exposure as possible to the world beyond his father's church, she recommended her daughter, Rollie, as a diligent and responsible baby-sitter for the boy.

It was therefore in the capacity of friend of the baby-sitter that I first met the Bedfords, when my father drove me there late on a Saturday afternoon to keep Rollie company while she took care of Foogie that night. Rollie had been there since breakfast, while the Reverend and Mrs. Bedford were in southern New Hampshire at a Twin State Baptist conference. Although they weren't Baptists, Asa was usually able to find a family or two at these sorts of weekend retreats who would listen with interest to his beliefs, and consider an invitation to his church.

Their house was modest and old, and buried in deep wood at the end of a long dirt road. A century ago the woods had been meadows and farmland, my father observed the first time he drove me there, motioning out the window of the Jeep at the squat, mossy stone walls we passed as we bounced down the road. I couldn't imagine such a thing; I couldn't imagine someone clearing forest this thick in an era before chain saws and skidders.

Although most Vermont hill farmers were careful to construct their homes on the peaks of their property, there were some who for one reason or another chose valleys—perhaps because a dowser had found a shallow well there. Whoever had built the Bedford place a hundred years ago was among those exceptions. I could feel myself lurching forward in the Jeep as we descended deeper into the woods, and the vehicle's lap belt pressed against my waist.

My first impression of the Bedford place—an impression garnered two months before my thirteenth birthday—was that someone with little money or carpentry skill was working hard to keep it tidy. The grass was high in the small lawn surrounding the house, as if it hadn't been cut yet that spring (Memorial Day was just over a week away), but someone had laid square pieces of bluestone in a path from the dirt road to the front door so recently that I could actually see the prints from a human palm pressed flush in the dirt against the stones' edges. Two of the windows on the first floor had long cracks sealed with white putty, but behind the panes were delicate, lacy curtains. Many of the clapboards were rotting, but the nails that were slammed through them to keep them attached to the exterior walls were so new that the sides of the house were sprinkled with small silver dots.

The place was a compact two-story box, its roof's angle wide and gentle, its walls the yellow of daffodils. The paint had begun to flake, but it was still bright enough that when the Reverend Bedford started up his car to drive Rollie and me home that night, the beams from his headlights gave the house a sulfurous glow.

The Saturday I met the three Bedfords—Foogie in late afternoon and the Reverend and his wife close to ten o'clock at night—the cluster of cells that would become Veil (spelled with an *e* for reasons I imagine only Asa fully understood) did not yet exist, but would be formed very soon.

Whatever fears of or enthusiasms for the apocalypse Asa harbored inside him were not usually apparent in his appearance. His face was almost as round as his eyeglasses, and his hair had receded back far on his head; what hair he had, however, was thick and reddish brown. Most of the times that I saw him he was wearing crisp, well-ironed white shirts, fully buttoned. He was, like my father, a man who I assumed had been quite thin when he was young, but was now growing wide and heavyset around the middle.

He looked like the sort of rural businessman I might observe in St.

Johnsbury or Montpelier: not as sophisticated, in my eyes anyway, as the executives I'd see on television or, of course, my own father.

He was also one of those rare and special adults who was capable of being every bit as silly as children. And Foogie adored him for it. I saw Asa pretend to be a mule and walk the lawn on his hands and knees, snorting and neighing and carrying his delighted son on his back. I witnessed the preacher waddling like a duck for Foogie, and making up rhymes to teach the boy how to spell certain sounds:

"Fox! Box! Boston Red Sox!"

"I was sent for the rent on the polka-dot tent!"

"I wish the fish would eat from a dish, because now there's fish food on the floor!"

Around Rollie and me he was gentle and serene; I understood on some level that he was considered a little strange by most people, but my family and the McKennas certainly didn't object to us being around him or his family. The Northeast Kingdom has always had its share of cults and communes, and Asa's little church was simply one more essentially harmless example.

On the other hand, although I never heard him preach, I imagined he was partial to what I would now call the spider-and-fly school of sermons. Sometimes he would allow himself the sort of remark in front of Rollie and me that certainly would have alarmed our parents had we shared it with them. One particularly dark night when he was about to drive the two of us home after we'd taken care of Foogie, he stood on his bluestone walk and looked up into the black sky and murmured, "Soon night shall be no more. Soon we'll need no light of lamp or sun."

On another occasion, when Mrs. Bedford was upstairs putting Foogie to bed and he saw that the only mail he had received that day were bills from the phone and gas companies, he said to the envelopes— unaware that Rollie and I were within earshot—"I am indeed happy to render unto Caesar what is Caesar's, especially since I know you will all burn that second death in the lake of fire."

He had a thick southern accent, which made his sentences always sound like songs to me, even if some of those songs could be unexpectedly frightening.

Charlotte Bedford was a petite, fragile-looking woman, barely bigger than Rollie and me as our bodies approached their teens. She was not tall, and there was little meat on her bones. Her skin always seemed almost ghostly white to us, which I don't believe was a look Charlotte cultivated. (A few years after the Bedfords had passed through my family's life like a natural disaster, I was in college in Massachusetts. During my sophomore year I became friends with a proud belle from a town on Lake Pontchartrain, Louisiana, who did in fact strive to look as pale as paste, so I am confident I know the difference.)

But she didn't behave as though she was sickly, and that would obviously become an important issue at the trial. My mother believed there was a critical difference between fragile and sickly. She discouraged many women with histories of medical illness from having their babies at home, but those sorts of women who simply strike us all as frail when we see them in shopping malls or drugstores but do not in reality have a diagnosed, physiological problem—those sorts of women my mother was happy to help when they became pregnant. My mother believed a home birth was an extremely empowering and invigorating experience, and gave fragile women energy, confidence, and strength: They learned just what their bodies could do, and it gave them comfort.

And I know my mother figured out pretty quickly that Charlotte was not prepared for the short days, numbing cold, and endless snow of a Vermont winter. Especially a Vermont winter not far from the northern border of the state. As early as October, when Charlotte was in her second trimester and visiting my mother at the office in our home in Reddington for her monthly prenatal exam, she became frightened and morose when she talked of the weather.

"I just don't know what we're going to do up here, I just don't know how we're going to get by," I heard her telling my mother. "Asa hasn't even had time to get himself a snow shovel, and I just don't know where to begin finding proper boots. And it's all so expensive, just so frightfully expensive."

They had arrived in Vermont at the best possible time of the year to become lulled into the mistaken belief that the state has a hospitable, welcoming, and moderate climate. I can imagine her thoughts when they arrived in mid-April, just after that year's awful mud season, when the rocky hills of Vermont—hills thick with maple and pine and ash—explode overnight in color, and the days grow long and warm. She probably imagined the mythic winters were indeed just that: myths. Sure, it snowed, but the state had plows. Maybe the rain sometimes froze, maybe the driveway would get a little muddy in March . . . but nothing a minister and his family couldn't handle.

But her introduction to fall in Vermont was nasty and winter harsher still. There was a killing frost that year in late August, and she lost the flowers she'd planted by the bluestone walk the previous spring; there was a light snow during the second week in September, and almost nine inches were dumped on the state the Friday and Saturday of Columbus Day weekend.

Charlotte had eyes as gray as moonstone, and thin hair the color of straw. She was pretty if you didn't mind the subtle but unmistakable atmosphere of bad luck that seemed to pulse from that pale, pale skin.

Rollie and I spent the Fourth of July at the Bedfords', baby-sitting Foogie. We spent the afternoon in T-shirts and shorts, watching Foogie run back and forth under the sprinkler in his bathing suit, and then spraying the boy with the hose. He loved it. Like his mother, he had white, almost translucent skin, but he had Asa's red hair and round head. He was a sweet boy, but as ugly as they come.

Rollie was menstruating by then, but I wasn't. She was in the midst of her fourth period that weekend, a fact she shared with me with no small amount of pride: the agony of the cramps she was stoically enduring, the flow that she claimed was so strong she'd have to leave me alone with Foogie almost every hour, while she raced inside to insert a fresh tampon.

Once when Foogie wasn't within earshot, I teased Rollie by suggesting she was fabricating her period for my benefit.

"How can you say that?" she asked.

"Your white shorts," I answered. "When I get a period, there's no way I'll wear white. What if the tampon leaks?"

"Tampons don't leak," she said firmly, and in a tone that implied I didn't have the slightest idea what I was talking about. "Besides, why in the world would I want to pretend I was having my period? It's not like this is some French class I want to get out of."

I shrugged my shoulders that I didn't know, but I did. Or at least I thought I did. Rollie and I were both pretty girls, but I had something she didn't: breasts. Not so large that boys would tease me or I had ever been embarrassed about them, but apparent enough that someone like Rollie would notice. Perhaps because of my mother's candor about bodies and birth and how babies wind up in a womb in the first place, Rollie and I were aspiring tarts. We couldn't talk enough about kissing and petting and contraception—rubbers, the pill, the diaphragm, and something that struck us both as incomprehensibly horrible, called an IUD.

Standing among the dog-eared paperback mysteries Rollie's parents kept in a bookcase in their bedroom was a well-read copy of *The Sensuous Man* and—behind the rows of paperbacks, against a back wall of the bookcase—a hardbound copy of *The Joy of Sex.* Rollie and I read it together often at her house, and garnered from it what I have since discovered was a frighteningly precocious comprehension of cunnilingus, fellatio, and all manner of foreplay. We imagined our lovers someday performing the recommended exercises in the books: sticking their curled tongues deep into shot glasses, doing push-ups for hours. I had yet to see a real penis then, and I had a feeling an actual erection might scare me to death when I did, but between the anatomic details of how the male and female apparatus functioned that I'd gleaned over time from my mother, and the pleasure to be found in those organs suggested by the McKennas' books, I think I was much less squeamish in the summer between my seventh and eighth grades about sex than most girls my age. Rollie, too.

We both expected that when we returned to school in the fall, the boys would begin to notice us. We weren't too tall, which was important, and we didn't have pimples. We were smart, which we knew would intimidate some boys, but not the sort we were interested in: Probably nothing, we thought, scared a boy like Tom Corts, and certainly not something as harmless as an interest in books.

And, fortunately, we looked nothing like each other, which we also assumed was a good thing: It would minimize the chance that the same boy might ever be interested in both of us, or we in him. We understood from our years of riding and playing together that we were a competitive pair, and the fact that I was a blonde and she a brunette, that I had blue eyes and she had brown, would decrease the chances that a boy would ever interfere with our friendship.

Or, as Rollie explained it that Fourth of July, "Boys look at us like we look at horses: color, height, eyes, tail. They can't help but have preferences." Her horse was a chestnut brunette, and in Rollie McKenna's cosmology of preference, this meant she would probably always prefer chestnut horses as long as she lived. Human nature.

That afternoon Rollie helped me plot ways to maintain contact with Tom Corts until school resumed in September and we would be together in the same section of the brick Lego-like maze that someone thought was a functional design for a school. Tom had a job that summer that I interpreted as one of those signals (like, in some way, his seemingly endless wardrobe of dark turtlenecks) that he wanted more from the world than the chance to fix cars in his family's beat-up garage, or to joust on motorcycles until the rescue squad had to rush him to the hospital with a limb dangling by a tendon. He was working for Powder Peak, the nearby ski resort, cutting the lawns around the base lodge where the company also had its offices, and assisting the maintenance crews as they tuned up the chairlifts and grooming machines. He was about to turn fifteen (just as I would soon turn thirteen), and he could have hung out at the garage with his brothers and father, he could have spent July and August smoking an endless chain of cigarettes with his brothers' and his father's friends, but he didn't: He hitchhiked up to the mountain every morning and found a ride home from an adult member of the crew every evening. And while mowing lawns and oiling chairlifts isn't neuroscience, the fact that he was doing it some miles from home suggested to me ambition.

Of course, it also kept him away from the village most of the time. And while Tom and I had kissed only once, and that one time had been three and a half months ago, I was sure we could have a future together if one of us could find a way to bring our bodies into a reasonable proximity. I was convinced that Tom hadn't tried to kiss me again for two simple—and, in my mind, reassuring—reasons. First, he was two years my senior, and therefore feared with the gallantry of a man who was kind and wise that I was too young to kiss on a regular basis. In addition, the fact that he was two years older than I was meant our paths simply didn't cross with any frequency—certainly from September through June, when we both attended the union high school but had a full grade between us as a buffer zone, and now in the summer as well, since he had an adult man's commute to the ski resort.

If Rollie wasn't as convinced as I that Tom Corts was my destiny, she at least agreed he would be a good boy to date. He was intelligent, independent, and cute. And since it would be no more likely for Tom's and my paths to cross in the fall, when he would be in the tenth grade and I in the eighth, Rollie believed we had to attempt to move the relationship forward in the summer. In her now barely thirteen-year-old mind, this meant simply being visible before Tom so he could again take some sort of initiative.

"The creemee stand," she suggested thoughtfully that afternoon.

"You have to hang out at the creemee stand once you figure out when he goes there."

"I'm not going to hang out at the creemee stand. I'll get fat."

"You don't have to eat anything. You just have to be there."

"No way. I think I'd get sick inhaling all the grease from the French fries."

"You don't inhale grease."

"And I'd wind up with pimples."

"You probably will anyway as soon as you get your period."

"You didn't!"

"I wash my face seven or eight times a day. Every two hours."

"Then I will, too. What do you think I am, a slob?"

"I think you're making excuses not to run into Tom because you're shy."

"I don't see you going after anyone special."

"There aren't any boys I'm interested in right now."

I shook my head, as Foogie aimed the sprinkler at a vacant hornet's nest near the awning of the house. "I am not going to hang out at the creemee stand, it's that simple."

"Do you have a better idea?"

"The general store, maybe. He has to buy his cigarettes before he goes to the mountain."

"Or when he gets home."

"Right."

"You can't just hang out at the general store, you know."

"But I can be there when he is."

And so it went for most of the day. We were still outside, sitting on the front steps and awaiting the Bedfords' return, as the afternoon slowly gave way to evening. Through the living-room window we could hear Foogie watching reruns of old situation comedies on television, while crashing a plastic flying saucer over and over again into the plush pillows on the couch.

The stories that the attorneys and newspaper reporters would choose to tell—although in my mind, certainly not my mother's story— began that afternoon. The Bedfords arrived just before six, well after most barbecues in Vermont had begun to smoke but hours before the night sky would be lit by the glowing, spidery tendrils of fireworks. As the Reverend Bedford was paying Rollie (a fee she would share that day with me, although she was the official Foogie-sitter), Mrs. Bedford pulled me into the kitchen.

In a voice that was whispery and soft, in a tone that suggested she was discussing a vaguely forbidden subject, she inquired, "Your mother, Connie: Is she truly a midwife?"

FIVE

I've helped birth the sons and daughters of two bakers, but no bankers.

My mothers have been painters and sculptors and photographers, and all sorts of people blessed with really amazing talents. Three of my mothers have been incredibly gifted fiber artists, and two hooked the most magical rugs I've ever seen in my life. When parents have been artistic but poor, I've been paid with quilts they've made themselves, and paintings and carvings and stained glass. Our house is beautiful because of barter.

And there have been lots of musicians among both my mothers and my fathers, including Banjo Stan. And Sunny Starker. And the Tullys.

There have been young people who farm, carpenters— probably enough in number to have built Rome in a day— wives of men who run printing presses, women who make jewelry, throw pots, roll candles from beeswax. If I look back through my records, I can find a few schoolteachers, a newspaper editor, journeyman electricians, a woman who grooms dogs, a man who cuts hair, the wives of auto mechanics, the husbands of laboring waitresses, a couple of ski instructors, chimney sweeps, roofers, pastors, loggers, welders, excavators, a masseuse, machinists, crane operators, a female professor, and the state's first female commissioner for travel and tourism.

But no bankers. No lawyers. And no doctors.

No people who make ads for a living, or fill cavities, or do other people's taxes.

No people, like Rand, who design houses or office buildings or college science centers.

Those sorts of people usually prefer hospitals to home births, and obstetricians to . . . to people like me. That's cool. They think it's safer, and while the statistics show that most of the time a home birth is no more risky than a hospital one, they need to do what's right for them. That's totally fine with me.

Sometimes I just think it's funny I've never birthed a baby banker.

—from the notebooks of SIBYL DANFORTH, MIDWIFE

WHEN AN AIRPLANE CRASHES, USUALLY FAR MORE THAN ONE THING HAS GONE wrong. The safety systems on passenger planes overlap, and most of the time it demands a string of blunders and bad luck for a plane to plow into a forest outside of Pittsburgh, or skid off a La Guardia runway into Flushing Bay. A Fokker F-28 jet piloted by two competent veterans might someday dive into the historic waters of Lake Champlain seconds before it is supposed to glide to the ground at nearby Burlington Airport, killing perhaps fifty-six air travelers and a crew of four, but such a crash would in all likelihood necessitate a litany of human errors and mechanical malfunctions. A wind shear could certainly take that Fokker F-28 and abruptly press it into the earth from a height of two or three thousand feet, and someday one might, but it would probably need some help.

It might demand, for example, that the captain had been ill when he was supposed to have attended his airline's recurrent training on wind shears—when to expect one, how to pull a plane through one.

Or perhaps it had been a smooth flight from Chicago to Burlington, and although there were now rolling gray clouds and thunderstorms throughout northwest Vermont, the gentle ride east had lulled the pilots a bit, and they were ignoring the FAA's sterile cockpit rule prohibiting extraneous conversation below ten thousand feet. Perhaps the pilot was commenting on how much his children liked to hike the deep woods northeast of Burlington at the exact moment the wind shear slammed hard into the roof of the jet, his remark about woods postponing by a critical second his decision to power the engines forward and abort the landing.

Or perhaps at the exact second the cockpit's wind shear alert screamed its shrill warning and the pilot was instinctively turning the jet to the right to abort the landing, the air-traffic controller in Burlington's tower was telling him of the shear and to climb to the left; in the chaos of warnings—one mechanical, one human—there was just that half-second of indecision necessary for the gust to send a jet built in the 1970s into the waters rippling over hundreds of eighteenth- and nineteenth-century ferries, rowboats, and wrought-iron cannons.

I am telling you this because it was the sort of thing my mother's attorney talked about a great deal when he first agreed to defend her. He could go on this way for a long time, always coming to the same point. The shit, so to speak, had to really hit the fan for a plane to auger in.

My mother's attorney had been a ground mechanic in the air force in the Vietnam War, but had wanted desperately to be a pilot: He was both color-blind and nearsighted, however, and so his eyesight prevented him from this. As I recall, his analogies in 1981 revolved around icy wings instead of wind shears, or—a personal favorite of his—the incredible chain of events that would usually have to occur for a jet to crash because it ran out of fuel. But he loved his airplane analogies.

As he sat around our dining-room table amidst his piles of yellow legal pads or as he paced the kitchen, occasionally stopping before the window that faced the ski trails on Mount Chittenden, his point was unchanging throughout those days and nights when he first began rolling around all of the variables in his mind: It would take the same sort of string of misfortune and malfeasance for one of my mother's patients to die in childbirth as it did for an airplane to crash.

And it certainly seemed so, at least initially, in the death of Charlotte Fugett Bedford. She died in the middle of March, after a nightmarishly long labor. The black ice that fell and fell during the night had trapped my mother and her assistant alone with Asa and Charlotte: Even the sand trucks and plows were sliding like plastic sleds off the roads. The phones weren't down for particularly long on March 14, but they were down for just about four crucial hours between twelve twenty-five and four-fifteen in the morning.

And for a time Charlotte had indeed shown signs that had led my mother to fear a placental abruption: The placenta detaches itself from the uterine wall, so that the mother may slowly bleed to death. There was a moment when Charlotte bled profusely from her vagina, and the pain inside the woman seemed more serious than the more natural agony that is labor. But the bleeding slowed to a trickle, then stopped, and if there had been an abruption, apparently it had clotted and started to heal itself.

And at another point Charlotte's blood pressure had dropped, falling briefly to seventy-five over fifty, while the baby's heartbeat had slowed to between sixty and seventy beats per minute. My mother and her assistant had only been together three months that March, and Anne Austin still had a lot to learn: When she—a young woman barely twenty-two—placed the metal Fetalscope upon Charlotte's stomach and heard how slowly the baby's heart was beating, she cried out for my mother to listen, which of course led Charlotte to cry out in fear.

Clearly there was chaos in that bedroom well before the worst would occur.

Consequently, when Vietnam veteran turned Vermont litigator Stephen Hastings first agreed to represent my mother, he concluded that it must have taken a combination of inclement weather, downed phone lines, and bad luck for Charlotte Bedford to die. In his mind, had there not been black ice on the roads, my mother would have driven her patient to the hospital in Newport. Had the phones been working, she would have called the rescue squad, and they might have rushed Charlotte there. And, of course, my mother would have done everything possible had Charlotte gone into shock due to a placental abruption. My mother had been prepared to administer oxygen. She'd already instructed Anne to pull from their calico birthing bag the plastic tubing and needle and clear bag of fluid she would inject into Charlotte intravenously to keep her hydrated . . . but Charlotte suddenly stabilized.

No, the cause of death had not been placental abruption, as the autopsy would later confirm. And my mother understood this well before the real crisis began: what looked for all the world to her like a ruptured cerebral aneurysm somewhere deep inside Charlotte's brain.

Sometimes I would overhear my mother try and explain to Stephen that while there had been moments of turmoil and confusion that night, the chain of events that cost Charlotte Fugett Bedford her life was nothing so complex as the sort of thing that pulled planes from the sky and people to their deaths. She would try and tell him it was more cut-and-dried than all that, and he would gently remind her that it wasn't.

Or at least, he would say, it would not be in the eyes of a jury. And then once more they would discuss what had occurred in that bedroom that was indisputable.

Charlotte Fugett Bedford went into labor with her second child on Thursday, March 13, 1981. It was late morning when her contractions began coming in earnest, and Charlotte decided that her back pains had nothing to do with the way she had lifted the vacuum when she had finished cleaning the living room. At one thirty-five she phoned her husband at the office at his church and spoke to him for three minutes. At one-forty she phoned my mother, reaching her as she was leaving the house to have the oil changed in her station wagon. Charlotte and my mother spoke for six minutes.

My mother knew that Charlotte's labor had been relatively easy with Foogie, although the first stage—that period when the cervix dilates to ten centimeters, and the contractions become longer, more frequent, and more pronounced—had taken a day and a half in Alabama heat. The second stage, however, had been brief: Once Charlotte was ready to push, she had Foogie through the birth canal in twenty minutes.

Although there is no recorded transcript of my mother's and Charlotte's conversation on the telephone, the prosecution never doubted her version. She said that Charlotte told her the contractions early that Thursday afternoon were still easily twenty minutes apart and lasting perhaps thirty or thirty-five seconds. My mother therefore decided to have the oil changed in her car as she had planned and then head north to the Bedfords'. She figured she would be there by three or three-thirty, and she was.

Nevertheless, she did phone her new apprentice and ask Anne to drop by the Bedfords' right away. She wasn't sure when Asa would return, and she wanted to be sure that Charlotte had company.

I remember getting off the school bus in Reddington that afternoon just as the skies were starting to spit a cold March rain. There was still a thick quilt of snow on the mountains, freshened perhaps every other night, but the only snow in Reddington that particular day were the drifts along the shady sides of the buildings. The temperature still hovered most afternoons in the twenties or thirties, but we knew winter was winding down and mud season would soon be upon us.

I was not surprised that my mother was gone when I walked inside our house. I didn't have to read the note she had scribbled in blue with one of the felt-tip pens that she loved, to know she was up at the Bedfords'. I had been expecting that note for days.

At about the same moment that I was returning home from school, one of Asa's parishioners stopped by the Bedford house and picked up Foogie. The Bedfords' home was small, and Foogie's parents had agreed it would be best for the boy to be someplace else when his brother or sister arrived.

The first stage of Charlotte's labor was much longer for the second child than most midwives or doctors would have expected. My mother arrived at the Bedfords' in the middle of the afternoon, and testified in court that she anticipated that Charlotte would deliver her baby soon after dinner. She said she never went into a delivery with any sort of expectations, or hourly objectives in her mind: a first stage that should last ten hours, for example, followed by ninety minutes of pushing. She said no midwife or doctor did. But when pressed by the state's attorney, she said if she had any expectations at all, she might have thought Charlotte's cervix would be fully dilated by six or seven in the evening, and the child pushed into the world by nine or ten that night—at the latest.

Fifteen minutes before midnight, when Charlotte was eight centimeters dilated and the baby's head had descended below the ischial spines to the first positive position—when there was, in my mother's mind, no longer a chance that the umbilical cord could slip past the baby's skull through the cervix, endangering the child—my mother carefully ruptured the membranes damming Charlotte's amniotic waters.

"I don't understand why you did that," Anne whispered to my mother, concerned that the intervention had been unnecessary.

"It was time," my mother answered with a shrug.

At midnight it started to rain, and the droplets turned to ice when they hit the cold ground. At that moment it was thirty-three degrees Fahrenheit at the weather station at Lyndon State College. At twelve twenty-five, the phones between Newport and Richford, between Reddington and Derby Line, went dead, brought down by the weight of the ice forming on the phone lines, and some ill-timed gusts of wind. My mother and her apprentice had no idea the phone lines were down then, but they would discover it soon.

Charlotte was fully dilated by one in the morning. Her first stage had lasted a solid thirteen hours. Charlotte's transition, that nightmarish period for many mothers just before they must begin the desperately hard business of pushing, those moments when many mothers fear with a horror that's visceral that they will not survive this ordeal, was rocky. Both my mother and Asa Bedford testified that Charlotte began sobbing through her pain, insisting that the being within her was going to rip her apart. She begged them to help her, telling them this felt different than it had with Foogie, this was killing pain, this was a torture she could not endure and she would not survive.

"I can't do this, I can't do this! God, I can't do this!" she wailed.

And, in at least one regard, Charlotte was right when she said it felt different than it had with her first child. Unlike during her first delivery, that day and night in Vermont she was experiencing the rigors of labor with a baby in the right occipitoposterior position: The child's head was pressing against the sacrum, the bone in the rear of her pelvis. Instead of the child facing down as it crowns, it was possible it would emerge sunnyside up.

But this wasn't alarming my mother. Often the baby rotates at the end of the first stage of labor or at the beginning of the second. And to increase the chances that the child would spin—and to decrease some of Charlotte's back pain—my mother had Charlotte on her feet and walking around between some of the contractions, and she had her laboring often on her hands and knees. Sometimes she asked Anne to apply hot compresses or towels to Charlotte's back; occasionally she had Charlotte squat.

Between one and one-thirty in the morning, when Charlotte was most miserable and her sobs were loud and long and filled with despair, Asa prayed. My mother said under oath that she still viewed the delivery as normal, and nothing had occurred that would have alarmed any obstetrician or midwife anywhere in the world. Charlotte's labor to this point had been hard, but it hadn't been life-threatening or dangerous for the child inside her.

Asa prayed softly at first, his voice even and calm, but as Charlotte's wails grew more plaintive and horrid, his praying grew more animated and intense.

Both my mother and Anne testified that he prayed to the Holy Father to help His child Charlotte through this ordeal, to give her the strength and the courage to endure it, and to protect her throughout it. He was most eloquent when Charlotte was most quiet: When Charlotte would open her mouth wide and yell, he was often reduced to repeating the Lord's Prayer over and over.

Sometimes Charlotte tried saying the Lord's Prayer with him, but she was never able to get through it before she would have to stop to breathe through her pain.

And my mother kept trying to reassure them both—and, as the night grew long, her own assistant as well—that back labor was hard and painful, but it wasn't fatal.

Shortly after one-thirty, not long after my mother had asked Asa to climb on the bed and sit behind his wife while she pushed, my mother noticed the blood. She told herself it was mere bloody show, but the timing of the flow and the quantity of the stream made her own heart beat in a way that made her nervous. She and Anne had just put the clean, oven-sterilized sheet on the bed on which she expected they would catch the child, and the stain spread on the white sheet like a glass of red wine toppled upon fresh table linens.

Charlotte surprised my mother by heaving her body with such force that she almost rolled off the bed, and by the time my mother had caught her and told her that she was doing fine, the blood had smeared across Charlotte's thighs and her buttocks, and the palm of her hand where she had slapped the bed in her pain.

Her suffering seemed extreme, and when my mother took her blood pressure, she saw it had fallen during the hour: The systolic reading had dropped to eighty, and the diastolic to sixty. Charlotte's pulse was up into the one-twenties, then the one-thirties, but the baby's heartbeat was as infrequent as ninety small beats per minute.

My mother decided she would not have Charlotte begin to push for another few minutes, while she monitored her. If Charlotte's blood pressure continued to fall, if she thought the woman was slipping into shock or she saw any further signs of fetal distress, she planned to call the town rescue squad and have her taken to the hospital. If for some reason they were unavailable, she would drive her there herself.

Three minutes later Charlotte's blood pressure had slipped to seventy-five over fifty, and the baby's heartbeat had slowed to sixty or seventy beats per minute. The vaginal bleeding had become a small, almost imperceptible trickle, and then stopped completely . . . but the wet sheets were a reminder of the size of the earlier wave. And so my mother said to the two parents in the room with her that it would be in both Charlotte's interest and the child's interest to have the baby in a hospital. She said—and apparently her words were at once appropriately dispassionate and concerned—there was a chance the placenta was detaching itself from the wall of the uterus. This meant, she explained, both that their little baby wasn't getting the sustenance it needed, and Charlotte might be bleeding inside.

My mother never came quickly or lightly to the decision that one of her patients should go to a hospital, but she also never hesitated to have a woman in the midst of dangerous complications deliver her baby with modern medicine's extensive safety net unfurled below her. For one reason or another, Sibyl Danforth took roughly one out of every twenty-five mothers to the hospital before March 14, 1981.

Both she and Asa later testified that had the phones been working that night, things might have ended differently. Unlike some parents who would plead with my mother to let them keep trying, parents who either loved the idea of a home birth so much or hated hospitals with such extreme loathing that they would labor for hours despite the danger, the Bedfords readily agreed they would venture to the mechanized, metal-railed birthing beds and sterile operating rooms of the North Country Hospital in Newport.

My mother picked up the phone in the bedroom to dial the rescue squad (and back then most phones in the Northeast Kingdom indeed demanded that one literally dial them) and discovered there was no purring tone. Reflexively she pressed the twin buttons in the receiver's cradle and she checked the connections: the connection of the cord to the telephone itself and the jack near the base of the wall. When she saw that both were attached, she suggested that Anne test the phone in the kitchen downstairs. A moment later Anne called up the stairs to inform my mother that the phone on the first floor wasn't working either.

"It's gone, too!" she cried up to them, and both my mother and Asa detected panic in the young woman's voice, panic they hoped Charlotte hadn't heard. Clearly, however, she had.

Rain and hard crystals of ice had been rapping against the bedroom windows for well over an hour now, although my mother said she had only become aware of the sound immediately after Anne yelled the bad news from the small entryway at the foot of the stairs. After the apprentice had discovered conclusively that the phones were down, Charlotte grew quiet with fear, and the insistent rain and ice against the glass sounded, my mother would say on the witness stand, "like someone was heaving handfuls of gravel as hard as they could, as if they were trying to shatter the glass."

My mother called Anne back to the bedroom to keep Charlotte and Asa company while she went outside to warm up her car: Her station wagon was bigger than the Bedfords' little Sunbird or Anne's tiny Maverick, and Charlotte would be most comfortable in it.

How slippery had the ground become? My mother's struggle across the bluestone walk Asa had built and across fifteen yards of driveway to the spot where she had parked her car would have been comical if it hadn't been so painful. Three days later, on Monday, her attorney had the bruises—still black and blue and ugly—along both of my mother's legs photographed. They also took pictures of the long cuts along the insides of her hands, and the sprained and swollen ankle around which she would wear an Ace bandage for weeks and weeks.

She fell four times, she said, before she crawled on her hands and knees to her automobile, and then pulled herself to her feet by holding on to the front door's metal handle. Yet she still planned on driving Charlotte to the hospital, and began by attempting to bring the car right up to the front steps of the house—yard and bluestone be damned—so Charlotte wouldn't have to walk along the ice rink that had overtaken the Bedford property. As she pressed her foot down slowly upon the accelerator, the car's tires spun in place like immobile carnival wheels, before abruptly pushing the automobile forward and then twisting it almost three hundred and sixty degrees. It slid into the remains of an ice-covered snowbank one of Asa's parishioners had built while plowing the driveway throughout the winter. And although my mother's car wasn't damaged, she knew it would be impossible to drive to the hospital.

If my mother cried—and it seemed to me that she had every right to as she pushed open the car door and rolled onto the ground to begin her return to the Bedfords' house—she had stopped by the time she rejoined Charlotte and Asa and Anne. But she said later she'd cried. She had birthed dead babies before, little stillborn things whose souls, in her mind, had gone to heaven before their flesh had known a world bigger than a womb, but experience didn't make the ordeal any less sad. She said she always cried for those babies and for their parents, and she feared now that the baby inside Charlotte would die, and the Bedfords would lose their second child. (Later, the State's investigation would reveal that babies had died three times in my mother's care prior to March 14, 1981, or almost exactly as often as it happened to women in the care of obstetricians.)

My mother testified that although the ground was slick with ice, there was a dusting of snow sticking to the grass, and when she saw it she imagined the vernix covering the body of the Bedfords' spiritless, unbreathing little baby. She imagined that baby was a boy.

But although my mother feared they would lose the baby, she said it never crossed her mind that Charlotte Fugett Bedford would die. She knew she could stop the bleeding once she had delivered the baby (dead or alive), and surely the phone lines would be quickly fixed. She reminded herself that the woman would have to lose six or seven or even eight pints of blood before cardiac arrest would occur, and that, in my mother's view, was a lot of blood.

And she knew in her birthing bag she had syringes, and glass vials of Pitocin and Ergotrate—drugs that caused the uterus to contract hard, and could sometimes control internal bleeding. Of course, it was illegal for her to have these regulated substances in her possession, but every midwife carried them. My mother wasn't unique.

Nevertheless, the image of Sibyl Danforth running around northern Vermont with a big bag full of illegal drugs and syringes wasn't a helpful one in a court of law.

Ironically, when my mother returned to the Bedfords' bedroom, Charlotte seemed better. Her blood pressure was returning to normal, as was her baby's heartbeat: one hundred, one-ten, then a reassuring one hundred and twenty little thumps per minute. Charlotte had stopped bleeding, and she certainly wasn't showing any symptoms of shock. Her skin wasn't clammy, her complexion seemed fine, her attitude was good. There would be no need, after all, for oxygen or an intravenous drip. There would be no need for Pitocin.

"I believe I am fine now, Sibyl," she said, the weariness in her voice tinged with hope.

Charlotte may have meant to convey nothing more with this statement than the idea that her pain, for the moment, had become tolerable. Bearable. Endurable. But in Charlotte's tone my mother had heard more. In Charlotte's voice my mother had heard a loving testimony to the power of prayer: As my mother had been slipping so badly outside among the falling drops of cold water and ice that each step since had caused her an excruciating splinter of pain, Asa and Charlotte and even Anne had prayed. Asa had knelt by the side of his wife's bed, her long, pallid fingers wrapped in his hands, and together they had prayed for her bleeding to cease and her pain to subside; they had prayed that the baby inside her would live, and their lives would be blessed by its presence.

Anne said at the trial she had never heard as much love in a man's voice as she did in Asa Bedford's that early morning.

My mother was at once comforted and moved. She no longer feared placental abruption. "Well," she said simply, "let's get that little baby out of you." It was, according to the note that she scribbled, three minutes after two in the morning.

My mother sat Charlotte up on the bed between Asa's legs and had her lean against him once more: Her back was against his chest, and his back, in turn, was against the headboard. Asa's arms could reach the inside of his wife's thighs and hold her legs apart as she pushed, so the baby would have room to descend. Charlotte's head and neck and spine were aligned, and she sat upon a firm throw pillow my mother had recently purchased at a tag sale, then washed, so her bottom was a couple of inches above the mattress.

My mother did not believe the baby had spun during its descent. Consequently, she anticipated the child would emerge facing the ceiling, instead of the ground, and the back of its head would continue causing Charlotte pain as it made its final journey through her pelvis.

Charlotte had labored once before and she had attended some of my mother's birthing classes, so she knew how to breathe and push. She knew how to ride a second-stage contraction, and make the most of each one. She knew when to hold air inside her and push, and when to relax and take shallow, light breaths.

For an hour Charlotte pushed through each contraction, with my mother and Asa and Anne encouraging her to push an extra second or two each time:

"You can do it, a little more, a little more, a little more, a little more!"

"You're doing fine, just fine! Perfect!"

" 'Nother second, 'nother second, 'nother second!"

"My, oh my, you're great, Charlotte, the best, the best!"

"You can do this, you're doin' great, doin' great, doin' great. Doing great!"

"Come on, come on, come on, c'mon, c'mon, c'mon, c'mon!"

I saw my mother deliver enough babies to know she was an inspiring coach and a mesmerizingly energetic cheerleader. And I also saw the way a majority of fathers would allow my mother to provide most of the verbal confidence. My mother was just so good at it.

But who said what between two A.M. and six A.M. would matter greatly to the State, and they insisted—and my mother and her attorney never denied—that Asa and Anne said most of the "You're doing fines," while my mother said most of the "Little mores" and " 'Nother seconds."

Charlotte would close her eyes and clench her teeth as she pushed, and the lines on her face extending out to her temples would grow sharp. Like all mothers about to deliver a baby, Charlotte strained and struggled and no doubt worked as hard as she possibly could. Sometimes her face grew blue when my mother pressed her to bear down even harder.

" 'Nother second, 'nother second, 'nother second!"

"My, oh my, you're great, Charlotte, the best, the best!"

After Charlotte had been pushing for almost a full hour, my mother had her rest for twenty minutes. Charlotte was again experiencing the fear that she wasn't going to be able to push this baby out, and she was scared. My mother reassured her that the baby was doing fine, and so was she.

The baby's head, my mother said in court, had made progress during that hour, although the autopsy would be inconclusive. The medical examiner could never be sure how far the baby had descended, and it was certainly impossible for him to say with confidence where it had been at three or four or five in the morning.

At three-fifteen, Charlotte resumed pushing. With her jaw locked tight but her lips parted, she continued trying to push her baby into the world. Sometimes her head would be back against Asa's shoulder, and sometimes her chin would fall down toward her own chest.

"You can do it, a little more, a little more, a little more, a little more!"

"You're doing fine, just fine! Perfect!"

She tried, my mother said, as hard as any woman she had ever seen. The surges sweeping through Charlotte's body were long, and my mother persuaded her to make the most of each peak.

And between them Charlotte would catch her breath, and then she would try again.

"Come on, come on, come on, c'mon, c'mon, c'mon, c'mon!"

A few minutes past four in the morning, my mother had Charlotte rest a second time. She could see Charlotte was exhausted, and she could see Charlotte's confidence was failing.

There are two general medical definitions for prolonged second-stage labor: a second stage that has lasted two and a half hours, and a second stage that has continued a full hour without further descent of the head.

My mother insisted that the baby had indeed descended during Charlotte's second effort. By four in the morning, she said later, the child had negotiated the ischial spines and much of the pelvic outlet: It had merely to navigate the pubic bone and then it would crown.

Near four-thirty the urge to push became overwhelming, and Charlotte told my mother and her husband that she wanted to try once more. And so she did. She pushed as hard as she could, she pushed with all of the strength she could find, she pushed so hard that when she would finally exhale, she would grunt like a professional tennis player at the moment her racket is slamming ferociously into the ball on a baseline backhand.

For brief seconds at the height of Charlotte's pushing, my mother could see tufts of the child's dark hair, but the baby always seemed to slip back.

Did my mother consider giving up, and attempting what she knew was probably impossible—navigating the icy roads that separated them from the hospital? My mother said that she did, although she never suggested such a thing to Anne. But even Asa testified that between five and six o'clock in the morning, my mother limped to the bedroom window and pulled the gauzy drapes away to look outside.

"Was that a sand truck I heard?" she asked once in that hour, a remark that her attorney argued was proof she was daydreaming longingly of a cesarean delivery performed by a doctor in Newport.

But from the Bedfords' bedroom window, the driveway still glistened like glass, and the rain and ice had continued to fall. My mother's car still sat by the snowbank, a grim reminder of what the roads were like, and she had only to glance down at the cuts on the palms of her hands to remember how difficult it was to move on foot on that ground.

And, Stephen Hastings pointed out, my mother had not actually heard a sand truck: No town trucks had tried venturing onto the roads in or around Lawson between two-fifteen and six-thirty in the morning. And even at six-thirty, Lawson road crew member Graham Tuttle would testify, the roads were "just plain awful. I drove right on top of the yellow line, sanding and scraping just a single lane. I didn't dare stay on my side of the road, or I'd have wound up in a ditch."

Obviously Charlotte had no choice but to try and push the baby out in her bedroom, and so while my mother may have wished with all her heart that they could go to the hospital, she never suggested the idea to Asa. She never broached the idea of a cesarean section at North Country Hospital, because she knew they had no real hope of getting there.

Besides, my mother really believed Charlotte was making progress. The baby was close, she thought. It might be just one more contraction and determined push away.

And so Charlotte tried. She never pushed again for very long, she never worked through wave after wave of contractions. But as the sun was rising somewhere high above the rows of clouds bringing ice and rain to their corner of Vermont, rising somewhere so far behind the curtains of black and gray that the skies wouldn't lighten until close to seven in the morning that day, Charlotte used all the strength she could muster to try and push her baby past the pubic bone.

Sometimes my mother changed Charlotte's position. Sometimes Charlotte labored squatting. Sometimes she labored with her back upright, but lying slightly on her side.

"You can do it, you can do it, can do it, can-do-it, can-do-it, do-it, do-it, do-it, do-it!"

At ten minutes past six, in the early minutes of her fourth hour of pushing, Charlotte Fugett Bedford suffered what my mother was convinced was a ruptured cerebral aneurysm—or what she would refer to in her own mind as a stroke. She imagined that the intracranial pressure of Charlotte's exertions had caused a small vessel inside the poor woman's brain to burst.

Asa and my mother, right up until that moment, were still telling Charlotte she could do it, she could get that little baby through her and into the bedroom with them:

"My, oh my, you're great, Charlotte, the best, the best!"

" 'Nother second, 'nother second, 'nother second!"

Asa had moved between his wife's legs to catch the child, while Anne and my mother were at her sides, holding her. Abruptly, while struggling in the midst of a contraction, Charlotte's chin shot up from her chest as she pushed with whatever energy she had left, she opened her eyes, and then exhaled with a small squeal. Her husband saw her eyes roll up, then close. My mother and Anne felt the body grow limp in their arms as Charlotte lost consciousness.

She seemed to go fast. Respiratory distress began almost immediately. My mother was about as well trained as the volunteers on the town rescue squad, and she tried to revive Charlotte. She knelt beside her and blew deep into the woman's lungs through her mouth, attempting to restart her breathing; she pushed down hard upon Charlotte's chest with the heels of her hands, shouting, "*One* and *two* and *three* and *four* and *five* and *six* and *seven* and *eight* and *nine* and *ten* and *eleven* and *twelve* and *thirteen* and *fourteen* and *fifteen*!"

Fifteen compressions and two breaths. Fifteen compressions followed by two breaths.

There didn't seem to be a pulse, and my mother pleaded with Charlotte to breathe as she worked. She was crying as she counted aloud, and she begged the woman to fight for her life.

"You can do it, dammit, I know you can, you can, you can, you-can! Please!" Anne said my mother demanded of the apparently dead woman.

Did she perform at least eight or nine cycles as my mother said, or four or five as Asa recalled? That is the sort of detail that was disputable. But at some point within minutes of what my mother believed had been a stroke, after my mother concluded her cardiopulmonary resuscitation had failed to generate a pulse or a breath, she screamed for Asa and Anne to find her the sharpest knife in the house.

Asa would say in court that he did as she asked without thinking, he would say he had no idea what my mother intended to do with the knife. He would say he believed at the time that my mother was going to use the knife to somehow try and save his wife's life. My mother was a midwife and he was not, my mother knew CPR and he did not. My mother was in charge. And he was not.

Perhaps he was anticipating a tracheotomy. Perhaps not. Perhaps in reality he knew. Perhaps not.

Anne would insist she went with Asa for different reasons at different times. Once it was because she couldn't bear to stay in the room with the dead woman. Once it was because she was afraid to stay in the room with my mother: My mother suddenly seemed insane to her.

For whatever the reason, Asa and Anne ran downstairs to the kitchen together, and Asa pulled from the wooden block back on the counter beyond Foogie's reach a knife that was ten inches long, six of which were a steel blade, rounded along the cutting edge like an arrowhead. The handle was wood, stained the dark green of an acorn squash to match the block that held it.

When they returned, my mother said through her tears, "I can't get a pulse, Asa. I can't bring her back."

"Can't you do more CPR?" Asa asked, dropping the knife on the foot of the bed.

"Oh, God, Asa, I could do it for days, but she'll still be gone. She's not coming back." My mother was sitting beside Charlotte, who was still flat on her back on the bed.

As Asa had much earlier that evening—the night before now, really—he knelt by the side of that bed. He rested his head on his wife's chest, and staring up at her face, he stroked her bangs, still wet from the sweat of her hard labor. He murmured her name, and my mother squeezed his shoulder once.

And then my mother moved with a suddenness that frightened both Asa and Anne.

"Let's go," she said, still sniffling, "we've got no time." With the same hand that had squeezed his shoulder only seconds before, she picked the knife up off the sheets.

What she did not do—and when the state's attorney went over this in the courtroom with Anne, her testimony made even me doubt my mother for a brief moment—was ask Asa what he wanted to do. She never asked the father if he wanted her to try and save the baby. If he had said no, she could have done it anyway, if that's what she wanted; but if he had said yes, she at least would have had complicity.

And she never placed the Fetalscope back upon Charlotte's stomach to see if there was still a fetal heartbeat. Of course, the baby would prove to be alive, but not checking one last time before she did what she did—it surprised and shocked even the novice midwife.

And from the moment Asa and Anne returned to the bedroom

until the moment my mother began to cut, she never checked one last time to see if Charlotte had a pulse or a heartbeat. Maybe she had—as she said under oath—checked just before they returned with the knife. But neither the father nor the apprentice witnessed my mother make sure Charlotte was dead before she plunged a kitchen knife into the woman.

"What do you mean?" Asa asked my mother, after she said to him that they had no time. He saw her wipe her eyes, and he would say later there was something about the motion that suggested to him my mother had just had some sort of breakdown. It was a frantic gesture, as if she thought she could heave tears across a room.

"The baby's only got a few minutes, and we used most of them on Charlotte!"

"What are you going to do?"

"Save your baby!" My mother's voice was shrill, both Asa and Anne thought, and Asa said in court he wondered if she was hysterical. My mother insisted that if her voice was shrill, it was not because she was hysterical: It was because she wanted to snap Asa to attention.

"Save the baby?"

"Save *your* baby!"

My mother had already pushed the old nightgown in which Charlotte had been laboring up around her neck when she had been trying to restart her heart, so there were no clothes to remove before performing the cesarean section. Asa stood up and walked behind my mother as she turned on the reading lamp by the bed for the first time that night.

"Is she dead?"

"God, Asa, yes! Of course!"

Was she? We'll never know for sure. The medical examiner would be one of many state witnesses who would say it was medically possible that Charlotte Fugett Bedford's heart may have stopped for a moment, but my mother's diligent CPR had revived it—and, for a time, revived the woman. But there was no doubt in Asa's or Anne's minds that my mother believed Charlotte was dead.

When my mother said to Asa that—yes, of course!—his wife was dead, he nodded, and my mother took that motion as an assent. Certainly Asa made no effort to stop her. He lumbered slowly to the window without saying a word and looked into the sky, which seemed destined to remain dark forever.

◆　　◆　　◆

My mother would say later that in the early-morning hours of March 14, she performed the emergency cesarean because she couldn't bear to see two people die. She just couldn't bear it. And Charlotte was dead without question.

Was my mother wrong? Anne thought so, just as the medical examiner certainly believed there was room for doubt. Asa was standing by the window when my mother made the first cut, but he said later that—like Anne—he saw blood spurt.

Blood powered, the state's attorney would insist, by a pumping heart.

But Anne said nothing at the time, too young to be sure of what she had seen. It would be hours before she would pick up the phone, confused, unable to sleep, and call my mother's backup physician. She would later say she could not believe blood would have spurted like that from a dead woman, but my mother's attorney said there was probably another reason she called Dr. Hewitt: Stephen Hastings always viewed Anne as a nervous rat jumping from the *Titanic*.

She made that critical phone call late in the morning, while miles away in Burlington the medical examiner was in the midst of his autopsy, trying—and failing—to find a sign of the cerebral aneurysm.

My mother ran a fingernail in an imaginary line from Charlotte's navel to her pubic bone. Her hands were shaking.

She remembered reading somewhere that a surgeon could pull a baby from its mother in a crisis in twenty or thirty seconds, but that didn't seem possible to her. All those layers. Cutting into a human. Not wanting to cut the fetus. It just didn't seem possible.

Although she believed intellectually that she could do Charlotte no harm, she still moved carefully, as if she feared nicking an organ. She pretended the line she had sketched below Charlotte's navel was real and then pressed the tip of the carving knife hard into the dead woman's skin.

Blood burst from Charlotte at the point of incision in rhythmic spurts. These were not, Anne said, the powerful geysers one would expect from a healthy, beating heart, but the little spasms one might get from a weak one. Nevertheless, the blood seemed to Anne to be pulsing through Charlotte, and pumping from her where my mother had made the cut.

When she saw the blood spurt momentarily into the air—splattering my mother's fingers—the idea first began to form in Anne Austin's mind that my mother was performing a cesarean on a living woman.

But Anne hadn't noticed Charlotte's body move, she hadn't seen a reflexive spasm or twitch. And quickly the pulsations stopped, and the blood merely flowed. A thin string appeared, then grew wide. My mother pressed the blade further into the woman, through skin to fat to fascia, and pushed against the layer of muscle that was the only part of Charlotte's body resisting the steel intrusion. And then she drew the knife down toward Charlotte's vagina.

The blood rolled down the woman's belly, coating pale hips and thighs, and spilled onto the sheets on the bed to create fresh stains.

My mother pressed a pillow onto the wound for a brief moment to soak up some of the blood so she could see inside the incision. As she held the pillow there, she said later, she decided that she hadn't actually made something that resembled a surgical incision so much as she'd made a gaping, unclosable hole in Charlotte Bedford's abdomen. It suddenly seemed gigantic to her, monstrously big, and she heard her teeth begin chattering inside her head before she actually felt and understood what the noise was. Somehow, she was sweating.

When she pulled the pillow away, she saw the hemisphere from a salmon-pink kickball, the smooth, shining half shell of the uterus. Globular. Clean. Almost fruity. There it was, steaming amidst fat that was luminous, and meatlike strips of moist muscle. My mother wasn't squeamish, but she said the sight made her dizzy—not so much because it would be warm and slippery, but because here was life at its most visceral. Most primal. Here was life in the womb.

She ran her fingertips over the fundus until she understood where the baby was, and then grabbed the knife off the mattress. Using its tip like a pin, she pricked the uterus like a balloon in a spot far from the fetus. There was little amniotic fluid left, and her fear that it would spout into the air and coat her arms and her face and her hands had been unfounded. She'd ruptured the membranes earlier, she remembered; there was nothing left to splatter.

She then placed a finger into the uterus and tore it open gently with both hands, afraid to sever it with a knife: The baby was too near.

She would recall in the courtroom that tearing the uterus was as easy as tearing damp pastry dough, but she was nevertheless finding it hard to breathe as she worked.

When the opening was large enough for her hand, she reached deep inside and felt the baby's face. Her palm grazed its nose, and she ran her hand across its skull, its neck, its spine, until she had discovered one of its fat, pudgy thighs. She slid her hand up its leg until she had one foot, and then reached in her other hand for the child's other foot.

She then ripped the body from its mother, and in the air of the bedroom the fetus instantly became in my mother's eyes an infant. A boy. And when she had sucked the mucus from his throat with an ear syringe and he slowly came around—gasping, then breathing, then finally howling—he became for his father a living reminder of Charlotte Fugett Bedford's life and death and unspeakable ordeal.

MIDWIVES
PART TWO

SIX

Eleanor Snow arrived this morning, and she is the most amazingly lovely little thing. Eight pounds, one ounce, twenty inches. Her nose is a gentle little ski jump. The tiny rolls of baby fat on her arms make little bracelets at her wrists. And her hair, at least this morning, is strawberry blond.

Her eyes are gray today, but I think someday they'll be blue.

Dottie Snow's labor was quick: Anne and I got there about six-fifteen in the morning, and Dottie was already ten centimeters dilated and ready to rock and roll. I don't think she pushed for more than half an hour, and the joy in that room as she worked was just unbelievable. Unbelievable! She had her two sisters with her, her mom, and of course Chuck was there. Chuck had also been present for the birth of his first two children, and he is just the gentlest coach. He and Dottie were smooching and hugging between each surge, and he was always rubbing her breasts and shoulders. I really get off on that kind of love.

But what made the aura in that room so powerful was the combination of husband-wife love, sister love, and mother-daughter love. Dottie's sisters were hugging her, they were hugging each other, they were hugging Chuck. It was magnificent. I wish I could have bottled the vibes in that room and saved a little for some of the lonelier births.

Lonely births are the saddest things in the world. They can bring me down for days.

Charlotte Bedford's birth might be a lonely birth. At least the potential's there. Charlotte has no family anywhere near here, except Asa. And Asa is a sweet man, but he's so involved with his congregation he doesn't seem to have enough energy left for Charlotte.

And I don't think I've met a single female friend of hers. Female or male! She's met very few people outside of her husband's congregation, she says when we talk, and they keep a certain respectful distance because she's the new preacher's wife. I may be her closest friend up here, and so her prenatal visits go on forever.

No doubt about it, hers could be a lonely birth. And a lonely postpartum. I hope Asa's parish will look out for them. I have to believe they will, they're good people. But I wish I knew more people up in Lawson or Fallsburg.

Maybe I'll meet some before the baby arrives. Maybe I'll make an effort and try.

—*from the notebooks of* SIBYL DANFORTH, MIDWIFE

MY MOTHER WASN'T HOME FROM THE BEDFORD BIRTH BY BREAKFAST, AND AS my father and I ate our toaster waffles, we discussed how it looked as though poor Charlotte was in the midst of one of those eighteen- to twenty-four-hour marathons.

School had not been canceled that day, but the first classes had been pushed back two hours to allow the road crews time to turn the winding ice rinks throughout northeast Vermont back into roads. And so my father left for work before I left for school.

Charlotte Fugett Bedford and her son Veil went their separate ways soon after Veil was born. Charlotte's body was rushed in the funeral director's van to Burlington after the state's attorney and the medical examiner had surveyed the bedroom, and the state police had taken the sorts of postpartum photographs that are blessedly uncommon. The medical examiner informed my mother that he would be performing an autopsy when the body and he had returned to Burlington, but he said it was a standard practice and nothing that should alarm her.

My mother, Asa, and Anne actually left the Bedfords' before the men in suits and uniforms. They were still roaming around the bloody mattress and dropping items—wet rubber gloves, dry specks of herb tea, a clean syringe, a bloody washcloth—into clear plastic sandwich bags when Veil was taken to North Country Hospital in Newport, where pediatricians could examine him carefully. It was from the hospital that my mother phoned my father at his office and told him what had occurred. Her plan was to tell me in person when I returned home from school.

Like everything else surrounding the birth of Veil Bedford, it didn't work out as my mother expected. News of accidental death, especially when it is grisly, travels fast in our corner of Vermont. Collisions involving pickup trucks and cars that result in fatalities, logging disasters with chain saws or skidders, drownings in the deep waters of the nearby gorge all encourage conversation. When people die, people talk—especially teenagers.

Consequently, I learned of Charlotte Bedford's death during gym class, just before lunch. We had played volleyball that morning.

When I first heard the news, the story did not include my mother. Perhaps if the strange ways in which rumor and reality are linked could ever be severed and the separate parts dissected, their histories would show that I was the individual who first incorporated Sibyl Danforth into the tale—at least in my school, at least among the teenagers in our county.

I was changing from my gym shorts to blue jeans when Sadie Demerest told me, "That weird preacher up in Lawson lost his wife—that one from the South." Her voice was unconcerned and natural, as if she were telling me of another student's fashion faux pas—a girl with a sweater that was a tad too formal for school, or an unnatural streak of black in her hair that was just a bit too punk.

"She died?" I asked.

"Yup. In childbirth."

And I murmured aloud a thought that I do not believe had yet passed through Sadie's mind, although it certainly would have soon enough. "I wonder if my mother was there," I said.

Sadie paused on the bench before her locker, her own jeans still in her lap.

"Your mom was her midwife?" she asked after a long moment, and I nodded. The sounds in the changing room—the water rushing in the showers a few yards away, the giggles and laughter from the other girls, the tinny thump of the metal lockers as they were opened and closed—seemed to disappear as Sadie stared at me. At that moment I did not understand the full magnitude of the way my life was about to change, but the first dark inklings were beginning to coalesce.

I could see that the idea that my mother might have been present frightened Sadie and changed her perception of the story dramatically. Suddenly, this was no longer a tragedy with anonymous players, a horror story sufficiently distant to allow casual appreciation of its core grue-someness. This little nightmare involved Connie Danforth's mother. Connie Danforth's mother had been with the dead woman. Connie Danforth's mother had not only been with the dead woman, she had been helping her have her baby.

And people weren't supposed to die having babies, not even in our rural corner of the Kingdom. And so Sadie asked me the question that everyone in the county would ask one another for months, the question that no one was able to answer fully at the trial and no one has been able to answer conclusively ever since. In Sadie's case, it was a rhetorical question, an inquiry she had to know I could not possibly answer. But it was a question she—like everyone else—was unable to resist asking.

Twisting the legs of her jeans in her hands, her skin growing pale before my eyes, Sadie asked, "Connie, what happened?"

When I got home from school, my father was in the kitchen. My mother was sleeping.

"How was school?" he asked. He was wearing the dress slacks and shirt he'd worn to work, but his necktie was gone—probably long gone by three-thirty in the afternoon. I imagined he'd been home for hours.

"Fine."

"Good, good," he said, his voice a numbed and distant monotone. I saw on the counter that someone had made a pot of coffee since I had left for school, but it didn't look as if anyone had touched it.

"You'll need to be gentle with Mom for a while," he then added.

"Because of what happened?"

He sat back in the wooden kitchen chair and folded his arms across his chest. "What have you heard?"

"I heard Mrs. Bedford died."

He shook his head sadly. "Why don't you put your books down and tell me what you know. Then I'll tell you what I know."

"The details?"

"If you don't already know them."

Throughout the afternoon, two notions had prevented me from hearing a word my English or history teachers had said. The first was that Foogie was now without a mother, and I couldn't imagine how the little boy would endure. At that point in my life, I had never met a child who didn't have a mother. The second was my fear that my family would suddenly become poor.

At thirteen I did not understand the details of how malpractice insurance worked, but I knew that Vermont midwives didn't carry any: There were no companies that offered it to them in the state. And I knew this was an issue on occasion between my parents, usually after my mother would return home from what she would describe as a complicated birth.

I think the afternoon after Charlotte Bedford died, this was my father's chief concern as well: a civil suit. I don't believe the idea that state troopers would be arriving at our home within hours had crossed his mind.

"So what have you heard?" he asked again when I had sat in the chair beside him. "What are people saying?"

"No one knows a whole lot. Mostly just that the southern preacher's wife died."

"In childbirth? Do they know she died in childbirth?"

"Uh-huh."

"Do they know your mother was attending?"

"Yup, they do." I didn't mention the fact that I was responsible for dropping that detail into the story as it circulated through the school.

"What else?"

"No one knew if the baby died, too. Did it?"

"No, the baby's alive and doing fine. They had a little boy."

"That's good, at least."

"It is, yes."

"What did they name it?"

"Reverend Bedford named him Veil," my father said, emphasizing the pronoun so that the object I'd called "it" would have a gender in my mind. "What else are people saying?"

"Like I said, no one really knows much. All I heard was that Mrs. Bedford had died in childbirth, and it was incredibly bloody. But I know childbirth is always bloody, and no one seemed to be able to tell me why."

"Why . . ."

"Why it was so bloody."

He toyed with one of his sideburns and then brought his fingers back to his chest. I realized I was sitting on my hands. "Who told you?" he asked.

"Sadie."

"Were a lot of kids talking about it?"

"Yup. By the end of the day, anyway."

"On the school bus?"

"I guess."

"Were the kids asking you a lot of questions?"

"No, just one. They kept asking me if Mom was there."

"And you told them she was?"

I nodded. "Was that okay?"

"God, Connie, of course. Of course it was. Your mom did absolutely nothing wrong. Nothing. Sometimes women die in childbirth, just like sometimes people get sick and die. It doesn't happen often, but it happens. Mrs. Bedford just happened to have been one of those few people who dies. It's sad—very sad—but these things happen."

"Unfortunately."

"Yes. Unfortunately."

He looked at the coffeepot and seemed to realize for the first time it was full. I expected him to stand and pour himself a cup, but he didn't move from his chair.

"Was it bloody?" I finally asked.

Resting his elbow on the table and his jaw on the palm of his hand, he nodded. "Yes, it was very bloody."

He might have told me then that my mother had performed a cesarean section, but in the hallway above us we heard footsteps. We both realized Sibyl was awake, and she was on her way downstairs. My father would leave it to her to tell me a few sketchy details of what had occurred in the Bedfords' bedroom early that morning.

When my mother entered the kitchen, her hair was still wild with sleep, and her eyes were so red they looked painful. She was wearing her nightgown, something she rarely did in the middle of the day even when she napped after a long nighttime birth, and her feet were bare. She looked old to me, and it was not simply because she was limping or because there were dark bags under her eyes. It was not merely because she looked tired.

That aura, to use one of my mother's favorite words, of limitless enthusiasm that seemed to surround her had dissipated. The energy—part optimism, part patience, part joy—that sometimes seemed to fill whole rooms when she entered had vanished.

It was also clear that my mother had not slept long, and whatever sleep she had been granted had not been deep. Those nights when sleep would come easily, those afternoons when naps would come quickly, those hours when her dreams would be untroubling and serene, were gone forever.

SEVEN

Clarissa Roberson's mother, Maureen, is a very together woman. She was a hospital baby, and so were all of her children (including, of course, Clarissa).

But David Roberson was born at home, and he wanted his children born at home. And so there little Clarissa was, all 137 pounds of her—137 pounds at nine months and a week!—laboring away on the bed in her bedroom, and her mom was right there beside David and me, helping her daughter through it.

And it was a long labor, and Maureen must be close to sixty now. But she was terrific. Tireless.

And while I've had lots of moms present at their daughters' deliveries, watching as their little girls made them grandmothers, I've never had one who wanted to be as involved as Maureen. Or involved in such an astonishingly loving and knowing and supportive sort of way. Some mothers get a little queasy or nervous when their own babies are in labor, and I think that's totally understandable. The surges can be breathtaking and scary, and the blood can be intimidating. I think that's why a lot of the mothers who help their daughters have babies limit themselves to things like brewing the tea, or cheering them on from the head of the bed.

But not Maureen. She was right in there with me. At one point between surges I put the Johnson's down to ask David a question, and when I turned around, there was Mau-

reen up to her elbows in baby oil as she massaged her little
girl's perineum.
    It was beautiful. Incredibly, incredibly beautiful.

    —from the notebooks of S<small>IBYL</small> D<small>ANFORTH,</small> <small>MIDWIFE</small>

M<small>Y</small> <small>MOTHER SAID VERY LITTLE IN THE HOURS BETWEEN WHEN</small> I <small>RETURNED HOME</small>
from school and when the state troopers arrived.

    She sat on the couch in the den in her nightgown, with a quilt
draped over her shoulders. The little room smelled like cinnamon from
the herbal tea she was sipping. Whenever the phone rang—and it must
have rung three or four times that afternoon—my father answered it and
dealt with the caller.

    About five-thirty the sun broke through once and for all, not long
before it would disappear for the night into the western horizon. But for
a few minutes sunlight filled the den, and the fire my father had started
in the woodstove earlier in the day seemed unnecessary.

    Twice my mother asked me how school had been that day, but I
knew neither time she heard my response.

    Once she asked my father for more aspirin for the pain in her
ankle, and when he brought her the pills and a glass of cold water, he
had to remind her that she herself had requested them.

    "Let's have that ankle X-rayed tomorrow," my father suggested.

    "Yes. Let's," my mother said. She rarely looked at my father or me.
She stared at the fire through the glass windows in the woodstove, she
stared at the tea in her mug. Sometimes she put her tea down on the table
by the couch and looked at the cuts on her hands.

    "Was that Anne?" my mother asked my father one of the times he
returned from answering the phone in the kitchen.

    "No. It was just Sara. She was hoping you could bake a cake for the
fire department's potluck next weekend."

    "The fund-raiser."

    "Right."

    "She hadn't heard?"

    "Apparently not."

    But most of the time the three of us sat in silence. For some reason
I was afraid to leave the house, and I was afraid to be upstairs alone in
my room. And so I sat with my parents in the den. I believe we all

understood on some level that we were waiting for something to happen; we all had an intuitive sense that something well beyond our control was about to occur.

My father and I saw the state police cruiser rolling slowly up our driveway Friday night around dusk, and I believe that we saw it at about the same time. The rack of lights along the roof was off, but I don't think anyone can see a green police car coast to a stop by her house and not be alarmed. Especially the daughter of ex-hippies Rand and Sibyl Danforth.

I was flattening ground meat into hamburgers, and my father was beside me, reaching into the cabinet for a skillet. My mother was still in the den, unmoving and silent but awake.

"I'll see to that," my father said quietly to me, perhaps hoping he could shoo the police away as if they were a pair of vacuum cleaner salesmen.

I assumed I would have to remain by the counter beside the sink, hoping to overhear at least the key details, but my mother heard the knock on the door and grew more alert: She put down her tea and sat up, and craned her head toward the door. When she realized who had come to our house, she rose from the cushions and pillows into which she had burrowed, and somehow found the strength to amble into the front hall. And so I ventured there, too.

"I really believe this can wait until tomorrow," my father was saying.

"I'm sorry, it can't," one of the officers said, although his voice suggested that he certainly understood my father's desire to give my mother a night of peace. "But I promise," he added, "this won't take too long."

The officers were tall, and both well into middle age. One had a white mustache trimmed so severely it looked a bit menacing. The other had the sort of sharp, deep creases across his face that I always associated with farmers—the sort of wrinkles that come from driving a tractor into autumn winds for days and days at a time. Their jackets were buttoned against the March chill, their collars folded up around their necks. When the fellow who would do most of the talking that evening—the one with the mustache—noticed my mother and me approaching in the hallway behind my father, he removed his wide-brimmed trooper's hat, and the other officer immediately did the same. They nodded at my mother as if they knew her, and I got the impression they'd probably met her at the Bedfords' that morning.

It was just after six-thirty, and our porch light was on: Sometimes it would make the badges on their jackets sparkle.

"In that case, do you need to come in?" my father asked.

"We do, yes. But just for a few minutes."

He motioned them inside, and they wiped their shiny black shoes diligently on the mat near the stairs. I tried to remind myself that these two powerful-looking men were not evil, focusing in my mind on the gentle way the one with the mustache had spoken to my father. They both wore wedding bands, which meant they had wives, and if they had wives, they probably had children. And if they had children, then they were fathers themselves. Just like my dad. Remove the trooper's hats and the holsters, the guns and green jackets, and they were just regular old guys. There was no reason I should be frightened of them.

But, of course, I was.

"I'm Sergeant Leland Rhodes," the one with the mustache began, "and this is Corporal Richard Tilley."

"Rand Danforth," my father said, extending his hand first to Rhodes and then to Tilley. When he turned, he saw my mother and me standing in the hallway behind him.

"Connie, why don't you go upstairs. This shouldn't take long," he said, his voice even.

"I could finish cooking dinner," I offered.

"You could, but you don't have to," he said, and I felt my mother's hand on my shoulder, pushing me gently (but without ambiguity) in the general direction of the stairs.

My mother made them coffee. That was the first thing that surprised me: I had barely reached the top of the stairs, and I heard her asking the state troopers if they would like some coffee or herbal tea. They both chose coffee, and while my father escorted the pair into the den, my mother went to the kitchen to make a pot.

The next day, I gather, Stephen Hastings would think that was one of the strangest things he had ever heard. "Coffee," my father said the lawyer repeated over and over. "You made them coffee."

The officers were courteous, and Sergeant Rhodes began by explaining that they were simply gathering information that evening about the tragedy my mother had witnessed.

"We just want to know what you saw," Rhodes said, as if my mother were a mere spectator, someone who had happened to see two cars collide at an intersection. "We want you to tell us what happened, while the memories are still fresh."

"I don't think my memories of last night will ever go away," my mother responded, and years later my father would tell me that one sentence made a huge difference in what happened next. Apparently my mother's eyes grew watery as she spoke, and my father feared she might finally—and suddenly—break down. He became so fixated on her, so worried about her emotional well-being, that he failed to cut short the interview when he had the chance during the next exchange, or inform both the troopers and my mother that there would be no further conversation until they had an attorney present. He told me the idea had already begun to form in the back of his head that they would need a lawyer, but in his mind it would be to defend against a civil suit, not a criminal charge. Not the sort of felony that would bring state troopers by our house on a Friday night.

"That's probably true, Mrs. Danforth, but Bill Tanner and I have both found over the years that some details are more . . . crisp when you talk about them right away," Rhodes said.

"Bill Tanner?" my mother asked. "Why do I know that name?"

"He's the state's attorney for Orleans County. You met him this morning," the sergeant answered.

Once the troopers had left, my father told my mother he hadn't realized the state's attorney had been at the Bedfords' that morning. Either my mother had forgotten to tell him that detail or she hadn't realized who William Tanner was—or why the fellow had joined the medical examiner at the Bedfords' house.

And so when Rand Danforth interrupted with the question any husband-protector might ask in that situation, he asked it timidly, without conviction: "Should we have our attorney present?" he wondered aloud.

"Sure, if you'd like. But all we're doing right now is filling in the blanks in the story," Rhodes said, his voice casual and unconcerned.

Would things have ended differently if my mother had remained silent at that moment, or if my father had persevered—insisted, perhaps, that they postpone any discussions with the state police until they had an attorney present? It's possible, but it isn't likely. In all fairness to my parents, even Stephen Hastings decided there was little that was particularly incriminating in the portion of the affidavit gathered that first evening. The troopers hadn't known what was involved in a home birth, and so they hadn't asked the sorts of questions that might have elicited long, informative, and damning responses: After Asa brought you the knife, did you examine Charlotte one last time to make sure she was dead? Did you check for a fetal heartbeat before cutting? Did you ask Asa for permission to slice open his wife?

Mostly the troopers had simply allowed my mother to tell her side of the story, to present what she believed had occurred. Stephen did make a pretrial issue of what he called the "interrogation," but he also told us before the suppression hearing that the State would probably prevail—which it did.

Besides, my parents didn't even have an attorney that night. They had used lawyers just twice before in their lives: once, almost a decade and a half earlier, to write their wills in the days immediately before I was born, and then a second time when my father started his own architectural firm and wanted a legal incorporation. They had used the same attorney on both occasions, an elderly friend of my grandmother who lived in St. Johnsbury and died soon after helping my father found his firm.

And the fact that the two troopers did not actively encourage my parents to have a lawyer present would actually prove helpful to Stephen in one small way when the case finally came to trial: He used that fact to help bolster his contention that the State had a vendetta against home birth, and was more interested in putting midwives out of business than protecting my mother's civil liberties. The troopers did not have to "Mirandize" my mother at that moment or inform her of her rights, the judge had ruled, there was nothing illegal about the way they took her statement; but Stephen nevertheless was able to suggest that Rhodes's portrayal of himself as a "good cop" that night was morally ambiguous at best.

In any event, my mother said both to the two police officers and to my father after he broached the idea of a lawyer, "I haven't done anything wrong." Her voice was incredulous, not defensive, as if she couldn't believe an attorney would ever be necessary. "I'll tell you exactly what happened. What do you need to know?"

At some point soon after my mother started to speak, Corporal Richard Tilley began taking notes. He wrote fast to keep up with my mother, and the few questions his partner asked usually began, "Could you repeat that, please, Mrs. Danforth?"

Eventually Tilley filled eleven pages of lined yellow paper, and my mother's story stretched from the moment early Thursday afternoon when Charlotte Bedford phoned her with the news that she was in labor to the time Friday morning when my mother leaned exhausted against a pay phone at North Country Hospital and called my father. The state troopers stayed in our den for over an hour, nodding and scribbling and sipping my parents' coffee.

A little after seven-thirty, Sergeant Rhodes looked over at his partner's pad. "And then you went home?" he asked my mother.

"No, then I went back to the Bedfords'. I had to get my car."

"Oh, that's right, it was still in the snowbank."

"Sort of. The snowbank had begun to melt."

"Who drove you there?"

"To the Bedfords'? I don't remember his name. He worked for the rescue squad."

"Your car was okay?"

"It was fine. The hardest part was backing around the police car."

"There were troopers still on the scene?"

"I guess so. One of their cars was still there."

"Did you speak to an officer?"

"I didn't see one to speak to."

"Were you alarmed?"

"Alarmed? Why would I have been alarmed?"

Rhodes apparently answered my mother's question with a question of his own: "So you didn't go into the house?"

"No."

"You went straight home."

"Yes. I went straight home. And then straight to bed."

There was a long silence. Finally Rhodes took the pad from the corporal and passed it across the coffee table to my mother.

"Why don't you read this, Mrs. Danforth, and make sure we have everything right," he said, as Tilley handed my mother his pen.

My mother read through the pages, but she said later she didn't read them particularly carefully. Most of the time she could decipher Tilley's penmanship, but she was exhausted and so when she came across a word or a sentence that was incomprehensible, she just ignored it and moved on. Tilley had usually captured the gist of what she had said, and it seemed to her that was all that should matter at that point.

"Is the story accurate?" Rhodes asked her when she was through. "Did Richard here even come close?" he continued, smiling.

"It's more or less what happened," my mother said.

"Good, good," Rhodes murmured. He then made the request of my mother that would finally lead both of my parents to realize they needed a lawyer, and they needed one right away. It didn't matter that it was between seven-thirty and eight o'clock on a Friday evening; it didn't matter that it was the start of a weekend. They needed an attorney. A criminal attorney. And they needed one immediately.

Nodding as if his request were small, a bit of minor and inconsequential protocol, Rhodes looked at the bookshelves over my mother's shoulder and asked, "Would you swear to the truth of it for us, please? And then sign it?"

EIGHT

*Charlotte spent a half hour today looking at all of the pictures
of babies and moms on my wall. She'd noticed the photos during her very first visit, but today was the first time she really
wanted to see them.*

*"Look, Foogie," she said to her little boy, pointing at
the first photo ever taken of Louisa Walsh. "Maybe your baby
sister will look like her."*

*"Or maybe my baby brother will look like that one,"
Foogie said, pointing at a picture of another baby he must
have assumed was a boy. It wasn't. He was actually looking at
Betty Isham at three hours, wrapped in blue swaddling because
that's what her parents happened to have handy. Of course I
didn't tell Foogie that.*

*Anyway, Charlotte says she wants a girl, Foogie says he
wants a boy, and Asa just wants a healthy baby. Charlotte tells
me that's all Asa prays for from the birth: another healthy
child. That's all he says that matters. A healthy baby.*

*Charlotte's taking good care of herself. I'm sure he'll get
his wish.*

—from the notebooks of SIBYL DANFORTH, MIDWIFE

MY MOTHER DID SIGN THE AFFIDAVIT. MY FATHER TRIED TO STOP HER, TELLING
the troopers, "She'll be happy to sign it once our attorney has reviewed
it," but my mother believed that she had done absolutely nothing wrong.

"I'll sign it," she said to my father, and she did, scrawling her name in large, proud letters along the bottom of the eleventh page.

Saturday morning my parents were up and around well before me. I struggled downstairs in my nightgown sometime around eight o'clock, and my mother and father were already fully dressed and finishing breakfast. Unlike most Saturdays, my father was wearing slacks and a necktie, and my mother was wearing a skirt and a blouse. She was sitting with her right leg stretched out straight, and even through her thick wool tights I could see how swollen her ankle had become.

"How did you sleep?" my mother asked me, her voice a forced attempt to be cheerful.

"Okay," I mumbled, noting through my own morning fog that neither she nor my father looked particularly well rested. I imagined they had slept, but it had been fitful at best.

"Up to anything special today?" she continued.

I shook my head, suddenly self-conscious as I stood before them beside the refrigerator. Quickly I reached for the milk and a box of cereal and joined them at the kitchen table.

At that point I knew the basics of my parents' agenda for that day, but none of the details. I knew they were seeing lawyers, little more. As they sipped their coffee, I was able to pick up the rest.

Friday night my father had spoken by phone to attorneys at three firms, two in Montpelier and one in Burlington. The pair of attorneys in Montpelier were casual friends of our family, the sorts of people my parents would see at big Christmas parties and townwide summer picnics and whose company they probably enjoyed. But we weren't especially close to either one, so my father's phone calls had probably caught them off guard the night before. Nevertheless, each lawyer was happy to meet with my parents and try and understand if he could help them.

The third attorney was Stephen Hastings, a friend of Warren Birch, one of the Montpelier lawyers my parents were visiting that morning. Hastings was a young partner in a Burlington firm, and Birch thought he was an excellent criminal lawyer—something Birch suggested he himself wasn't.

And so my parents' plan was to meet with the two Montpelier-based attorneys before lunch and then see Hastings at his firm in Burlington in the afternoon. They left soon after I'd finished my breakfast, and I spent most of that day in a daze.

Tom Corts and I had been going steady by then for close to four months, although we hadn't formalized the arrangement with anything as symbolic as an ID bracelet or ankle chain. In our part of Vermont, ID bracelets were passé by 1981, and the only girls who wore metal around their ankles were a trio of especially fast young things led by a newcomer to the Kingdom from Boston.

Tom and I were supposed to have gone to a dance together Friday night, a shindig at the American Legion post in Montpelier of all things. The Legionnaires had been holding "alcohol-free" dances every other Friday that winter for the high-school kids, hoping to decrease the number of us who drank too much before rolling our daddies' pickups into ditches, or slamming our already-dented Novas into trees. Obviously I was years away from driving that spring, and the privilege still eluded Tom by five months. And, of course, we were nowhere near old enough to drink legally in Vermont.

But Tom's friends in the tenth and eleventh grades had discovered that while the dances may have been alcohol-free in the Spartan dance hall inside the Post, there was almost always at least one unemployed quarry worker from Barre or laid-off lathe operator from the furniture factory in Morrisville hovering around the nearby convenience store who would buy a kid a six-pack if he could keep one or two of the beers for himself. And so small groups of us would stand in the shadows of the Legionnaires' Post or the convenience store, stamping our feet to stay warm and holding chilled beers that were nowhere near as cold as the night air around us.

Usually one of my parents or Rollie's mother would drive us to the dances that winter, but we always had one of Tom's older brothers pick us up. We feared our breath or my babbling would give our drinking away. I've never held alcohol well, and in eighth grade it only took a beer and a half to give me the giggles.

I had not gone with Tom to the dance that Friday night, however, because I had suspected in school that I had best be home in the evening. By the time most of us started piling into school buses to go home at three, Tom had heard that one of Sibyl Danforth's mothers had died. We discussed it briefly before each of our last classes began, and his take was at once characteristically prescient and prickly:

"That preacher's probably upset, but it's the doctors who'll come after her. Doctors think they know everything."

And then after a long pause, he added, "They scare me, doctors do. They're like pack animals. Wolves. They surround their prey and go right for the throat."

Tom had called me late Friday night, close to eleven, from the pay phone in the convenience store's parking lot. He said our line had been busy most of the night, and I explained to him that my father had been talking to lawyers. I could tell he'd been drinking, but he was still far from drunk. He said he couldn't come by my house Saturday morning because he'd agreed to help an older cousin move into a new apartment in St. Johnsbury, but he said he'd be by in the afternoon. I told him that would be fine.

When my mother and father left for Montpelier Saturday morning, they told me they wouldn't be back until late in the day, and that I should screen incoming calls: As a midwife, my mother had probably been one of the first people in the county to purchase an answering machine, and so our family had used one for years. I was an old hand at screening phone calls.

They were concerned that newspaper reporters would phone us, and their fears were well founded. *The Burlington Free Press,* the state's largest daily paper, was the first, but the reporter who called only beat the *Montpelier Sentinel* and the *Caledonian-Record* by minutes. A fellow from the Associated Press in Montpelier left three messages, and I will always believe he was the person who then called every ten minutes until lunch, hanging up each time when the answering machine's recorded message clicked on.

I spent most of the day in a fog, listening to the messages reporters and family friends and other midwives would leave on the answering machine, and waiting for Tom to come by. Usually if I was expecting Tom when my parents weren't home, I'd anticipate that we would wind up quickly on the couch in the den, where we would neck until Tom would start trying to pull up my sweater and I'd have to slow the proceedings. We both knew it was only a matter of time before I'd finally take off my sweater and let him do battle with my bra, but we hadn't reached that point yet.

The Saturday that my parents went searching for a lawyer, however, the idea that Tom and I might make a beeline toward the couch never even crossed my mind. I knew I was happy Tom was coming by, and I knew I was scared—scared as if one of my parents were desperately ill. But I had no concept of how the two emotions might overlap when Tom finally appeared at our front door: Was he supposed to hug me or bring me a beer? Was he supposed to grill me for the details of what I knew or mindfully talk about everything but home birth? And if he happened to be at our house when my parents returned, would either of us have the slightest idea what to say to them—especially to my mother?

Just before lunch Rollie came over, and for about an hour the two of us listened to the calls coming in to the answering machine. Had my parents even imagined the dozens and dozens of people who would use the phone to besiege me, they might have taken me with them and then sent me shopping in Montpelier and Burlington while they met with their lawyers. But none of us expected the deluge that began just after nine o'clock:

"Good morning, my name is Maggie Bressor, I'm a writer with the *Burlington Free Press*. I would like to speak with Mrs. Sibyl Danforth as soon as she returns, please. I'm sorry to bother you, but I'm writing a story about the . . . the birth up in Lawson, and I only need a few moments of your time, Mrs. Danforth. I am on a deadline, so I may try you again this afternoon. My number here in Burlington is 865-0940. Thanks a lot."

"Hi, Sibyl, hi, Rand. Molly here. I heard about the, um, tragedy, and I'm thinking of you. Travis and I both are. Call us when you feel up to it. And let us know if there's anything we can do. Bye for now."

"Hello, I'm looking for Sibyl Danforth. This is Joe Meehan with the *Sentinel*. Just thought I'd see if you were home. I'll call back."

By the time Rollie arrived, I'd had to put in a second cassette tape to preserve the messages. And still people called.

"Sibyl? Are you there? If you're there but not picking up, please pick up! It's me, Cheryl. I have a whole file of legal stuff from MANA I want you to see. It's huge! Okay, you're not there, I believe you. But call me when you are. Or maybe I'll just drop the stuff by. There are even the names of some lawyers in it—all, of course, in places like Maryland and New Mexico—but they might be able to give you the name of one in Vermont. A good one. If you need one. Talk to you soon."

Rollie sipped her soda and asked me what MANA was.

"It's one of Mom's midwife groups. They're in the Midwest somewhere," I answered. I learned soon that the acronym stood for the Midwives' Alliance of North America, the closest thing lay midwives had then to a national trade association.

"Hi, guys, Christine here. Call me. I'm worried about you."

"Sibyl. Hello. This is Donelle. I know another midwife I want you to talk to. She witnessed a mother die in a home birth, so she understands the pain you're probably feeling. She lives in Texas, and I know she'd be happy to talk and listen all you wanted. Bye-bye."

"Timothy Slayton with the Associated Press. Thought I'd try again."

It really was endless. Eventually even Rollie grew tired of listening to the calls, and went home about one-thirty. Tom didn't get to our house until close to three, and in the hour and a half in between I continued to stare at the answering machine and watch its red eye blink when the tapes for incoming and outgoing messages weren't turning. Only once did I pick up the receiver and talk to someone, and that was when I heard my father's voice speaking from a phone in the attorney's office in Burlington.

"How are you doing?" he asked me.

"Oh, fine."

"What have you been up to?"

"Reading," I lied. I was afraid he and my mother would worry if they knew the truth and envisioned me sitting with my arms wrapped around my knees, transfixed by the telephone answering machine.

"Schoolwork?"

"Yup. Schoolwork."

"Well, it's Saturday, so don't work too hard. Life goes on. Have you been on the phone?"

"A little, I guess."

"Any calls for your mom?"

"A few."

"Friends or reporters?"

"Both."

"Okay. When your mom and I are done with Mr. Hastings, we have one more stop. Since we're in Burlington anyway, we're going to go by the hospital to get your mom's ankle X-rayed." He had tried to downplay the importance of the hospital visit, implying that they prob-ably wouldn't have bothered with an X ray if they hadn't been in

Burlington anyway, but it's hard to make light of a visit to the emergency room.

"It still hurts her?" I asked.

"A bit," he said.

I think the only time I moved between the moment Rollie left and the moment Tom arrived was when I stood up to see what the small thuds were in the kitchen. It turned out to be one of those normally wondrous harbingers of spring: A male robin had returned to the bird feeder outside one of the kitchen windows after a winter away, and the fellow was doing battle with his reflection in the glass. That Saturday, however, the robin's homecoming was merely an irritation, just another mesmerizing example in my mind of the idiocy of the natural world: Birds banged into glass, mothers died giving birth.

I probably looked like eighth-grade hell to Tom when I opened the door for him. I was as vain as any girl just shy of fourteen, but I hadn't combed my hair once that Saturday, and I don't believe I had remembered to brush my teeth. I had gotten dressed shortly before Rollie came over, but I certainly hadn't dressed for Tom Corts. I was wearing jeans that were much too baggy and loose, and one of my mother's old hippie sweaters that she had knit herself. She has used perhaps eleven shades of yarn, and while the effect was supposed to be psychedelic, even she used to say it was merely chaotic, as if the colors had been chosen by a preschooler.

But if Tom was appalled by what he saw when I opened the door, he kept his disappointment to himself. And I was indeed glad to see him. He wrapped his arms around the small of my back and pulled me to him, and gave me a kiss on the lips as gentle and chaste as the first one we'd shared a year earlier in the mud of the McKenna family's small paddock.

And then he just rocked me for a long moment, an awkward sway that felt just right for that time. I pressed my forehead against the cotton from his shirt that peeked through his partly zipped parka, lulled if not wholly reassured. I don't recall how he finally separated our two bodies and moved us inside, but somehow he managed without traumatizing me.

It was quickly apparent that Tom, like me, had absolutely no idea of how much or how little he should speak of Mrs. Bedford's death or my mother's involvement. He understood a hug would be good, but the spoken sentiments he'd have to ad-lib as he settled in for his visit.

"My cousin lives in a pit," were his first words to me after we had walked into the kitchen. "That boy is as stubborn as a pig on ice, so there was no changing his mind. But, my God, has he moved into a dump."

"What's so bad about it?"

"Aside from the fact it's got about two windows and they're only as big as record albums, nothing. Except, maybe, it's only two rooms and a bathroom, and the floor's about rotted out in the bathroom. And I could only find one outlet in the whole darn place."

As we walked through the kitchen to the den, he stopped before the refrigerator. "Can I get myself a soda?"

"Sure."

"I just have no idea what that boy thinks he's doing," he went on as he reached inside the white Kelvinator for a Coke.

"Is the apartment in town, or outside it?"

"It's in a house by the maple syrup company. The one that cans all the stuff from Quebec."

"A nice house?"

"Hah! 'Bout as nice as a car accident. It's dark and old and in need of either a good carpenter or a well-placed bolt of lightning."

He sat down on a corner of the floor by the stereo and began thumbing through the record albums and tapes lined up to one side.

"How's your mom today?" he asked, careful to look intently at an album cover instead of at me.

"I think her ankle hurts more than she'll admit."

"Her ankle?"

I told him how in addition to everything else she had endured up at the Bedfords', she had injured her ankle.

"She picked out a lawyer?"

"I don't know."

"How many are your folks seeing?"

"Three."

He nodded approvingly. "My cousin said he guessed your parents make too much money to get a public defender. But he said he had a good one once."

We may not have had particularly crisp reception back then in our part of Vermont, but I had nevertheless seen enough television to know what a public defender was.

"He did?"

"Yup, in St. Johnsbury. He said the guy was real sharp."

"What'd he do?"

"My brother or the lawyer?"

I shrugged. "I guess both."

"My cousin was drunk and stole a car to go joyriding and then hit a telephone pole. Wrecked the thing."

"Whose car?"

"Belonged to a guy from Boston. A Saab. Problem was, it was the second time he'd gotten smashed and taken somebody's car. So he ended up spending thirty days in Windsor. But he said it would have been a lot worse than thirty days if his lawyer hadn't been such a fast talker."

"Stealing a car when you're drunk gets you thirty days?" I asked.

"That's what it got my cousin."

In the kitchen the phone rang, and when I didn't move to answer it, Tom looked up at me and offered to get it.

"Let the answering machine deal with it," I told him, and explained how up until perhaps an hour earlier, the phone had been ringing nonstop. Not surprisingly, it was merely a reporter calling yet again.

"There'll be a lot in the newspapers tomorrow, won't there?" Tom said.

"I guess."

"Has your mom spoken to any newspapers yet?"

"I don't think so."

He sighed and looked down at the pack of cigarettes in the breast pocket of his shirt. I could tell he wanted one, but he wasn't allowed to smoke inside our house.

"Do you think she should?" I asked.

"I don't know. Maybe. Get her side out there."

"Her side? What do you mean her side?"

He slipped an album back into the line of records wedged between the wall and one of the speakers, and clasped his hands behind his neck.

"Look, Connie, I don't know much about any of this stuff. I can't even fake it when it comes to lawyers and newspaper people. So I could be completely wrong about all this. But here's the thing: A lady's dead. And she died having a baby. She didn't die because she was hit by lightning, or because she crashed her car into a rock, or because her house burned down in the middle of the night. She didn't die because she was too fat for her heart, or because she broke her neck on a snowmobile. She's dead because of something that happened while she was having a baby."

"So?"

"So, they're going to have to blame someone. Look at all the reporters who've started calling already."

I heard the robin outside the kitchen window, back to beat up on his reflection. I tried to focus for a moment on what Tom was saying, but I kept coming back to his cousin and the time the fellow spent in the state prison in Windsor. The sentence kept forming in my mind like a word problem in a math class:

If a man steals a car and is given thirty days in jail, how much time will a midwife get when one of her mothers dies during a home birth?

"Who was your cousin's public defender?" I asked.

"I don't remember his name."

"But it was in St. Johnsbury?"

"Yup."

If a man steals a car and is given thirty days in jail, how much time will a midwife get when one of her mothers dies during a home birth? The man is drunk, the midwife is sober.

"Not Newport?"

"Not Newport."

"Think Newport has its own public defender?"

"It's a different county. Probably."

If a man steals a car and is given thirty days in jail, how much time will a midwife get when one of her mothers dies during a home birth? The man is drunk, the midwife is sober. When you do the math, don't forget that the midwife cut open the mother after she died.

"Mrs. Bedford died up in Lawson. The people who went by their house yesterday morning were all from Newport."

"Look, I'm sure the Newport guy's good, too."

"I hope so."

"Besides, even if your mom does end up needing a lawyer, your parents are the type who'll shop around. They'll probably use one of the guys they meet today."

"And that's if my mom even needs one," I added hopefully, echoing his earlier words.

He nodded his head and murmured, "Yup, that's right: if. If she even needs one," but I could tell that deep down he was convinced that she would. Behind us the phone rang again, and this time Tom didn't even look up. He just kept staring at the knees of his blue jeans, as yet another unfamiliar voice asked my mother to call him back when she returned.

NINE

Fifteen years ago, I always expected I'd be arrested one day. I marched against the war, I called police officers "pigs," I smoked more than my share of pot.

But I guess I never got mad enough or wild enough or stoned enough to do something really crazy. Maybe I would have if I hadn't been blessed with Connie. I knew plenty of girls then who would give a trooper the finger while holding their baby in their other arm, but that wasn't me. My baby was always too precious to me to screw around like that.

I remember that Rand was picked up once and herded into a wagon. He was one of dozens and dozens of guys arrested in a Washington, D.C., protest, and I probably would have been with him if I hadn't been five months pregnant at the time. But I was carrying Connie, and the last thing I wanted to do was spend a day in a cramped van driving from Vermont to Washington, and then another day standing around in the D.C. heat, screaming my lungs out with thousands of really, really angry people.

I think Rand only spent a night in the jail, and he was never charged with anything.

And unlike me, he never had to wear handcuffs.

This afternoon when Stephen was making sure I didn't have to go to jail, the judge and the state's attorney—Tanner—made me feel like I'd shot someone while robbing a house. Stephen said it was all a formality, but I don't think anyone who's ever had state troopers show up at her house and arrest her would call "handcuffs" a formality. And while I was expecting the troopers, I certainly wasn't expecting the handcuffs.

"Now, I don't really think that's necessary, do you?" Stephen asked the two officers.

"We don't have a choice, Stephen, you know that," the fellow with the mustache said, the one who I think is named Leland.

And so right there on my own front porch, they made me put out my arms so they could "cuff me."

I just don't know how criminals ever get the hang of handcuffs. They really weren't that tight, but I guess I don't have much flesh or fat around my wrists. Every time I wiggled my thumb, the bones in my wrist rubbed against the steel. If I did it enough, I think it would have started to peel the skin.

The weirdest thing about the handcuffs was this rubber guard someone put around the chain between the bracelets. It was like a five- or six-inch length of clear garden hose. Here they design these scary, ugly, painful metal shackles for people's wrists, and then they put a rubber sleeve around the chain.

It struck me as the most surreal part of a completely surreal experience. There I was, sitting in the backseat of a state police cruiser in this spring dress covered with blue irises, with my hands folded demurely in my lap because I was wearing handcuffs in a garden hose.

—from the notebooks of SIBYL DANFORTH, MIDWIFE

STEPHEN HASTINGS HAD NOT HAD MANY DEFENDANTS IN OUR COLD, REMOTE corner of the state. He usually worked in Burlington, where the sorts of crimes that might result in the need for a high-powered—by Vermont standards, anyway—attorney were most likely to occur. Stephen had defended the power company executive who was accused of drowning his wife in Lake Champlain, and the high-school English teacher who was charged with having sex with two fifteen-year-old girls from one of his classes. With Stephen's help, they were both found not guilty.

And while he lost as many visible cases as he won, the fact that he

won any at all made him a lawyer in some demand. After all, no one
thought he had a chance with the hospital administrator who virtually
decapitated the bookkeeper who had apparently figured out he'd been
embezzling hundreds of thousands of dollars. ("The means and mere
gruesomeness of the death suggested premeditation," Stephen told us the
judge had remarked to him one evening when that trial was finished.)
Everyone in the state knew a particular motel owner in Shelburne would
be convicted of trafficking drugs, and the woman who left her infant
twins to freeze atop Camel's Hump would be found guilty of first-degree
murder.

Although Stephen's murder, rape, and drug trials garnered the
most ink, he had also defended a bank president who had doctored his
institution's reported assets and liabilities, an entrepreneur who had
stolen from her investors, and a pair of Vermont officials who had
accepted bribes from a construction company bidding on a state office
complex. Vermont rarely endures more than a dozen murders a year,
and most of those are the sorts of drug-related homicides or domestic
nightmares that wind up with the public defender. Consequently, it was
only natural that a firm like Stephen's—and Stephen himself—would
handle all sorts of less visible (and less grisly) white-collar crime as well.

While Stephen may have rarely wound up in the Orleans County
Courthouse in Newport, he still knew the county's state attorney fairly
well. Vermont is a small state, and Stephen and Bill Tanner ran into each
other at formal bar association functions in Montpelier, and informal
receptions at the law school in Royalton. They had mutual friends in
Burlington and Bennington, and once spent a Saturday skiing together
at Stowe, when they ran into each other in a lift line early that day.

Consequently, the scene I inadvertently witnessed one morning
during the trial shouldn't have surprised me. But of course it did. I
viewed Bill Tanner as an almost psychotic sort of villain, a fellow bent
upon the destruction of my mother and my family for reasons I couldn't
begin to fathom. He was, in my mind, especially menacing because he
was so unfailingly mannered.

In any case, one morning before the trial began for the day, I was
standing outside the two lacquered wooden doors that led from the
courthouse hallway into the courtroom itself. It was still very early, but
through the porthole glass windows I could see that Stephen and Tanner
and Judge Dorset were already inside. Dorset wasn't wearing his robe,

and his necktie hung loose around his neck like a scarf: He had not even begun to tie it.

Tanner was eating a banana and Stephen was munching on dry cereal, his whole hand and part of his arm disappearing periodically inside the large cardboard box. The three men were hovering around the defense table, and Tanner was actually sitting in the chair that usually belonged to my mother. The jury had not yet been brought in, nor had the bailiff or the court reporter arrived. The newspaper writers hadn't struggled in, nor had most of the other spectators who filled the courtroom during the trial: my mother's friends and supporters, curious members of the State Medical Board, and Charlotte Bedford's family—a small group at once inconsolably sad and unmollifiably angry. The only two people I saw in the gallery that moment were the two young adults who—based upon the thick books of state statutes they were reading, and the yellow markers they used to highlight passages in their dense law journals—I assumed were law students.

My mother was in the women's room on another floor of the building at that moment, and my father was with her—probably pacing the corridor just outside the bathroom.

Something about the sight of the two lawyers and the judge together prevented me from plowing into the courtroom as planned. The acoustics in the courtroom were sound, and through the thin crack between the double doors I could hear their conversation.

"Oh, God, I almost laughed out loud when I saw the paper this morning," Tanner was saying, chuckling just the tiniest bit.

"Was Meehan at the same trial we were?" Stephen said, and it took me a moment to remember why I knew the name Meehan. And then it clicked: He was the gaunt, blond fellow covering the trial for the *Montpelier Sentinel,* the man who always looked so tired.

"I just had no idea it was going so damn well, Stephen," Tanner continued, pressing the yellow and black peel from his banana into an empty Styrofoam coffee cup.

"Meehan's an idiot," Dorset said. "You both know that."

"Maybe. But if the jury has seen it so far the way he has, I have really screwed up here," Stephen said.

"No one sees things the way Meehan does," Dorset said.

"I hope so. Otherwise, it's going to be a very long couple of days for my friend Sibyl," Stephen said, shaking his head with mock drama.

"But a very short deliberation," Tanner quickly added, and he punched Stephen lightly on the arm.

I think what distressed me most at that moment wasn't the idea that Stephen feared the trial was going badly, although I'm sure that contributed to the queasiness I felt most of the morning. It may not even have been the way the attorney who was supposed to protect my mother and preserve my family was fraternizing with the enemy that I found so disturbing.

No, looking back, what I believe upset me the most that day was the casual, lighthearted way the three men were bantering. This trial had become everything for my family, it was our lives; it was in our minds every moment we were awake, and I can't imagine my mother escaped it in her dreams. I know I didn't. The penalty for involuntary man-slaughter was one to fifteen years in prison, and Tanner's relentless attacks on my mother had made it clear to us all that should she be found guilty, the State would press hard for the maximum penalty. (I had done the math instantly the morning the charges were brought against my mother: If she was found guilty and sent to prison for a decade and a half, I would be twenty-nine years old by the time she got out, and my mother would be close to fifty.)

For Stephen Hastings and Bill Tanner, however, for Judge How-ard Dorset, this trial was merely their job. It was, in fact, just one of the many jobs they would have in their lives. One more house for a home builder. One more flight for an airline pilot. One more baby for an obstetrician or a midwife. The stakes may have been high for my family, but for the men arguing about my mother's character and capabilities, it was just another morning out of the office, another afternoon in court.

I didn't have a crush on Stephen Hastings, but it would have been understandable if I had. I imagine a lot of girls in my situation would have fallen madly in love with the fellow, given the fact that he was about as close as our family was going to get to having a white knight or cavalry officer ride into our lives and rescue us. And, of course, my hormones were the chemical mess that everyone's are at thirteen and fourteen years old, an explosive combination of elements with a tendency to combust—at least here in Vermont—in the damnedest places. A pickup truck with a pile of clothes or old blankets tossed casually in the bed. The mossy, hidden crevices that dot the rivers as they switchback through the woods. Cemeteries.

Perhaps because so much granite is pulled from quarries in Barre and Proctor, a lot of teenage boys in Vermont come to believe adamantly (albeit mistakenly) that graveyards and tombstones affect teenage girls like aphrodisiacs.

Rollie often teased me that I had a crush on Stephen, but I think that was because she herself was so attracted to the man. That didn't surprise me then; it doesn't surprise me now.

Stephen was my father's age the summer and fall he defended my mother, and two years older than Sibyl. The men around me that year were thirty-six, the woman who was my world was thirty-four.

I didn't read newspapers much before my mother's name started to appear in them on a regular basis, so I had never heard of Stephen before he entered our family's life, but I realized quickly that most adults around me had. If they didn't know his name, often they recognized his face once they met him. He was photographed frequently. Back then cameras weren't allowed into courtrooms when trials were in progress, so the typical Stephen Hastings pictures were what he once referred to around me as either "grip and grins" with a defendant on the courthouse steps after he had won, or "solo frowns of righteous indignation" when he was announcing the inevitable appeal after a defeat.

His hair was just beginning to gray along his temples and across the pair of graceful boomerangs that served as eyebrows. It was more black than brown, and he kept it combed and trimmed with the discipline one might expect from an air force veteran. Small wrinkles had begun to wave from the corners of his mouth, but otherwise his face was lean and sharp. Since I saw him most of the time in the late afternoon or evenings, he always had a shadow of stubble, a dark and natural makeup that in my memories suggests he was especially hard-working and wise.

He was about my father's height, an inch or so short of six feet, and he was slightly heavier—not fat, not even meaty, but he'd never lost the muscles he'd found while training for Vietnam.

He was recently divorced when he met my mother and father, but the marriage hadn't lasted very long or led to any children. My mother said that when he was especially preoccupied, he sometimes rolled the thumb and index finger on his right hand around the finger on his left where he had once worn a wedding band, but I never saw him do it myself.

Perhaps because I was a teen with a fairly predictable interest in clothing, I noticed that Stephen always seemed to be dressed slightly better than the men around him: If he was surrounded by attorneys in blazers and slacks at a Tuesday-morning deposition, he would be wearing a suit; if the gentlemen around him at a Saturday-night cocktail party were wearing khaki pants, his slacks would be gray; even one Sunday at a picnic that summer, before which the adults must have decided en masse that they would all appear in blue jeans, he alone chose to wear chinos—twilled, yes, but ironed and crisp and beige.

"One click above," he explained that day to my father and me, rolling his eyes and laughing at himself, after my father had made some comment about his habit of always dressing a tad better than the world around him. "To win at what I do—and let's face it, charge what I charge—demands dressing exactly one click above everyone else. Not two clicks, because then I look like an idiot. One. One click makes me look pricey. And, I hope, worth it."

"I hope so, too," my father agreed, the tone belying a tension otherwise veiled by his words.

Stephen never treated me like a child, which at that age meant a great deal to me. Twice he brought me punk albums from a record store in Burlington that wouldn't find their way to the Northeast Kingdom for months. Once after he heard Tom Corts expressing an interest in the American West, he brought him a paperback monograph of Ansel Adams prints. He always seemed enormously interested in my father's work, and I think by the time the trial began he knew so much about home birth he could have delivered a breech in a bedroom by himself.

I know that sometimes my father felt Stephen had become too much a part of our family's life, but that seemed to me a reasonable price to secure my mother's acquittal. Looking back, I think Stephen simply decided that—or as in actuality these things tend to work—*discovered* that he cared for my mother, and he wanted to be around us all as much as he could. His gifts, in my mind, were always genuine, his embraces avuncular and sincere.

Barely forty-eight hours would slip by between the Saturday my parents met Stephen Hastings in Burlington and the Monday evening he appeared at our home in Reddington with a photographer, and I was introduced to him. Apparently my parents had taken an immediate liking to Stephen the day they had met, and he'd agreed on the spot to represent my mother if—as he said to them—it proved necessary. And while we all held out hope as the State conducted its investigation throughout March that Bill Tanner would decide not to prosecute, Stephen was adamant that my parents should prepare for the worst: a charge of involuntary manslaughter stemming from my mother's reck-lessness or extreme negligence.

"Bill may even make some noise about it being intentional," Stephen had warned that Saturday afternoon.

"What does that mean?" my father had asked.

"In actuality it will mean nothing. But as the State's top gun in Orleans, Bill needs to act like he's one tough cowboy," Stephen began, before turning in his chair to address my mother directly. "If he suggests you acted intentionally, it means he believes he can win with a charge of voluntary manslaughter, not merely involuntary. Maybe even second-degree murder."

My mother simply nodded in silence, my father told me much later, and he said he couldn't think of anything to say. And so he just reached over and covered her hand with his.

Fortunately Stephen continued quickly, "Of course, it won't come to that. I don't think Bill could find a precedent for such a thing on God's green earth. I'm just warning you he might make noise to that effect early on."

Stephen wanted to take steps right away to begin building a de-fense—just in case—and my parents agreed. He wanted photographs of the scrapes and bruises my mother had received on the ice that Friday morning in Lawson, and the sprained ankle upon which she was hob-bling. He wanted to examine Charlotte Bedford's prenatal records with a physician, and he said he'd probably bring on board an investigator right away. And he gave my mother some advice: "Don't talk to anybody about this, not a soul. Don't tell anybody anything—and don't tell me everything. I'll ask you what I need to know as we move along. And try not to worry. I know you will, but you shouldn't. In my opinion, the State should damn well be giving you a medal for saving that baby's life, not threatening you like a gang of legal thugs."

Of course, there were signals right away that should have told my parents clearly and concisely that any hopes they had that the State would not press charges were unfounded, any optimism unwarranted. Throughout the Friday, Saturday, and Sunday that followed Charlotte's death, my mother kept expecting Anne Austin to call. My mother was genuinely concerned that her young apprentice had been so deeply scarred by what she had seen, she would give up her plans of becoming a midwife herself someday. Consequently, my mother phoned her on Saturday morning before she and my father went in search of attorneys, and again when they returned at the end of the day. She called Sunday morning, and again Sunday night.

Like us, Anne had an answering machine, and my mother left a message each time. When Anne had still failed to call back by the time we had dinner Sunday night, my mother wondered aloud if Anne had gone to Massachusetts to visit her parents, and put some literal distance between herself and the house where Charlotte Bedford had died.

"And for all we know, she's tried reaching you a dozen times and gotten nothing but busy signals," my father added.

The Sunday newspapers, too, should have been a pretty good indication that the State would prosecute. Saturday morning there had merely been a couple of three- or four-inch articles in the *Burlington Free Press* and the *Caledonian-Record* noting that a woman named Charlotte Fugett Bedford had died during a home birth, but there was no mention of Sibyl Danforth. Anyone who came across either article would have assumed from the stories that while the woman's body had been taken to the medical examiner, it was just a formality and there was no reason to suspect anything other than death from a natural cause.

Sunday's stories, however, were very different. They were lengthy, more detailed, and grisly. They also lacked my mother's perspective on that long night in the Bedfords' bedroom, because she had chosen not to return any of the phone calls from reporters that Saturday. And while Stephen explained to my parents that they should forward press inquiries to him, they didn't know that as they sat in his office the first time, and so there were no comments from Stephen Hastings in Sunday's stories either.

Consequently, the articles that ran on Sunday were not only gory, they were one-sided and wrong. They were filled with quotes from doctors and midwives who hadn't been in the room with my mother, people who were willing to conjecture about what "must have happened" or what "might have occurred." The ob-gyn from North Country Hospital who greeted Veil soon after he was born was happy to talk both about what he knew (the boy was fine) and what he didn't (why the mother wasn't).

"We've all been lulled into believing that birth is as safe as having a cavity filled or a broken arm set," Dr. Andre Dumond told reporters. "Obviously, as this incident proves, it's not. The list of things that can go wrong in a home birth is frightening and it is endless. That's why doctors prefer the technological and institutional support of a hospital."

Even as a thirteen-year-old I can recall thinking as I read this remark that I personally wouldn't have had my teeth filled at home or a broken arm set in my bedroom, but I still understood his point. And I knew other people would as well.

Dumond was also asked by the reporter from the Associated Press whether Charlotte Bedford specifically would have died had she had her baby in the hospital, and his response to the question should probably be studied by public-relations executives and law students who understand the role the media can play in a trial:

"At this point I have no idea whether the poor woman would have died in a hospital. I don't know all the details yet of what happened. Would she have had her stomach ripped open with a kitchen knife? Of course not. Would she have had to endure a cesarean section without anesthesia? Of course not."

Of the half-dozen doctors who could have met my mother and Veil when they arrived at North Country Hospital, Dumond was the worst choice from my family's perspective. My mother and Dumond knew each other, and they disliked each other. I have no doubt that Dumond was a fine obstetrician, but he was in his mid-fifties then, and he was the sort of doctor midwives referred to euphemistically as "interventionist." He believed that birth was a dangerous business, and it demanded constant monitoring and lots of drugs. My mother and the other midwives sometimes called him "Ol' Doctor Forceps" and the "Electrolux Man"—a reference to the skull cap–like vacuum physicians such as Dumond would apply to the infant's cranium to help pull the child from the vagina—because he was so quick to make baby skulls look like turnips with his delivery room toys.

My mother thought it was absolutely ridiculous (but completely predictable) when Dumond convinced a pediatrician to keep Veil at the hospital over the weekend for observation. The two doctors went so far as to place the healthy, howling eight-and-a-half-pounder in the closest thing the hospital had to a neonatal intensive-care unit: a special, sealed room they set up beside the nursery with oxygen, monitors, an incubator, and bilirubin lights available. The baby even slept on a mattress through Sunday with an alarm inside that would sound if he stopped breathing.

In some articles, an anonymous official in the state's attorney's office, in all likelihood Bill Tanner himself, explained that Vermont was investigating the death. "We won't know for a while whether there's a basis for criminal charges, or whether it's merely a civil matter," the source said, suggesting that even if the State didn't press charges, my mother could expect to be sued for every penny she had.

Only the reporter from the little *Newport Chronicle* tracked down Asa Bedford for a short statement. The reverend hadn't exactly gone into hiding, but he had taken Foogie with him Friday night and spent the next few days at the home of one of his parishioners. Saturday morning or afternoon he told the newspaper writer that he was still in shock on some level, and he had nothing to say about my mother or his wife's labor:

"I am very, very grateful that I have been blessed with another child. But I don't even know how to begin to convey my grief over Charlotte's death. I just don't have those words. I'm sorry. I shouldn't say anything more."

He didn't preach on Sunday morning. He wasn't even in church. In fact, he never preached in that church again. He attended services there twice more, but by early May he had left Vermont and returned to Alabama, where he had family.

Some weeks later his expression "I shouldn't say anything more" would take on a life of its own for my father. For a time he became convinced that either Bill Tanner or some ambulance-chasing attorney had told Asa to say that, to make sure the reverend didn't say anything that would come back to haunt the Bedfords when they took the Danforths to court. And even if the words hadn't been suggested to Asa by a lawyer, the Sunday morning we saw them we should have realized they—along with the observations of Dr. Dumond and the source in the state's attorney's office—meant that my mother was going to trial.

My mother and I almost never made dinner together, and yet, ironically, that is essentially what we were doing late Monday afternoon when

Stephen Hastings and his photographer rang our doorbell. My mother was sitting at the kitchen table, trying her best to stay off her feet. Despite the Band-Aids on three of her fingers, she was attempting to peel the skins from the red peppers we'd roasted, while I chopped vegetables on the cutting board by the sink.

It was barely four-thirty, so my father wouldn't be home for at least another hour.

My mother knew her lawyer was coming by at any moment to talk with her some more and to pick up whatever papers from her records he deemed important. Perhaps because the state police had sent two men to our house Friday night, one who asked questions and one who took notes, I answered the front door expecting to find on the other side a fellow roughly my parents' age in a dignified suit, and a much younger person—probably dressed more casually—whose sole responsibility would be to capture the conversation on paper.

Instead I saw a man in slacks and a blazer, no necktie, and a slightly older man in blue jeans, a flannel shirt, and a down vest. Like a pack animal, the fellow in jeans had camera bags slung over both of his shoulders, and in his hands were coils of extension cords and a pair of large metal lights.

The press, I feared, had decided to descend upon our house since my mother had refused to return their phone calls.

"I don't think my mother wants to speak with you," I said, standing tall and straight in the doorway.

The photographer turned to the other man, and although the photographer's beard was as thick as steel wool, I could see him frown. He raised his shoulders in a way that made the straps from his bags slide in toward his neck, and he sighed deeply with disgust.

The fellow in the blazer extended his hand to me and smiled. "You're Connie, aren't you?"

I refused his hand, but I nodded. I liked his voice and his tone—confident and serene, unaffected—but the last thing I wanted to do was to get involved in a protracted conversation with reporters when my mother's attorney was due at any moment.

"I'm Stephen Hastings," he continued. "I met your mother and father Saturday afternoon. This is Marc Truchon. He's with me to take some pictures."

Truchon nodded, as I reflexively took Stephen's hand.

"I thought you were reporters," I said, and I tried to laugh, but the

noise sounded more like a grunt. Even today I'm not especially good at
smoothing over social gaffes, and as a teenager—as awkward and self-
loathing as most—I would sometimes blush a pink so deep I looked like
I was choking. As I escorted the two men back into the kitchen, a
moment's humiliation had probably cooked my skin so that it looked as
if I'd spent a week in the sun.

My mother rose from her seat as we entered the room, holding on
to the back of another chair for support.

"God, Sibyl, don't get up!" Stephen said, using his hands to motion
her back into her seat as if he were directing traffic. When she was sitting
down again, he grinned and added, "On second thought, why don't you
get back up and jump around a bit? Let's get that ankle as big as a
grapefruit."

For almost thirty minutes Marc Truchon photographed my mother
in the living room, snapping pictures of parts of her body against a small
white backdrop he had brought with him inside one of his bags. He
recorded lacerations that ran along the palm of her left hand like lighthearted swoops, including a gash that ranged from the edge of her
wedding band to her thumb. He took pictures of her inventory of
abrasions and bruises, many with dozens and dozens of pinpoint-small
dots formed by fresh scabs.

At first I was surprised that Marc began with my mother's arms
and hands, since her legs were much more seriously beaten up and
bruised. But then when he said, "Okay, Mrs. Danforth, shall we do the
legs?" and Stephen wandered back toward the kitchen mumbling something about a glass of water, I understood: That afternoon my mother
had been wearing a long paisley peasant skirt, a modest dress that fell
almost to the floor when she stood, and she was now going to have to
pull that dress up practically to her hips. In addition to her sprained
ankle, she had bruises dotting both of her legs, including what I understand was a strawberry on her thigh so painful she was unable to wear
jeans, a contusion so deep it was considerably more black than blue.

Quickly I followed Stephen into the kitchen to give my mother and
the photographer their privacy. Besides, I didn't want to see the worst of
my mother's bruises.

"Where do you keep glasses, Connie? I really would love a drink
of water," Stephen said, wiping his eyeglasses with a white handkerchief.

I opened the cabinet door and reached for two glasses. Then,
remembering how my mother was always offering people coffee and

herbal tea, I pulled down the metal container in which my mother kept tea bags. "Would you like coffee instead? Or herbal tea?"

"Does your family own stock in some coffee or tea company?"

"I don't know," I answered, not realizing until after I'd opened my mouth that this was a joke.

"No," he went on, "water would be perfect right now."

I filled each glass from the kitchen sink.

"Eighth grade, right?" he asked.

I nodded.

"Up at the union high school?"

"Yup."

"They send a school bus up here, or do your parents have to drive you back and forth?"

"Oh, no, there's a school bus."

He shook his head. "Must be a dream in mud season."

"It's hard to stop a school bus."

"Do you know Darren Royce?"

"Mr. Royce, the biology teacher?"

"One and the same."

"Sure, I know him."

"Is he one of your teachers, or do you just know who he is?"

"I have him for biology. Fifty minutes a class, plus all the labs."

"Is he a good teacher?"

I realized as we spoke that I had begun to stand up straight, a response to the fact that Stephen's posture was perfect. I stepped forward from the counter against which I'd been leaning and squared my shoulders.

"Are you two friends?" I asked.

"Ah, answering a question with a question. Very savvy."

"Ah, answering a question with a compliment. Very savvy."

"Yes, we're friends."

"Yes, he's a good teacher."

"Like him?"

"Sure. How do you two know each other?"

"Air force. Want to have some fun at his expense?"

"Maybe."

"The next time you see him, tell him L-T says hi from Camp Latrine."

"L-T?"

"He'll know."

"And Camp Latrine: Was that what you called your base in the army?"

"Air force. Yup. It was one of them, anyway."

"Was this in Vietnam?"

"It was."

From the living room we would occasionally hear either my mother's or Marc's voice, and then the click the camera made every time he took a photograph. The door was shut no more than halfway, and each time the flash went off the kitchen would whiten as if summer lightning had brightened the sky outside.

"Your father home?" he asked.

"Not yet. He usually gets home around five-thirty or six."

He glanced at the skinned peppers on the kitchen table and the vegetables, some diced, on the counter.

"Dinner looks good. What are you making?"

"I'm really not making much of anything. I'm not much of a cook. I'm just chopping what Mom needs chopped. I think the end result will be some sort of stroganoff."

"Well, I hope we don't keep your mother too long."

"What are you doing next?"

He removed a tape recorder about as long as a postcard from one of his blazer's front pockets, and half as wide. "I'm just going to ask her a few questions. Nothing too tough tonight."

"You're not going to take notes?"

"Oh, good Lord, no."

"That's what the police did. My parents said the police took notes."

He opened the recorder and showed me the tiniest audiocassette I'd ever seen in my life, a tape little bigger than a postage stamp. "Well, the police have their methods, and I have mine. And you know what?"

"What?"

"Mine are a whole lot better."

It may have been the confident way that he spoke, and it may have been the ramrod way that he stood. It may have been the way he was dressed, that one-click-above blazer. It may have been all of those things combined. But I went to sleep that night absolutely convinced that if my mother indeed needed a lawyer—and, in all of our minds, that still wasn't a sure thing—she had the best one in Vermont.

TEN

Connie had a cup of coffee with breakfast yesterday. First time, but I think it's going to become a regular thing. I didn't ask her if she liked it because that would have been just too much like a parent. And I didn't stop her, although the idea crossed my mind. She isn't even fourteen yet.

I remember what I was doing when I was fourteen. It was a lot worse than coffee, and somehow I made it to fifteen. So I told myself this coffee thing is okay, she knows what she wants, and tried to chill out.

She must have put in two whole packets of Sweet'n Low. And I'll bet the coffee still wasn't as sweet as my girl looked to me. She was still in her nightgown, and she had on those slipper socks on her feet: big wool socks with leather soles. Rand was already up and out the door—until this whole horrible thing is over, I think the only time he'll ever get any work done is before the rest of the world is even awake—and she just shuffled into the kitchen, shuffled across the floor, shuffled over to the coffee mugs on the pegs by the toaster, and started pouring herself a cup.

I think I must have been staring by the way she stopped mid-pour and then looked over at me.

"Okay if I have a cup?" she asked.

And that's when this really weird sentence formed in my head, the sort of sentence I can hear my own mother saying to me: Don't you think you're a little young?

So I just nodded like, you know, no big deal. And while on the one hand it isn't—it's coffee, and she sees her dad and mom practically mainlining the stuff—on the other hand, it is. It's one more step for our girl.

I want to write "little girl." But she hasn't been a little girl in years. I probably shouldn't even think of her as a girl anymore. The person in a nightgown and slipper socks is a young woman. (God, wasn't it just yesterday she was calling them "slippy socks"? Probably not. It was probably half a decade ago.) And I don't just mean she's a young woman physically, though it's clear as she stands in her nightgown that her body has changed. Height. Hips. Breasts.

I mean she's becoming this young woman emotionally. She's always been very mature for her age, but she has some moments these days when she seems totally grown up to me. She still sounds pretty kid-like when she's on the phone with Tom Corts, and from a distance she still looks pretty kid-like when she's grooming the McKennas' horse with Rollie. But the way she's handling the bigger things right now is amazing to me. That's when she seems like this little grown-up person. Like when she was reading all those horrible newspaper stories Sunday morning. She was practically dissecting them like she was one of those Sunday-morning news commentators on TV.

Or when she met my lawyer last night. That's a perfect example. When she met Stephen. She was this little diplomat, making sure he had whatever he needed, asking him these really good questions, and telling him these really funny stories.

She even asked him if he could stay for dinner. Just like a little diplomat. Just like a young diplomat. Not little. Young. And while he couldn't stay for dinner last night, I have a feeling he will be having dinner with us other nights this spring. Connie will have to see a lot of him, which is only unfortunate because of what he does, not because of who he is.

I know Connie's scared. I know I'm scared. I don't know what to do about that in either of our cases.

Here's what I think I'll do about the coffee. She can have coffee in the morning before school, but not after dinner. If she wants to start the day with a cup of coffee, that's cool.

But none before bedtime because she is still growing, and she does need her sleep. That's how we'll handle this coffee thing.

—*from the notebooks of* SIBYL DANFORTH, MIDWIFE

WHEN CHARLOTTE FUGETT BEDFORD DIED, THE MIDWIVES WERE SCARED. THE lay midwives, that is, the ones without any medical training, the ones who did the home births. Not the nurse-midwives: They worked with doctors and delivered babies in hospitals, and had no reason to be frightened.

But the lay midwives feared—rightly, it would prove—that the medical community would try and use the woman's death as an indictment of home birth in general. As winter slowly gave way to spring, however, and my mother was charged with a crime and treated like a criminal, when the midwives learned the conditions of my mother's bail, their fear quickly grew into anger. Fury, to be precise. And while the midwives I have met in the course of my life have many, many strengths, an ability to have a dispassionate conversation about home versus hospital birth or a willingness to discuss the conduct of one of their own with anything that resembles an objective detachment is not among them. Moreover, if—as Tom Corts had put it—doctors are predatory pack animals like wolves, then midwives are herd animals like elephants: Attack one, and the others will rush to the wounded animal and do all that they can to defend it.

In the months after Charlotte Fugett Bedford died, our house was filled with midwives. Sometimes they came with food as if someone in our family had died, sometimes they came with flowers: When May arrived, our house grew rich with the sweet aroma of lilacs; in June the dining room and kitchen were filled with the scent of sweet honeysuckle and narcissus. Occasionally they brought with them the names of other midwives around the country who had also experienced a—to use the midwife's euphemism for virtually any fatality, deformity, or grotesque malformation—"bad outcome." Sometimes they appeared with the names of those women's lawyers, a gesture which initially I assumed Stephen Hastings would find threatening. I was wrong. He was thrilled.

Early on he asked my mother to share with him the names of these midwives and their attorneys so he could discuss with them *their* trials and *their* defense strategies. From a lawyer in Virginia he got the name of one of the forensic pathologists who would eventually testify on my mother's behalf; from a midwife in Seattle he heard the story of the midwife in California who had been tried for practicing medicine without a license after she injected Pitocin and Ergotrate into a woman in labor.

The midwives who visited us came from all over New England and upstate New York, and a few traveled distances that absolutely astonished me, just for the opportunity to meet and console my mother. When some of the news articles about her were sent over the wires, midwives in places as far as Arkansas and New Mexico read about her plight, and one from each of those states ventured to Reddington as a show of solidarity.

These women, regardless of whether they were from a rural corner of northern New Hampshire or an urban neighborhood in Boston, regardless of how well they knew my mother, were huggers. They never shook her hand when they met her, they always embraced her. This went for my father, too, if he happened to be home, and for Stephen Hastings if he happened to be visiting. They, too, would be hugged. Moreover, these were not the sort of mannered little squeezes society matrons or youthful debutantes might share at dining clubs or cotillions in Manhattan, these were emphatic bear hugs of impressively long duration. These were the sorts of decorum-be-damned greetings that begin with arms opened like wings, which then close around one like a straitjacket. I hate to think of the sort of damage they might have done to their clothes if these midwives or my mother had been the sort who wore makeup.

The Vermont midwives, all of whom knew my mother, rallied around her like Secret Service agents around a president who's been shot. They brought her casseroles and stews; they left in our kitchen absolutely mammoth tureens of gazpacho, escabèche, or sweet pea and spinach soup. They baked multigrain breads and blueberry muffins, gingerbread cookies and decadent chocolate tortes. They wrote my mother poems. They penned editorials for the opinion pages of Vermont newspapers; they wrote letters to legislators and the state's attorney. They conducted "teach-ins" to explain home birth at public libraries in St. Johnsbury and Montpelier. Cheryl Visco and Donelle Folino organized a quilt sale to raise money for my mother's legal defense fund, while Molly Thompson and Megan Blubaugh wrote hundreds of fund-raising letters on her behalf. Midwife Tracy Fitzpatrick's sister and brother-in-law owned a vegetarian restaurant in Burlington, and she convinced them to have a

special fund-raising dinner one night, with all of the proceeds going toward my mother's defense.

Some midwives dedicated births to her, and I don't believe there was a baby born at home in Vermont over the next six or seven months whose picture wasn't presented to Sibyl as a boost to her morale: *This,* said those snapshots and portraits of boys and girls born in bedrooms and living rooms, *is what you're defending. This is why you must fight.* I know of at least three young women living in Vermont today who are named Sibyl, each of whom was a baby born at home in the summer or fall of 1981, their names a not insignificant homage to my mother.

And, of course, the midwives helped out my mother by accepting her pregnant clients as patients, once the State insisted she stop practicing, at least temporarily, as a condition for bail. Often they actually conducted the prenatals in the women's homes to save them the additional burden of traveling after the trauma of losing their midwife.

Most of the time, I think, my father was glad to see my mother receiving all of this support from the midwives. It took some of the pressure off him. Sometimes it boosted his spirits, too. And as a family we really did eat very well that spring and summer. But there were other times when my father grew irritated, tired of the way his home had become a coffeehouse for a New Age world of women in sandals, for tireless earth mothers in wraparound paisley skirts. I think he found Cheryl Visco especially annoying.

The day after Charlotte had died, literally moments after my parents had returned from a Saturday spent with lawyers and emergency-room doctors, she appeared at our house with a ragged manila envelope overflowing with legal information she had amassed over the years from the Midwives Alliance of North America: the names of the women who had been tried for one reason or another, the outcomes of the cases. Bad copies of ancient newspaper articles. Lists of insurance companies. Law firms.

And in the weeks immediately after the death, when it was becoming increasingly clear that the State was slowly and methodically building a case, Cheryl would drop by almost every other day for no other reason than to offer moral support. Sometimes she'd appear with one flower, sometimes with a note card she thought was funny. Sometimes she'd have the name of a book my mother should read, sometimes she'd have the book itself.

When she arrived late on a weekday afternoon, she would stay for

dinner. When she arrived on a weekend morning, she would stay for lunch. The days were indeed growing longer as March became April, but—as my father said—when Cheryl was there they seemed to last forever.

Cheryl was probably in her early fifties then, but she was still a beautiful woman. Her hair was gray, and unlike most gray hair it still looked magnificent long. It fell like curtains down her back, usually draping a tight black sweater or the top of a long-sleeved but close-fitting black dress. Cheryl was close to six feet tall, more slender than most women half her age, and the subject of all sorts of rumor and gossip: She had three children from three different fathers, only one of whom she had actually bothered to marry. While some people assumed the relationships failed for the reasons the marriages of many midwives go bad—ridiculously long hours and a completely unpredictable schedule—others attributed the fact that Cheryl was a three-time loser in love to a flighty morality and a loose set of values. If she had had one husband and two significant partners over the years, the gossips whispered, she had most certainly had thirty lovers. Maybe three hundred.

Personally, what I believe did her marriages in was her truly astonishing ability to speak for hours at a time without stopping to breathe. She could tell whole stories without ever inhaling, recount lengthy anecdotes without so much as a pause. It drove my father crazy, just as it probably drove most men in Cheryl's life away. In my experience, men aren't particularly good listeners, and to be around Cheryl for any length of time demanded patience, passivity, and an insatiable interest in Cheryl Visco's life.

Of course, Cheryl adored my mother, and in those weeks when my mother was still reeling from the death up in Lawson, Cheryl was the perfect friend: present but undemanding, company that necessitated no effort. My mother could simply sit still and listen, perhaps nod every so often if it felt right.

"*Chance* is the strangest word in the world, isn't it?" Cheryl might begin, speaking slowly at first but gathering momentum like an obese teenager on skis. "One syllable, six letters. It's a noun, it's a verb. Change one letter and it's an adjective. And everything about it scares the bejesus out of so many people; it's this thing they try to avoid at all costs. Don't travel to the Middle East these days—there's a chance something could happen. Don't get involved with that new fellow on Creamery Street—I

hear a lot of mud was scraped off his floor after the divorce. Don't have your baby at home—there's a chance something could go wrong. Don't, don't, don't . . . Well, you can't live your life like that! You can't spend your entire life avoiding chance. It's out there, it's inescapable, it's a part of the soul of the world. There are no sure things in this universe, and it's absolutely ridiculous to try and live like there are! There's nothing that drives me crazier than when people say home birth is chancy or irresponsible or risky. My God, so what if it is? Which, in my opinion, of course, it isn't. What's the price of attempting to eliminate chance, or trying to better the odds? A sterile little world with bright hospital lights? A world where forceps replace fingers? Where women get IVs and epidurals instead of herbs? Sure, we can cut down the risk, but we also cut off a lot of touching and loving and just plain human connection. No one said living isn't a pretty chancy business, Sibyl. No one gets out of here alive."

Although Cheryl lived over an hour away in Waterbury, she would sometimes stay until ten or eleven o'clock at night. Some nights when I would go upstairs to do my homework or call one of my friends around eight or eight-thirty, I would leave her lecturing my parents. I'd hear my father escaping soon after, trudging upstairs with the excuse that he was tired. Later, when Cheryl had finally gone home and my mother had struggled upstairs herself, I'd hear my father comment angrily on Cheryl's uncanny ability to outstay her welcome. Some nights his tone was more caustic than others; some nights his voice was louder.

On the quieter nights he might simply remark, "She can't keep a husband because she can't shut up." But when he was particularly disgusted or he'd had an extra scotch during dinner, I might hear him raise his voice as he said, "We have enough stress in our lives without her! The next time she shows up and won't leave, call me. Call me and I'll sleep at the damn office."

My mother would then shut their bedroom door, and I would wait silently at my desk, listening, wondering if tonight the fight would blow up or blow over.

We learned on Monday night what had happened to Anne Austin, my mother's apprentice. We didn't learn because the woman herself called my mother back, or because she finally answered the phone one of the many times my mother called her. We didn't learn because she appeared at our door after Stephen Hastings and his photographer left, or because we ran into her while shopping at the supermarket.

We learned because B.P. Hewitt—Dr. Brian Hewitt—called from the hospital during dinner and said he wanted to drop by when he finished his rounds. My parents said sure, and much of our conversation as we finished our meal revolved around why my mother's backup physician wanted to come by our house. As far as I knew, he'd only been here once before, and that was three years earlier when it seemed half the county was in our yard for the "graduation" party of sorts my mother held for Heather Reed, an apprentice who'd been with my mother for at least half a decade and was about to embark on a career of her own.

"How much does he know?" my father asked, pushing the skin of a baked potato around his plate with his fork.

"About Charlotte?" my mother asked.

"Yes," my father said, after inhaling deeply and slowly so he wouldn't snap at her. But the sound of that breath murmured clearly, *Of course. What the hell else could possibly be on his mind?*

"I told him what I remembered. I told him the basics."

"When did you talk to him? Was it Saturday or Sunday? Or today?"

"As a matter of fact, it was Friday. Friday morning. I called him from the hospital before I even went home. Why? Do you think it matters when I called him?"

"Maybe. I don't know. I was just wondering whether he heard the story first from you, or from that . . . that creep who met you at the emergency room with the baby. The one who said all those ridiculous things to the newspapers. Dumond. *Doctor* Dumond." He said the word *doctor* as if he thought the fellow had earned his medical degree by mail, as if he had found the school on the inside of a matchbook cover.

"He heard it from me." Categorical, but defensive. A tone that would color more and more of my mother's remarks that year. And while that tone was wholly understandable, the combination of absolute surety and righteous stubbornness made it sound a bit like a whine, and I believe on occasion it did her no good.

◆   ◆   ◆

I knew Dr. Hewitt's first name was Brian, but I had never heard him referred to as anything but B.P. Although he was more than a decade older than my parents, he still wore the nickname well he'd been given in medical school: B.P., a natural for a man hoping to become a doctor, whose first and middle initials were the abbreviation for blood pressure. His hair—vaguely camel-colored—was always flying around his forehead and flopping over the tops of his ears, and I can't recall ever noticing a line on his face. He had four sons, two of whom were close enough to my age that it was not uncommon for me to see the doctor around town: In my mind, I can still see his hair sticking out from underneath baseball caps, bicycle helmets, and the straw hat he wore one summer to a county fair in Orleans. It always seemed appropriate to me that he was the kind of doctor who delivered babies.

B.P. delivered his patients' babies in hospitals, of course, and he would testify that he believed hospitals were the safest place for newborns to arrive. But he also said he understood that some women were going to have their babies at home regardless of what he believed, and he was happy to back up the "right sort of midwife."

My mother, apparently, was the right sort of midwife. As her backup physician, he agreed to be on call to go to the hospital when my mother transferred one of her own patients there. Since my mother took women to the hospital only when she feared a complication—a slowly evolving difficulty such as a labor that just wasn't progressing, or the sudden and gut-wrenching chaos of fetal distress—this meant that the majority of the time B.P. met my mother there, he was anticipating a cesarean section.

In the nine years that B.P. had backed up my mother, the records would show that twenty-eight times my mother had transferred a patient to the hospital. Of those twenty-eight transfers—a small number, yes, but of course behind the vagaries of those digits lurk the terror and disappointment of twenty-eight women being rushed by ambulance or car from the warmth of their homes to the unknowns of a hospital, fearing with every movement (or pause) in their womb that their baby is dying—B.P. had been available twenty-six times. And of those twenty-six days or nights when he had met my mother at the hospital, on twenty-four occasions he had brought the laboring woman—usually silent with fear, although never, never numb—into an operating room and surgically removed the infant.

All but once the baby had been fine. Once the baby was stillborn. Born dead.

Never did a mother die.

And on that occasion when the baby was born dead, B.P. and the medical examiner were quite sure that the baby—a boy the parents would name Russell Bret—would have been born dead even if his mother had endured her labor in a hospital. If anyone believed that Russell Bret's parents made a mistake by attempting to have the child at home, I don't believe anyone said so. At least publicly. And no one, as far as I know, ever hinted that my mother might have been somehow to blame.

When B.P. arrived at our house that Monday night, he looked tired and preoccupied. I was immediately struck by the realization that this wasn't the carefree father I'd seen in the high-school bleachers watching his son play second base, or the serene dad I'd noticed bicycling back and forth with other sons on Hallock Street. He gave me a smile as my father walked him into the living room, but it was the sort of desperately wan grin I've since learned is the precursor to particularly bad news. I've always imagined that—along with doctors—accountants, mechanics, and the attorneys who handle death row appeals have a need for that grin often.

While he told my parents why he had stopped by, I cleaned up the kitchen. I was careful to make just enough noise that my parents would assume I was focused upon the dishes, but not so much that I couldn't hear most of what the adults were saying.

"She called about an hour after you did, Sibyl. Maybe forty-five minutes," B.P. told them.

"Friday morning?" my mother asked.

"Yup. Friday morning."

"She was that concerned?"

"Evidently."

"Why didn't she just call me?"

"Didn't she?"

"No."

"You two haven't spoken to each other since . . . since the birth?"

"Sibyl's been trying to reach her for three days," my father said. "Over the last three days, Sibyl has probably left a half-dozen messages on the woman's answering machine."

I slowed the water pouring from the tap to a trickle and dried my hands on the dish towel by the sink. I began to feel dizzy, as if I had stood up too quickly after kneeling for a long moment. They were talking about Anne, I realized, my mother's new apprentice. The woman who'd been with my mother at—to use B.P.'s term for the event—the birth.

I reached for the edge of the counter with both hands and leaned forward, trying to take some of the weight off my feet.

"You two haven't spoken, you two haven't seen each other?" The doctor's voice again. In it was something like surprise, something like concern. Concern for my mother.

"Nope," my mother said. "Not one word."

"I asked her to call you. Talk to you," B.P. continued.

"She didn't."

"Is she still in Vermont?" my father asked.

"I believe so."

"Then I'll see her tomorrow," my mother told B.P. "I have pre-natal exams all afternoon, and Anne will assist me. We can talk about this whole affair then."

"Oh, I don't think so, Sibyl," B.P. said slowly, and I assumed the reason he had begun to speak at a slower speed was because he wanted to buy the time to find the right words for the point he was about to make. "If Anne hasn't already called you, I wouldn't expect her tomorrow."

"What exactly did Anne say to you?" My father. Suspicious.

"Tell me something first. If you don't mind. How well do you know Anne?" the doctor asked, and I could tell he was directing the question at my mother.

"I believe I know her well."

"But she hasn't been your apprentice very long."

"No, not long at all."

"About six months?"

"Not even that long. Three. Maybe four. We started working together in December."

"You're stalling, B.P., you're avoiding the issue. What did the girl say to you?" my father asked once more, his patience fading.

B.P. sighed. Finally: "When you made the incision into Mrs. Bedford to rescue the baby, she says she saw blood spurt. A couple of times. She says she thinks Mrs. Bedford was alive."

There are expressions to convey silence; there are all the old clichés. There are the poetic constructs and affectations. A silence deep as death, a silence deep as eternity. Quiet as a lamb, a quiet wise and good. The silence of the infinite spaces, the silence upon which minds move.

After B.P. spoke, did the living room grow so quiet we could have heard a pin drop? Rooms are often that still, and the floor of that particular living room was hardwood painted gray. We could have heard pins drop in the quiet of that room most days and nights. No, the stillness that overtook the three adults and me, the stillness that fell upon our house was very different from silence. It was not the silence of thought, the quiet of meditation. It was not the silence that grows from serenity, the hush that flowers around minds at peace.

It was the stillness of waiting. Of preparation. Of anticipation tinged—no, not tinged, overwhelmed—overwhelmed by gloom.

How long we all remained still—the adults in the living room, I in the kitchen—was probably far different in reality than it feels to me now in memory. I remember the stillness lasting a very long time; I remember leaning over the sink on my arms for what seemed a great while. But I was so dizzy I feared I might become ill, and in reality the stillness may have lasted mere seconds. A pause in the conversation—albeit one in which everyone present understood that our realities were changed by B.P.'s news, that our lives before and after his remark would be very different—but a simple pause nonetheless.

And then it broke. The stillness brought on by words was done in by words.

"If you'd like," my mother said simply, "I'll talk to Anne tomorrow and put an end to this."

"She won't be here tomorrow, Sibyl, I'm telling you that."

"Why are you so sure? Did she say something to that effect?"

"She didn't have to. But it's clear. It's clear from the fact she hasn't connected with you since . . . since the woman died. She's avoiding you."

"Avoiding me." More of a statement than a question. My mother sounded more incredulous than concerned.

"Avoiding you. Yes."

I took in a few deep breaths to try and calm myself, to settle my stomach. But my knees were going and so I gave in, I allowed my body to slide to the kitchen floor. I fell slowly, as if I were slipping serenely underwater, my back sliding against the cabinet under the sink as I collapsed.

"What did you say to Anne when she called?" I heard my father ask, and for a brief moment the voices sounded so far away I feared I would faint, but the moment passed.

"I told her I doubted what she said was true. I told her I'd already spoken to you and Andre, and my sense was she probably saw a lot of blood and it was probably very frightening. But she hadn't seen you cut open a living woman. It just wasn't possible, given who you are."

"Who I am," my mother murmured. An echo.

"Yes. An experienced midwife. A woman with excellent emergency medical training."

"And then?" My father again.

"She seemed to understand, and I hoped that would be the end of it. I suggested she call you and get it all off her chest. Get it all out in the open between the two of you."

"But she never called me," my mother said, and in her voice I heard as much hurt as I heard fear.

"Apparently not. But later that day, she did call Reverend Bedford."

"She called Asa?"

"And then she called the state's attorney's office."

"And she told them she thought this woman had been alive when Sibyl did the C-section?" my father asked.

"So it would seem. What she probably told the state's attorney—and this is why I wanted to come by tonight—is that she and Asa both saw blood spurt when you made your incision. In her opinion, the heart was pumping when you began the operation."

"Then why didn't she say something?" my mother said, raising her voice for the first time that evening. "No, she knew Charlotte was dead—and Asa did, too!"

My mother wasn't frantic, but her tone suggested she understood clearly that Asa's perception of the tragedy affected everything. My father, perhaps with some cause, feared that frenzy was just another revelation away, and asked quickly, "B.P., why are you here tonight? This moment? Did something happen today?"

"I was interviewed. I guess that's the right word. Interviewed. I was interviewed today by a couple of state troopers. They wanted a statement. And based on their questions, I got the distinct impression that everyone—state's attorney, medical examiner, father—believes that somebody's dead right now because a midwife performed a bedroom cesarean on a living woman."

Later that night my mother knocked on my door and asked if I was awake. She probably knew that I was because she could see the light on under my door, and I was never the type to fall asleep while reading. Through the register in the floor I could hear my father downstairs, adding a last log for the night to the woodstove.

"Come on in," I said, rolling over in bed to face the doorway, and tossing the magazine I was reading onto my night table.

I was surprised that my mother hadn't yet gotten ready for bed. B.P. had left hours ago; it was probably close to midnight. But my mother was still dressed in her loose peasant skirt, and she still had her hair back with a barrette. She limped across the room and sat on the edge of the bed. Outside my window the moon was huge, an oval spotlight one sliver short of full.

"You're up late," she said.

"It's the coffee," I told her, teasing. I'd seen how closely she'd watched me that morning when I'd decided to test one of my limits. It was a completely spontaneous exploration, absolutely unplanned. I simply saw Mr. Coffee, and my arms and hands did the rest.

She picked up the magazine, one for women in their twenties, and thumbed through its pages. That particular issue had articles on super summer shorts and the pros and cons of tanning salons, as well as a special pullout section on birth control. There was no woman in the state of Vermont with a figure as perfect as the Texas blonde on the cover, and no girl with hair that big.

"Anything interesting in here?"

My mother knew exactly which parts of the magazine I found interesting.

"There are some shorts I like on page 186," I told her, not a complete fabrication, but not exactly the truth either.

She nodded and smiled. "They'd look good on you."

"Yeah. But they are sort of yachty," I said, making a word up when I couldn't find the right one. "I think you'd have to live on the ocean to get away with them."

"Probably."

"Or be some rich guy's mistress," I added, an inside joke between us. Whenever we saw a young woman in Vermont who was mind-numbingly overdressed for our little state, one of us would whisper to the other, "Over there—some rich guy's mistress," drawing out the word *rich* until it became almost two syllables: *ri-ichhhhh.*

"Oh, good, there's an article on how to choose the right tanning salon. That should be very, very helpful," my mother said.

"There is one now in Burlington, you know."

"No, I didn't know."

"Yup."

"We're becoming pretty hip up here in the hills."

"Mostly I just look at the ads. To see what's cool."

She skimmed the headlines and captions in the section on birth control. "How are you and Tom doing?"

"Fine."

"Was it strange not going to the dance with him Friday night?"

"Strange?"

"Did you miss him?"

"We talked on the phone. And he came over Saturday afternoon, you know."

"I know. But I'll bet it's not the same as hanging out with him at a dance."

"Nope. Not exactly."

She looked down again at the magazine, and with her eyes on the section about diaphragms she said, "Don't ever forget: When you think it's time, you tell me. We'll go straight to the clinic." The clinic was our word-saving shorthand for Planned Parenthood.

"I will."

"Promise?"

I rolled my eyes. "Mom!"

She rolled her eyes and threw back her head histrionically in response.

"Promise?" she asked again, a reference to the vow she'd asked me to make when I turned thirteen that if I ever thought there was even the slightest chance I might be having sex in the foreseeable future—even if that chance was as statistically remote as being hit by lightning in late December—I would tell her, and we would visit Planned Parenthood and get me fitted for a diaphragm. Short of dealing heroin to our schoolmates or shooting a teacher, I think the only thing Tom and I could have done that year that would have truly disappointed and upset my mother would have been to have had the sort of tumble together that results in an unexpected teenage pregnancy.

When I told some of my friends about this promise, girls like Rollie and Sadie, they decided that there was no mother on the planet as cool as my mom. Most mothers then wouldn't even say the word *diaphragm* to their thirteen-year-old daughters, much less offer to drive them to the clinic where they could get one. In the eyes of my friends, the attitudinal advantages of having a midwife for a mother dramatically outweighed the inconveniences brought on by long labors and midnight deliveries.

"I promise," I said.

"Thank you." She rolled the magazine into a tube and held it primly in her lap like a diploma.

"You're welcome. How does your ankle feel?"

"It feels okay." She shrugged. "Painkillers."

"They work?"

"You bet."

"What did Dr. Hewitt want?"

"You weren't listening?"

"I couldn't hear everything."

"He's a good friend," she said instead of answering my question. I don't think it was a conscious evasion, but she quickly continued, "I think I'm on my own for the prenatals tomorrow."

"Anne doesn't do much yet anyway, does she?"

"She does her share. She's learning."

"It sounds like she's got a lot to learn."

My mother looked at me for a long moment, and I worked hard to maintain eye contact. I think she realized in that second just how much I understood: how much she needed to share with me, and how much she didn't. She didn't blink, and if the cluster flies in our walls were not dormant that moment, they would have seen my mother's head nod just the tiniest bit. *Yes,* that nod agreed, *she does.*

Downstairs my father added water to the kettle atop the wood-stove, pushing the wrought-iron lid against the brass handle. I knew the clang it made well. A second later my mother and I both heard the brief sizzle from the drops of water that spilled down the sides of the kettle onto the soapstone surface of the stove, hot enough to turn that water to steam in an instant. He then pulled the chain of the reading lamp by the couch, and we knew he was about to come upstairs.

Finally I looked down at the edge of my quilt, unable to meet my mother's gaze any longer.

"Sleep well, sweetie," she said. "Sweet dreams."

"You, too, Mom," I answered, and somewhere inside her she found the strength to murmur the lie that she would.

ELEVEN

$25,000. A two and a five and three zeros—five zeros if you're using a decimal point. Not a whole lot less than it took to buy this whole house not that many years ago. The cost of two years of college for Connie. The cost of my baby's entire college education, with change, if she decides she wants to go to the University of Vermont.

Until today, Rand and I had never written one check that big. Technically, I guess, I still haven't. It was Rand who actually tracked down a pen in the kitchen drawer and wrote out the words "Twenty-five thousand dollars" on that line checks have right below "Pay to the Order of." Then he scribbled the two and the five and all those zeros.

And that $25,000 is just the beginning. "The retainer to get the clock started," Stephen Hastings said. "The money to feed the meter." And now the meter's running.

I was very disturbed by the amount at first, and I found myself wishing we were eligible for the public defender, but we're not. I kept hearing these words in my head, this sentence: "Man, that's a lot of bread." That's what we used to say: "A lot of bread." Grass might be a lot of bread, or a car—used or dented or wrecked by some sort of really hideous orange paint that someone thought was psychedelic—or a pair of stereo speakers.

I told Rand it was too much money, especially since we'll need a lot more if this thing drags on. It's almost our entire life savings, almost all of the money we've squirreled away for over a decade for Connie's college or our retirement or both.

Besides, I haven't done anything wrong. And so I said to Rand maybe we didn't have to have the best attorney we could find, or the best lawyer money could buy. It's not like I was caught robbing a bank with a machine gun.

But Rand disagreed, and said it didn't matter whether I'd done anything wrong, that wasn't the point. The point was that a woman had died doing something we all know the state hates, and that was having her baby at home. And so someone will have to be held accountable.

In the old days, of course, he would have called the state "the establishment."

In my mind, I can see Rand shaking his head and I can hear him saying, "Man, it will take a lot of bread to beat the establishment, but pay up we must." He didn't say that, of course. He wouldn't, not these days.

What he said was, "We want the best, and apparently that's Stephen Hastings. We shouldn't be surprised that he's the most costly."

Rand is probably right. But given who I am and what I do, Stephen Hastings is a very ironic choice. In the world of law, Stephen's as pricey as they come: He's polished and high-tech and very, very slick. Meanwhile, in the world of babies, I'm about as inexpensive as you get, a fraction of the cost of an ob-gyn. And I try hard to be unpolished and low-tech and . . . earthy.

And it sounds like Stephen was in Vietnam, based on something he said to Connie. I find that very weird, too. Imagine this: It's a single day fourteen years ago. On one side of the planet, I'm in Plattsburgh in my "Drop acid, not bombs" T-shirt, putting daisies all over the wire fence at the air base and in the gun barrels of the soldiers who keep telling us we have to stop. And somewhere on the other side of the planet it's nighttime, and there's this guy from Vermont named Stephen Hastings who's up to his hips in some swamp or rice paddy. And now that guy's defending me.

I do believe this will all be fine in the end, at least partly

because Stephen seems to be such a good lawyer. But also be-
cause I was trying to do the right thing when I decided to save
Veil.

Stephen seems to understand that. He may be polished
and slick and a high-tech kind of guy, but I can see myself
delivering his wife's or girlfriend's baby someday in their home.
Maybe Stephen will be my first lawyer daddy. That'd be cool.

I know he doesn't have any children yet, and I know he's
no longer married. I wonder if he has a girlfriend back in
Burlington.

—*from the notebooks of* SIBYL DANFORTH, MIDWIFE

HOW HIGH DOES BLOOD SPURT FROM A BEATING HEART? FOR MY MOTHER, THE
question lost its rhetorical or theoretic flourish, and became instead one
of pathological and clinical detail: In her mind, there was a tangible,
perhaps even mathematical, connection between the power of the pulse
and the height of the geyser at the point of incision.

For Stephen Hastings, however, the issue became one of mere
staging and lighting: logistics, not pathology. It didn't matter to him how
high into the air a beating heart could arc a fountain of blood, or whether
the red crescent was narrow or squat—a water pistol–like squirt, or the
burp of a water balloon burst with a pin. Although my mother's fate
would indeed depend in large measure upon who would win the battle
of the experts Stephen waged with Bill Tanner—his doctors versus the
State's, his midwives versus theirs—on this one question he didn't worry
much about medical testimony. He worried instead about blocking, and
where Asa Bedford and Anne Austin were standing when my mother
took a kitchen knife and first pierced Charlotte's skin:

STEPHEN HASTINGS: And then you asked if your wife was dead?
ASA BEDFORD: Yes, sir.
HASTINGS: And Sibyl told you she was?
BEDFORD: That's right.
HASTINGS: So what did you do next?
BEDFORD: I didn't do anything.
HASTINGS: I believe, Reverend Bedford, we've already established
that you went to the window. Correct me if I'm mistaken.

BEDFORD: No, I didn't understand the question. I thought you wanted to know if I did something . . . medical.

HASTINGS: You went to the window?

BEDFORD: Yes.

HASTINGS: To look outside?

BEDFORD: I guess.

HASTINGS: You looked out the window. Did you watch it snow?

BEDFORD: I don't remember, but I probably did. At least for a second or two. But then I looked back at Charlotte.

HASTINGS: From the window.

BEDFORD: Yes, sir.

HASTINGS: (motions toward easel with overhead drawing of the Bedford bedroom, *State's 8* for identification) How far is the window from the bed?

BEDFORD: Not far. A couple of feet.

HASTINGS: Two feet?

BEDFORD: No, further.

HASTINGS: Three?

BEDFORD: No.

HASTINGS: Five?

BEDFORD: Maybe. It might be more.

HASTINGS: Seven?

BEDFORD: I don't know, I've never measured it.

HASTINGS: But you think it might be as much as seven feet away?

BEDFORD: Or as little as five.

HASTINGS: (at easel) Using the State's diagram and the State's scale, it's six feet, eight inches from the center of the bed to the glass. Does that sound right to you?

BEDFORD: It sounds . . . fine.

HASTINGS: Thank you. Was the sun up?

BEDFORD: No, sir, it was still dark out.

HASTINGS: So you did look outside.

STATE'S ATTORNEY WILLIAM TANNER: Objection. Asked and answered.

JUDGE HOWARD DORSET: Sustained.

HASTINGS: It was still night?

BEDFORD: It was still dark. It wasn't night. It was dark because of the storm. The clouds.

HASTINGS: And so the only light in the room came from the lamps?

BEDFORD: Yes, but I could see Charlotte.

HASTINGS: (motions toward diagram) Was the floor light on? The one in the corner?

BEDFORD: Yes. That one had been on all night long.

HASTINGS: What about the one on the night table?

BEDFORD: Yes, that one was on, too. Sib— Mrs. Danforth had turned it on just before she began the . . . the operation.

HASTINGS: Where was Sibyl standing during the operation? On which side of the bed?

BEDFORD: The far side. The side away from me.

HASTINGS: Here?

BEDFORD: Yes, sir.

HASTINGS: (presses a bright blue dot onto the drawing beside the bed) This is Sibyl. (Presses a red dot onto the drawing just inside the window) And this is you. Is this accurate?

BEDFORD: I think so.

HASTINGS: In other words, your wife was in bed, and the bed was between you and Sibyl.

BEDFORD: Exactly. From the window, I had an unobstructed view.

HASTINGS: (presses a yellow dot on top of the night table behind the defendant) And this is the light Sibyl switched on just before she rescued your baby?

BEDFORD: Yes.

HASTINGS: (presses a second yellow dot in the corner of the bedroom behind the defendant) And this is the light that was on most of the night?

BEDFORD: Right.

HASTINGS: Is it a bright light?

BEDFORD: No, it's soft. And it only had a low-watt bulb in it, which is why we used it for the birth. Mrs. Danforth wanted the lights to be low.

HASTINGS: And the lamp by the bed. Was that a bright light?

BEDFORD: In my opinion, it was. It was our reading light.

HASTINGS: Bright enough to cast a shadow?

TANNER: Objection. Calls for speculation.

DORSET: I'll allow it. The witness may answer.

BEDFORD: I guess.

HASTINGS: A hundred-watt bulb?

BEDFORD: Most of the time.

HASTINGS: Most of the time?

BEDFORD: If the bulb blew and we had a hundred-watt bulb in the house, that's what we'd use. If we didn't, we'd use the next best thing. Maybe a seventy-five-watt bulb.

HASTINGS: The night Veil was born, you had a hundred-watt bulb in that lamp, is that correct?

BEDFORD: Yes, I think so.

HASTINGS: It was intense?

BEDFORD: Yes, sir.

HASTINGS: (at State's diagram, presses a finger on the dot signifying Mrs. Danforth and a finger on the dot representing the lamp on the night table) And we're in agreement that this is the right spot in the room for the lamp, and the right spot for Sibyl?

BEDFORD: Yes.

HASTINGS: And the lamp was on?

BEDFORD: The lamp was on.

HASTINGS: Where was the shadow?

BEDFORD: The shadow?

HASTINGS: A lamp bright enough for reading will always cast a shadow. Isn't that right?

BEDFORD: I guess so.

HASTINGS: Well, Sibyl had a lamp with a hundred-watt bulb in it right behind her, and when she hunched over your wife—her upper body exactly between that lamp and your wife—there had to have been a shadow. Correct?

BEDFORD: It would seem so.

HASTINGS: The night your son was born—Veil—where would the light from the hundred-watt bulb behind Sibyl have cast its shadow?

BEDFORD: On the bed.

HASTINGS: Please look at the diagram of the bedroom. Where on the bed would that shadow have fallen? (Presses finger in middle of bed) Here?

BEDFORD: Probably.

HASTINGS: Where is my finger?

BEDFORD: On the bed.

HASTINGS: What part of the bed?

BEDFORD: The middle.

HASTINGS: What was in the middle of the bed the night your son was born?

BEDFORD: My wife, of course. It's where she lab—

HASTINGS: The shadow from the lamp fell on your wife?

BEDFORD: Yes.

HASTINGS: On her torso?

BEDFORD: I guess.

HASTINGS: Thank you. Do you remember what Sibyl was wearing that night?

BEDFORD: I think she was wearing a sweater and blue jeans. A heavy sweater.

HASTINGS: A ski sweater?

BEDFORD: I've never skied.

HASTINGS: But a heavy sweater?

BEDFORD: Yes.

HASTINGS: Do you remember what color it was?

BEDFORD: No, sir.

HASTINGS: (shows article of clothing to state's attorney and Judge Dorset; sweater is admitted into evidence) Your Honor, Defense's three for identification. Is this the sweater Sibyl was wearing?

BEDFORD: I think so.

HASTINGS: What color is it?

BEDFORD: Navy blue. And the snowflakes around the shoulders and collar are white.

HASTINGS: But it's mostly navy blue?

BEDFORD: Mostly.

HASTINGS: (shows sweater to jury and puts it on evidence cart) We've established that Veil was born sometime between six-fifteen and six-twenty in the morning. Correct?

BEDFORD: Correct.

HASTINGS: Did you sleep at all the night before?

BEDFORD: No, I did not.

HASTINGS: Had you napped the day before? In the afternoon, maybe?

BEDFORD: No.

HASTINGS: Do you remember what time you got up the day before? Thursday?

BEDFORD: Not exactly. But it was probably around six-thirty.

HASTINGS: So you'd been up all night when your son was born?

BEDFORD: That's right.

HASTINGS: In fact, you'd been awake for just about twenty-four hours.

BEDFORD: Yes.

HASTINGS: Were your eyes tired?

BEDFORD: I don't remember thinking they were.

HASTINGS: Might they have been?

TANNER: Objection.

DORSET: I'll allow it.

HASTINGS: After being awake for twenty-four hours, might your eyes have been tired?

BEDFORD: It's possible.

HASTINGS: Thank you. Now, you've told the court that you think you may have seen this bit of blood spurt, despite the fact that you were almost seven feet away when it happened. Am I correct?

BEDFORD: Yes.

HASTINGS: And despite the fact that your wife's stomach was covered in shadow. Correct?

BEDFORD: Yes.

HASTINGS: And despite the fact that you would have been seeing this blood against the backdrop of a navy blue ski sweater. Right?

BEDFORD: Yes, but—

HASTINGS: And despite the fact that you had been awake all night long. No, not just all night. A full twenty-four hours. Is that the testimony you actually want the jury to believe?

BEDFORD: I know what I saw.

DORSET: Does counsel have any further questions for the witness?

HASTINGS: Yes.

DORSET: Then please proceed.

HASTINGS: Did you believe your wife was dead when you went to the window?

BEDFORD: Oh, yes.

HASTINGS: Did you love her?

BEDFORD: Of course.

HASTINGS: Were you sad?

BEDFORD: Good Lord, yes!

HASTINGS: Were you very sad?

BEDFORD: Yes.

HASTINGS: And was it in that frame of mind that you think you saw blood spurt?

BEDFORD: Yes, but I was not hysterical. I'm telling you, I know what I saw.

HASTINGS: And yet, did you make any effort—any effort at all—to stop Sibyl when you saw the blood?

BEDFORD: No, as I told Mr. Tanner, I thought it was normal. I assumed my Charlotte had passed away, and this was just . . . just what the body did . . .

Stephen had told my parents while they were discussing strategy the night before that there would be two issues with Asa's testimony: what the man *could* have seen, and what the man *would* have seen. Stephen was firmly convinced that no husband in his right mind would actually have brought himself to witness a knife going into his dead wife's belly, and that was the real reason Asa had gone to the window. But first, he told my parents, he would cast doubt upon what Asa could have seen from the bedroom that morning.

Stephen's cross-examination of the reverend began right after lunch and continued until we recessed for the day. There were moments that afternoon—brief but thrilling—when I was convinced with the confidence of a teenager that Stephen had persuaded every soul in the courtroom that it wasn't logical to believe Asa Bedford would actually have watched his wife's cesarean, and it was unlikely he could have seen blood spurt even if illogic had somehow prevailed. No man in Asa's position, I told myself, could be completely sure of what he had seen, and—perhaps more important—no man would have been willing to watch.

But when the cross-examination was over, the fact remained that Asa Bedford was still a clergyman: In our corner of the Kingdom in 1981, this meant his words had weight. Great weight, despite the eccentricities of his church's dogma. I thought Stephen's cross-examination had been wonderful, but when we all went to our separate homes for dinner, I nevertheless feared one cross-examination—even a good one—could not undo a week of damaging medical testimony and the memories of the minister.

When girls are little, their dolls are likely to be babies, not Barbies.

So said Stephen Hastings. Stephen, of course, had no children. But this didn't stop him from having strong opinions about how children thought and what they believed. After all, he said one night when my father challenged him, he had been one himself. Stephen would readily admit that he hadn't the foggiest notion of how one should raise a child—how to discipline one, or reward one, or simply smother one with love—but he insisted he understood well the logic that informed a child's mind. A girl's mind as well as a boy's.

And Stephen was convinced that little girls loved baby dolls—plastic infants that demanded no maintenance. No rocking, no feeding, no changing, no watching. No work. Only mock howls, play colic, pretend pangs of hunger. Imaginary dirty diapers. Make-believe mess. Eventually, he said, baby dolls would drop off the child's radar screen. Older dolls might or might not, depending upon whether the little girl discovered Barbie and Skipper and Ken. But plastic babies—and the instinctive desire to nurture something small and needy—did. Some girls got the nurture bug back when they began puberty, and used baby-sitting as a substitute. Others didn't rediscover the desire to mother until they were adults themselves, and the primordial need to dispose of the diaphragm and continue the species overwhelmed all reason.

And then, of course, there were those girls who became midwives: girls who could not get enough of the tiniest of babies—the newborn—girls who would grow into women who absolutely reveled in the magnificent but messy process of birth.

As spring became summer and Stephen steeped himself in the culture of home birth, he concluded that the principal difference between the woman who becomes an ob-gyn and the woman who becomes a midwife had less to do with education or philosophy or upbringing than it did with the depth of her appreciation for the miracle of labor and for life in its moment of emergence. Women who became doctors viewed themselves as physicians first, ob-gyns second. He felt that when these girls began focusing seriously on what they wanted to be when they grew up—in high school or college—they probably decided originally that they simply wanted to be doctors. Then, perhaps in medical school, they narrowed in on obstetrics.

Those girls who became midwives, on the other hand, knew midwifery was their calling at a very early age, or—as my mother's path suggested—had one profound, life-changing experience involving birth that pulled them in. Stephen was adamant that the women who became ob-gyns loved babies no less than midwives, but they were the type who were more likely at a young age to trade dolls that one dressed for toy cribs for dolls that one dressed for pretend formals.

Certainly Stephen was on to something in my case, at least when it came to dolls. My dolls stayed babies barely beyond my arrival in first grade; almost overnight that year they became a small world of Barbies obsessed with clothing and cars and the color of their hair. I even had a Nurse Barbie, although to be honest she spent most of her time with Ken with her clothes off.

Yet did I become an obstetrician simply because I wanted to be a doctor, and I happened to grow up in a house that made me comfortable with the anatomic terrain? I doubt it. And after watching the way some ob-gyns clinically picked my mother apart in the courthouse—using the third person as if she weren't sitting merely a half-dozen or so yards away—it's arguable I might have developed such a visceral distaste for the entire profession that I would have become anything but a baby doctor.

To this day, some of my mother's friends think I've betrayed her by becoming an ob-gyn. There are two midwives in Vermont who won't speak to me, or to the midwives who use me as their backup physician. But as I've said to all those midwives from my mother's generation with whom I've remained friends, or to those midwives of my generation with whom I've become friends, my choice of profession was neither an indictment of my mother's profession nor a slap at her persecutors. Clearly her cross was a factor in my decision—all my C-sections have been upon inarguably living women, each one properly anesthetized and prepared for the procedure—but as a friend of mine who's a psychiatrist says, motives don't matter: Most of the time we don't even know what our motives are. And while I learned from my mother that how babies come into this world indeed matters, I learned from her detractors the ineluctable fact that most babies come into this world in hospitals. In my opinion, I do a lot of good in delivery rooms and ORs, and while I don't use an herb like blue cohosh, I've never once had a prenatal exam that took less than half an hour. I get to know my mothers well.

Stephen brought in the specialists fast, even before my mother was charged with a crime. In addition to a photographer to chronicle the cuts and bruises my mother received crawling around the ice by her car, he immediately hired an accident reconstructionist to examine the slope and width of the Bedfords' driveway. He wanted to be sure there could be no doubt in a jury's mind that my mother had done everything humanly possible to try and transfer Mrs. Bedford to the hospital the night that she died, but the driveway had been a mess and the roads impassable: My mother did what she did because she hadn't a choice.

And he probably spent entire days on the phone those first weeks, tracking down midwives around the country who'd been tried for one reason or another—practicing medicine without a license, illegal possession of regulated drugs—and interviewing their lawyers. He found forensic pathologists and obstetricians who could serve as our expert witnesses should they be needed, some willing to come from as far away as Texas.

And although Stephen may not have been particularly interested in the specifics of how high blood might spurt, there were some medical issues that mattered to him greatly—including, of course, Charlotte Fugett Bedford's cause of death. Stephen wanted to be sure that we had our explanation for why the woman had died, especially after the autopsy was complete and it was clear that the State was going to contend there had been no cerebral aneurysm, and that the cause of death was therefore Sibyl Danforth.

With the help of his specialists, in those first weeks Stephen began developing lists: long litanies of the complications that can occur in any birth, home or hospital; anecdotes from my mother's professional history that demonstrated her unusually high standards of care; incidents that suggested that the medical community had a vendetta against home birth, and my mother was merely a scapegoat—tragic, but convenient.

The specialist who became most involved with us as a family, however, actually knew as little about home birth in the beginning as Stephen. She was, in fact, more of a generalist, since her specialty was getting information. Patty Dunlevy was a private investigator, the state's first female PI. Stephen Hastings chose her as his investigator first and foremost, he said, because she was without question the best in Vermont. But given the issues surrounding my mother's case, we all understood the fact that she was a woman wouldn't hurt either.

Patty fast became a role model of sorts for Rollie McKenna and me. We met her together, on a Wednesday afternoon less than a week after Charlotte Bedford had died. The two of us were grooming Witch Grass in the section of the McKennas' paddock nearest the road when Patty's white car—a squat but sleek foreign thing caked with mud, a good-sized ding on the door, a spiderweb crack in the windshield—squealed to a stop in the dirt by the fence. The woman driving leaned across the empty passenger seat, pulled off the mirrored sunglasses she'd been wearing, and rolled down the window to ask if either of us knew where someone named Sibyl Danforth lived.

New paranoias die even harder than old habits (especially when the paranoia's grounded in reality), and my immediate fear was that this woman was a reporter. So despite the mistake I had made only two days before when Stephen Hastings appeared at our front door, I responded to the woman's question with an inquiry of my own.

"Does she know you're coming?" I asked warily.

"Sure does. You must be her daughter."

"What makes you think so?"

"You're looking out for her. I'm Patty Dunlevy. I work with Stephen Hastings—your mom's lawyer."

The woman was in her late thirties or early forties, but her hair was still an almost electric strawberry blond. That afternoon she was wearing a golf-course-green headband to keep her mane from her face, and the sort of tailored black leather jacket one was more likely to find on the back of a Park Avenue debutante at a dance party than a biker at a Hell's Angels rally. But we'd learn quickly that Patty was a chameleon, which was one of the reasons she was so good at what she did. I know when she interviewed my mother's clients or other midwives that spring and summer she was likely to be dressed in billowy peasant skirts or broken-in blue jeans; when she visited physicians or hospital administrators, especially the hostile ones, she'd appear in madras skirts and low-heeled pumps, with crisp, well-ironed blouses. Patty clearly liked her mirrored sunglasses and black leather jacket, but she also understood they were a needless occupational encumbrance with many of her sources, and was careful to make sure her first impressions were perfect.

And once I understood that Patty Dunlevy wasn't a reporter, I liked her right away. Rollie and I both did. Her car was both a reflection of her work ethic—style tempered with labor—and the remarkable way the woman herself was one of those walking centers of inexorable gravitation: After I'd informed Patty that she was indeed looking for my mother, I did not simply provide directions to our home, I climbed into the car and served as copilot for the five hundred yards separating the McKennas from the Danforths.

"How's your mom doing?" she asked, as Rollie and Witch Grass grew small in the rearview mirror.

"I guess fine."

"What a nightmare. You don't know how awful I feel for her."

"What do you do with Mr. Hastings? Are you a lawyer, too?" I asked, settling into the bucket seat in her car.

"Nope. I'm an investigator."

"A detective?"

"More or less. I work with lawyers to get the poop they can't."

An image passed behind my eyes of Patty Dunlevy sitting in her squat little car in the parking lot of one of the motels out by the Burlington airport. She was using a camera with a lens the width of a bazooka to photograph illicit lovers through dusty, half-open venetian blinds.

"What sort of poop?" I asked.

Her answer suggested that she'd heard the apprehension in my voice.

"Oh, all sorts. It might be something incredibly mundane like getting a confirmation of a power outage from an electric company. Some phone records. Or it might be something a little more interesting like getting background on a hostile witness. The sort of thing that just might discredit someone a tad. But I'll tell you point-blank what I tell everyone: I don't do adultery and I don't do divorces."

"What are you going to . . . do for my mother?"

She smiled. "Well, for starters, I'm going to get from her the name of every single person on this planet who will say something nice about her if we ask them to testify. Then we'll begin figuring out exactly what I'm going to do for her."

"You'll have a long list, you know."

"Of people who like her? Terrific. It's always a special treat when Stephen actually has me working for the good guys."

I'm not superstitious now, and I wasn't in 1981. In my mind, it is merely ironic—not symbolic—that Charlotte Fugett Bedford went into labor on the thirteenth of March, and that the results of the written autopsy arrived on the first day of April. April Fools' Day. The former a day of bad luck, the latter a day of bad jokes.

April 1 was a Tuesday that year, and in my parents' attempts to give our lives a small semblance of normalcy, they had insisted I try out for the junior varsity track team as we'd discussed throughout the winter. I always thought I was a pretty good athlete, and I was confident my legs were strong from my years of riding Witch Grass. I hadn't yet begun to imagine whether I'd be running long distances or sprinting short ones, but I knew I'd like the way I looked in those shorts.

Tryouts began on Tuesday, and so I didn't get home that afternoon until close to dinner. But there had been enough conversation about the imminent submission of the written autopsy in our house in the weeks since Charlotte Bedford had died that I could tell instantly by my parents' silence and the presence of a bottle of scotch on the kitchen table that its final conclusions had offered only bad news.

As my mother rose from her seat and began to serve dinner—a beef stew that none of us touched, despite the fact that we all understood it would be the last heavy stew of the winter—my father told me what I already knew. The medical examiner had found no signs of a stroke, no indications of a seizure. Immediate cause of death? Hemorrhagic shock due to a cesarean section during home childbirth.

TWELVE

Birth is a big miracle foreshadowed by lots of little ones. Conception. Little limbs. Lanugo. A fingerprint, hard bones. The quickening. The turning. The descent.

I will never forget the moment of quickening with Connie. She was thirteen or fourteen weeks old. I was bundled up in this monster sweater that hung down to my knees. Lacey Woods had brought it back from somewhere in Central America, and it had this vaguely Aztec eagle on the back. It was beautiful, and so heavy that it kept me warm even outside on the sort of cold December day on which Connie made herself known.

I was sitting on one of the tremendous rocks in Mom and Dad's backyard, one of the ones that faced the ski resort on Mount Republic. Rand and I had decided by then we were going to get married, but the little one inside me wasn't the reason. She—of course, then it was still he or she, we hadn't a clue whether we'd be blessed with a boy or a girl—was just the signal that we might as well do it sooner rather than later.

The sun was already behind Republic, even though it wasn't quite four o'clock yet, and it was getting really chilly. They'd made some snow on the trails at the ski resort, but otherwise the ground was still brown, and so the mountain looked a little bit like a volcano that made this weird white lava.

I hadn't climbed those rocks since I was in high school, and sitting there made me feel like a very little girl. And then, suddenly, I felt this tiny flutter a bit below my belly button. A tadpole flicking its tail. A ripple, a wave. Instantly that image of the tadpole—an image I'd probably pulled from some high-school biology textbook—changed to that of a newborn baby. I knew my baby at that moment looked nothing at all like a newborn, but that was what I pretended was fluttering inside me. A psychedelic little person doing the breaststroke in a lava lamp. A bubble bouncing euphorically, but in slow motion, around in my tummy. I saw a newborn's pudgy fingers flicking amniotic fluid with a whoosh, I saw little feet smaller than baking potatoes gently splashing my own water against me, and I wrapped my arms around me and hugged my baby through my belly.

Oh my God, was I happy. I remember I just sat on that rock grooving on the little person—my little person—inside me.

Of all the little miracles that build to that big one, the birth itself, my favorite must be the moment of quickening. All these emotions and expectations and dreams for your baby just roll over you like so much surf.

And quickening *really is the perfect word to describe it, because your heart races, and the pace of the pregnancy just takes off.*

Some mothers experience the quickening as early as twelve weeks, others are much further along. Sixteen weeks is common in my experience, but some women don't feel it until they're through a good eighteen weeks. It really doesn't matter, except that those women who have to wait have to worry. It's inevitable, a mother can't help it. You want to feel your friend, you want to know he or she's there.

Of course, there may be one nice thing that comes with a later quickening. After all that anxiety, the high must be amazing when it finally arrives. Absolutely, unbelievably, out-rageously amazing.

—from the notebooks of Sibyl Danforth, midwife

April is neither wholly spring nor wholly winter in Vermont. It's common for there to be flurries—maybe even a few inches of heavy, wet snow—one day, and then hot sun and temperatures in the high sixties the next. The crocuses and tulips emerge, endure the schizophrenic weather about as well as everything else (they flower, they sag, they perk up and flower), blooming blue or yellow against brown grass one day, and then against green the next.

Vermonters don't manifest their reactions to the abrupt changes in weather as dramatically as flowers, but we do feel them inside and show them outside. We might not bother to shovel our walks or plow our driveways after an April snow shower—the snow will melt soon enough—but we will sweep it away from the front porch or front steps, and the idea of taking a broom to sopping white blankets when the rest of the world seems well into spring makes even the most resilient among us shake our heads with disgust. And with the exception of the sugar makers hoping for one last frenzied maple sap run, as a group we all sigh when we awake and discover that our roofs were covered once more with snow as we slept: By midmorning those drapes will slide off the slate or sheet metal, rolling like avalanches down the pitch, creating snowdrifts that torment us for days.

When the sun is strong and the air is warm, however, we shout greetings to one another down the lengths of long driveways and from the windows of our cars as we pass; we hold our heads high as we walk, staring up into the sky with our eyes shut and our faces widened by smiles. We breathe in deeply the summery air, but this sort of inhalation doesn't result in a sigh; it's a precursor to a purr, or the moans one might make during a backrub.

We no longer mope, we no longer grouse. We are filled with energy.

Although my family understood on the first of the month that my mother would be charged with a crime, it wasn't until a little later in the month that the State had determined exactly what that crime—crimes, actually—would be. Consequently, throughout the first week and a half in April our emotions rode a roller coaster with more pronounced peaks and dips than even our almost malevolently capricious weather could erect on its own.

Stephen had warned my parents on the very first day they had met that the State might suggest that my mother had willfully killed Charlotte Bedford, and she should therefore be charged with second-degree murder. The difference between second-degree murder and involuntary manslaughter was no small distinction: Second-degree murder came with a decade in prison *if* there were mitigating factors on the defendant's side, and up to a lifetime if there weren't. Involuntary manslaughter, the charge Stephen thought was likely, merely implied that my mother had acted with absolutely wanton or gross negligence, but at least she hadn't consciously decided to kill anybody. Murdering Charlotte Bedford was not her intention in this case, it was just an unhappy accident and therefore came with a mere one to fifteen years behind bars, and a possible three-thousand-dollar fine.

There was never any doubt about the lesser charge, however, the misdemeanor: practicing medicine without a license. That, Stephen said, was inevitable.

Nevertheless, despite Stephen's warning—and his reassurance that a charge of second degree was unlikely—the first time Bill Tanner suggested that the State might try seriously to build the case that my mother's actions were willful, my father grew furious, my mother grew frightened, and they both grew confused. I sat on the stairs of our house one night, listening as they spoke to Stephen on the telephone—my mother from the phone on the first floor, my father from the phone on the second.

"I know what the words *intentional* and *involuntary* mean to a normal person," my father was saying. "I want to know what the hell they mean to lawyers . . . I see . . . A precedent? Are you telling me this kind of thing has happened before? . . . Uh-huh . . . The woman was already dead, for God's sake. Why would Sibyl have thought a C-section would kill her? . . ."

A moment later my mother added, her voice almost frantic, "How can they say that? I'd already told Asa she'd died!" but I can't imagine Stephen got far into a response to her exclamation, because my father almost immediately cut in again.

"I thought if you killed someone you were supposed to have a motive . . . But there's no goddamn reason why she would have 'desired to effect the death' of that woman, there's just no reason! . . . That's stupid, that's the stupidest thing I've ever heard . . . Well, it's still stupid. I hope they do say that, because they wouldn't have a fucking chance of winning. Right? Right?"

When it was clear that the conversation was winding down, I left my perch on the stairs and went into the living room, and acted as if I'd been reading my biology textbook all along. Almost immediately my father came downstairs and joined my mother in the kitchen.

"I'm sorry I lost my temper," he said, and I heard him opening the cabinet with the liquor.

"You couldn't help it," my mother said softly. "Probably happens all the time to him."

"People blowing up?"

"I guess."

"He didn't seem to mind."

"Nope."

The freezer door shut with a pop, and the ice cubes struck the sides of the glass before splashing down in a puddle of scotch at the bottom.

"Let me make sure I've got this right," my father said, and he pulled one of the kitchen chairs away from the table, sliding it along the floor with a brief squeal. "They're going to say you killed Charlotte Bedford on purpose—"

"They might say that. Apparently they haven't decided anything."

"Okay, they might say you killed Charlotte Bedford on purpose."

"I guess."

"To save the baby."

"Yes. They might say I thought Charlotte was going to die, but I had to know full well she was alive when I did the cesarean."

"You had to . . ."

"I had to. I couldn't possibly do what I do for a living without being able to tell the difference. I couldn't possibly have made such a . . . a mistake."

"And you did it to save the baby . . ."

"The C-section? Yup. So they think."

A long silence. Then an echo from my father: "Yup. So they think."

I couldn't see either of my parents from my spot on the couch, but I envisioned my father swirling his drink in his hand, and my mother sitting perfectly still with her arms folded across her chest. I knew those actions and poses well.

"Sib?" my father continued after another quiet moment.

"Yes."

"I want to ask something."

"Of Stephen or me?"

"You. And I'll only ask it this one time, and I'll never ask it again. But I have to know. I have to ask—"

"Don't even think of it, don't even think of asking it. I can't have you doubting me, too."

"You answered it. That's all I wanted to hear."

"Don't doubt me, Rand."

"I don't."

My mother had spent almost uncountable days and nights bringing life into the world. It didn't seem fair to me that her trial revolved around the notion that she could mistake it for death in the end.

Here's how our emotional roller coaster worked: No sooner had my parents begun to pull themselves up from the almost debilitating despair and self-doubt inspired by the possibility of a second-degree murder trial than Stephen reassured them that the charge was unlikely. Instead of working their way slowly to the crest of the ride over days, they were yanked abruptly to the top in an instant—my mother first, in an afternoon visit from Stephen, my father that night when he came home from work.

Almost as if we'd been diagnosed with a terminal disease, the sort of news that would once have appalled us was thrilling. I'm in remission, I might have two whole years to live? That's wonderful! Involuntary manslaughter only? Oh my, that's great!

I was surprised when I came home from track practice one afternoon later that week to find my mother and Stephen sitting on the front porch of our house. It was one of those wondrous April days with a hot sun shining above cold, still-sloshy ground, and as late as five in the afternoon one could still sit comfortably outside on a deck or a stoop that faced west.

My mother and Stephen were each sitting with their backs against one of the white posts that supported the porch roof, their legs bent at the knees into pyramids. They stopped talking and smiled at me when they saw me at the end of our driveway, and I could sense the lawyer had arrived with good news.

Was I surprised that Stephen had come all the way from Burlington to meet with my mother—a drive closer to ninety minutes than an hour—rather than call? I was, briefly. And it was that night at dinner that my father made the first of a great many catty comments about Stephen that I believe he came to regret. But my first reaction when I saw Stephen sitting there that moment was that he would be a good friend for my mother, and he would certainly do his best to protect her. If he had feelings for her that most attorneys would have deemed unprofessional, that could only be to our benefit.

They both stood when I got to the beginning of the walkway, and my mother started forward as if to kiss me when I got to the steps. She stopped suddenly, however, as if she feared I'd be embarrassed if she kissed me in front of Mr. Hastings. She was right, I would have been. But I was probably equally embarrassed by the way she had bobbed her head forward like a wild turkey, and almost would have preferred she'd given me that kiss.

"How'd it go today, honey?" she asked, referring to practice.

"Good. Fine."

"Legs sore?"

"Nope. Not a bit."

"Your mom tells me you made the track team," Stephen said.

"Just the junior varsity," I told him, a meaningful correction in my mind.

"In eighth grade, that's still a mighty accomplishment," he said.

I nodded and stared at my sneakers, my way then of graciously accepting a compliment.

"Mr. Hastings is here to tell us what's going on," my mother explained.

"Us? Is Dad home?" I looked back at the driveway, wondering if somehow I had managed to walk past my father's Jeep without noticing it. I hadn't; there was no Jeep there. Just Stephen's dignified but boxy gray Volvo.

"No, not yet. I only meant us, our family."

"Oh."

"Mr. Hastings says I'm not in as much trouble as we thought the other night." She offered a tiny grin that seemed sincere and brave to me at the same time, but I think now was probably ironic. My parents had tried to explain to me as best they could the distinctions between second-degree murder and involuntary manslaughter, an intentional killing versus merely reckless and illegal behavior, and while much of what they had said made perfect sense, a lot of it was still completely unfathomable to me those first weeks in April, and I still reduced my mother's plight to one fundamental vision: Joan of Arc being burned at the stake. The exact image came from a painting in our encyclopedia, and it was horrid: a beautiful woman a bit younger than my mother, standing in a midwifelike peasant dress, her face stoic—almost superhumanly heroic—as yellow and red flames turned brown wood black. Joan's skin had not yet begun to blister, but the heat from the flames was causing her to sweat, and some in the crowd around her were standing atop her dead horse to get a better view of her death.

My mother was no saint in my eyes, even then: I was still troubled by the way her pregnant mothers always seemed to come before me. But I believed she had done absolutely nothing wrong in the case of Charlotte Bedford, and certainly didn't deserve to be consumed by the fire that suddenly surrounded her. And so when she said she seemed to be in less trouble—so much less trouble that Stephen had driven all the way out to our house in Reddington—I immediately assumed she must have been granted a complete pardon, and the bonfire was being disassembled. That man named Bill Tanner had come to his senses. Asa Bedford had come to his senses. That Anne Austin—despicable, lying, traitorous Anne Austin—had come to her senses.

"What happened?" I asked, and the expectant joy in my voice was so apparent that instantly both adults began shaking their heads to calm me down.

"It's good news, Connie, don't get us wrong," my mother said quickly, "but neither of us should start spinning cartwheels on the lawn."

I hadn't done a cartwheel in at least five or six years, and I couldn't imagine that my mother had done one in decades, but I kept the thought to myself. Perhaps if Stephen hadn't been present I would have said something flip, but he was there and so I simply nodded and waited for her to continue.

"There are still a lot of people out there who are even more freaked out about Charlotte's death than we are, if that's possible, but at least it looks like they don't think your mom is a"—and she paused as she pulled from within her the strength she needed to verbalize the word—"murderer."

And then quickly she grinned, and added through lips parted in sarcasm, "They just think your old lady's one really lousy midwife."

Stephen bent to wipe some dry dirt from his one-click-above, shiny black loafers, and said, "Sibyl, I don't think that anyone believes that."

"Pardon me. They just think I can't tell if a woman is dead or alive."

"They think that once—one time—you made a mistake."

"A gross mistake. A reckless mistake."

Stephen stared at my mother, and I could see by the expression on his face that he was trying to put the brakes on her emotions, to calm her down for my benefit. He then turned to me, his hands behind his back as he leaned against the post, and said, "Assuming this whole nasty ordeal ever goes to court, it probably won't be a murder trial. That's the news."

I thought for a moment, the words *murder* and *manslaughter* and *willful* a tremendous jumble in my mind. I tried to remember all the distinctions. Finally I gave up and asked, "What kind of trial will it be?"

"Involuntary manslaughter. At least that's what it looks like the charge will be right now."

"Do you understand what that means, sweetie?" my mother asked.

"Sort of."

"Sort of, but not completely?"

"Yup."

"What that means," Stephen continued, "is that the State is going to say your mom was responsible for Mrs. Bedford's death, and she acted illegally when she did the C-section. But it was an accident. She didn't mean to hurt anyone."

"If they think it was an accident, why are they bothering to have a trial?"

"Just because something is an accident doesn't mean it isn't also a crime."

"That's the manslaughter thing, right?"

"The involuntary manslaughter thing. That's right."

Fifteen years. For an accident. I stood there, trying to absorb a number of years longer than I'd been alive.

"When will the trial begin?" I asked.

"Months from now. Hopefully years," Stephen said.

"Years?"

"If it even goes to trial."

"Stephen, I don't want this thing to drag on for years," my mother said.

"Delay is our friend, Sibyl."

"Why?"

He shrugged. "A case like this always starts out with a lot of prosecutorial energy, and it always loses momentum over time. It's a fact of nature. Bill has to focus on prosecuting the real bad guys, not some nice lady midwife and mother like Sibyl Danforth. And all of those doctors who seem so angry right now will move on to other things. Let's assume nobody else dies in a home birth: Eventually they'll lose interest. Eventually the press will lose interest. Besides, the longer you're out on bail without any problems, the more likely you are to walk away with probation even if you're found guilty."

"Bail," my mother murmured, not so much a question as it was perhaps the first dawning comprehension that along with a charge would come an arrest.

"It's one of those strange absolutes no lawyer completely understands. But delay always benefits the defense. It really does. The last thing we want is for this thing to go to trial before Christmas—or even next spring."

My mother took long strands of her dirty blond hair between her thumb and fingers and contemplated the brownish lengths as if she disliked their color. Bringing the tips close to her eyes, she said to me, "We probably won't eat till late, honey, so why don't you go inside and make yourself a snack?"

I've never had any sort of weight problem, but like many teenage girls I snacked on low- and no-cal products. And so it was a diet cola and a bowl of freezer-burned chocolate ice milk that I brought with me to the dining room, the best room from which to eavesdrop upon a conversation on our porch. Just because my mother didn't want me to hear what she and Stephen were saying didn't mean that I didn't want to listen.

The storm windows were still sealed for the winter, but there was one on the far side of the curio cabinet close enough to the front steps that I could sit beneath it and hear clearly the adults' conversation through the two layers of glass.

I sat against the wall with my ice milk in my lap, careful that my head remained below the sill.

"What makes you think this thing might not go to trial?" my mother asked as I settled in.

"We just might not have to."

"Of course we will."

"What makes you say that?"

"I've delivered too many babies over the years, and pissed off too many doctors. They're not going to let me off the hook."

"First of all, Bill Tanner has a spine. He's not proceeding because some ob-gyn has a grudge against you—"

"We're not talking about *some* ob-gyn, we're talking about lots of them. We're talking the entire medical board."

"I understand that. I know there are some doctors who don't approve of home birth—"

"Or of midwives."

"Or of midwives. But whatever else I think or don't think about Bill Tanner, he's not the type who would proceed unless he honestly believed a crime had been committed. He's not doing all this just because you've pissed off some doctors."

"But that's a factor."

"At best, a small one. They may have alerted him on some level that in their eyes there's a problem, but it's his decision to go forward."

"Then why do you think we might not have to go to trial?"

"Perhaps we can settle things ahead of time."

The conversation went quiet, and I held my spoon in the air. I was afraid they knew I was listening, and I didn't want the sound of the spoon on the bowl to give me away. But then my mother spoke, and I realized she was just digesting the idea of a settlement.

"What does that mean?" she asked. "I pay a fine and I get on with my life?"

"No, it's more complicated than that."

"Tell me."

I heard Stephen laugh, a sort of self-deprecating chuckle. "You want to know too much too soon. You're moving too fast for me."

"I want to understand my options."

"It's too soon. I don't even know your options. It depends on what kind of case the State has. What kind of case we have."

"Give me an example, then."

"An example? An example of what?"

"A settlement."

"Settlement's a civil term. Not a criminal one."

"You used it, Counsel."

"If I did, I'm sorry. But I think I only said settle."

"You lawyers are all alike," my mother said lightly. "You'll argue over the smallest points."

"God, I hope you haven't had to deal with that many lawyers in your life that you can generalize with accuracy."

"Oh, a few. But it's usually just been to defend me those times I've killed people by mistake."

"Seriously, have you ever needed a criminal lawyer before?"

"I told you the day we met that I hadn't."

"I only asked if you had any prior convictions—not if you'd ever used a criminal lawyer."

"Good Lord, of course I haven't! When would I have needed a criminal lawyer?"

"I don't know. That's why I'm asking."

"No, Stephen, this is a new experience in my life, I assure you."

"I'm your first."

"You're my first."

"I'm flattered."

"An old lady like me can flatter you? God, you've been divorced too long."

"How old are you?"

"Thirty-four."

"A mere babe in the woods."

"Oh, I don't think so. I'm definitely too old to throw around expressions like 'old lady' and 'old man' the way I once did."

"I think it's the expressions that have aged badly. Not you."

"You're biased."

"Because I like you?"

"Because you weren't exactly a part of the counterculture."

"You don't think I was a revolutionary?"

"No way."

"A hippie?"

"Isn't that word awful? I can't believe we ever used it seriously."

"We didn't, Sibyl. At least I didn't."

"I'll bet you were a real hippie-hater back then. I'll bet we drove you crazy."

"I didn't hate hippies! I didn't even know any hippies. Why would you think I'd hate them?"

"Because you're so unbelievably uptight. Look at your shoes."

"I'm not uptight."

"You think so?"

"I do."

"Okay, let's see. Ever smoked grass?"

"Yes."

"A lot?"

"I didn't like it. So I didn't do it again."

"So you did it once."

"Or twice, maybe."

"In Vietnam or Vermont?"

"Vietnam."

"That doesn't count."

"Why?"

"I've always envisioned that place as so totally horrible you had to smoke dope like air just to survive."

"It was horrible if you were in the jungle. I wasn't."

"So you didn't have to smoke dope?"

"Well, at least not to survive."

"But you didn't want to either."

"It seems to me, Mrs. Danforth," he said with professorial gravity, "that any movement that uses an illegal drug as its principal criterion for membership or inclusion is a movement not worth joining."

"Okay. Here are some easy ones. Ever spent a week in a commune?"

"Thankfully not."

"Slept in a van?"

"Nope."

"Been barefoot?"

"Of course."

"For days at a time?"

"Hours. Maybe."

"Worn beads?"

"Not a prayer."

"That's fine. Let's get a little more serious: Ever tried to connect with the Black Panthers? Maybe help set up a volunteer breakfast program for hungry families in Boston?"

"You did that, I suppose?"

"I did. Ever put together prenatal information pamphlets for poor Vermont women, and then gone house to house and trailer to trailer for days to make sure people got them?"

"Did that too, eh?"

"I did. Or how about just feeling the most incredible, awesome love for people—all people—just because they're human and therefore amazingly magic? Ever felt that?"

"Probably not sober."

"Or just wanting the world to stop caring about *things?* Possessions? Status? Wanting us all to stop judging each other by what we own?"

"I like what I own, Sibyl," Stephen said, trying to make light of her passion, and then I heard him yell in mock pain.

"Do you always hit your lawyers?"

"That didn't hurt," my mother said, and she was laughing.

"Trust me, it did."

"I did those things, I felt those things," my mother said, ignoring him. "I was with people like Raymond Mungo and Marshall Bloom. I really believed the war was wrong."

"I believe you did."

"I grew up in Vermont—not Westchester County or some townhouse in Back Bay. I actually knew boys who went to Vietnam. A lot of them. Most of the boys in my high-school class went there. For me, the war wasn't just some trendy thing to protest against. I was worrying about boys I knew well—sometimes very well—as well as villagers I'd never met."

"Boys like me."

"Yes, boys like you. Being a hippie wasn't just about bouncing around without a bra, or having a lot of sex with boys you barely knew. It's really easy today to look back on those years and make fun of us for our clothes or drugs or silly posters. But at its best, the whole . . . era was about trying to make the world a little less scary."

A floorboard squeaked as one of the adults outside stood up. A shadow passed across the sill, and Stephen's voice grew closer.

"I didn't mean to make fun of the things you did," he said.

"You didn't make fun of anything. I was just telling you."

I then heard the wood shift under my mother's weight as well, as she stood up beside him. The two were silent for a long moment and I envisioned them watching the sun set, or staring into the shadows shaped like ice cream cones that were cast by the line of blue spruce at the western edge of our lawn.

"You never told me how we might settle," she said finally.

"I didn't, did I?"

"No."

"Okay, let's see," Stephen began, those first words offered at the end of a long sigh. "Here is where the idea of small-town Vermont has always been most real to me. Bill and I know each other, and we know the system. When I used the word *settle,* I meant negotiate. Or bargain. Depending on what the State has or doesn't have in the way of a case, I can imagine me sitting down with Bill at some point this spring and saying to him, 'Bill, we both know we can settle this thing now, or we can make all our lives unduly hard in six months with a trial.' "

"What would we be negotiating?"

"It might be the charge. And if we agree on that, it might be the sentence."

I flinched at the word *sentence,* and clearly my mother had, too. "The sentence?" she said, a tiny but unmistakable sliver of panic shooting through her voice. "I haven't done anything wrong!"

"Everything I'm saying here is conjecture, Sibyl. This is all just . . . just talk. Okay?"

"I don't think I like this kind of talk."

"Well, a sentence may not even be an issue. So let's not talk about it now. Fair enough?"

"No, I want you to go on."

"Are you sure?"

"Of course I'm sure. The idea that we're already sentencing me freaked me out there for a second, but I'm fine now."

"Okay. Here's one way we might settle this thing. We plead guilty to a charge of practicing medicine without a license—a misdemeanor— and we pay a fine. No big deal, at least not in the greater scheme of things. Then on a charge of involuntary manslaughter, we accept a deferred sentence. Let's say two or three years and another small fine, but no conviction at the end of the deferment. How does that sound?" Stephen asked, and I could tell that he thought he had just painted a wonderful scenario for my mother, one that he believed would restore her confidence and mood.

"Tell me what a deferred sentence is," she said simply.

"You plead guilty to involuntary manslaughter. Usually, that would mean imprisonment for one to fifteen years. Not in this case. A deferred sentence is a postponement of the sentencing by—in my example, any- way—two or three years. If at the end of that time you've met all of the conditions for the deferment, there's no jail time and no record. Just the fine."

"What's a condition? Something like house arrest?"

"God, no! You'd come and go as you pleased, your life would be completely normal. Maybe you'd do some community service. But mostly you'd just be expected not to break any laws during the deferment or—and I think this is inevitable—work as a midwife."

"And after two or three years?"

"It would be like nothing happened."

"It will never, ever be like that. Not under any circumstances."

"I mean in the eyes of the law."

"So if I give up my practice for a few years, the State will back off? Is that right?"

"That's one . . . possibility."

"And there'd be no record?"

"On the charge of involuntary manslaughter. In the stew I just cooked up, you've pleaded guilty to practicing medicine without a license."

"And that's a misdemeanor?"

"Astonishingly, yes."

"Is this . . . stew likely?"

"I don't know yet."

"But you don't think so, do you?" my mother said. We had both heard the doubt in Stephen's voice.

"Sibyl, I just don't know. For all I know, it's possible. Maybe probation is possible—"

"Probation?"

"Let's suppose the State has an airtight case, a case we just can't win. There's no way. In return for no jail time we plead guilty, and you get a suspended sentence and a couple years' probation. Again, your life goes on more or less as it always has, except there's this probation officer you see every so often, and you give up midwifery."

Slowly, sounding at once oddly drugged and unshakably determined—each syllable in each word a declaration itself—my mother said, "That's not an option, Stephen. I could never give that up. I never will give that up."

The sun was well below the evergreens now, and the room around me was growing dark.

"I doubt it will even come to that," Stephen murmured after a minute.

"You don't believe that. You believe that it will."

"I don't know. And I won't know for months."

"Months . . ."

"Perhaps even longer. Like I said, delay helps us a lot more than them."

"I don't want this to drag on."

"I understand."

"And I won't stop birthing babies."

I heard the sound of my father's Jeep as he pulled into our driveway and then turned off the engine.

"I think you'll have to, Sibyl. At least for a while."

"Until the trial?"

"Or until we settle with the State."

"And you say that could be months."

"At the very least."

The Jeep's door slammed, and I saw the shadow of my mother's arm as she waved at my father.

"Please, Stephen," she said, her voice not loud enough for my father to hear, "get this over and done with fast. As quickly as possible."

"The longer it—"

"Please, Stephen," she said again. "Fast. For the sake of me and my family: Get this over with fast."

Years later when my mother was diagnosed with lung cancer—an adenocarcinoma, the sort a nonsmoker's most likely to get—I saw my father become an exquisite caregiver. I saw a tender person inside him emerge and purchase a Vita-Mix blender, and prepare her broccoli shakes and carrot juice in the middle of each afternoon. My mother told me he did all the laundry and the grocery shopping when she became unable, and I saw how he filled the house with fruit. I know he drove often to the department store in Burlington to buy my mother turbans and hats and scarves. And, toward the end, on occasion I saw him sitting patiently beside her as she did crossword puzzles in bed, keeping her company as a listener at once active and serene. Sometimes that bed was in their bedroom, sometimes it was in the hospital.

He was, I can write without reservation or qualification, an exceptional cancer coach: part nurse, part dietitian, part partner and soul mate. Part Knute Rockne.

But, of course, my mother was not diagnosed with cancer in 1981, she was charged with a felony. She was accused of taking one life when she was supposed to be facilitating another's arrival.

Consequently, my mother didn't need a nurse or a dietitian or a cancer coach, she needed a lawyer. And so I think it was natural that to a large extent that role of caregiver fell more upon Stephen Hastings's shoulders than upon my father's, and that my father was jealous: He wanted to help. He wanted responsibilities. He wanted more things to do.

I watched my parents carefully the night Stephen stopped by with his news, and it was clear that my mother had lost sight of the good tidings he'd brought her behind the bad. Undoubtedly she was relieved that in all likelihood the State would charge her with involuntary manslaughter instead of second-degree murder, but this information had been overshadowed by the idea that she would have to stop birthing babies for some period of time. Perhaps forever.

Looking back, I realize my mother's reaction probably shouldn't have surprised me: A criminal charge was an abstract thing to her, something she couldn't fully comprehend. But midwifery was her calling, it was what she had chosen to do with her life. The very notion that she'd have to close her practice—even temporarily—caused her more anxiety than her lawyer's news about the charge brought relief.

"What am I supposed to do, tell someone like May O'Brien that I can't help her have her baby?" she asked my father that night as she picked at the food on her plate.

"I guess you'll have to refer her to someone else," my father said. "Maybe Tracy Fitzpatrick."

"Tracy lives in Burlington, for God's sake. She's too far away for most of my mothers."

"What about Cheryl?"

"Cheryl Visco doesn't have a moment to breathe; she couldn't possibly handle anybody else. Besides, she lives too far away, too."

"What about—"

"And I have relationships with these women—that's what counts! They trust me, not Cheryl or Tracy. They don't even know Cheryl or Tracy. And what about someone like Peg Prescott? She's due next month. What am I supposed to say to her? 'Well, Peg, it's no biggie. Just go to the hospital delivery room, and some doctor you've never seen before will take good care of you. No biggie, no biggie at all.' She will freak, she will absolutely freak."

Without looking up from his plate, my father asked, "What did Stephen say you should do?"

"He didn't have a solution."

"Really?"

"Really."

"We stumped the stars?"

"What's that supposed to mean?"

"I'm just surprised. I thought our hundred-dollar-an-hour lawyer had the answer to everything."

"Did I miss a step somewhere? Did Stephen say something to you today that pissed you off?"

"Do I sound pissed off?"

"Yes, you do."

I tried to remind my parents of my presence before their fight could escalate, rising from the table on the pretext of getting another glass of skim milk. I asked them if either wanted anything from the refrigerator while I was up.

"Honestly, did Stephen say something that angered you?" my mother continued after she'd told me she was fine and my father had remained silent.

"No."

"Then why this tone?"

"I just think it's . . . it's odd that he drove all the way out here this afternoon."

"What's odd about it? He's our lawyer."

"Maybe *odd* is the wrong word," my father said. "It just seems to me that he shouldn't be driving all the way out here to give you information he could just as easily give you on the phone. It seems financially irresponsible. It seems like he's awfully cavalier with money. With our money."

"Maybe lawyers don't charge for driving."

"And maybe there's a fish with wings out back in the pond."

"If I worked in Burlington, I'd want to get away as much as possible," I said as I sat back down. I didn't believe that at all—as a matter of fact, at that age I thought working in Burlington was positively glamorous—but it seemed to me the sort of thing my parents liked to hear, and it might help keep them civil.

"Is that so?" my mother asked me. She smiled slightly, and it was clear she didn't believe a word I'd said.

"Yup. Get away from all that noise. All those cars."

"All those record stores," she added. "That big mall with all those clothing stores on Church Street."

"I'm not saying a city's all bad," I explained. "It's just that if you're there every day, it's probably fun to come out here every once in a while."

"I agree," my mother said, touching my hair fondly for a moment.

My father tried to glare at me, but he appreciated my intentions too much to be angry at me for siding with my mother. He smiled, too, as he raised an eyebrow.

"Okay, fine. Maybe his little visit here this afternoon didn't cost us a penny."

"Obviously it cost something," my mother said.

"Oh, maybe not," my father said, a hint of sarcasm in his tone. He leaned across the table and kissed her once on the forehead. "Maybe April mud is a great lure for a poet like our lawyer. Maybe it's downright seductive. Maybe it was the beauty of our mud alone that drew Stephen here."

While my father and I were watching television together after dinner, we heard my mother on the telephone with one of her midwife friends in the southern part of the state. It seemed that one of my mother's newer patients, a college professor at the end of her first trimester, had been unable to hide her discomfort and nervousness around my mother at a prenatal appointment that morning. The woman's blood pressure had been much higher than the first time my mother had taken it, a month earlier.

After a lengthy discussion—*interrogation* was the exact word my mother had used on the phone that night—about all of the things that could go wrong during a home birth, the patient had started asking very specific questions about what had occurred up in Lawson. As Stephen had advised her, my mother had refused to talk about that. Apparently my mother and the professor had eventually agreed that she should reconsider her decision to have her baby at home, and think about whether she might be happier after all delivering the child with a doctor in a hospital.

Recalling the conversation with her friend had saddened my mother, and my father and I both heard my mother's voice go brittle. When she hung up the phone, my father went into the kitchen and rocked her in his arms for a long time.

THIRTEEN

I do the supermarket shopping, as if nothing happened. It's surreal. I push my cart up and down the aisles, and I nod at people and they nod at me. I pick out fruit, which is never easy this time of year, and I try and find things I think Connie will eat.

Yesterday Rand and I figured out the monthly bills, and we paid them. We made sure there was enough money in the checking account, as if life were still completely normal and our biggest worry was bouncing a check.

And today I ordered a pair of blueberry bushes from the nursery, and Rand ordered three cords of wood. He said he hoped we could have them by Memorial Day so he could have them stacked by the Fourth of July. That's Rand: only guy I know who has his winter wood stacked before summer's even gotten a serious dent.

Actually, the supermarket shopping is a little different now. It doesn't feel like it's taking longer, but I know I spent more time in the grocery store today than I have in years. It wasn't intentional, it just happened. I pulled into the parking lot around one-thirty, and it was almost three o'clock by the time I got out. An hour and a half. I think it usually takes me about forty-five minutes.

It's not that the lines were so long, or people stopped me to talk. If anything, it seems like people go out of their way these days not to stop me to talk. They nod when they see me, and then stare with this amazing intensity at the label on the canned peas or beans in their hand so they don't have to make any more eye contact with me than necessary and risk a conversation. It's weird.

So I don't know exactly why the shopping took so long today. I just went about my business, but I guess I was moving in incredibly slow motion. Me and my cart, just moseying along the store aisles. But I have a theory. I once read somewhere that work takes up as much time as you can give it. If you give a job thirty minutes, for example, you'll do it in thirty minutes. But if you can give it an hour, it'll take an hour. That makes sense. And I think that's what happened today at the grocery store. Normally I would have done the shopping in less than an hour because I'd have to be home for prenatals. I'd have two or three mothers scheduled between, say, two-thirty and five, and I'd have to be back to check weight and pee, and to listen to fetal heartbeats. I'd have to be back to measure bellies and look for edema.

Nope, not today, not anymore. At least not while I'm— and I love this expression—"out on conditions." What a concept. With a completely straight face, like he was explaining to me a tax code or something, the judge set five conditions for my "release." First, he said, I had to agree to appear in court and I had to keep in touch with my lawyer. Those two made sense.

But then, like I'm this hardened criminal and I go around holding up convenience stores on a weekly basis, he said I couldn't commit another crime (like I'd committed one in the first place!) and I couldn't do any illegal drugs (which I don't think was a reference to the fact that I'll smoke a joint when offered one if I'm not on call, but was merely one more way of getting in a dig).

The only condition that really bothers me—no, it doesn't bother me, it pisses me off and scares the hell out of me at the same time—is the midwifery one. I'm not allowed to practice my craft until this trial is over. That's the one that hurts. I'm not allowed to birth any babies, I'm not allowed to tend to any mothers.

So today instead of learning if May O'Brien had felt her little one kick or Peg Prescott's cervix had begun to thin, I did the grocery shopping. I bought beets. I looked at bottles of salad dressing. I picked out sodas with sugar for Rand, and sodas without sugar for Connie.

And I guess I did it all at the pace of a dead person.

—from the notebooks of SIBYL DANFORTH, MIDWIFE

MY MOTHER WAS CHARGED WITH INVOLUNTARY MANSLAUGHTER AND PRACTIC-ing medicine without a license on Wednesday, April 9, a little over a week after the medical examiner had filed the final autopsy report. We knew on Tuesday night she'd be arrested the next day, and I spent all of French class and most of algebra on Wednesday morning envisioning what was occurring at that moment at my home—as well as in a police cruiser, and at the courthouse to the north in Newport.

Stephen had come to our house again on Tuesday, arriving this time at the end of the day and staying through dinner. My father seemed less concerned with the idea that the lawyer's meter was running than he had been the week before, given Stephen's reason for coming to Red-dington and the gravity of his news. Moreover, that night he was able to walk us all step-by-step through the process my mother would endure the next day, and make it seem like a series of tedious but commonplace formalities, rather than a series of increasing indignities that could lead eventually to jail.

Nevertheless, the idea that my mother was being arrested fueled the darkest parts of my adolescent imagination, at the same time that it absolutely terrified the part of me that was still a little girl. One moment I saw my mother subjected to the sort of violent police brutality I had glimpsed on the news, and the next I saw myself as a motherless child, a lonely latchkey kid stretched tall in a teenager's body.

As the daughter of a midwife, of course, I had spent long hours and afternoons alone, so the idea of an absentee mother shouldn't have ter-rified me. But that morning in school it did, especially since my mother had adamantly refused to allow either Stephen or my father to drive her to Newport so she could discreetly turn herself in. Despite Stephen's assurances that turning herself in in no way implied guilt or culpability, she insisted that the State would have to come to Reddington to get her.

"If they want to arrest me, they'll have to come here," she had said Tuesday night, without looking up from the plate of food in which she had no interest.

Consequently, to prevent the worst visions from completely clouding my mind Wednesday morning, over and over I ran through the scenario Stephen had presented, trying to focus on the sheer banality of what my mother was experiencing at that moment.

A Vermont state police cruiser from the barracks in Derby was driving to our home in Reddington, twisting along Route 14 through Coventry, Irasburg, and Albany. The rack of lights on the roof was flashing, but the siren was silent. It was passing the cars that were sailing along at the fifty-mile-per-hour speed limit, and flying past the pickups and milk tankers lurching along at thirty-five. It slowed as it passed the general store and the church in the center of Reddington, and then turned into our long dirt driveway. It coasted to a stop behind my mother's station wagon and beside my father's small Jeep. Two green-uniformed officers climbed from their cruiser and walked up the path to our front door, perhaps the very same two fellows who had appeared at our home the month before: Leland Rhodes and Richard Tilley. Politely they explained to my mother exactly why she was being arrested, citing specific dates and formal charges.

For brief moments I would see my French teacher and the blackboard behind him, but he would quickly disappear as my mind drifted back to the events occurring at my house. One of the two officers was placing my mother in handcuffs, and the other was leading her into the backseat of the cruiser. My father and Stephen Hastings were not allowed to sit with her on the drive north to Newport and had to follow the police car in their own vehicles.

They arrived at the police station during my algebra class. As the rows of X's and Y's on the paper before me were transmogrified from variables and vectors into abstract line drawings, my mother's fingers were inked, her prints recorded, and her face photographed from the front and the side. With the tips of her fingers still blue, she was then brought to the courthouse to stand before a judge. Stephen was allowed to remain beside her, but my father had to sit in one of the rows of benches that formed two square blocks behind her.

I imagined the judge behind a desk that was not merely huge but elevated above the rest of the furniture in the courtroom with comic-book absurdity. I saw him staring down at this lawyer in a Burlington-type big-city business suit and this woman in a dress with blue irises and pearls and lipstick. At Stephen's suggestion, my mother had endeavored to look as suburban and unthreatening as possible, and so she was wearing the pearl necklace and lipstick that usually appeared only on special occasions like weddings and New Year's Eve dinner parties.

Stephen had taken great pains at dinner the night before to make it clear to us that my mother would not go to jail the next day for one single moment, so Wednesday morning I was at least saved from visions of steel bars and cell blocks. But I did hear the judge's voice as often as I heard my math teacher's, and that voice was stern: the sort of voice that can still be heard sometimes from the tall pulpits, reminding New Englanders that we are all sinners in the hands of an angry God. Sadly, I did not see the judge as a kind of impartial referee and arbitrator, someone who, it was conceivable, might actually become an ally of Sibyl Danforth's. Instead I conjured a judge who cared solely about conviction and punishment, and so when he spoke it was simply to agree with that unreasonably evil Bill Tanner, or to harangue my mother for taking the life of a patient.

The only snippet of conversation I heard in my mind that I knew reflected the reality of what was occurring in Newport was the response to the question from the bench "How do you plead?" Stephen was to speak for my mother at the arraignment, and so it was he who would answer, "Not guilty." My mother would have absolutely no lines that day in the drama of which she was the reluctant star.

At that point, I assumed, my parents and Stephen would leave the courthouse, and my father would drive my mother home.

The reality, I would learn later, had been in a small way somewhat better than my fantasies, but in one important way far worse. The small way? Judge Howard Dorset was no Jonathan Edwards–like preacher, no Calvinist voice from on high who took pains to inform my mother of the yawning, flaming pit before her. Months later when the trial was in progress, I would in fact discover that I rather liked the sound of Dorset's voice, especially the way as a native of northern Vermont he would occasionally stretch words like *stairs* and *pairs* into two syllables, or *business* into three.

Nevertheless, my mother had to endure one astonishing moment for which Stephen had not prepared her: the conditions of release.

Stephen had made it clear that my mother would have to give up midwifery until the trial was over or the case was settled, but otherwise he had led her to believe the discussion of bail wouldn't be contentious.

In actuality, it was.

Bill Tanner argued that "a midwife by her very nature demonstrates a reckless disregard for authority, and for the established medical norms of our society. A midwife is by nature an outlaw, someone who cavalierly puts women—and babies—at risk on a daily basis for no other reason than a mindless and backward distaste for the protocols of modern medicine." My mother was a good example: an irresponsible ex-hippie in a little hill town, tooling around northern Vermont in a beat-up station wagon. A woman with no formal medical training, she nevertheless ran around with syringes and surgical silk, with drugs like Ergotrate and Pitocin, while feigning the sort of expertise it took doctors years to acquire.

"Sibyl Danforth has a long history of challenging the State, first as a war protester and now as a midwife," Tanner said. "Given that history, and given the fact that she is now facing fifteen years in prison if convicted, the State believes there is a real and significant danger of flight."

"Your Honor, we all know there's no risk of flight. None at all. My client has lived in the same house for almost a decade, and in the same town almost her entire life," Stephen said.

"Moreover, Mrs. Danforth faces the loss of her practice—such as it is," Tanner interjected.

"And let's not forget she's a mother. She has a daughter in school here in Vermont whom she loves very much. And she has a husband with an established architectural practice. This is where her life is, this is where her roots have grown deep and taken hold. Mrs. Danforth isn't going anywhere."

"She has no job, Your Honor, her career's in shambles. Her reputation has been irrevocably tarnished. There are just so many reasons for her to leave the Northeast Kingdom that we know there's a very great risk of flight. And so we'd like to see bail reflect that. The State would like to see bail set at thirty-five thousand dollars."

"That's absurd," Stephen said. "Just ridiculous."

"Not at all. Your Honor, thirty-five thousand dollars is roughly half the appraised value of the Danforths' home. We believe it's a sum sufficient to ensure that . . . that nothing happens to all those deep roots."

Judge Dorset, my father told me, gave Bill Tanner what my family called the hairy eyeball: a chastising look in which someone rolls his eyes up so far into his head that the eyes and the brows become almost one.

"A tragedy has brought us all here," the judge said, "and we are probably about to embark upon a long road together. I, for one, can do without such hyperbole as 'outlaw' this early into the process, especially since I expect I will witness even more grandiloquent and dramatic license later on. My sense is defense counsel is correct when he tells me Mrs. Danforth has no plans on leaving, and I see no reason to impose a monetary condition for release."

Then in a voice that suggested he did this all the time—that most of the conditions were standard and he could recite the list by rote—Dorset outlined the terms of my mother's freedom.

It was the summer of motions. My mother had been arrested and charged in the first third of April, but the wheels of justice roll slowly indeed—a snowplow going uphill in a snowstorm—and it wasn't until early July that all of Stephen's and Patty Dunlevy's activity seemed to have any direction.

In July and August, however, the State's moves and Stephen's countermoves gathered momentum, and suddenly that snowplow was barreling downhill on completely clear, dry roads. Just after the Fourth of July weekend, Stephen filed a motion to have the case dismissed, arguing that even when all of the evidence was viewed in the best possible light for the State, there was still absolutely no case. He said we would lose on this motion, which we did, but it would give him an opportunity to hear Bill Tanner's arguments and listen to some of his experts.

Two weeks after that Stephen filed a motion to have my mother's statement from the night the state troopers came to our door suppressed—that conversation the State referred to with inappropriate glee as her confession. Stephen said the odds were we would lose this one, too, but he thought there was at least a small chance we could keep her first formal recollections of Charlotte Fugett Bedford's death from becoming evidence: The troopers, he insisted, had completely dominated the atmosphere in the house, yet had failed to make it clear to my mother that she should have an attorney present before she opened her mouth.

Had my mother raised the question of a lawyer that night in March instead of my father, we might have won; had my father brought the issue up before my mother was well into her statement, we might have won. Neither happened, and my mother's remarks became a part of the State's case.

Then Stephen filed a motion to obtain Charlotte Bedford's medical records going back to her childhood in Mobile, Alabama, and her years with Asa in Blood Brook and Tuscaloosa. This motion he won.

And he argued that we should be allowed access to the woman's correspondence that winter with her mother and her sister, as well as the audiotapes Asa made of the Sunday services at his church for the parishioners who were unable to attend due to weather or illness. After speaking to members of Asa's church, Patty had concluded that Charlotte was sicker than she had let on with my mother; Stephen wasn't sure whether this information would be relevant or, if it was, how we would use it when the time came, but it was information that mattered to him, and he wanted evidence. In those letters or in those services—as Asa or another parishioner asked for prayers for the sick or needy—might be a suggestion of the sort of frailty Charlotte hid from my mother.

Stephen won this motion as well, and Patty spent a weekend in August listening to tapes of Asa Bedford—fiery fundamentalist—and of his congregation.

And then there were the plea negotiations, although the two sides were always so far apart it never really looked as if a compromise or bargain was possible. At one point Stephen had my mother willing to plead guilty to involuntary manslaughter if the State would offer a deferred sentence of five years. The idea of my mother giving up midwifery for five years astonished me, but it seemed reasonable to my father and Stephen, and they convinced her to accept it. Pressured by the medical board and emboldened by angry ob-gyns, however, the State would not offer a deferred sentence.

But, Bill suggested to Stephen, the State might listen to a mere year in jail and then a suspended sentence with probation—perhaps six more years—if my mother was willing to pay additional fines, perform community service, and never practice midwifery again.

As soon as the State reiterated its demand that my mother give up midwifery, of course, the negotiations inevitably broke down. It wasn't the specter of prison that made it impossible to settle, it was my mother's unwillingness to relinquish her calling.

"Don't you get it, Stephen, a woman's dead," our attorney told us Bill would remind him—as if he'd forgotten why they were meeting or speaking on the telephone.

"I haven't lost sight of that, Bill," Stephen said he would usually respond, "and my client is as saddened by that fact as anyone. But my client didn't kill her."

Sometimes Bill would hint to Stephen that the rage his client had heard the day she was arraigned was absolutely nothing compared to what she'd have to endure throughout a trial. And Stephen did all that he could to make sure my mother understood this.

"Doctors are a funny bunch. They just don't approve of people without medical degrees delivering babies," Stephen said a number of times that summer, always as a warm-up to his warning that the State would say astonishingly mean things about midwifery and my mother. By Labor Day his expression "Doctors are a funny bunch" had become a running joke in our household, a bit of gallows humor as the trial loomed near.

For all of us, of course, that humor veiled both fear and anger. In July I began to experience the first shooting pains up and down the left side of my back that dog me still, pains that made it excruciating to ride Witch Grass some days or swim in the river with Tom Corts on others. But given the fact that Sibyl Danforth was "that midwife who did the C-section," I didn't believe I could trust a doctor that summer, and I did not want to subject my mother to what I imagined would be the tension of having to take me to see one.

I've always liked stories that end with parents folding their children into their arms, or tucking them into sleep at the end of a day. They are many and they are varied.

I longed to be tucked in the summer I turned fourteen, an odd desire only in that I hadn't had any longings of that sort in at least half a decade before then, but a yearning wholly explicable when I contemplated the loss of my mother and the dissolution of my family.

Afternoons when I was alone in the house, I'd blast my stereo as loud as the speakers and my ears could bear. I'd cocoon inside the music, the noise and vibrations sheltering me from the worst of my fears. Rock music has never been a particularly subtle form of expression, but it's unquestionably noisy and prone to anger. That summer, in most ways, I was much closer to woman than girl; being lost below waves of anger and noise was about as close to being tucked in as I could hope to get.

I spent lots of time with Tom, much more so than during the school year. We would spend evenings together when he returned from the ski resort where he was working once again, and whole afternoons on his days off. We swam together in the river, often with Sadie Demerest and Rollie McKenna and the boys who passed through their lives that summer. A road followed the river almost exactly, builders and pavers choosing to align the asphalt path with the aqua, but the water was hidden from the road by steep banks that slid twenty feet down, and by thick walls of maple and pine and ash. On a hot day, there might be thirty of us from the high school sunning ourselves on the rocks smack in the middle of the water, or bobbing in the deep pools between the boulders. On a cool or cloudy afternoon, there might be as few as four or five of us, depending upon whether Rollie or Sadie had brought a boy with her that day.

At any given moment that summer, I was as likely to be found experimenting with eyeliner with Rollie, as with marijuana with a half-dozen girlfriends at one of the places at the edge of the forest or far corners of the fallow meadows that had become our designated places to hang out.

Tom turned sixteen early in August and started to drive, which I think terrified my parents as much as anything that summer, because that meant we could actually drive ourselves to movies or one of the diners near the ski resort. Tom didn't have a car of his own, but an advantage of coming from a family that owned an automotive garage and graveyard was that he always had one at his disposal. Some were in better shape than others, but they all ran.

If my parents had not reached a point where they pined to see Tom someday as a son-in-law, they had grown from merely tolerating him to sincerely liking him. Once we had begun going steady during the school year, well before Charlotte Bedford had died, he began coming over to our house with some frequency. Usually my mother was busy with one of her patients in the part of the house that served as her office or she was off somewhere delivering a baby, and we always had the privacy to neck and listen to records. I think it speaks well of the young Tom Corts that he continued to come around even after Charlotte Bedford died. In the spring and summer between my mother's arraignment and trial, he dropped by especially often, both because he understood I needed him and because he wanted to show his alliance with my family. I know my parents appreciated that. My mother actually baked a cake for him the night before he turned sixteen.

And showing his alliance with my family demonstrated no small amount of maturity and spine. My mother's calling had always had the capability of eliciting strange and strong reactions in people, ranging from those parents who wouldn't allow their little girls to play at my house when I was very young because they feared my mother would whisk us all off to a birth, to my teenage friends who assumed—optimistically but mistakenly—that among the alternative or New Age herbs my mother used on a regular basis were marijuana and hashish. After one of my mother's mothers had died, all of the small communities in which I lived—my village, my school, my circle of friends—were split. Some folks saw Charlotte Bedford's death as an indictment of midwifery generally, and of my mother's irresponsibility specifically: *This was bound to happen, you know,* their gazes said when they ran into me at the front counter of the general store, or in the locker room as I got dressed after track. Other people would go out of their way to show their support for my family as we endured what they viewed as a lynching: *You're all in our thoughts and prayers,* they would tell me, sometimes giving me bear hugs at the pizza parlor in St. Johnsbury or as I helped my father empty our trash at the town dump.

The second group, I'm sorry to say, was considerably smaller than the first. I spent most of that calendar year under the critical gaze of assistant gym teachers, town clerks, checkout ladies at the supermarket, the fellows who pumped gas, and—all too often—the parents of the girls I thought were my friends, or the parents of the children for whom I baby-sat. I could never prove this, but I believe in my heart that Mrs. Poultney abruptly stopped calling me to take care of Jessica the last week of March because of the role she believed my mother had played in another woman's death.

Tom Corts, however, never wavered, and so some afternoons I daydreamed of him tucking me in at the end of the day, or sitting in the rocker beside my bed through the night as I slept. In hindsight those daydreams have led me to wonder on occasion if they were part of some peculiar attempt to forestall an adult sexual relationship with Tom, but most of the time I know that isn't the case. That summer we went well beyond the enthusiastic groping through sweatshirts and cardigans that had marked our spring, but Tom wasn't pressuring me to sleep with him and I was feeling no particular urgency either.

I think instead I daydreamed of Tom watching over me in a vaguely fatherly capacity because I could no longer be protected that way by my own father. Just as Tom had turned sixteen that summer, I had turned fourteen, and that meant I could no longer be held and embraced and cuddled by my dad in the way I once was. I would have used the word *weird* at fourteen to describe any such desire on my part or show of affection on his, well aware that the word was imprecise. But precision with the language of need is impossible at fourteen, and I feared anything I might say would be misconstrued—or, worse, would reflect a deviance inside me that was at once dangerous and unhealthy.

The fact is, despite the anger that coursed through my father at those moments when he viewed himself as abandoned by his spouse, the midwife, it was indeed my father who taught me how to tease a troll's neon-pink hair. It was my father who was there the Saturday I slid headfirst down a metal slide onto a tent stake and needed seventeen stitches along my cheek. It was upon my father's lap that I watched hours and hours of *Sesame Street* on a TV with fuzzy reception. My father was of a generation that had yet to understand the profound importance of the frequent squeeze, but he still knelt to hold me relatively often, and I can remember being lifted as a tiny girl into his arms and being hugged. To this day I do not mind at all being held by a man with some stubble on his cheeks.

For Tom's sixteenth birthday, I used up weeks of baby-sitting money to buy tickets to a rock concert in Burlington. Soon after his birthday we went, just the two of us for a change, and we had hours together alone going and returning in a giant Catalina of a car. I turned up the volume on the eight-track tape player that dangled underneath the glove compartment, and curled my legs up against my chest. The Catalina had a couch the size of the general store's freezer case, but Tom was near and the music was loud, and the trip to and from Burlington inside that car offered the sort of vaguely womblike escape I was craving.

Since we happened to be going to Burlington, my mother asked us to drop off an envelope with Stephen Hastings and pick up a banker's box of her files. Stephen had had the files for months, and had photocopied the materials he needed.

My mother probably expected me to peek inside the envelope, and

I didn't let her down. She was returning to Stephen Xeroxes of Charlotte Bedford's medical files, part of the history Stephen had petitioned the court that summer to see. My mother had scribbled her thoughts in blue pen on some of the documents, and now that I'm a physician and the trial has passed, the things she circled make sense. In the car that afternoon, however, the notion that Charlotte had been treated five years earlier for iron-deficiency anemia meant little, as did a Mobile, Alabama, doctor's prescription in 1973 for a drug I could not even begin to pronounce at the time: hydrochlorothiazide, an inexpensive diuretic used to control hypertension.

Apparently my mother had treated Charlotte for anemia while the woman was in her care, but not for high blood pressure; apparently Charlotte's blood pressure had not been high enough to alarm her. But, then, it also didn't appear that Charlotte had thought to share with my mother the fact that she'd been treated for the disorder in the past.

Stephen's law firm comprised two Victorian homes that shared a driveway at the edge of the campus of the University of Vermont. The buildings were in the hill section of Burlington, the mannered, elegant, and tree-lined streets at the top of the hill that towered over the commercial section of the city. In the nineteenth century, when Burlington was a thriving Lake Champlain lumber and potash port, the wealthier merchants and more successful businessmen had built homes for their families on the hill above the city proper.

I hadn't expected to see Stephen when we arrived. I had assumed I would simply drop off the envelope with a receptionist, pick up the banker's box, and leave. But after I explained to the woman at the front desk who I was, she said Stephen would be disappointed if he didn't get a chance to come out and say hello. She said he was in the middle of a meeting with an investigator, but the meeting had been going on all afternoon. When she went upstairs to find him, I went back out to the car to get Tom so he wouldn't have to sit there alone, baking in the sun while wondering where I was.

Stephen had been meeting with Patty Dunlevy, and the two of them came out to greet me, Stephen in a crisp navy-blue business suit, Patty in sandals and the sort of flouncy peasant dress I usually associated with my mother's midwife friends. It seemed odd for the woman I'd first met in mirrored sunglasses and a black bomber jacket to be wearing a styleless muumuu, and I must have stared. She took my elbow conspiratorially with one arm and, motioning toward her dress with the other, said, "Isn't this thing hideous? I bought it at a secondhand shop in the North End. But I spent the morning with some more of your mom's moms, and I figured I should look the part."

"The part?" I asked.

"You know, a home-birthy sort. Peace, love, tie-dye. Alternative medicine. Let's barter since I'm broke. I can't pay you, but my husband's a carpenter who will build you the most amazing bookshelves you've ever seen if you deliver my baby."

She talked fast, and her voice was filled with pleasure.

"You should have been an actress," Tom said.

"Brother, I am."

Stephen gave us a tour of the building we were in, and there were moments when I expected to find velvet ropes cordoning off some of the shining hundred-year-old tables and wooden breakfronts that served now to store files: I expected to be told, "George Washington sat here," or "Ethan Allen ate there." The couches were elegant but plush: I could have slept comfortably on any one of them. The chairs behind all of the desks were leather; all of the pens on the blotters were silver or gold. Computers were uncommon then, but they nevertheless seemed to be everywhere.

Finally we passed the conference area in which Patty and Stephen had been working. I don't believe he had intended to show us in, but I didn't realize that at the time; the two adults were a step behind us, and in my awkward fourteen-year-old sort of way I blundered into the dark paneled room, with Tom right beside me. Lit by a chandelier with grapefruit-sized globes, the area looked as if it had once been two separate bedrooms. There was a long, wide table in the center of the room, buried leagues below piles of yellow legal pads, file boxes, and newspaper clippings. The walls were covered with white poster paper on which Stephen and Patty had scribbled notes and names in Magic Marker. There must have been two or three dozen pieces of that paper hung on the walls with thick strips of masking tape.

Before Stephen or Patty could even begin to explain to us what they were doing or escort Tom and me back into the hallway, words and phrases and the names of people I knew popped out at me from the walls. I recognized that one sheet was filled with the names of midwives, and another with families whose children my mother had delivered.

There was a sheet filled with names of doctors, and then one beside it with only one: my mother's backup physician, Brian "B.P." Hewitt. There was a page titled "Pathologists," and another with the strange and ominous-sounding word "vagal." And while it crossed my mind that the word might be some sort of abbreviation or modest abridgment for *vaginal,* something about the words underneath it—bradycardic, blackout, CPR, C-section—led me to conclude it wasn't.

"Connie, do keep all of this to yourself, won't you?" Stephen said suddenly, when he realized I was staring and reading.

"Oh, sure."

And as quickly and as casually as Tom and I had mistakenly wandered into the room, he ushered us out, telling us, "We kept the kitchen downstairs. It's nice to work in a place with a kitchen. Know what I mean?"

After my mother had completed the cesarean, she took the time to sew up Charlotte Bedford's body. This has always impressed me. Yet in my mother's notebooks, especially in those long entries she wrote in the weeks after Charlotte's death when she was trying to understand what had happened, there is only one sentence about that particular moment in the tragedy:

"Her body was too big to wrap in a blanket, so I sewed it up the best I could."

Read in a vacuum, independent of the rest of the notebooks, the sentence seems somewhat peculiar: neither illogical nor insane, but slightly odd. As if my mother has made some connection understood only by her. As if a link or a clause between blankets and sutures is missing.

The link appears in a notebook entry written almost three years earlier, an entry about different parents and a different birth:

Their baby was born dead, and the poor, poor thing was the most deformed creature I've ever seen. His intestines were on the outside. But of course his parents wanted to see him. And so I swaddled him in this little baby blanket one of his aunts had made, wrapping the little guy from his feet up to his nose because—if everything else wasn't bad enough—he was also miss-

ing the lower half of his jaw. I didn't cry when I was delivering him, because I'd known for a few hours he would be born dead, but I did when I had him wrapped and was showing him to his mom and dad. He looked so peaceful and so happy. Suddenly I was weeping.

At some point after my mother had delivered Veil, she returned to Charlotte's body. It wasn't right away, because first she had to tend to the baby, initially a pale, limp thing that seemed likely to die. She had to, as some midwives say, "work that baby hard." Vigorously rubbing the newborn's back, suctioning mucus, hitting the bottoms of his feet. Suctioning more mucus. Talking to him, asking his father to talk to him.

I imagine my mother telling Asa, "Say something. He needs to hear your voice! Talk to him!" Neither Asa nor Anne ever mentioned such an exchange during the depositions or the trial, however, and my mother never told me of one.

Nevertheless, it is clear that in those first minutes after Veil arrived, my mother was focused solely on getting the child to breathe. Obviously she succeeded.

And when it was clear that the child would live, she handed Veil to his father and started ministering to him. She held Asa, first standing and then sitting. The two adults—with the boy in his father's arms—slid down the wall beside the window until they were on the floor, the small of their backs against the baseboard trim. My mother's arms never lost their hold on the pastor.

Anne said she heard my mother tell Asa over and over that the baby was beautiful, and might have said a couple of times, "It's all right. Shhhh. It's all right."

Asa was crying, his shoulders rising and falling as he gasped for air in the midst of his sobs.

And at some point on the bed, Charlotte's body stopped bleeding. When the autopsy was conducted, the medical examiner would find just about seven hundred and fifty milliliters of blood in the peritoneal cavity. Imagine more than two pints of milk. And then there were the unmeasurable waves of blood that had rolled from the incision—and overflowed from inside the abdomen—onto the bed, soaking the sheets and mattress and the pillow my mother had used like a sponge, until the white bedding looked burgundy.

When my mother finally stood and returned to that bed and the body upon it, no one looked at his or her watch or noticed the time on the clock on the nightstand. But given Asa and Anne and my mother's agreement that it had been ten minutes after six when something happened—when Charlotte's chin shot up as she pushed, and Asa watched his wife's eyes roll up into her head—everyone agreed it was probably between twenty to seven and quarter to seven when my mother stood for a long moment with her hands rubbing the back of her neck, and stared down at Charlotte's brutalized body.

If I have interpreted the remark in my mother's notebook correctly, the idea passed through her mind to simply wrap the body in a blanket. Perhaps she would have folded the skin back over the wound first. Perhaps not. But she wanted to cover the body; she didn't want it left exposed and cold and so very open.

But in my mother's mind the body was too big to be swaddled, and so she repaired it. There were still towels folded on a chair in a corner of the room, and my mother took one and patted the area around the incision dry. Sterility no longer mattered. She then put the towel on a corner of the mattress at the foot of the bed and went to her birthing bag for her catgut. Her tweezers. Her curved needle and needle holders.

And she began to work. Sealing the wound took three packages of dissolvable sutures.

When the medical examiner testified, he noted that my mother had not concerned herself with repairing the damage to the uterus; she had not stitched the spot where she had torn open the womb. He didn't present this information as an indication that my mother's work was shoddy, or to convey the idea that she was disrespectful of the dead. On the contrary, he said my mother's sutures were "professional and tight. Her work was perfectly capable."

His point—the State's point—was simply that my mother was not attempting to save Charlotte's life when she sewed the body back together; she understood that Charlotte was dead. By that point, my mother was simply concerned with the cosmetics.

When my mother was giving her own testimony, Stephen asked her why she had bothered to sew up a body she knew was dead.

"I couldn't leave her like that," my mother said. "It wouldn't have been fair to her, and it wouldn't have been fair to her family."

"Her family?" Stephen asked, expecting her to clarify that she had meant Charlotte's husband, or, perhaps, Charlotte's husband and her family in the South.

"Asa and Veil," my mother said, beginning one of the many exchanges between the two in which Stephen thought he knew exactly what my mother was going to say, while my mother assumed that whatever she was going to say was completely harmless. Sometimes she was right, sometimes she wasn't.

"But mostly Veil. How we come into this world means more than any of us understand," my mother continued. "So I wanted to be sure that Veil saw his mother: I wanted to be sure he had a picture with him for life of how incredibly sweet and pretty and peaceful—just amazingly peaceful—her face was. Even then. Even after all she'd been through. Even at the very, very end."

MIDWIVES

PART THREE

FOURTEEN

Stephen and Rand want me "pumped up." "Fired up." "Psyched." They want me ready for a fight.

I think they're talking like that because it's football season, and we hear those expressions all the time. But it sounds very strange coming from Rand, because he's never really been into football. Like me, he's always seen it as this totally bizarre form of organized violence.

But he's a man, and so I think that's the only language he has to inspire me; those are the only words that he knows.

Of course, the sport is everywhere suddenly. At least it seems that way in this part of the county. The football team at Connie's high school has won its first three games this fall, which wouldn't be a big deal in some areas, but it is around here. Someone told me this is a team that never wins, and suddenly it's won three games in a row, and it's won them in a big way. I gather the victories were very one-sided.

Stephen's a little better about the "Get psyched!" stuff, probably because he sees people like me who are scared all the time. It's part of what the guy does for a living. He has to keep me from completely falling apart, and so he seems to know just how far to push me with questions when we're together, and exactly when to back off and give me some space.

He's also a bit of a mimic. That's not the right word at all, because it makes him sound like a parakeet or a monkey. Or some sort of entertainer. All I mean is that it's clear he listens to me very carefully, and not just what I say: He listens to how I say something, the exact words I use. And then, a few minutes later, I'll hear a word or expression come back to me.

I was at his office this morning, and I was explaining to him what goes on in my opinion in the first stage of labor. I said to him how each surge has the potential to change a mother, and eventually one will. I told him how a woman at that stage might go from being this totally serene person in touch with everything around her, to this frenzied animal unaware of anything but her own physical reality. Her surges. The way her body is changing. And that's part of the deal, the giving up of everything—and I mean everything—but the demands of labor. A woman's body knows what it's doing, I said, and she just has to let it do its own thing.

Maybe ten or fifteen minutes later we're talking about this ob-gyn who actually believes in home birth—of course his practice is nowhere near Reddington, that would be way too much to ask—and what he's going to say on the stand. And Stephen says to me, "He's this totally serene guy. You'll like him." And then, a couple minutes later when we're talking about the time he's devoted to researching my case, he says, "I've done this often enough that I know instinctively how deep to dig into something, and instinctively when to let something go. It's just a part of doing my thing."

Does Stephen do this on purpose? Damned if I know. But I like it, it makes me feel good. And it's a whole lot better than the football stuff, which—like Rand—he sometimes resorts to, especially now that the trial's about to begin and he's afraid I'm not "fired up" enough.

I want to tell him—I want to tell him and Rand both—that it's hard to get "fired up" when most of the time I'm just too busy being scared to death. But I think all they'd do then is worry about me even more than they already do, and try and "pump me up." Get me ready to fight or hit back or whatever it is football people do.

Besides, I think if I told them how frightened I am, the floodgates would open. Suddenly I'd be telling them that I'm scared I'm going to jail. I'm scared I'm going to have to give up my practice. And—and this fear wasn't so bad in the spring, it's only in the last month or so that it's really crept up on me—sometimes I'm scared I might have made a mistake in March. It's possible. What if Charlotte Bedford really was still alive?

—from the notebooks of SIBYL DANFORTH, MIDWIFE

NEWPORT SITS AT THE SOUTHERN TIP OF LAKE MEMPHREMAGOG, A THIN, COLD lake that stretches thirty miles north to south. Perhaps a third of the lake is in the United States, while the rest is north of the border in Canada.

Before my mother's trial began, I hated that lake. By the time it was over, I loathed it.

As a child there were some obvious reasons to despise it. It was hard to spell and impossible to pronounce. I know now that the name is the Abenaki term for "beautiful waters," but in grade school it was merely a long chain of syllables, at once incomprehensible and unpleasant.

Even as a teenager, however, even when I was no longer intimidated by the phonetics of the word, I disliked the lake. It always looked to me like the sort of lake that liked to swallow swimmers and small boats whole. Those few times when I was taken swimming there with my friends, its waters always felt more frigid than its neighbors'— especially inviting little places like Crystal or Echo Lake—and its currents more dangerous.

And I don't think I ever saw the lake when its waters weren't choppy.

There were also myths about Memphremagog, some involving a giant lizard much more menacing than the benign monster said by some to swim in Lake Champlain, and some involving a particularly gruesome thing that could live as comfortably on the shore as it did underneath those dark waters, and would mutate into the form of its prey: fish or dogs or baby deer. That's how it killed them. Although I never believed any of these tales, they did reinforce in my mind my conviction that the lake was an unhappy place of which I wanted no part.

Most people aren't like me, however; most people think highly of Lake Memphremagog. And most people who spend any time at all in the courtroom of the Orleans County Courthouse are very glad the city of Newport meets the lake where it does. The courthouse sits on the top of the bluff on Main Street, and the courtroom is on the third—and, therefore, highest—floor of the century-old stone-and-brick box. The courtroom has three monstrously large windows facing the lake, a mere three blocks to the north. Jurors are granted a panoramic view of the waters, and the shapes and summits of Owl's Head and Bear Mountain in the distance. I imagine in trials less demanding or notorious than my mother's, jurors have stared themselves to sleep as they gazed at those waters.

Even during my mother's trial, however, jurors on occasion used Lake Memphremagog as a place upon which to focus when they wanted to be sure to avoid eye contact with my mother, or when an exceptionally grisly piece of evidence was on display. For me, this was just one more reason to hate the lake.

As the defendant, my mother had a spectacular view of the waters: She and Stephen shared a table by the window, and Stephen always took the seat toward the center of the courtroom so that he could rise and pace without having to climb around my mother or draw undue attention toward her. And as the defendant's daughter, I sat in the front bench— the one directly behind her—which meant the lake was an unavoidable and inescapable presence in the corners of my eyes as well. Even when my father took the "window seat," the shadow of the lake remained with me: The windows were that tall and wide and clean.

Fortunately, my mother did not share my dislike for Lake Mem- phremagog. With an awareness of how the media approached her trial and the role image would play in its history, she said something to my father and Stephen and me one night when we were leaving the court- house that indicated in her mind the lake was not merely an impartial witness to the events occurring on the third floor of a building a few blocks from its shore, it was actually an ally of hers of sorts. The sun was low as we walked to our cars, but it had not yet set. It was probably close to five-thirty.

"Look where she's standing," my mother said, and she motioned toward the reporter from the CBS affiliate in Burlington who was speak- ing at the moment to a TV camera, "and look what's going to be in the background. That's where they all stand. Have you noticed? Day after day, every single one of them. Even that lady from the Boston station who only spent an afternoon here. Isn't that something? They all stand right over there somewhere."

We had not noticed it before—at least I hadn't—but we all understood instantly what my mother meant: The woman was standing across the street from the courthouse, instead of in front of the building itself, or on its steps. Someone—either the reporter herself or her partner with the camera—had apparently decided they would rather have the lake in the background than the Orleans County Courthouse.

"Everyone who isn't here who thinks about this will remember that water," my mother continued, "everyone who sees it on TV. Tomorrow or next week or whenever, that's what they'll remember when they picture this whole thing. That lake. That amazing and mysterious lake."

Any hopes Stephen had that the trial would not commence before Christmas had evaporated by the time the Labor Day weekend approached. We all knew it would be a fall affair. And only two days after Labor Day itself, the first Wednesday of September, we were officially informed of the date of the trial. It would begin Monday, September 29, and Stephen expected it would last at least two weeks. Maybe three.

During that unusually hot, arid summer—a July that wilted flower gardens early and stunted the corn, and an August that dried up a good many of our neighbors' wells—the case never lost what Stephen had referred to once around my mother as its "prosecutorial energy."

If anything, that person named Tanner seemed to me more rabid than ever as autumn arrived, as interested in persecuting my mother as he was in prosecuting her. And while in hindsight I know this was largely the perception of a teenager who didn't understand that "deposition" is merely a lawyer's term for court-sanctioned harassment, or the ways both the defense and the prosecution leverage court appearances for pretrial publicity, I know also there was some validity to my paranoia: Bill Tanner really was furious, Bill Tanner really was out for blood.

Neither Tanner nor his staff could believe that my mother had rejected the State's offer of a mere year in jail (of which she'd probably only serve six or seven months) and six years of probation in return for a guilty plea on the charge of involuntary manslaughter. If six years on probation sounded like a long time, they still thought it was a tremendously magnanimous and merciful offer: Despite the fact that Charlotte Bedford was dead, my mother would go to prison for barely half a year.

Yes, she was expected to give up midwifery, but to them, that was a small price. It just didn't get any better than this, they must have thought; a deal couldn't get much sweeter.

Meanwhile, when the rumor of Tanner's offer circulated throughout the medical community, many doctors—especially obstetricians— were livid. Absolutely livid. The whole idea that a hippie midwife had killed some woman with a bedroom C-section (and in their diatribes, this was indeed the essential scenario) and might only go to jail for a few months had a good number of physicians enraged beyond reason. It seemed to me that some of them were spending more time writing editorials or letters to newspapers than they were practicing medicine, and Stephen took to calling the State Medical Board "the Furies," a shorthand reference even I understood.

Looking back, I still find it astonishing that so many doctors were so clearly unwilling to heed their own advice about stress.

From the window in my parents' bedroom, the one that faced our backyard and—in the far distance—Mount Chittenden, I watched my mother and Stephen sit back in two Adirondack chairs in the corner of the lawn by the porch. They'd moved the chairs so they were side by side and they could see the sun set through the damp fall air.

"Being pretty can be a disadvantage with a jury," Stephen was saying, and he stretched his legs through the leaves on the ground by his feet.

"You think too much. You think too much about the damnedest things."

"That's my job."

"Well, I don't think we need to worry that I'm so pretty we're at a disadvantage."

"It will be a factor in the voir dire. That's all I'm saying."

"The what?"

"The jury selection."

"The way your mind works. Unbelievable."

"I hope that's a compliment."

"I'm not sure. I just find it incredible."

"My mind?"

"This process. The very idea that because you think I'm pretty—"

"It's the idea that the jury will think you're pretty. What I think is irrelevant."

"Hah!"

"They will, Sibyl. You are an undeniably pretty woman. Undeniably. And with some jurors that will be an asset. With others, it will be a problem we'll have to overcome."

My mother and Stephen dangled their arms over the sides of their chairs, and their fingers picked at the grass just this side of dormancy and the fallen leaves that had begun to dry. Sometimes the tips of their fingers touched, occasionally the backs of their hands grazed. I wondered if they were savoring those brief, brief seconds when their skin brushed together.

"You're really going to let Connie watch?" my grandmother asked my mother one Saturday in mid-September, as if I weren't there having lunch with the two of them at our kitchen table.

"We're really going to let Connie watch," my mother said.

I imagine in her younger days my grandmother had been an extremely tolerant woman. Her daughter, after all, had dropped out of Mount Holyoke to live with an older man on Cape Cod, and then spent a winter with the Black Panthers in Boston. When Sibyl had finally returned to Vermont, she got pregnant before she got married, and she'd done both very young. And even if this *had* been "the sixties"—an umbrella rubric for a variety of excesses and an excuse for all sorts of otherwise antisocial behaviors—one might have expected a certain amount of mother-daughter tension. But they always insisted there had been none, a point of family history my father says he can corroborate from at least the moment he entered my mother's life.

By the time Charlotte Fugett Bedford died, however, my grandmother had grown more conservative. Her own husband, my grandfather, had died ten years earlier, and a decade of living alone had made her slightly skittish, wary, and quick to frown or find fault. And, of course, the woman who watched her daughter on trial was considerably older than the woman whose daughter had dropped out of college: She had aged from her early fifties to her mid-sixties, and she was no more exempt from the anxieties of age than anyone else.

Nevertheless, my Nonny—my name for her, even at fourteen—was still a warm and energetic woman when I was growing up. My mother's tendency to hug friends on sight was at least partly genetic, and I'll never lose my love for the vaguely floral, vaguely antiseptic smell of my Nonny's hair spray: I'd get a strong whiff of it with every embrace.

In any case, when it was clear that the charges against my mother would not be settled without a trial, Nonny tried hard to convince my parents to keep me away from the courtroom. She thought it would be a scarring experience, and while there were certainly people attending the trial who would have agreed with her—especially in light of my eventual breakdown—my parents knew how desperately I wanted to be there. Moreover, I think they realized that it would be equally scarring for me to hear important details second-hand in the girl's bathroom at school. And so it didn't matter that I'd miss two (and perhaps three) weeks of classes; it didn't matter that I'd see all sorts of frightening pieces of evidence; it didn't matter that I'd hear truly terrible things said about my mother, or have to watch a variety of witnesses in all likelihood sob on the stand.

No one, after all, expected Asa Bedford to keep his composure throughout the entire proceedings, or Anne Austin to endure without tears what Stephen himself said would be a "withering search-and-destroy, free-fire, relentlessly savage" cross-examination. And I think both my father and Stephen had begun to wonder by September how even my mother would do. We could all see she was growing quiet and morose—not so much gloomy, as tired beyond the rejuvenating powers of sleep—and in their own ways they were constantly trying to rally her spirits.

Yet absolutely none of this mattered, because my parents understood how badly I wanted to attend the trial. It seemed to me I had a moral responsibility to be present; in my mind, my appearance was an important show of solidarity with my mother.

Besides, Stephen wanted me there.

"Stephen thinks Connie here will be very helpful," my mother said to her mother, and she gave my arm a small squeeze. *Don't you worry about Nonny,* that squeeze said: *You're going.*

"Helpful? Helpful how?"

"Connie will be a constant reminder for the jury that I'm not just some faceless defendant. I'm not just some midwife. I'm a mother. I have a daughter, a family."

Nonny had turned the last carrots from her vegetable garden into a salad with raisins and walnuts, and while the carrots were supposed to be shredded, the blender my grandmother used was older than I, and the salad still had a great many large orange chunks. I watched Nonny methodically chew one of those pieces while she thought about my mother's explanation, and noticed there was some dry dirt on the cuffs of her light-blue cardigan. From her garden, I thought. She'd probably harvested the carrots we were eating that very morning.

Her voice more quizzical than dubious, more puzzled than angry, Nonny finally said, "And that means they'll have mercy?"

"This is not about mercy!" my mother snapped back.

"It's about—"

"I don't need mercy."

"Then what does that lawyer of yours mean? Why does he want Connie there so badly?"

" 'That lawyer of yours'? Mother, must you put it that way? It sounds horrible. It sounds like you think he's some sort of charlatan."

Nonny sighed, and rubbed the arthritic bulbs of her long fingers. My mother and I both knew that Nonny did not think Stephen was a charlatan. How could she? If she meant anything at all by her diminution of Stephen Hastings to "that lawyer of yours," if there was anything at all behind the remark, it was probably a vague apprehension triggered by the way my mother's voice seemed to rise whenever she said the word *Stephen*, the way the word was tinged with promise and colored by hope when it came from her lips.

"I just don't think Connie should be there," Nonny said after a moment, wrapping her hands together in her lap. "If you don't need . . . mercy or sympathy or something, I don't see why you should bring a fourteen-year-old girl into that courtroom."

"It makes Mom a real person," I chimed in, paraphrasing a remark I had overheard Stephen make to my parents earlier that week. "And that makes it harder to convict her. Juries don't like to convict the kind of real people who might be their neighbors."

Both of the adults turned toward me.

"You weren't doing your homework Wednesday night, were you?" my mother said, trying hard to look stern.

"I did my homework Wednesday night."

"Yeah, after Stephen left you did your homework," she said. She then turned to my grandmother and continued, "Connie will be with me because I love her and I want her there—as long as she wants to be there. She's come this far with us, she may as well see it through."

◆   ◆   ◆

I woke up in the middle of the night a few days before the trial began, and through the register in the floor I could see the light on in the den below. It was almost two in the morning. For a moment I assumed my mother or father had simply neglected to turn off the light before coming upstairs, and while that would have been uncharacteristic behavior from either of them, these were unusual times. We all had a great deal on our minds.

I rolled over, hoping to fall quickly back to sleep, but I thought I heard something in the den. Something as intangible as a rustle, as imperceptible as a draft. An eddy, perhaps, whorled, drifting up from the basement through the cracks between the floorboards. Had the curtains merely shivered? Or had someone exhaled, a faint tremor in his or her breath?

I climbed out of bed and crouched by the register in my nightgown. If there were people in the den, they were not on the couch, which—along with the coffee table and a part of the woodstove's hearth—was about all I could see through the wrought-iron grate.

I was neither frightened nor cold, but when I decided I'd go downstairs, I started to tremble: Connie Danforth, just like a heroine in one of those ridiculous slasher movies my friends and I were always watching, that idiot camp counselor who went alone into the woods at night, shining her flashlight before her as she practically beckoned the psycho killer in the hockey mask to come get her.

The stairs remained silent as I walked upon them, largely because I knew exactly where to step to avoid their idiosyncratic creaks and groans. I told myself I was going downstairs to get a glass of milk. If anyone asked what I was doing—and why would someone, it was my house—I would say just that: I'm getting a glass of milk.

The lights were off in the dining room and the kitchen; I saw the mudroom was dark. Perhaps my parents really had simply left the light on. Perhaps I had heard nothing more than one of the strange breezes that blow through an old Vermont house as the seasons change or the northern air grows cold.

I paused outside the kitchen entrance to the den, my back flush against the refrigerator, and felt its motor vibrate against my spine. I half-expected to hear a voice call out to me. I wondered if I'd hear, suddenly, an exchange between people in that room. Hearing neither, I pushed off the refrigerator with the palms of my hands and turned toward the den.

There I saw my father, alone with easily a dozen small stapled packets of papers scattered around him on the floor in one corner. Xeroxes of some sort. He was still wearing the business shirt he had worn to his office that day, and the same light-gray slacks. He was sunk deep into the rocking chair by the brass floor lamp.

"What are you doing up, sweetie?" he asked when he saw me in the doorway. He looked worried that I was awake.

"I'm getting a glass of milk."

"Couldn't sleep?"

"No. I mean, I woke up. And I decided I wanted a glass of milk."

He nodded. "Know what? I think I'll have one with you. Then I should probably go to bed myself."

"Is that work?" I asked, motioning toward the clusters of papers surrounding him on the floor.

"These? No, not at all. They're precedents. Legal precedents. They're some of the cases your mom's lawyer had researched while putting her defense together."

I picked up one of the stapled packets, a sheaf of nine or ten pages titled "*State* v. *Orosco.*" I skimmed the lengthy subtitle, an incomplete sentence that seemed to me a study in gibberish: "Certified questions as to whether information and affidavit in involuntary manslaughter case were insufficient following denial of motions to dismiss and to suppress statements."

"You've been reading these?" I asked, astonished that he would punish himself so.

"Yup."

"Why?"

He shrugged. "Because I love your mother. And I want to understand what Stephen's doing to defend her."

He stood and led me to the kitchen where I'd been only moments before, my mind rich with unspeakable suspicions, and pulled from the refrigerator a cardboard container of milk.

FIFTEEN

I didn't think I'd be scared once this thing began, but I am. I thought I'd get over it once I got here, once I was settled down in my chair. I was wrong. Or maybe I was just kidding myself the last few weeks.

All day long I tried to focus on the little things in the courtroom to take my mind off the big ones, even though I know I'm supposed to be paying attention like there's no to-morrow.

"No tomorrow." I wish I hadn't thought of that expres-sion. It's hateful.

But there were times I couldn't do it, times I just couldn't pay attention. Or maybe I should say I wouldn't— there were times I just wouldn't pay attention. Some moments, I just found it easier to think about nothing but the incredible chandelier this courtroom has than the idea that I might be in prison somewhere when my sweet baby is in college or when she has her first baby.

I want to be there when she has her first baby so much. I want to be there when she has all her babies.

And when the idea that I might miss out on something like that crossed my mind today, I'd zone out as fast as I could and focus on something else. Anything else. Like that chandelier. I'd seen the courtroom before when I was charged back in the spring, but I hadn't looked around that day and so I hadn't noticed the chandelier. After all, all I'd really done that morning was breeze in in my little spring dress while Stephen said, "Not guilty, Your Honor." Took about two seconds.

But I saw the chandelier today, I couldn't miss it. And it's a beauty, it really is. A huge wrought-iron thing that hangs down from smack in the center of the ceiling. The bulbs sit inside these delicate glass tulips, and the metalwork is a series of the most amazingly graceful curlicues and swirls. A lot of times, it was just so much easier for me to get a picture in my head of those tulips or those swirls than the faces of the people being asked all sorts of questions about home birth and midwifery. Stephen and Bill Tanner must have talked to thirty or thirty-five people today, and they still haven't agreed upon who will be on the jury and who won't.

So, as Stephen said, "We get to do this again tomorrow." I just can't believe it.

I think there were four or five people up there today who hated me without even knowing me. That wouldn't have bothered me once. Before Charlotte died, I don't think it fazed me a bit when I came across a person who hated me for what I did. I think I viewed it as their problem, not anything I needed to lose sleep over. It was like, "Hey, you deal with it. That's your trip, not mine."

But it really freaked me out today. It really frightened the hell out of me.

From where I sit, I can see Lake Memphremagog, and every so often this afternoon when a possible juror was explaining how all of his children had been born in a hospital because it's safer, I'd try to get a picture of the water in my mind. Then I could stare at the guy and look like I was listening, when all I was seeing was the lake.

I'll bet that water's cold right now, incredibly cold.

This just isn't a good time of the year for a trial like this. At least for me. Everything's dying, or going brown. I didn't used to mind the fall. I do this year. That's another thing that seems to be different with me since Charlotte died. Suddenly I dislike the fall.

There were moments today when I found myself staring

at the water in the lake and getting the chills when I thought about where I might be when it freezes.

—*from the notebooks of* SIBYL DANFORTH, MIDWIFE

DOCTORS DO NOT PROTEST, THEY LOBBY. THEY ARE NOT THE SORT OF PEOPLE who will stand around outside a courthouse with placards and sandwich boards, or hold hands and sing rally songs. Midwives, on the other hand, are. Midwives are exactly the sort of folk who will use public spectacle to make a political point.

And so while doctors made their presence felt in a variety of powerful ways before and during my mother's trial—they just loved to testify—they did not stand on the steps of the Orleans County Courthouse.

That responsibility fell upon the midwives.

The Monday my mother's trial began, my family was greeted in Newport by somewhere between sixty and seventy people, counting the midwives and their clients. There were women whose faces I recognized, like Cheryl Visco and Megan Blubaugh, Molly Thompson and Donelle Folino, and there were a great many women and men I'd never seen before, but who, apparently, believed passionately in a woman's right to labor in her own bedroom. There were some of my mother's patients there as well, faces I remembered from prenatal exams at our house as recently as the previous winter. Inside, we'd soon discover, were even more of my mother's clients, quietly knitting or nursing in the three back benches.

We saw the supporters as soon as we drove down Main Street that morning, standing like a phalanx along both sides of the courthouse steps and in long lines on the grass that extended out from the walkway to the front door. We had driven to Newport in my mother's distinctive old station wagon, and so we were recognized immediately, and a cheer went up as we coasted into the parking lot between the courthouse and the lake.

"Set Sibyl free, let babies be!" was the first chant we heard from the group, and we heard it the moment we emerged from our car. Of all the chants we'd hear over the next few weeks (and we'd hear many), that one was my least favorite. It implied my mother wasn't free; it suggested prison and confinement and my family's destruction.

Unfortunately, to this day it's the one I hear most often in my head. The others—either doggerel that linked hospitals with laboratories, or ditties that elevated home birth to a religious rite—come back to me when I think hard about those weeks, but they don't pop into my head today like bad songs while I'm seeing patients or brewing coffee.

As planned, Stephen and a young associate from his firm were already waiting for us in the parking lot when we arrived. There had been a frost the night before, so even though the sun was well up by eight-thirty, the air still felt cool and I could see Stephen's breath when he spoke.

"You have some fans," he said, motioning toward the demonstration across the street.

My mother smiled. "Are you behind this?"

"God, no! We made sure we'll have some friends once we get inside the courtroom—quiet friends—but those campers over there came on their own. Don't get me wrong, I'm perfectly happy they're here, but I had nothing to do with it."

The adults all shook hands, and I was introduced to Stephen's associate, a man a few years his junior named Peter Grinnell. Peter lacked Stephen's polish, and it was clear he had a liking for fried dough and sausage heroes—the epicurean specialties of the town and county fairs that begin in Vermont in early August and continue until the first weekend in October. His hair was thin, his skin unhealthy, and he needed to lose a good thirty or forty pounds.

I couldn't imagine where this fellow fit into the dignified—downright intimidating—law firm I'd seen a glimpse of that day in Burlington; I was surprised someone like Stephen even wanted him working there. Peter was wearing an overcoat, so I couldn't see his suit, but I found myself hoping it was, as Stephen would say, one click above whatever Bill Tanner would be wearing.

"How do you feel, Sibyl?" Stephen asked.

My mother shrugged. "I can feel my heart beating pretty fast. But I think I'm okay."

"Fired up?"

"No, Stephen, you know I'm not," she said, shaking her head, and she sounded almost resigned. "I'm not a fired-up kind of lady."

"They are," he said, and he pointed with his thumb like a hitchhiker at the midwives and home birthers behind us.

"They're not me."

"Well, you look—" Stephen stopped himself midsentence, a pause that was at once awkward and uncharacteristic for my mother's lawyer. "You look like you're ready," he said finally.

What Stephen meant to say, I've always assumed, was that my mother looked beautiful. Or heroic, perhaps. Or courageous. Because my mother did look, at least to me, like all of those things. She seemed tired and she was pale, but looking back, I think I understand in a twisted way why at least one nineteenth-century convention of female beauty was vaguely tubercular—why, even at the end, Bram Stoker's Lucy Westenra and Mina Harker were still considered lovely. My mother had a cornflower-blue clip holding back her blond hair, and she was wearing a modest, almost schoolgirl-like green kilt she'd bought specially for the occasion. Unlike the other midwives both inside and outside the courthouse, she wore leather loafers and stockings.

But I think Stephen stopped himself because my father was present. He probably would have told my mother exactly how attractive he thought she was had the two of them been alone.

"Sure, I'm ready," my mother said. "I don't really have a choice now, do I?"

"No. Guess not."

My mother nodded, and my father wrapped his arm around her shoulders.

"It's cold out here," he said to the lawyers and me. "Let's go inside."

"Grandma's not here yet," I said, speaking to no one in particular.

"Is your grandma the type who could find her way into the courtroom?" Stephen asked.

Before I could answer, my father said he would walk with us as far as the front door of the courthouse and then wait for grandma there. And so amidst the aroma of fresh paint and poster board, the five of us made our way through a small sea of women in paisley peasant skirts and babushkas, men with beards that fell halfway down their chests, and dozens and dozens of male and female feet in heavy wool socks and sandals.

I hadn't realized that Charlotte Fugett Bedford had a sister and a brother-in-law. Somehow I had missed the detail that she had a mother.

And no one had told me that the three of them had traveled from Alabama to Vermont to sit in a bench behind Bill Tanner and his deputy and watch my mother's trial.

But when I walked into the courtroom, I knew instantly who they were. No one had to tell me. The two women had more than a vague resemblance to their dead kin, and the way the younger woman leaned into the younger man for support suggested marriage. And all three of them were wearing clothing too summery and thin for Vermont in the last week of September.

I saw them before they saw me, and so that first morning I was able to look away before our eyes met and I would have to acknowledge the sadness that had scarred their faces. Although I don't believe I had ever viewed the Fugetts or the Bedfords as possessing the sort of evil Bill Tanner embodied, somehow that summer I had managed to forget or ignore that my mother was not the victim in this tragedy, or that—in most people's eyes—she was not the only one who was suffering.

Twenty-eight possible jurors were sat by the bailiff in four rows of seven: Two of those rows were in the raised jury box itself, and two more were in wooden chairs with cushioned seats directly before it. That meant the first two rows were lower than the pair in the jury box, and so that side of the courtroom looked a bit to me like a movie theater. The seats had a downhill sort of slope.

In addition, another dozen possible jurors were seated in the two benches in the courtroom nearest the jury box, and as the morning progressed and Bill Tanner asked a seemingly endless number of questions, some of them took the place of their peers in the rows along the side of the courtroom.

The goal was to find twelve jurors and two alternates whom both Stephen Hastings and Bill Tanner would accept. Each side was allowed to strike up to six people without offering the judge a reason, which meant that if there were only one or two challenges for cause—the elimination of a possible juror for reasons as dramatic as an admitted bias, or as pedestrian as a doctor's appointment during the trial that simply could not be rescheduled—a jury could be built from that first group of twenty-eight people.

Of course, it rarely happened that way, and my mother's trial was certainly no exception. There was no limit to the number of possible jurors who could be eliminated for cause, and the lead attorneys on both sides seemed to be quite good at rooting out reasons to have people excused that would not demand they use any of their six precious preemptory strikes.

Perhaps somewhere in the files in the basement of the Orleans County Courthouse, or on a floppy disk or computer in one of the offices on the building's second or third floors, exist the names of the couple of dozen women and men who were part of that original late-September pool. Perhaps not. But many of the names of that first twenty-eight (and of the reinforcements who joined them, as one by one Stephen or Bill Tanner excused someone after eliciting yet another reason why that individual could not objectively or logistically sit in judgment upon my mother) have blurred in my mind with the names of the final fourteen.

Not the faces, however; I still know the faces and features of that final fourteen well. Moreover, I know—or at least I believe I know— exactly whom Stephen was happy to have sitting in the jury box for two weeks, and exactly who made him uncomfortable.

"Would you want people on the jury who love the idea of a home birth, or people who think it's an incredibly foolish notion?" Stephen asked my parents and me the Thursday night before the trial started. Stephen had taken my family to dinner at a French restaurant in Stowe, the sort of place that had me pulling blouses and skirts from my closet for forty minutes before I found a combination that I thought was at once appropriately elegant and sufficiently cool. Stowe was slightly closer to Reddington than Burlington, but it was still vaguely equidistant between the two, and I imagine Stephen was hoping a dinner out would rally my mother's spirits before the trial finally began.

We had finished eating and the three adults were sipping their coffee when Stephen broached the subject of the jury's configuration. As if he were a law school professor and the Danforth family a small group of students, he continued, "What do you think: Would you want a group who thought home birth was a perfectly safe proposition, or a group who thought it riskier than landing an airplane in a hurricane?"

"I suppose I'd want people who approved of home birth," my father said quickly. "They'd be more sympathetic."

"More sympathetic to Charlotte or Sibyl?"

"Sibyl," my father answered, and instantly I began to fear that the conversation was about to take one of those turns that I dreaded. I couldn't tell if my father's answer was wrong and his mistake would embarrass—and then anger—him, or if the discussion would deteriorate simply because the subject was so volatile. But I knew I didn't like the way Stephen put down his coffee cup and shrugged after my father blurted out my mother's name.

"Maybe those are the sort of people we'll want," Stephen said slowly, "but maybe not. Obviously my partners and I have gone around and around on this one. Personally, I want to see the jury stacked with people who believe home birth is a reasonable way to have a baby. But I have two partners who are quite convincing when they argue that I should try and get a group who thinks the idea of having your baby in your bedroom is a terrifically stupid stunt, a group who . . ."

"A group who what?" my mother asked Stephen when he paused.

"Forgive me, Sibyl," Stephen said, taking a deep breath before finishing his thought. "A group who thinks the idea of home birth is so . . . dangerous that Charlotte Bedford got what she asked for."

My mother tilted her head and rested the fingers of one hand on the small of her neck. I remember that all of the tables in the restaurant—filled that evening with the sort of wealthy, elderly couples who packed Vermont in the fall to watch the leaves grow yellow and gold and fantastic shades of red—seemed to become quiet around us, and suddenly I no longer even heard the tapes of classical music that had been playing throughout our meal. I heard a high ringing in my ears, and I wondered what would happen first: Would my mother cry, or would my father snap at Stephen?

I was wrong; neither occurred. I believe my father might have been about to tell Stephen angrily that his remarks were out of line, but my mother spoke first. Though tired, though unwilling to buck up in the sort of physical, visible ways the men around her wanted, my mother was still very strong.

"I don't think that would be very smart," she said, her voice soft but firm. "I don't think it will do any of us any good to make my mothers or me look like idiots."

Stephen nodded, and the music and conversation and the sound of silverware on fine china returned. "I agree. I'm just telling you what some of my peers believe," Stephen said.

My father sat back in his chair. "So I was right. You'll fill the jury with people who believe in home birth."

"I doubt I can 'fill' it with them. But if I find people who seem to think that way, I'll try and keep them." He turned to face my mother directly and continued, "I'm sorry. I was simply hoping to convey how complicated all of this is, even for me."

"Even for you," my father said. "Imagine."

"As a lawyer, Rand. That's all I meant."

"I understand."

Stephen sighed. "I've probably swallowed half my shoe already. But at the risk of putting even more in my mouth, I'll tell you something else: Right now I probably understand better who I don't want on the jury than who I do."

"And that is?" my father asked.

"Well, let's see. First of all, I'm going to try and stay away from women of childbearing age. I'm not sure they could separate themselves from the victim. And I don't want any nurses or doctors or EMTs. No volunteers from town rescue squads. The last thing we need are people who aren't nearly as knowledgeable as they think they are trying to second-guess Sibyl. And, of course, there won't be a soul on the jury who's ever been anywhere near a bad birth experience—ever had one, or seen one, or heard about one real close to home. That I can assure you."

"Will you want more men or women?" my father asked. My mother's fingers were still resting upon her neck, and although she was staring right at Stephen—and probably had been since he apologized a moment earlier—I don't think she saw him. I'm sure on some level she was listening, and I'm sure she would have jumped back into the conversation if she needed to defuse a bomb smoking between her husband and her attorney; otherwise, however, she seemed content to sit quietly and let the two men waste energy on conjecture.

"It's not as simple as a male-female thing. I wish it were. I think in this case it's more important to get smart people."

"Because of the experts?"

"Yup. A smart person will hang in there when they're hearing testimony about something like standards of care. Or what the autopsy showed—and didn't show. And smart people won't automatically assume that the State's doctors or experts have more credibility than ours."

And so when the lawyers began building a jury—asking question after question of the farmers and store clerks and elderly loggers who comprised the pool—I understood whom we wanted on the panel and whom we did not. I sat in the first row of benches directly behind my mother and Stephen and Peter Grinnell, with my father on one side of me and my grandmother on the other, and I made a list in my mind of who I hoped would be left in the end in the jury box.

A pair of law clerks from Stephen's firm and Patty Dunlevy sat with my family on our bench, but the three members of Charlotte's family had their bench to themselves. People wanted to give them their space. Otherwise there were no free seats in the courtroom.

The Danforth and Fugett family benches were in the same row, but our families were buffered by a wide aisle and the private investigator and the clerks. Only when I was studying the pool of jurors sitting along the part of the wall nearest the door was there any risk that a part of the Alabama contingent might turn a head and I'd be caught staring, or I'd have to look instantly away to avoid what I feared would be a hateful glare.

One of the few times I was watching the Fugetts, however, a moment just after the original group of twenty-eight jurors had been seated, I realized one important part of their family was absent. I leaned around my grandmother and asked the clerk beside her, a young woman I'd been told was named Laurel, "Where's Reverend Bedford?"

"He'll be testifying," she whispered, "so he's sequestered. He won't be in the courtroom until we get to the closing arguments."

"Will Foogie come?"

"Foogie?"

"The little boy," I answered, and then, remembering there were actually two little boys now, added quickly, "the older boy."

"You mean Jared, don't you? No, he won't be here. At least I wouldn't think so."

I fell back against the bench relieved. It was bad enough having to sit within ten or twelve yards of Charlotte's sister and mother; it would have been almost unendurable to watch a lonely widower with one of the two young sons he was now forced to raise on his own.

"This is no small distinction," Bill Tanner said to the jury pool, pacing slowly between his table and the high bench behind which the judge sat.

"An important part of your job will be to understand the difference between reasonable doubt and all conceivable doubt—there's a difference—and to render a verdict accordingly."

I had no idea whether Tanner was a fly fisherman, but I knew enough adult men in Reddington who fished that I imagined at the time that he was: He walked as if he were wading through shallow water, stepping high and moving with care. He was tall and thin, and in front of a jury he spoke like a grandfather. He seemed patient and methodical, the sort of fellow who would tie a fly with meticulous care and then stand happily in a river casting his line for hours.

I had heard Tanner's voice twice before on the television news, but that morning was the first time I heard it live, and the first time I heard him speak at length: It was hard to believe this pleasant man was capable of saying the terrible things about my mother he already had, or that he would soon say much worse.

His hair was mostly gray, and his face deeply lined. He often held his eyeglasses by an earpiece in one hand as he spoke, exposing deep red marks along the sides of his nose where they usually rested. I guessed he was somewhere in his late fifties.

"What about you, Mr. Goodyear? Would you feel you had to have one-hundred-percent certainty of a person's guilt before you could convict him, or would the elimination of all reasonable doubt do?" he asked.

"Nothing in this world is a one-hundred-percent sure thing," he answered. Earlier in the morning he had mentioned he was a pressman for a printer in Newport, and his fingertips were discolored by ink.

"Except taxes," Tanner said. Although he was holding his eyeglasses in one hand, he was holding a piece of paper with a grid on it in the other. The grid listed the possible jurors by row, so Tanner knew all of the people by name.

"Do you have any children, Mr. Goodyear?"

"Two boys."

"How old are they?"

"One's ten and one's seven. No, eight. He's about to turn eight. Next week."

"You're married?"

"Yup. For twelve years."

"What does your wife do?"

"She works two days a week at the school cafeteria. And the rest of the time she raises the boys."

"You grow up around here?"

"I did."

"Lucky man," he sighed. "We have here one of the most beautiful parts of the state."

"I think so."

"Where were you born?"

"Newport."

"In this very city?"

"Yup."

"Hospital?"

"Uh-huh."

"Your boys? How about that? Where were they born?"

"Same hospital."

"North Country?"

"Yup."

These days, we envision lawyers using podiums and microphones. Back then in our corner of rural Vermont, that wasn't the case. Like stage actors, the lawyers spoke loud enough to be heard, and they did it without seeming to raise their voices. They held their notes in their hands when they spoke, and if they needed a place for papers, they used their tables.

"Were the labors easy? Hard? Somewhere in between?"

"They were easy for me," Mr. Goodyear said. "I was at my wife's sister's house eating dinner one time, and in the waiting room with both our families at the other."

"Were they easy for your wife?"

"I guess they were. We got two good boys out of 'em."

"Did you and your wife consider having the boys at home?"

"You mean instead of a hospital?"

"Yes. That's exactly what I mean."

Goodyear smiled. "No, sir. I don't believe that idea even crossed our minds."

"Let's see," Tanner said. "I haven't visited with Golner. Julia Golner. How are you this morning, Mrs. Golner?"

"I'm fine."

"Do you work, Mrs. Golner? Or have you retired?"

"Oh, I stopped working seven years ago. I'm sixty-eight years old, Mr. Tanner."

"Does your husband work?"

"He passed away."

"I'm sorry. Was this recent?"

"No. Nineteen seventy-five."

"Do you have children?"

She beamed. "Seven. And fifteen grandchildren—my lucky number."

"Were you born in Vermont?"

"Yes."

"In a hospital?"

"No. I was born in nineteen thirteen. I was born before the World Wars. Both of them!"

"So you were born at home?"

"I was born in my mother and father's bedroom, in the farmhouse they lived in for years and years in Orleans."

"How about your children? Were they born at home, too?"

"No. Some were. But not all."

"Would you tell me about that?"

In a saga of live births and miscarriages that would have continued without pause for two decades had her husband not enlisted in the army in 1943, Mrs. Golner offered an informal history of labor in the Northeast Kingdom between 1932 and 1951, and its migration from home to hospital. She told the court she had had four children before the Second World War in her bedroom, and at least that many miscarriages. She had then had three children after the War, and two more "souls" who never made it through the first trimester.

Those postwar babies had arrived in hospitals: "I don't know why that was," she said. "I guess we all just decided after the War it was better that way. Safer, I guess."

"I spent three years in the Pacific. I fought on Iwo Jima."

"Wounded?"

"Nope. I was lucky," Mr. Patterson told the state's attorney. A burly man in a turtleneck and a blue sweater that clung to his bulk like a second skin, he sat with his arms folded defiantly across his chest.

"Your time in the Pacific: Is that why you say you have little . . . patience with people who opposed the war in Vietnam?"

"No. Even if I hadn't been given the opportunity to serve my country, I would expect others to step forward when asked. And we both know a lot didn't."

"Step forward."

"That's right."

"In the sixties and early seventies."

"Yes."

"Suppose there was a witness you didn't like, Mr. Patterson. Personally. Could you be fair?"

"What do you mean?"

"Well, let's say one side or the other has someone testifying who rubs you the wrong way. Would you listen to their testimony with an open mind?"

"Yes. It seems to me I would have to. It would be my duty," Mr. Patterson said, but before he had even finished speaking I knew Stephen would draw a line through the fellow's name.

When we left the courtroom for lunch, we passed by a row of women in the back bench who were starting to nurse their babies. The littlest ones had not been delivered by my mother, since she had stopped practicing almost six months earlier. But there were two babies there my mother had caught in the weeks or months before Charlotte Bedford died, bigger infants between six and nine months old. I watched them at their mothers' breasts for a moment before I saw something infinitely more interesting to me: Some of the reporters, even the female ones, were trying desperately to talk to members of the group during the recess without allowing their eyes to fall below the nursing mothers' foreheads. It was as if they were trying to interview the wall behind them.

My mother had cinnamon toast and hot chocolate for lunch in a diner, and insisted we stop by the florist on Main Street to look at the fall wreaths on display. When she spoke, she talked of the foliage that year, and the lines of cars with out-of-state plates parked in some spots along the country roads. She thought the maples were a more vibrant red than usual, and clearly this pleased her.

Stephen and his little staff never left the courthouse, with the exception of the law clerk named Laurel. She stayed with us when we went to lunch, and it seemed to me her principal responsibility was to help us push by the reporters and tell them with a smile that we had nothing to say.

"I think you're all doing very well," she told us as we stood for a moment on the sidewalk outside the flower shop's glass window. "I think you make a very good presentation as a family."

My grandmother beamed and my mother nodded, as if she found great meaning in Laurel's observation. She gave the clerk that smile she had developed like new wrinkles over the past half-year—a smile that was part incredulity and part patience. "Well, you know," she said, her voice completely serious, "we've had a lot of years to get that look just right."

Once, weeks earlier, I'd peeked out my parents' bedroom window to watch my mother greeting Stephen as he arrived at our house at the end of the day. I had heard a car pulling into our driveway, and so I'd put my homework aside and crossed the house to one of the rooms that faced the front of our home. At breakfast my father had said he wouldn't return until seven or seven-thirty that night, and I'd wanted to see who was stopping by at five in the afternoon.

It was Stephen. By the time I got to the window, my mother was already outside, strolling down the walk to greet him. She was moving slowly, with the gait of a sleepwalker, or someone preoccupied beyond reason. But I was nevertheless struck by the fact that she had left the house to meet his car: She may have lacked the giddy stride of a young girl in love, she may have been worn down by the wait for the trial, but she still had some desire to give air to those few pleasant sparks life would yet drop before her.

When Stephen emerged from his car, my mother was already there. She let him take both of her hands in his, and they stood there for a moment with the car door open, the proximity of their legs curtained from me by gray steel.

"Who has the burden of proof?" Stephen asked Lenore Rice, a young woman who worked at the Grand Union in Barton. Lenore was probably six or seven years older than I was, but she didn't look it: She was a small person with petite, barely pubescent features.

"I don't know what that is," she answered.

"Burden of proof is a legal term," Stephen began slowly, but without condescension. "We have two sides in this courtroom, the defense and the State. I represent the defense, and sitting over there, Mr. Tanner represents the State. One of us will have to prove something inside these walls over the next few weeks, and one of us won't. Am I the one who has to prove something?"

"Why, yes," she said. "Of course."

"And what would that be?"

"That your person is innocent."

Stephen nodded, and sat for a moment at the edge of the defense table. Peter handed him the grid listing by row the prospective jurors before he requested it.

"Mr. Anderson, do you agree with Miss Rice?" Stephen asked after glancing at the sheet of paper. "Do you agree that I have to prove something in these proceedings?"

"Nope."

"Why not?"

"A person is innocent until proven guilty."

"Indeed," Stephen said, standing and walking toward the first row of the panel. "That's exactly right. What do you do, Mr. Anderson?"

"I'm an electrician."

"Thank you. Don't go anywhere, we'll talk some more in a moment. Miss Rice, what do you think of what Mr. Anderson has just said? Have you changed your mind?"

"About what?"

"About whether I have to prove my client is innocent."

"Well, he says you don't."

"Actually, it's not Mr. Anderson who says I don't, it's our entire philosophy of jurisprudence. Our system of justice. In this country, a person is innocent—absolutely innocent—until proven guilty. If you are a juror, you need to begin this trial with the presumption that the defendant is innocent. Are you okay with that, Miss Rice? Can you do that?"

She looked down into her lap. "I don't know," she mumbled.

"You don't know?"

"It seems to me someone wouldn't be here if he didn't do something wrong."

Stephen turned to Judge Dorset. "Your Honor, may I approach the bench?"

The judge nodded, and both Stephen and Bill Tanner stood before the high wooden barricade and whispered with Dorset for a long moment. When they were finished, the judge murmured something to the bailiff. Tanner then retreated to his seat, and Stephen returned to the edge of his table.

"Miss Rice, you are excused. The court thanks you very much for your willingness to spend the day with us," Judge Dorset said.

The young woman stood, looking more recalcitrant than relieved, and the bailiff called juror number thirty-two to come forward from one of the rear benches to take her place. Lenore Rice was the fourth person either Stephen or Bill Tanner had not wanted to see among the final fourteen jurors, and had managed to have excused for cause.

"It's made from organic soybeans," Nancy Hallock said.

"And you use it instead of milk?" Stephen asked.

"Yes. We don't have any animal products or by-products in our house."

"No meat?"

The woman shivered. "Yuck. God, no."

"Your family are all strict vegetarians?"

"Well, my husband and I are. We don't have any children."

"May I ask how old you are?"

"You may. I'm forty-one."

"Do you plan on having children?"

"I think there are enough people on this planet, don't you? If we decide to have any children, we'll adopt them."

When I wandered into my mother's office to kiss her good night after the first day of jury selection, she was scribbling in her personal diary at her desk. She had never hidden the fact that she'd been keeping a journal for years, and the loose-leaf binders she used—thick three-ring notebooks covered with thin layers of blue fabric, just like mine—filled the lowest shelf of a bookcase behind the desk. She trusted my father and me to respect her privacy.

"Do you want more hot water before I go upstairs?" I asked, and motioned toward her half-filled mug of tea.

"No, I'm okay," she said, and she put down her pen and sat back in her chair. "You were so quiet at dinner tonight. Everything okay?"

I shrugged. "Guess so."

"What did you think of your mom's first day in court? Pretty dull stuff, isn't it?" she said, hoping to downplay the significance of what I was witnessing.

"I thought it was pretty cool."

She smiled. "At your age, you're only supposed to think rock concerts and cute boys are cool."

"They are, too."

"Have you spoken to Tom tonight?"

"Uh-huh."

"Did you tell him about today?"

"Only the things Stephen said it was okay to discuss," I lied. In actuality, I had told Tom every detail I could remember.

"Glad you're there?"

"Yeah, I am."

She put down her pen and stretched her arms over her head and behind her back, and her fingertips grazed the bookcase. In addition to her personal notebooks, the bookcase was filled with treatises on birth—books with titles like *Spiritual Midwifery* and *Heart and Hands*—and the journals in which my mother kept the medical records of her patients. I knew there were even more records in the wooden filing cabinet beside the bookcase, many of which had been taken by subpoena by the State.

"I'll bet it makes you want to be a lawyer when you grow up," she said, and she rolled her eyes.

"Or a midwife."

"Right. Or a midwife."

From where I stood I could see the lines and lines of blue ink that rolled over the white pages like waves. She wrote on the front and back of each sheet, so when the notebook was opened flat the effect was vaguely reminiscent of a very large book.

"Think this will be over soon?" I asked.

"Oh, I think so, sweetheart," my mother said, her voice tinged with concern for me. Instantly I regretted my question. "Stephen says the trial should only last two weeks."

"And I'm sure we'll win," I said, hoping to give her the impression I was so confident that—on top of everything else—she needn't worry about her fourteen-year-old daughter.

"Oh, I'm sure we will, too," she said.

"And then everything will get back to normal."

She opened her mouth to speak, and I heard in my mind the echo—*Sure, Connie, sure. Then everything will get back to normal*—but no words came out, not even a whisper. Instead she nodded, but we both knew in our hearts that Charlotte's death had changed everything forever. For my mother, nothing would ever be normal again.

SIXTEEN

They finally finished selecting the jury this afternoon. I think the lawyers would have kept asking questions into Wednesday, but the judge had heard enough by lunchtime today, and both sides agreed at three o'clock to make their picks.

Vermont is a small state, and Stephen was sure that a lot of the group would be excused because they knew me or Charlotte, but that only happened one time. And it wasn't like the guy really knew either of us. He'd gone to visit Asa's church one Sunday to see if it would be a good congregation for his family—he'd decided it wasn't—and he'd shaken Asa's hand when the pastor was greeting everyone as they filed out after the service.

There are two people on the final jury who were born at home, but that's just because they're in their sixties—they were born when it was still pretty rare up here to go to a hospital to have a baby.

There were also a couple of people in the big pool at the beginning who had had their babies at home, one who I'm pretty sure used Molly Thompson, but they were both dismissed. Behind me, I heard Rand swear under his breath when their numbers were called and they were excused, a little "Damn!" that I'm sure only Peter and I picked up, but I turned around anyway to give him a little wink that said, It's okay, it doesn't matter.

But of course it does.

Stephen doesn't want me turning around to wink at my family or look at the people behind us, but I still do sometimes. I can't help it, it's like a reflex. Sometimes I just have to see Connie. I winked once at her today, too. Just because.

I wish Connie were little again. I wish she were little and I were young—maybe not newborn little, although I did love swaddling the warm and gurgling and incredibly tiny thing she once was. I wish Connie were maybe two or three again, when she was this beautifully funky little person who loved to dance and spin and climb all over the couch like it was a mountain, and was always singing words to songs with the little twists Rand and I made up:

"Twinkle, twinkle, little moon. Won't you brighten Connie's room?"

Connie was the best hugger when she was two. Just the best. She'd wrap her little arms around my neck and squeeze and squeeze and squeeze: "Hug, Mommy!" I loved that so much.

And when Connie was two, all of this stuff I'm putting my family through right now was still years and years away. I wish it could be that way again. I wish my life weren't this record album someone gave me that's almost over, and only the first couple of songs were any good.

Does that sound selfish? I'm sorry if it does, because I don't mean to sound selfish, or like I'm this pathetic victim who's been screwed by some cosmic disc jockey or record producer. I know what mistakes I've made, I know where I've screwed up.

Sometimes this week I've turned around to look at Charlotte's family, too, at her sister and her mother. Charlotte's sister bites her nails just the way Charlotte did. She keeps her fingers straight. We made eye contact a couple of times today, and I thought she was just going to break down and sob when we did.

Seeing her face and sitting so close to her has made me feel absolutely pregnant with guilt. I feel it growing inside me, I half-expect to touch my tummy with my left hand and feel something move. A little kick. One of those hiccups.

Charlotte's sister despises me. Both she and her mom despise me. It's a terrible feeling to be despised, and alone in my room when the world is asleep—at least my world—it seems like I've earned this.

And yet the weirdest thing is, Charlotte's family probably wouldn't hate me so if I hadn't tried to save Veil. The nephew of one, the grandson of the other.

Stephen says by the time this thing is over, everyone will understand that. He says he'll make sure everyone will see that I could have let that little baby die right there inside his mother, and if I had, none of us would be here right now. He'll show them it would have been an even worse tragedy because two people would have died instead of one, and yet no one would be sitting around inside a courtroom all day long pointing fingers at everyone else.

I haven't seen Veil since he was born. Will he, too, grow up to despise me? Will he, too, blame me for killing his mother?

—*from the notebooks of* Sibyl Danforth, midwife

ALL SUMMER AND INTO THE FALL I HAD BEEN AFRAID THAT BILL TANNER could send my mother to prison and destroy my family. But it wasn't until the first Wednesday morning of the trial when I looked out the window of the courtroom and saw the gunmetal gray clouds rolling in from the northwest that I began to fear the man was sufficiently powerful to control the weather, too. The skies darkened and the room grew dim as he launched into his opening argument, and to this day the state's attorneys in Orleans County shake their heads and laugh when they tell stories of the way Bill Tanner timed his outline of the case against Sibyl Danforth to coincide with a cloudburst.

Outside of the courtroom, of course, to the shoppers on Main Street in Newport or to the leaf peepers wandering the back roads in Jay, it was just another rainy day in autumn. It was only to those of us in the third-story courtroom with the panoramic views of lake and mountains to the north that it seemed to have unnerving supernatural significance.

"No one is going to tell you that Sibyl Danforth is an evil person. No one is going to tell you that she is a cold-blooded murderer," Tanner said. "If anything, you're going to hear from the defense what a fine person she is . . . what a remarkable person she is. For all I know, they're going to tell you she's an excellent mother, the perfect wife. Maybe she is. Maybe she isn't. For your purposes, however, none of that matters. None of it.

"Sibyl Danforth has been charged with practicing medicine without a license, and she has been charged with involuntary manslaughter. No one is saying she murdered anybody. But she did kill someone. That's a fact, and that's what matters.

"A young woman is dead and buried in an Alabama cemetery because of Sibyl Danforth, and a father is faced with the daunting task of raising two small boys on his own. Imagine: Little Jared Bedford only enjoyed the unique and nurturing love of his mother for seven years. Seven short years. Even worse, his baby brother, Veil—a baby who, mercifully and miraculously, survived both Mrs. Danforth's incomprehensible negligence and her cavalier use of a kitchen knife—will never, ever know the woman who should have raised him: Charlotte Fugett Bedford."

Tanner shook his head and sighed before continuing. "Charlotte Fugett Bedford is dead because of Sibyl Danforth. Undeniably. Indisputably. Incontrovertibly. A twenty-nine-year-old woman is dead because of Sibyl Danforth's criminal recklessness. And if Mrs. Danforth is not the sort of person who would take a handgun and shoot one of you over money or drugs or . . . or in a crime of passion, it is upon her shoulders that the death of Charlotte Bedford rests. Sibyl Danforth killed her. Pure and simple: Sibyl Danforth killed her. That's why we're all here right now."

The fly fisherman looked at specific jurors as he spoke, as if he were eulogizing a river they'd once fished together that was now dry or polluted beyond use. For emphasis, he would occasionally pause and look out the window at the storm clouds, but he always seemed to turn back toward the jury when he had a particularly dramatic point he wanted to make.

"The defense is going to try and convince you that this is a complicated case with a lot of gray in it, and they are going to parade into this courtroom a whole lot of so-called experts who have probably never set foot in Vermont before. Never. But you will soon see this case isn't so complicated.

"We will show you that from the moment Charlotte and Asa Bedford sat down with Sibyl Danforth to discuss the notion of having their baby in their home, Mrs. Danforth behaved with the sort of gross irresponsibility that could only result in tragedy.

"Should Charlotte Bedford have even been allowed to have her baby in her bedroom in the first place? We will show that other mid-wives—as well as probably every single reasonable physician on this planet—would have said no. The risk was too great.

"Did Charlotte and Asa understand this risk? It is clear they did not. Either Mrs. Danforth did not appreciate the risk herself or she chose not to share her knowledge of the risk with her clients; either way, she never warned the Bedfords of the dangers of their decision.

"On the day that Charlotte Bedford went into labor, did Sibyl Danforth even demonstrate the common sense to consider the weather? No, she did not. Did a woman born and raised right here in Vermont, a woman who must know the . . . the orneriness and capriciousness and downright uncertainty of Vermont weather, discuss with the Bedfords the chance that they'd be trapped in their home in the event that some-thing went wrong? No. She did not."

The rain had not yet begun to drum against the wide glass win-dows opposite the jury box, but I noticed a few of the jurors looked past Bill Tanner at the ominous sky outside. I couldn't help but do so, too.

"And then that night," he said, "when she realized that because of her own astonishing lack of foresight she and a woman in labor were cornered in a bedroom miles and miles from the help a hospital would have provided, what did Mrs. Danforth do? She had Charlotte push . . . and push . . . and push. Hours beyond what any doctor would have allowed, she had Charlotte push. Hours beyond what a healthy woman could have endured, she had her push. Without anesthesia. Without painkillers. She had her push."

My mother moved little during the onslaught. Occasionally she turned toward the lake, and she might have been watching the whitecaps the storm had churned up, but she sat stolidly with her hands clasped before her on the table. Once in a while Stephen or Peter wrote some-thing down, but my mother never even reached for her pen. It was as if she were anesthetized, or had grown inured to hate. Although my father and I both grew flushed with rage, she seemed to be somewhere else entirely.

"Sibyl Danforth had the poor woman push for so long that she thought she had killed her! She actually believed she had had one of her mothers push for so long, so nightmarishly long, that the woman had finally died. Pushed to death, so to speak. The irony? Sibyl Danforth hadn't pushed her to death. She almost had. But not quite. Charlotte Bedford did not die from pushing. It took a ten-inch knife with a sparkling six-inch blade to do that.

"You will all see—and I am sorry beyond words to say this—when we are done, that one woman is dead because the individual sitting at that table over there took a kitchen knife and brutally gouged open Charlotte Bedford's stomach in the poor woman's own bedroom, and she did so while the woman was still breathing."

He eyed my mother and then shook his head in disgust. My mother didn't flinch, but beside me my father did. He crossed and recrossed his legs.

"This crime is appalling on many levels, but you will find two especially galling: Charlotte Bedford would not have died in a hospital. This is clear. And Charlotte Bedford would not have died had she been cared for throughout her pregnancy by a physician. Obviously, Sibyl Danforth is not a doctor. She is a midwife. And while the women who call themselves midwives claim to have all sorts of arcane knowledge, while they claim to be able to deliver babies, in reality they know little more about medicine than you or I. Sibyl Danforth has never been to medical school. She has never been to nursing school. She does not have a license to practice medicine. In fact, she has so little medical training of any kind that between six and six-thirty on the morning of March fourteenth, she couldn't even tell the difference between a living woman and a dead one! Let's face it, Sibyl Danforth is no more certified to deliver babies than the woman at the stationery store who sold me my newspaper this morning, or the teenage boy who filled my car with gasoline!"

Tanner paused to let the vision grow real in the jurors' minds: a teenage boy with acne and a baseball cap and grubby hands delivering a baby.

In the momentary silence, however, I heard the sound of a baby about to nurse in the back of the courtroom, and I was glad. An adolescent grease monkey was a powerful image, but it seemed to me it paled before a nursing newborn. The little thing behind us cried briefly with hunger, then cooed when her mother opened her blouse and she saw the breast from which she was about to eat.

When Tanner resumed, he stood up straight and rested one hand on the rail of the witness stand, then empty. "The defense might insist that this trial is about the way the medical profession has stolen the process of birth from the women to whom it rightly belongs," he said, his voice growing more animated as he approached what I assumed would be a crescendo of sorts. "Well, that's hogwash. They might argue that this trial is about the right of pregnant women to choose to have their children at home. That's hogwash, too.

"This trial is about one thing, and one thing only: Sibyl Danforth's pattern of irresponsibility and misjudgment, a pattern that led inevitably to the mistake that cost Charlotte Bedford her life. The definition of involuntary manslaughter in Vermont is clear—you have heard it from the judge—and the case before you is a horrifying but altogether perfect example: Sibyl Danforth was grossly negligent. Sibyl Danforth engaged in conduct which involved a high degree of risk of death. And on the morning of March fourteenth, 1981, she indeed caused the death of Charlotte Fugett Bedford—as the statute says, 'another human being.' "

Tanner might have been about to say more, but the storm spared him the effort: Almost on cue, perhaps a second after quoting the statute, a gust of wind slammed the first sheet of rain into the picture windows behind him with such force that it sounded like thunder and shook the glass.

I was only one of many women and men in the courtroom who gasped.

At my high school, we were allowed to miss study hall up to three times a quarter if we had a valid excuse like a doctor's appointment or—apparently—the involuntary manslaughter trial of one's girlfriend's mother. By passing on the study hall before lunch and skipping the history class that came after, Tom was able to string together almost three consecutive hours to drive up to Newport and surprise the Danforth family as we emerged from the courthouse. My parents invited Tom to join us at a restaurant, but he had brought with him sandwiches and soda and a vision of an autumn picnic for two, and they let us go our own way for an hour.

"Just don't talk to any reporters," Stephen said to us as we left the adults. "Please. In fact, don't talk to anyone . . . please."

It was still pouring, so Tom and I ate our sandwiches in the front seat of the rusty Sunbird his older brother had finished repairing but would not be picked up by its owner until the end of the week. He had double-parked beside the Newport Library, an austere brick, almost imposing monolith across Main Street from the courthouse.

During most of our lunch we didn't speak of the trial, although I don't believe either of us was explicitly or consciously avoiding the subject. He'd asked how it was going as soon as we were seated in the automobile, and I'd told him what a mean son of a bitch Bill Tanner was, but then we'd moved on to other subjects: The fact that Sadie Demerest was going to break up with Roger Stearns. The fear we had that our football team would lose its first game that Friday night to St. Johnsbury, a much bigger school with, we had to assume, a much bigger and better team. The idea that Chip Reynolds was experimenting with the little tabs of acid his older brother was always bringing back from Montreal, and our firm belief that he was headed for trouble.

The rainstorm I'd watched that morning in the courtroom had come in from the north, and Tom told me of the armies of Canadian geese he'd seen flying south before it: I imagined great honking gray Vs in the sky, and in my mind I saw them flying overhead in wave after wave. He told me his uncle had gotten his first partridge of the year that day, a quick shot up on Gary Road just before breakfast, and he laughed at his uncle's pride in shooting a bird that "probably weighed about as much as a Snickers bar."

Before we parted, as I pushed the wax paper I'd crumpled into a ball into the bottom of my brown bag, I asked him if people in school were talking about the trial.

"I know one class, senior humanities, talked about it for a good forty-five minutes this morning. Made a lot of us wish we were a year older."

"You mean in class? They talked about it in class?"

"Honest to God. Garrett Atwood told me," he said, referring to a senior basketball player who was dating my precocious friend Rollie.

"And they were talking about the trial?"

"Not so much the trial," he said, pressing the smoldering tip of his cigarette into the ashtray, "as the way it's all so . . . so tragic. Mrs. Bedford being married to a minister and all."

I don't believe the word *irony* was a part of either of our working vocabularies back then, but I knew exactly what he meant.

"Did Garrett tell you how it ended?"

"I don't think the discussion really went anywhere, except a couple of girls ended up crying."

"For Mrs. Bedford? Or her husband?"

"Both. And for you and your mom."

"That's so sad."

"The whole thing's sad. Of course, Mr. Rhymer's a smart guy, and he kept everyone from getting hysterical. But Garrett said everybody still left feeling like this is one of those horrible things we're just not meant to understand."

"What about outside of class? Were people talking about it outside of class, too?"

"Well, yeah. Because you're not in school. But let's face it, if you were there, people would probably still be talking—just not when you were around," he added.

"What are they saying?"

He shrugged. "Oh, mostly that they think it's unfair what's going on. Most girls are saying they think it's A-OK to have a baby at home, and someday they probably will."

He didn't look at me as he spoke; he stared straight at the still-smoldering butt of his cigarette, and I knew instantly he was lying. I knew it with an intuitive, instinctive conviction. I knew, in fact, that exactly the opposite was true. The girls, when they spoke of me or my mother's situation at all, were sharing their fears about childbirth in general, and their astonishment that anyone would be stupid enough to try such a thing in their home.

"Like many midwives, she was probably viewed by the village with a mixture of awe and envy, fear and respect," Stephen said, referring to a late-eighteenth-century midwife whose diary he had studied. The woman had practiced in central New Hampshire, and her two-hundred-year-old diary had been discovered and published when I was in the sixth grade. Although I had not read the book, my mother and her midwife friends had, and the woman—Priscilla Mayhew of Fullerton—had become both a small saint and a large role model in their eyes.

"That's how it's always been with midwives," he said with dignified authority, pacing calmly before the jurors. "To some people, they're witches—or, these days, strange and somehow dangerous throwbacks to another era. But in the eyes of other people, they're healers. Not surprisingly, it always seems to be the women who see them as healers, and the men who are quick to cry witch. Or shaman. Or meddler. Midwives, by their very nature and profession, have always challenged authority; they've always been a bit too independent—in the eyes of men, anyway. The history of midwifery in America is filled with the names of women lionized by their own gender and ostracized by men. Names like Anne Hutchinson. That's right, Anne Hutchinson. The first religious leader in Colonial America who was a woman was also a midwife.

"In addition to having a brilliant mind, Anne Hutchinson had the strong heart and gentle hands of a midwife. And she had followers. So what happened to Anne? The men—*the men*—of Massachusetts banished her to the rough woods that with her help would become the fine state of Rhode Island.

"Did they ask the mothers how they felt about this? No. Of course they didn't," Stephen continued, and he shook his head and smiled at the jurors, offering them a grin that said, *I'm not surprised, are you?*

I followed his gaze to the group, hoping to see that they were as disgusted as he. I couldn't tell. Vermonters would make good poker players if they ever decided to give up military whist, and this particular batch of farmers and florists, schoolteachers and chimney sweeps, loggers and secretaries and journeyman carpenters was not atypical: They sat unmoving, many with their hands in their laps, their faces almost uniformly reserved, businesslike, and indecipherable.

There were seven women and five men on the jury. Both alternates were women, and so the box looked deceptively female. No one in the group had ever tried to have a baby at home, although I knew two of the three older women on the jury had themselves been born there. There were no doctors or nurses in the box, as Stephen desired, but obviously there were no midwives either, or people who were even related to midwives.

One man knew one midwife, but not very well, and another fellow—the part-time chimney sweep and part-time roofer—scraped the creosote regularly from the chimneys in one midwife's house. But he couldn't recall the two of them ever discussing birth while he was there.

Nobody on the jury worked at food co-ops or frequented natural-food grocery stores. Nobody said they had ever lived on communes.

There was one woman of childbearing age on the jury, the principal demographic Stephen was hoping to avoid. She was a woman in her late twenties with stylish red hair and the sort of makeup one usually saw in Vermont only on tourists visiting from New York City. She was a mother with children three and six years old, and plans to have more. She worked as a secretary at a ski resort, but none of us thought she did it for the money. Moreover, her grandfather had been a physician, and so she worried Stephen as much as anyone on the jury. She was smart, articulate, and properly—or improperly—inspired, she was the sort who could dominate deliberations.

Unfortunately, there had been panelists far worse from our perspective, and so she had stayed.

Stephen held up Priscilla Mayhew's diary for the group again, a hardcover book with a glossy dust jacket. There was a painting of a wooden birthing stool on the front, which was a source of endless frustration for my mother. Apparently it was highly unlikely Priscilla Mayhew had ever used such a thing, and a careful reading of the diary made that clear.

"Now, by the standards of late-twentieth-century America, was Mrs. Mayhew's maternal mortality rate high?" Stephen asked the jury rhetorically.

"Yes. By our standards it was. By our standards it was unacceptably high. Mrs. Mayhew witnessed one maternal death for every one hundred and ninety-two happy, healthy babies she delivered. Roughly two hundred years later, in 1981, barely one in ten thousand mothers dies while giving birth. And yet as recently as 1930, as recently as fifty years ago, in the United States one woman in one hundred and fifty died as a result of childbirth. One out of one hundred and fifty. You can look it up at the National Center for Health Statistics. Is there an irony here? You bet.

"In the United States in 1930, most of those women were laboring in hospitals, and they were laboring in the care of physicians.

"In other words, Priscilla Mayhew, eighteenth-century midwife, had a dramatically lower mortality rate than physicians practicing as recently as 1930.

"And while obstetrics has made impressive leaps in the last fifty years, the statistics show that today a planned home birth is every bit as safe as a hospital one—for babies as well as for mothers," Stephen said, striding toward the table where my mother and Peter were sitting. Peter handed him a piece of paper with columns of figures.

"The numbers in this research may surprise you, but here they are. In a recent study, one-point-three babies died out of every one thousand born at home, while one-point-seven died out of every one thousand born in some Minnesota hospitals . . . or two-point-four in one particular New York State hospital.

"My point? The people who are prosecuting Mrs. Danforth are going to be insisting that home birth is not merely irresponsible, it's insane. Well, you're going to see that they're wrong. It may not be the right choice for some women, but it's no more dangerous for most than a hospital birth. Let's face it, women have been having babies in their homes since, well, since the beginning of time. And until recently, they were cared for by the likes of Priscilla Mayhew: knowledgeable, tireless, loving midwives. Women who dedicated their lives to their sisters in labor. Who were these women?

"There's one sitting right before you. Sibyl Danforth. As you know, Sibyl Danforth is a midwife. You will learn that she is a knowledgeable midwife. A tireless midwife. A loving midwife.

"Most important, you will learn that she is an excellent midwife.

"You will learn that statistically her babies did every bit as well as babies born at North Country Hospital, and her mothers actually did better. That's right, her mothers did better. They had fewer episiotomies, fewer lacerations, and fewer surgical interventions," he said, meaning cesarean sections. He had explained to my family that he was going to use euphemisms wherever possible in the beginning—words like *lacerations,* for example, instead of *perineal tears*—and he was going to avoid the word *cesarean* at all costs. That word, and all it connoted, would become a fixture in the trial soon enough, he had said.

"In all of her years of delivering babies and tending to mothers, only one woman died. Charlotte Bedford.

"And please understand, we are not going to tell you that her death isn't a tragedy. It is, my God, of course it is," Stephen said, and he ran his hand over the lacquered wood at the edge of the court reporter's desk. Almost all of the wood in the courtroom was so sleek that it shined, especially the dark amber posts that bordered the doors like Doric columns.

"And no one is sadder about that fact than Sibyl Danforth. Is Charlotte Bedford's family devastated by the loss? Yes. Any family would be. But Sibyl Danforth is devastated, too. After all, Sibyl Danforth saw her die. She was there, she was present in the room. She saw the woman die.

"But Sibyl Danforth did not kill her, and that is what this case is all about," he said, and he paused. For a long moment he stood perfectly still before the jury box in his banker's gray, one-click-above business suit, unmoving. His back was absolutely straight, his hands were at his sides, and for the first time that day I was reminded that Stephen was a war veteran.

And then abruptly he spread both arms to his sides, and with a sudden flourish brought them down hard onto the rail before him, so near to one juror that the young man flinched when they hit.

"For God's sake, Sibyl Danforth didn't kill someone," Stephen said, "she saved someone. Sibyl Danforth didn't take the life of one young woman that morning in Lawson, she saved the life of one baby boy. That's what happened, that's the truth: She rescued a baby from his dead mother.

"The State, of course, is claiming otherwise, insisting that Charlotte Bedford was alive when Sibyl Danforth performed the rescue. Where did this allegation come from? The opinion of a terrified, exhausted, and naive twenty-two-year-old woman, that's where: a woman who hadn't yet seen a dozen births, but had just endured the drama of her young life. The State is going to ask you to take the word of this twenty-two-year-old apprentice over that of the defendant, an experienced midwife who has safely delivered over five hundred babies. A woman who probably knows more about cardiopulmonary resuscitation and emergency medical treatment than most paramedics.

"Make no mistake: Sibyl Danforth knows about birth, but she also knows about death. She is too well trained to confuse a live person with a dead one. Charlotte Fugett Bedford was dead when Sibyl Danforth saved the life of the child in her womb."

He turned toward my mother and pointed at her: "This woman isn't a felon, she's a hero! Her actions weren't criminally negligent, they were courageous! She's courageous!"

It hadn't rained since just before lunch, but the skies showed no signs of clearing. Stephen paced toward the window, looked briefly at the clouds, and then stared at the jury from across the courtroom.

"There are risks to birth, and there are risks to home birth," he said, his voice even, almost wistful. "You know that, and so did Charlotte

Bedford. Both she and her husband knew the risks. The State insists that Mrs. Danforth did not share with them the risks. We will show you the State is wrong.

"The State says what Mrs. Danforth did was practice medicine without a license. We will show you that she did only what any decent and courageous person—perhaps any of you—would do, given the same horrifying choice: Two deaths. Or one.

"Finally, the State is going to tell you that Charlotte wouldn't have died had she labored in a hospital. We'll never know that. But it doesn't matter. It doesn't matter because Charlotte Bedford made the informed decision to have her baby at home. And you will see that when Charlotte Bedford's labor failed to progress the way my client would have liked, my client indeed did everything in her power to get the woman to a hospital. Everything. Unfortunately, ice and wind and rain conspired against her.

"Charlotte Bedford's death is a tragedy. We know that. The State knows that. But given Charlotte and Asa Bedford's desire to have their child at home, a right protected by the state of Vermont, it was unavoidable—as you will see.

"The only reason my client is even on trial is because we have doctors in this state who want to see home birth disappear as an option; they want the whole idea to go away. They want to see every baby in this state born in a hospital. The whole idea that a midwife can do what they do—and do it better—drives some of them crazy, and so they're persecuting my client. A woman who is an excellent midwife. And I use the word *persecute* advisedly: They're not just prosecuting Sibyl Danforth, they're persecuting her. Her and her . . . kind.

"Doctors are doing now to Sibyl Danforth exactly what men have done to midwives for centuries, since the days when Anne Hutchinson was exiled from Massachusetts. They're trying to drive Sibyl Danforth away. And they're trying to do it by charging her with crimes she didn't commit."

He nodded at the judge and then murmured a soft thank you to the jury. He then took his seat beside my mother and rested his chin in his hand.

At the time I thought it had been a powerful and impressive argument, and although almost two weeks of testimony still loomed, I certainly would have resolved to acquit my mother of all charges had I been sitting in the jury box. But there was something gnawing at me when Stephen sat down, and it wasn't until my family was driving home and I was alone with my thoughts in the backseat of the car that I figured out what it was: Although Stephen had said in a variety of eloquent ways that my mother did not kill Charlotte Bedford, he never did say exactly why the poor woman had died.

S E V E N T E E N

I could probably figure out roughly the number of times I've reread what I wrote on March 15. I'd just have to count on a calendar the number of days that have passed since then to get a good estimate, because few days have gone by when I haven't looked at that entry. I think I started writing about four-thirty in the morning because I couldn't sleep, and I don't think I stopped until Rand got up a couple hours later. It was the Saturday we met Stephen.

That entry's like a car accident to me. I'm drawn to it, I find myself staring at the words.

When Stephen and Bill Tanner were giving their opening arguments today, they each had their own versions of what happened, and I kept thinking of mine—what I wrote on the fifteenth. After all this time, it seems to me that mine's become just one more version, too. I have a version, and Asa has a version, and Anne has a version. And we expect these twelve people to make some decision about what really happened, when even we can't agree.

Did I really love catching babies once in my life? God, I know I did, because I did it for years. And my diary is filled with the ways I loved it; I can run my fingers over the words —my words. But I haven't caught a baby in months now, I haven't felt a mother's surge while she's in labor since the spring.

And I just can't remember anymore what it felt like.

All that pleasure I once experienced has gotten to be like pain, the sort of sensation you just don't remember very well when it's over and done with. Very few of us really remember pain when it's gone; we can't recall how awful it was. That's what all the pleasure I once got from birth has become: a vague word that doesn't mean very much.

Next week I'm going to sit on the witness stand and I'm going to tell everyone what I think happened, and I'll probably find it in me to be really cool and together about it. I'm sure I'll be every bit as confident about what happened as Stephen wants me to be, because that's what I have to do now for my family.

But the truth of the matter is, I just don't have any idea anymore what really happened.

—from the notebooks of SIBYL DANFORTH, MIDWIFE

IN THE WEEKS BEFORE MY MOTHER'S TRIAL AND THE WEEKS OF THE TRIAL itself, it was all my parents could do to take care of themselves. Their teenage daughter was certainly not the lowest priority in their lives, but, understandably, their attention was not focused upon me.

During the nights the trial was under way, I was supposed to be home in my room doing the sort of reading that the adults around me had concluded did not demand either class discussion or an academic's explanation. The school's guidance counselor had met with my teachers and my mother the week before the trial began, and everyone had agreed I'd try and keep up with my English and history, and then catch up in math and science and French when all this had passed.

Looking back, I'm astonished that anyone would have demanded such a thing. The adults were exhausted after each day in court, and so was I: After watching my mother savagely attacked for six to eight hours, I was in no condition to work.

Likewise, my parents were too tired to discipline me, too spent to even remind me that I was supposed to be doing my homework.

Consequently, I spent a good part of the night after the opening arguments, the first Wednesday of the trial, in the McKennas' barn with Rollie and Tom and Garrett Atwood. The four of us were so stoned by ten o'clock that we were actually cupping our hands around the snout of

poor Witch Grass and trying to blow the dope we'd just held in our own lungs into hers.

The horse got a little giddy, but not like us. The day's rain had left the inside of the barn damp, but Tom and Garrett had the testosterone-driven insight to bring blankets with them as well as marijuana, and Tom and I curled up to neck in one corner of the barn, while Rollie and Garrett found a nook of their own. Most of the clouds had moved on to the east, and a magnificent harvest moon lit the sky through the few that remained.

By the time I staggered home shortly before midnight, the only lights on in our house were upstairs in my parents' bedroom. I assumed they were waiting up for me, and would descend upon me the moment I opened the front door. And so with the inspired logic of a stoned teenager, I wandered around to the back of our home and pulled open the storm window on the side of my mother's office. I'd always suspected by the way my father surrounded the metal edges with caulking and Mortite each fall that the storm window didn't close properly, and I was right. It was easy to open it from the outside, and easy to pull myself over the ledge and crawl into the room.

Beside the window was my mother's desk, and in the moonlight I could see that one of her notebooks was open upon it. Earlier that evening she had apparently been writing.

I pushed shut the door, pressing it silently into its frame so no light would escape when I switched on the desk lamp. Had I not been stoned, I like to believe I would have respected my mother's privacy and left her diary alone, but I can't say for sure that's the case. And regardless of whether drugs can or should excuse bad behavior, there's no question they can often explain it. Hunched over the desk, I started to read, and when I saw what my mother had written about March 15, I flipped back the pages a full half a year.

In my parents' minds, I hadn't come home until two in the morning, because that was the time I finally stopped reading and decided to come upstairs. And though their room seemed silent when I started up the steps, their door opened the moment I reached the landing, and I realized they were both awake.

Had my mother not been on trial that moment, I probably would

have been grounded through Thanksgiving. But she was on trial, and as angry as my parents were at me for worrying them and behaving irresponsibly, it was clear that they attributed my behavior to the strain of the trial and the long days spent in court. They blamed themselves more than me and took some comfort in the knowledge that I'd been no farther from home the whole time than Rollie's barn, and I'd been there with a group of other kids.

We were all cranky at breakfast the next morning from too little sleep, and only I had an appetite, but otherwise Thursday began the way the rest of the week had: My parents discussed what Stephen had said was likely to occur that day in the courthouse, and I listened and learned and worried.

The first witness Bill Tanner put on the stand wasn't a state trooper or doctor; it wasn't the medical examiner or a midwife.

It was a weatherman. The first person I saw testify under oath was the voice of Vermont Public Radio's twice-daily "Eye on the Sky," the principal source of weather information back then for most of us in the Northeast Kingdom. The fellow was shorter than I had imagined, but he was also much cuter. Listening to his voice in the car or some days over breakfast, I'd always envisioned a tall geeky man with glasses, when in reality he was a strong, stocky fellow with wavy blond hair and apparently perfect eyesight.

He couldn't have testified for more than twenty minutes; he was probably gone from the courtroom by nine-thirty. I was fascinated by the way one bailiff led him into the room and another swore him in. Tanner then made sure everyone on the jury understood that this man was probably Vermont's foremost expert on weather—a meteorologist who not only forecast the weather but also taught meteorology at a college in the northern corner of the state—and he'd spent all of March 12 and 13 warning his listeners about the rains and the cold that were approaching, and the tremendous likelihood that highways would freeze.

"Did you ever suggest that people should stay off the roads?" Tanner asked him.

"I did," he answered. "Wednesday afternoon and all Thursday I said the storm would be nasty and there would be lots of black ice. I said the conditions would be extremely hazardous."

Then for good measure Tanner played the weatherman's two-minute forecast from Thursday the thirteenth's lunchtime edition of the "Eye on the Sky," and we heard a taped version of the fellow saying exactly that.

"Her body was under a sheet, and it was pulled up to her neck," said Leland Rhodes, the state trooper who to this day comes to mind whenever I see a trooper's green car fly past me on the interstate. He sat on the stand with his shoulders straight and his wide-brimmed trooper's hat in his lap. His uniform was so crisp and well ironed that the fabric looked as unbending as the clothes painted on plastic dolls. Whatever distrust people have these days for police officers was untapped in our small corner of the Kingdom in 1981, and Rhodes was a powerfully honest figure.

Besides, as Tanner had gone to great pains to make clear to the jury, Rhodes had no reason to exaggerate or to lie.

"You knew she was dead?" Tanner asked.

"We knew from the radio call that she was dead before we arrived."

"The dispatcher had informed you?"

"That's right."

"Describe the condition of the bedroom," Tanner said, and beside me my grandmother flinched.

Before Rhodes could begin, however, Stephen stood to object: "Your Honor, this line of questioning is completely gratuitous."

Judge Dorset shook his head and said he would allow it. With the help of an occasional question from the state's attorney, Rhodes then told the jury what he had seen when he arrived at the Bedfords'. His voice remained forceful but calm, even when he was recalling particularly grisly details, and he spoke for close to an hour before he finished and Stephen was allowed a cross-examination.

Rhodes began with his discovery of the way my mother's station wagon was lodged in a snowbank, and how he and his partner had to walk slowly across the yard to the front door: They had thought the grass would offer better footing than the bluestone glazed over with ice.

No one answered the door when they knocked, but they had expected that, and they let themselves in and shouted up the stairs from the front hall. My mother called from the bedroom to join them on the second floor.

Although Rhodes noted that his watch said seven thirty-four, the drapes were still drawn in the bedroom, and only the floor lamp in the corner was on. The room, in his opinion, was depressing and dim and quiet except for Asa Bedford's hiccuplike sobs.

He said Anne Austin was seated in a chair against one wall, rocking the baby in her arms. He thought the baby was asleep. Asa was sitting on the bed by his wife, his body partway hunched over hers, and my mother was sitting behind him, rubbing his shoulders as he cried.

Rhodes usually spoke directly to the jury or to Tanner. After watching other witnesses over the next week and a half, it became apparent even to me that Rhodes—like many police officers—testified often and was comfortable in the witness stand.

"Tell us about the items you found in the room," Tanner suggested, and Rhodes obliged. He began with the basics of any home birth, the sorts of things that might just as easily have peppered the aftermath of an experience my mother would have viewed as exquisitely beautiful: A box of fresh sanitary pads, and a wastebasket filled with used ones. A rectal thermometer. A bulb syringe, still partially filled with mucus. An opened tube of a jelly lubricant. A glass of water with a straw in it. Metal clamps. A Dixie cup of orange juice. Scissors. A pie plate in which the placenta would have been received. A needle. A vial of Pitocin. Paper towels. Three brown paper grocery bags in which the Bedfords had sterilized the sheets and blankets and towels they had carried into the bedroom, and then all of those linens themselves, some folded and fresh, some dark red with dried blood.

He said he saw a pillow that he imagined belonged on a couch downstairs, because it was such a deep crimson it didn't match anything in the bedroom, but then he realized the pillow was soggy with blood. A moment later he noticed an empty packet of sutures on the nightstand, and the blood on the sheet upon Mrs. Bedford, some of the patches so thick that Rhodes said they looked more like scabs than stains.

"Did you see the knife?" Tanner asked.

"Not right away."

"Why not?"

"It had been removed from the bedroom."

"Do you know who removed it?"

"Mrs. Danforth said she did."

"Where did she take it?"

"We found it in the kitchen."

"Did she tell you why she brought it there?"

"She said she didn't want the woman's husband to have to continue looking at it."

"What condition was the knife in?"

"It was completely clean. All the blood and tissue were gone from the blade, and there were still soap bubbles in the sink."

Tanner then strolled back to his table, and his deputy handed him a clear acetate filled with handwritten papers. At the table before me Stephen reached for what I assumed was a photocopy of the same document.

He brought the acetate forward to Rhodes and said, "Let me show you what has been marked State's seventeen for identification. Do you recognize it?"

"I do. It's the statement Corporal Tilley and I took from Mrs. Danforth the night of the incident."

Tanner nodded, and moved for the admission of the statement into evidence. Stephen immediately objected, arguing as he had in a motion that summer that the statement was inadmissible because it had been taken without an attorney present. But he was overruled because in the judge's opinion the issue had already been resolved, and Rhodes took the court through what my mother had told the troopers that very first night.

"Did Anne Austin say anything to you that might have led you to believe Sibyl was responsible for Mrs. Bedford's death?" Stephen asked Rhodes shortly before lunch.

"Do you mean the morning we got there?"

"Yes, I mean that morning."

"No."

"What about Asa Bedford? Did he tell you he thought my client had done something . . . wrong?"

"No."

"Could he have? Did he have an opportunity?"

"I guess."

"But he didn't."

"No."

"Not even when you two were alone in the kitchen around ten after eight."

"No."

Stephen stared at him but remained silent, and allowed the trooper's answers to linger in the room a long moment.

Once when Leland Rhodes was testifying, as he and Stephen were arguing over whether the trooper had even viewed the Bedfords' house as a crime scene when he first arrived, Charlotte's sister began to sob. These were not unobtrusive tears, these were the sorts of whimpers that left unchecked would grow loud.

Almost simultaneously Stephen and Tanner approached the bench, and for a short moment the judge and the lawyers whispered with their backs to us. When they were through and the lawyers had returned to their tables, Judge Dorset said to the courtroom, his eyes roaming from one side to the other, that he understood well the way trials tend to provoke strong emotions, but everyone present needed to keep their feelings to themselves, and anyone who couldn't would be asked to leave the courtroom.

Charlotte's brother-in-law hugged his wife against his chest with one arm, and slowly she settled down. Stephen and the trooper resumed their debate, and although my mother was absolutely convinced that the idea hadn't even crossed Rhodes's mind that morning that a crime might have occurred, the trooper just kept repeating, "A woman was dead, and I knew the medical examiner would be the one to determine the cause of death."

Later that day Peter Grinnell told me that as pleased as Stephen had been when Charlotte's sister finally quieted down, Bill Tanner was probably even happier: The last thing the prosecution wanted was a mistrial because some family member couldn't stop crying.

Two weeks before the trial began, I listened to my mother on the phone with Stephen Hastings. It was late: The dinner plates were tucked in the dishwasher, my father was upstairs in bed. My mother had already taken a bath.

"Sure, I've met male midwives," she was saying, and I wondered if she knew I was nearby. She was curled up on the couch in the den in a cotton nightgown, and I'd come downstairs for a history book I'd left on the kitchen counter.

"No, not anymore," she continued. "I don't think there are any more right now in Vermont or New Hampshire. The few there were went on to other things."

I might have gotten the textbook and then left, but I heard her giggle, and the sound of her laughter had become so rare that I was unable to leave without hearing more.

"You'd be terrible, Stephen, just god-awful. You view breasts like a teenager. I hate to think of the way you'd handle a prenatal! You'd have too much fun . . . Yes, but it's not that kind of fun . . . Maybe someday I will, sure . . . With books and pictures . . . With books and pictures only . . ."

I'd seen my mother flirt lightly with the men she and my father had known for years, the male halves of the couples that formed their circle of friends, but I'd never imagined her flirting with one on the phone. Perhaps because my father was absent, perhaps because she was wearing a thin, almost transparent nightgown, this seemed more illicit to me, and I found myself frozen in something like wonder.

"It's not an aphrodisiac, I promise. I don't think male ob-gyns go home hot and bothered, do you? . . . Well, you're a pervert . . . Then maybe you're all perverts! But I don't really think so. Fortunately, the kind of men who become midwives or ob-gyns don't have your uniquely weird one-track mind," she said, and for a brief moment her voice had the sparkle that once brightened most of her conversations.

"Hold on, will you, Stephen?" she said suddenly. "Connie? Is that you, sweetie?"

I stood perfectly still until she started speaking again. When she did, finally, I turned and tiptoed back up the stairs as fast as I could.

Perhaps because I had a vision in my mind of how most of my mother's midwife friends dressed—the jeans and the sweaters, the big boots and the sandals, the endless number of peasant skirts that must have come from walk-in closets the size of bedrooms—I was unprepared for the two women who testified just after lunch: a midwife, followed by an ob-gyn who had once been a midwife.

The midwife, Kimberly Martin, even looked like a doctor to me. She was wearing a woman's blue business suit, and she had short, fashionably teased hair. It was easy to see her in loose hospital scrubs.

I also noticed she had an engagement ring on her finger but no wedding band, which surprised me as well: She was probably a good ten years older than my mother, and apparently about to be married.

"How long have you been a certified nurse-midwife?" Tanner asked her.

"Fourteen years."

"Would you tell us what it means to be a certified nurse-midwife?"

"First of all, we're all registered nurses. That's basic. We have formal medical training. Secondly, we've all graduated from one of two dozen advanced-education programs around the country that focus on women's health care and midwifery. Third, we've all passed the certification exam given by the American College of Nurse-Midwives. Finally—and personally, I believe this is very important—we all meet the requirements of the health agencies or medical boards of the state where we practice."

"And you have still more training, don't you?"

"Well, yes, I have a master's. From Marquette."

"Are you a member of the American College of Nurse-Midwives?"

"I am. This year I'm also part of the Division of Accreditation."

Tanner smiled as if he was pleasantly surprised, and I wondered if he hadn't known this detail. "How many nurse-midwives are there in this country?" he asked.

"About twenty-five hundred."

"Do most nurse-midwives deliver babies at home?"

"Oh, no, just the opposite's true. The vast, vast majority of us work in hospitals or birthing centers—almost ninety-five percent of us."

"What about you?"

"I have delivered babies at home, but I haven't since I was much younger. I prefer birthing rooms in hospitals."

"Why did you stop delivering babies at home?"

"In my opinion, it's needlessly risky."

"Did you have a bad experience?"

"Thank God, I didn't."

"What made you think it was dangerous?"

"Education. The more I learned about obstetrics, the more I realized that allowing a woman to have a baby at home exposed everyone—mother and infant—to completely unnecessary hazards."

◆   ◆   ◆

"You said roughly ninety-five percent of nurse-midwives work in hospitals and birthing centers. So that means roughly five percent don't?" Stephen asked Kimberly Martin.

"Yes."

"That five percent: Do they work in homes?"

"Yes."

"Do they have a higher infant mortality rate than the rest of the group?"

"No, they don't."

"About the same?"

"The numbers are small, so it's hard to make a statistical comparison."

"Bearing in mind the numbers are small: About the same?"

"Yes."

"How about maternal mortality? Do you see a greater incidence of maternal mortality among midwives delivering babies at home?"

"No."

"In fact, did any nurse-midwife in your organization see any woman die in home childbirth last year?"

"I don't think so. But that doesn't diminish—"

"In fact, none died, Miss Martin," Stephen said, cutting the woman off before she could elaborate on her answer. "Did you know Bell Weber?" he then asked.

"I did."

"Would you tell us who she was?"

"She was a nurse-midwife. She died this summer in a car accident."

"Did she deliver babies at home?"

Martin nodded. "In Maryland."

"Was she a member of your group?"

"Until she died."

"Was she on the Division of Accreditation with you?"

"Yes."

"Was she on any other committees for the American College of Nurse-Midwives?"

"She was chairing the home birth committee."

"Your organization has a home birth committee? Really?"

The midwife looked annoyed with Stephen, disgusted at the flip-pant way he'd asked the question. "Obviously we have such a commit-tee."

"Is that because some midwives in your group still choose to prac-tice there?"

"Yes."

Stephen nodded. "Does the American College of Nurse-Midwives formally oppose home birth?"

"No."

"Thank you."

Kimberly Martin was followed by another woman who had once caught babies in people's bedrooms, and then, apparently, decided this wasn't a particularly good idea. A few minutes after she began answering Bill Tanner's questions, I must have looked worried or nervous, because Patty Dunlevy turned to me and whispered that we had experts, too, and ours would be every bit as impressive as these people.

But that afternoon it was hard for me to believe we'd have anyone as accomplished as Dr. Jean Gerson. Thirty years earlier Jean had been a young midwife delivering babies at home; now she was an ob-gyn affiliated with a teaching hospital in Boston, a faculty member at Boston University's School of Medicine, and the author of two books on prenatal care.

She had also written extensively about the history of birth in Amer-ica. It was she who reminded us early in her testimony that while labor is natural, it's dangerous: "Let's face it," she had added, "there was a time when women and babies died all the time in labor."

Dr. Gerson had reviewed the medical history Charlotte Bedford had supplied my mother the summer Veil was conceived, and she had examined the records my mother had kept, charting the woman's progress. And she told the jury that no responsible person, doctor or midwife, would have allowed Charlotte Bedford to labor at home. It was clear based on her first labor that she was a poor candidate for home birth, and it was evident during the pregnancy that she was too frail for the ordeal. She wasn't gaining enough weight, and she was anemic.

Moreover, Dr. Gerson was positively telegenic. She was a hand-some, dignified woman who smiled when she spoke, the sort of person who was instantly likable at even the sort of distance—figurative as well as literal—that separated defense and prosecution tables in a courtroom. Years later when I was in medical school, I would recall her face and her voice, and I would find myself wishing I had gone to B.U.

Ironically, a part of my mother's defense was the fact that Charlotte was indeed an imperfect candidate for a home birth, but not because she was anemic: Stephen planned on making an issue of the fact that Charlotte had been treated for hypertension in Alabama but had never shared this information with my mother. And so when he stood to begin his cross-examination of Dr. Gerson at the end of the day, the sun so far to the west that the courtroom was lit almost solely by the big chandelier and the sconces along the walls, we all expected the two would have a brief and perfunctory conversation.

"Are many pregnant women anemic?" Stephen asked her, and I was surprised by the energy that still filled his voice. It may have been because I had been up so late the night before, and it may have been due to the stress, but I was exhausted. I couldn't imagine where Stephen got his strength.

"I wouldn't say many are 'anemic,' but I would say that many experience some small degree of anemia," she answered.

"Why is that?"

"When a woman is pregnant, her blood volume increases. Sometimes it increases by as much as half. And so there's a natural dilution, and a natural anemia."

"Is it treatable?"

"Yes."

"How?"

A newborn baby in the back of the courtroom started to whine and fuss, and I heard the sound of the long zipper on the front of his mother's dress. I saw many of the jurors glance reflexively in the woman's direction, and then Judge Dorset looked that way, too. Almost instantly all of the men turned away when they saw the woman place the nipple on her full breast into the infant's mouth, deciding to stare intently at Stephen or the doctor instead.

"Iron tablets. Ferrous sulfate, usually."

"Any side effects?"

"Indigestion sometimes. Often constipation."

"You said you've reviewed how Sibyl treated Charlotte Bedford's anemia, correct?" Stephen asked.

"That's right."

"What did Sibyl do?"

"She had her take iron tablets."

"Did her condition improve?"

"Not enough to merit—"

"Did Charlotte Bedford's condition improve?"

Dr. Gerson offered a broad smile that suggested to me—and I have to imagine to the jury as well—that she wouldn't stoop to Stephen's level of discourtesy and debate. If he wanted to interrupt her and cut her off, her smile said, fine. It made no difference to her.

"Yes," she said.

Stephen asked the court officer who was standing beside the rolling cart upon which Bill Tanner was piling his evidence for the medical records the State had just entered. He then handed the physician two sheets of paper lined with boxes and graphs.

"Do you recognize these?"

"They're the records your midwife kept of the deceased."

"These are the records you examined?"

"A part of them, yes."

"What are their dates?"

She adjusted her eyeglasses slightly and then answered, "One is from September fifteenth, 1980, and one is from February twelfth, 1981."

"I want to focus on the hematocrit values," Stephen said, referring to the term the medical community uses to describe the percentage of blood occupied by red corpuscles. All of us in the courtroom had learned the term during the first part of Dr. Gerson's testimony. "What was Charlotte Bedford's hematocrit value in September?"

"Thirty-one percent."

"What is it normally?"

"Oh, around forty-two in most women. Slightly lower in a pregnant woman."

"How about February? What was the woman's hematocrit in February?"

"Thirty-five."

"Is that an improvement?"

"A slight one."

"When one of your patients—a pregnant woman—has a hematocrit value of thirty-five, do you anticipate a bad outcome?"

"That's an odd question, and I'm not sure it's relevant. After all, I deliver babies in hospitals. If you mean, would it affect my handling of the woman's preg—"

"I'll repeat the question: Would you anticipate a bad outcome?"

Dr. Gerson was silent for a moment. Finally she said simply, "No."

"Thank you."

"You're welcome."

Stephen paced toward the windows with his hands behind his back. When he had put some distance between himself and the witness, he turned back toward her and asked, "You told us earlier that Charlotte Bedford's blood pressure was slightly higher than normal. Am I correct?"

"Yes."

"How would you have treated it?"

"I would have watched it very carefully. Perhaps placed her on bed rest. I don't know if I would have prescribed an antihypertensive. I might have."

"Would you have looked for protein in the urine?"

"Yes indeed."

"Based on those records, did Sibyl?"

"Apparently."

"Thank you. Is there any indication in Charlotte Bedford's medical records that she had ever been treated for hypertension in the past?"

"I didn't see any."

Slowly Stephen began to walk back toward her. I'd seen him do this enough during the day that I knew it was all part of a strategy of irritation and intimidation: He was about to invade the good doctor's personal space, practically leaning into the witness box with her.

"Am I correct that there's a box on the form that says 'Patient's History'?" he asked as he approached.

"Yes, there is."

"And it lists a variety of . . . conditions?"

"It does."

"What has been circled in the box?"

The doctor looked at the form and then read from it, "Bladder infections. German measles." When she looked up, Stephen was directly beside her, standing catty-corner so the jury could see both of their faces.

"That's it?"

"That's right."

"Have the words 'high blood pressure' been circled?"

"No."

He nodded and prepared for the kill. Sometimes, of course, even the best hunter misses his mark; sometimes the lion charges abruptly and flusters even the coolest rifleman. This would be one of those moments. And while Stephen would ask to have Dr. Gerson's remarks stricken from the record, and while the judge would agree, the jury had not missed what occurred and I could not imagine they would forget it when they were deciding my mother's fate.

"There is no indication that Charlotte Bedford shared her history of high blood pressure with Sibyl, is there, Doctor?"

"Bottom line, Counsel," the doctor said, speaking quickly but calmly, her voice gently condescending, "is that the records show the poor woman had symptoms of both anemia and high blood pressure. Both. No doctor or midwife in her right mind would ever have allowed that woman to labor at home."

We drove home Thursday night with the car's heater on, and I sat in the backseat with my knees curled up to my chest and my coat draped over me like a blanket. The heater in my mother's car could still warm the car like a woodstove, but during the previous winter it had developed a tendency to rattle, as if a piece of thick paper were caught somewhere in a vent.

My parents said little to each other, as they had most of the week. I imagine they were too spent to talk, and even if they had the energy, I doubt they would have known what to say. Occasionally my father would try and cheer up my mother by observing how Stephen had done a fine job taking apart one witness, or how the damaging testimony of another would be negated when Stephen began our defense.

Usually my mother would just mumble her agreement and stare at the trees we could see in the twilight.

When we got home, however, there were glass vases of roses awaiting my mother on the kitchen counters: a bunch of red ones, a bunch of yellow, a bunch of pink. My father had had them delivered during the day, and each vase had a large card beside it he'd made himself with old photos of the two of them, architectural blueprint paper, and the binder clips I knew he used for capabilities presentations for prospective clients. The cards were beautiful, and my mother was touched.

Later that night when they were passing my bedroom on the way to theirs, my mother was still talking about the cards and the flowers, and I found myself bragging about my father in phone calls to Rollie and Sadie and Tom.

Friday morning began with the testimony of a woman whose little baby my mother had hoped to deliver, but who had wound up giving birth via cesarean in a hospital instead. It had been a hard, unpleasant labor, and she said my mother had demanded she push for almost half a day: ten and a half hours of pushing and resting, pushing and resting, before my mother had finally—to use this woman's word—"allowed" them to leave for the hospital.

We were then treated to a man who insisted my mother had never warned him or his wife that there were greater risks involved with a home birth than with a hospital one. According to this fellow, he and his wife would never have tried to have their child at home had my mother been appropriately candid. Although the State was not allowed to ask the fellow how his baby's birth had turned out, my parents and I had to sit in agony throughout his testimony, aware of the fact that his infant was one of the tiny few whom my mother caught dead.

And, as lunch approached, the State squeezed in one more witness, a doctor who explained to us all what a prolonged second-stage labor meant, and the dangers it posed for the mother. The doctor was a researcher with the American College of Obstetricians and Gynecologists in Washington, D.C., an organization of which I am now, ironically, a dues-paying member. Like Dr. Gerson, he viewed labor as a dangerous circus stunt: He was the witness who in one especially rare moment of rhetorical flourish compared a hospital to a car seat, and then jumbled a car accident and a kitchen appliance.

But it was clear the jury got the point, and thought Dr. Geoffrey Lang was a wise and compelling man.

In another particularly brutal exchange from my mother's perspective, he managed to simultaneously explain why pushing too long endangered a woman, while casting yet one more aspersion upon my mother's competence: "It's perfectly reasonable that someone with the limited training of a midwife would suspect a ruptured cerebral aneurysm. Obviously, that's not what occurred in this case, but someone with only rudimentary obstetric education might think such a thing."

"What did occur?" Bill Tanner asked, and for the first time I heard spoken the word I'd seen written the month before on a wall in Stephen's office. *Vagal.* It was one of the words and expressions Tom Corts and I had seen scribbled in sprawling Magic Marker letters on the large sheets of white poster paper.

"She—and this is a shorthand term some doctors I know use in conversation—vagaled. She vagaled out." With clinical formality, he then began laying the groundwork for the testimony we would hear that afternoon from the medical examiner.

"You went easy on Farrell," my father told Stephen as we picked at our food during the recess for lunch. Farrell was the father who said my mother hadn't been clear about the risks that come with a home birth.

"He really wasn't all that damaging," Stephen said, and he asked Peter Grinnell to pass him a paper napkin from the metal box against the diner's wall.

"He made it sound like Sibyl hides things," my father continued.

Stephen touched a tip of the napkin to his tongue and then rubbed the moist paper over an ink smudge on the back of his hand. "Think so?"

"Yeah, I do. Don't you?"

Stephen looked at the skin on his hand and folded the napkin again and again until it was roughly the size of a quarter. "It seemed a lot worse to you than it was. The jury doesn't know that he and his wife had one of those bad outcomes."

The food on my father's plate, a grilled cheese and coleslaw, looked exactly as it had when the waitress brought us our lunches. The sandwich remained a pair of flat, butter-burned triangles, and the mound of coleslaw still held its ice-cream-scoop shape.

"What about that doctor?"

"Lang? I thought we went at it pretty good."

Peter signaled for the waitress to bring the check to our booth. "I wish we'd done more."

"I made sure the jury understood that every word he said was conjecture. And I made sure they realized the guy never even saw the woman's body. Tell me, what more would you have wanted?" There was no edge to Stephen's question, no trace of irritation.

"He was a horse's ass. I wish we'd made that clear."

Stephen nodded, letting my father's frustration roll over him like a wave. When he saw the waitress drop the bill on the table by Peter, he reached inside his suit jacket for his wallet.

"Well, we'll get 'em this afternoon then," he said, and he sounded to me like my high-school track coach.

"Look," my mother said, her voice strangely groggy as she gazed out the window at Lake Memphremagog. "There must be something flat floating out there. Look at the seagulls."

Perhaps a hundred yards into the lake, dozens of seagulls were standing on the surface of the water—not floating or bobbing as one might expect, but standing with their small legs extended below them on pieces of driftwood. We all turned, and as I did I looked at my mother's eyes, and something about them suggested she hadn't heard a word my father and Stephen had said.

EIGHTEEN

I doubt I'll ever talk to Anne again, so I guess I'll always be wondering: What did she think would happen when she picked up the phone and called B.P. Hewitt? Did she expect something different? Or did she get what she wanted?

—*from the notebooks of* SIBYL DANFORTH, MIDWIFE

ANNE AUSTIN HAD NOT WORKED WITH MY MOTHER FOR VERY LONG, AND SO SHE had not become a part of our lives the way her predecessors had. Heather Reed, for example, was no substitute for a big sister, but she spent close to six years on the periphery of our family—days and days doing prenatals in the room off the kitchen, dinners at our house almost weekly, the evenings she would baby-sit me when my mother and father would be out someplace together—and there was little of importance I wouldn't have shared with her when I was in elementary school. Heather always seemed to know when I'd been fighting with Rollie or Sadie, she was an unfailing source of help with my homework, and she was a strong shoulder in times of trouble.

But I had barely known Anne Austin when Charlotte Bedford died. Over the years it has become difficult for me to differentiate my opinion of the woman after the turmoil from my opinion of her before it, and to remember that I did not always despise her. But the fact is, Anne had only been a part of our lives for one winter when Charlotte died; she had only been assisting my mother since the previous December. She'd had dinner at our house two or three times, and on occasion

I'd seen her coming and going on those days my mother had pregnant women stopping by for their checkups. She had struck me, I believe, as a sweet but mousy thing with brown hair she kept short: the sort of woman I came across once in a while in college who would trade a party on a Saturday night for an evening bent over books in the science library, yet would still fail to do very well on the exam. The trade, more often than not, was triggered by shyness rather than drive, and an organic chemistry test was merely a reasonable excuse to avoid loud music and aggressive boys.

But I don't think when I first met Anne I thought she was self-righteous or smug; I don't think I thought she had it in for my mother. That impression grew during the summer and fall as my mother's trial approached, and I'd hear the adults discussing once more what had occurred the night of the thirteenth and the morning of the fourteenth.

"And that's when you broke her water," Stephen said to my mother on one of those occasions, referring to Charlotte, when the two of them were alone in the kitchen.

"That's right."

"And what did Anne ask?"

"She didn't ask anything."

"But she said something . . ."

"She said, 'I don't understand why you did that.' "

"And it wasn't meant as the sort of question an apprentice might ask her midwife? It wasn't a . . . a part of the learning process?"

"No. She was irritated with me. She thought I was intervening."

"Intervening?"

"Interfering with the natural process."

"Was that the first time she had gotten mad at you?"

"She didn't get mad at me. She was just annoyed."

"First time?"

My mother laughed. "Good Lord, no!"

"She was often annoyed with you?"

"Anne has just read too many books and been around too few births," my mother said, and although I was listening from a perch on the steps in the front hall, I was sure she was rolling her eyes.

Anne was twenty-two when she came to my mother, and until that winter she hadn't seen a baby crown or caught a newborn once in her life. But she had visions in her mind of what a perfect birth was like, and it was clear from the dinners we shared that she had indeed read copiously about the subject. Under my mother's tutelage she studied hard, and my mother thought she was a fine apprentice, despite Anne's periodic frustration with what she viewed as my mother's tendency to intervene. Anne wanted desperately to become a midwife, and there was no reason to believe that someday she wouldn't succeed.

By the time the trial began, however, she had grown in my mind from a mousy little midwife-wannabe to an arrogant traitor of almost theatric proportions: pietistic, self-important, and—for reasons I couldn't fathom—bent upon the destruction of my family. She had left Vermont the weekend Charlotte Bedford died, apparently coming back only twice before the trial: once for a deposition and once to pack up the possessions she had left in the room she was renting from a college professor in Hardwick.

But when she had first phoned B.P. Hewitt—my mother's backup physician—six and a half months earlier, I doubt she hated my mother. I doubt she hated her even after B.P. tried to reassure her that she had not witnessed a cesarean on a living woman. When she picked up her phone to call the physician, I tend to doubt she even understood the fusion she was about to trigger, the linear progression of events she was about to unleash—a progression which, in hindsight, could not possibly have had a good end for my family. But for all I know, her intentions may even have been kind, her desires noble: A woman was dead, and something had to be done.

Yet the stakes must have grown large for Anne Austin that morning, and I would not be surprised if even today she cannot fully explain why she did what she did. Perhaps she thought that B.P. would share her first phone call with my mother, and that would effectively end her apprenticeship. After all, how could my mother ever trust Anne again after she had called her backup physician behind her back?

And so she had to convince herself that she was right, my mother was wrong. She'd call Asa Bedford, find out what he'd seen. And then, once she had broached her fears to the husband, fears reinforced by his own horrific memories—spurts of blood from the woman on the bed— she had to call the state's attorney. She had to. Perhaps she feared that the reverend would if she didn't, and then she herself might be charged as an accessory to a crime. She was, after all, the midwife's apprentice. She'd even gone with Asa to get the knife.

No, I really don't believe Anne Austin hated my mother when she started her phone calls that bitter morning in March. But I do believe she grew to hate her over the summer; I do believe she learned to despise her. She had to; her mental health demanded it. How else could she have justified the pain she was inflicting upon my mother and upon my family? How else could she have lived with herself?

By the time the trial began, I am quite sure in Anne's mind my mother was a sloppy and dangerous midwife, and deserving of the punishment before her.

I could see it the moment she arrived in court Friday afternoon, just after we'd all stood for the jury and judge and then retaken our seats. She marched to the witness stand, careful to stare straight ahead, but I could still see the loathing she had for us all sparkle in her round dark eyes, and the way she had her jaw set against us.

She and my mother hadn't spoken since they left the hospital in Newport that Friday morning in March; they hadn't said a single word to each other. I watched my mother study Anne as she was directed across the front of the courtroom and sworn in by one of the court officers, and it was as if my mother were seeing for the first time a twin she hadn't known before existed, or a rare and frightening animal in a zoo—the sort of creature that would cause one to run or cringe were there not steel bars as a buffer. My mother slowly swiveled her chair so she was facing Anne directly, and for one of the few times in the trial I actually saw her whispering to Peter and Stephen when the shock of seeing Anne finally wore off.

My mother seemed to be more perplexed than angry. Occasionally she shook her head slightly, a small gesture that seemed to me to be asking Anne, *Why are you doing this to me?*

Anne's voice had a slight trace of Boston I hadn't recalled from the winter, and it made her seem stronger, more authoritative. She was small-boned and she looked tired, but the young woman—a mere eight years older than I—sat up straight and spoke well, telling the jury in measured tones of the horrors she had witnessed, and how my mother had used a kitchen knife to cut open the stomach of a living woman in Lawson.

It was during Anne's testimony that the jury began growing uncomfortable, and began to steal glances at my mother. Although Anne did not begin speaking until the afternoon of the fifth day, the trial's first Friday, and although the panel knew well the outline of what had occurred in the Bedfords' bedroom, they had not yet heard an account from an eyewitness. And as Anne answered question after question Bill Tanner asked, I think Charlotte Bedford grew real for the first time in some of the jurors' minds.

In all likelihood, that was Tanner's plan. All of the individuals the State had put on the stand so far were mere warm-ups for the final three, a troika of powerful witnesses who in theory would seal my mother's fate. Anne Austin and the medical examiner on Friday afternoon. The Reverend Asa Bedford on Monday morning. Even at fourteen I understood instantly the logic of this progression: The first witness, the one who had initiated the litigious part of this saga, recounts the nightmare she saw. The second, an expert with powerful credibility, explains the exact cause of death. And the third, the one who had lost the most, serves as the medley's anchor.

What I did not appreciate until later that Friday (and what I might not have appreciated for years had Patty Dunlevy not explained it to me) were the subtleties of Tanner's order. The last witness the jury would hear before the weekend—two full days during which they would stew upon all they had seen and heard the first week—would be the coroner giving the State's version of the cause of death. Then, if the State had any fears that their case had lost momentum over the weekend, they knew that on Monday morning they had the widower left, a grieving but articulate pastor who was—to take liberty with a cliché—very much accustomed to public speaking.

By the time Stephen had an opportunity to cross-examine Anne, most of the jurors must have had a picture in their minds of Sibyl Danforth as an alarmingly slipshod midwife, a woman whose carelessness would eventually cost one mother her life. Moreover, when they envisioned my mother on the morning Charlotte Bedford died, they must have imagined her as a lunatic: a midwife who became hysterical and panicked, a woman who temporarily lost her mind and grew capable of hacking apart a living woman in the final stages of labor. (Would things have ended differently if insanity had actually been my mother's defense? They might have for me, perhaps, but in the long run the outcome would not have been much different for my mother. And though I did not know then that Stephen had once broached the idea of temporary insanity as a possible defense, at the time my mother still

believed she would resume her practice once the trial was over, and
vetoed the discussion instantly. No one, she told Stephen, wanted a
midwife who went certifiable under pressure.)

Like my mother, Anne dressed for court in an uncharacteristically
conservative outfit: a white blouse, cardigan sweater, and gray skirt. No
midwife-wannabe work shirts for her that day; no baggy dresses with
monster pockets. She looked like a young bank teller from Burlington.

Throughout her testimony she had avoided looking at my mother,
and I noticed that when Stephen stood up to begin his cross-examination,
he remained behind his table so Anne would at least have to stare in my
mother's general direction.

"Prior to Veil Bedford's delivery, you had only seen nine births,
correct?" he asked.

"Yes."

"And none of them resulted in an emergency situation, right?"

"That's right."

"Veil Bedford's was the first, wasn't it?"

"Yes."

"Prior to March fourteenth, had you ever been in an emergency
situation?"

"Like what?"

Stephen strolled behind my mother's chair so Anne would see her.
At first she turned toward the lake and stared at the puffy white clouds
floating by over Canada instead. "A car accident, maybe. Ever been in a
car accident where people were badly injured? Or come across one?"

"No."

"Plane crash?"

"Of course not."

Stephen shrugged. "Train wreck? Man with a heart attack? Baby
falling into a pool?"

"No, nothing like that."

"Never?"

"Never."

"And you've never been with an EMT or rescue squad volunteer
in a life-and-death crisis, have you?"

"No."

"Charlotte Bedford was the first, wasn't she?"

"Yes, she was."

"And you've never witnessed surgery of any kind, right?"

"Like in a hospital?"

"Yes. Like in a hospital."

"No."

"Do you have any formal medical training?"

"You mean like at a college or something?"

"Yes. Exactly."

"Not yet, but I'm planning on—"

"Thank you, Miss Austin. You've never even taken an accredited first-aid course, have you?"

"No."

"And you don't know CPR, do you?"

"I know it a little. A few days after Charlotte died, I was going to start—"

"Are you formally trained and certified to administer CPR?"

"No."

Stephen raised an arm and I thought for a moment he was going to rest his hand gently upon my mother's shoulder, but he didn't. Instead he merely reached inside his suit jacket for a pen. "Was Charlotte Bedford the first person you ever saw die?" he asked, and for the first time that afternoon he raised his voice a notch and sounded ready for one of the confrontations he seemed to relish.

"Yes."

"When you saw the blood that resulted from Sibyl's attempt to save the baby, was that the first time you'd ever seen a body opened?"

"I'd seen pictures in textbooks."

"Please, Miss Austin, I didn't ask if you'd ever looked at a body in a book. Was that the first time you'd ever seen a body opened?"

"I guess."

"Yes?"

"Yes."

"Thank you." Stephen took the pen and began tapping it lightly against the table for a moment, perhaps hoping to distract Anne into looking his way. "So prior to the early-morning hours of March fourteenth, you had never seen the quantities of blood that might or might not flow in that situation. Correct?"

"Yes."

"You'd never seen blood spurt from a living or a dead body?"

"No."

"In that case, what in your background led you to make the wild assumption that the blood you saw that moment was coming from a living woman?"

"It was the way it spurted."

He shook his head. "I'm not asking you what you think you saw. I'm asking you what in your background led you to think that based on the bleeding Charlotte Bedford was alive?"

"You didn't see it. If you had been—"

"Your Honor, please instruct the witness to answer the questions," Stephen said abruptly.

Judge Dorset looked down at Anne and said simply, "Miss Austin, you will answer the questions."

"But if any of—"

"Miss Austin," the judge added, and he sounded almost as annoyed as Stephen, "answer the questions as they are asked. Please. Mr. Hastings, proceed."

"What part of your training led you to think that the blood you saw was coming from a living person?" Stephen asked, and he continued to tap the tip of the pen slowly on the table.

She folded her arms across her chest. "I don't recall."

"Is that because you have none—absolutely no medical training?"

"I guess."

"Am I correct in saying that any conjectures you made about the blood were founded on absolutely no experience—no first- or second- or even thirdhand experience?"

Finally she looked in Stephen's direction and when she saw my mother she shut tight her eyes against tears, but they were too much. She sniffed back some, but her answer was still filled with her sobs. As if Stephen hadn't asked her a question, as if he weren't even present, she cried with the suddenness of lightning at my mother, "God, Sibyl, I'm sorry, I'm sorry, but I had to do it, I had to call! You know you killed her—"

Stephen tried to cut her off. He demanded the remarks be stricken from the record, and Judge Dorset slammed his gavel down on his bench a thousand times harder than Stephen had tapped his pen on his table a moment earlier, but before breaking down and triggering a recess, Anne managed to sob once more, "I'm sorry, Sibyl, I am! I know you didn't mean to, but we both know you killed her!"

◆   ◆   ◆

My mother sipped water from a paper cup in a small, windowless conference room during the recess, and my father held her hand. She looked a little paler than she had before Anne's outburst, and sometimes she simply pressed the rim of the cup against her lower lip.

"She is a little witch, isn't she?" Peter murmured, I think trying to do little more than make conversation.

"No," my mother said, "she isn't really."

"That's awfully big of you, Sibyl. You're with family and friends here; you don't need to be noble," Stephen told her, and he seemed as angry as when the judge had called the recess fifteen minutes earlier.

"I'm not. Anne's just . . . she's young, and she's gotten herself in too deep."

"Well, then," Stephen said, "she's about to drown. It will be short and sweet, but we're about to take her down for the third time."

"Miss Austin, you will focus solely on the question Mr. Hastings is asking, and Mr. Hastings, you will allow her to answer each question fully. Do we have an understanding?" Judge Dorset asked when we had reconvened.

Stephen nodded, and moved out from behind his table and began pacing the room as he had with most other witnesses. He asked the court reporter to read back the last question he had asked, the one about first- or second- or even thirdhand experience.

"That's right," Anne answered. Her eyes were red from crying, and her words were no longer draped in poise.

"But nevertheless, when Sibyl made the first incision, you decided Charlotte Bedford was alive."

"When I saw the blood, yes."

"Did the body show any other signs of life as the incision was made—or, for that matter, after?"

"Like what?"

Stephen shrugged. "Did the woman cry out with pain?"

"No, she was unconscious."

"Did the body . . . shudder?"

"I didn't see that."

"You didn't see it shudder?"

"No."

"It didn't move at all, did it?"

"Not that I saw."

"Does that mean that the only indication you had that the woman might have been alive was the blood?"

"Yes."

"But that was enough to alarm you?"

"It was."

"So what did you do when you were alarmed? Did you try to stop Sibyl from proceeding?"

"No."

"Did you say to her, 'Don't do this, Sibyl, she's alive'?"

"No."

"Did you try and take the knife out of Sibyl's hand and—"

"Objection. This is just badgering," Tanner said.

"Overruled."

"Did you try and take the knife out of Sibyl's hand?"

"No."

Stephen nodded, and walked the length of the jury box. "So despite your contention later on that Charlotte Bedford was alive before the incision, you did absolutely nothing to try and save the woman's life. Did you, at the very least, share your fear with the father while the two of you were still in the room?"

"No. Not then, I didn't."

"You testified earlier that you were surprised Sibyl never checked for a fetal heartbeat. Did you suggest to the midwife that perhaps she should?"

"No."

"So am I correct in saying that despite your claim after the fact that Charlotte Bedford had been alive before the incision, you did absolutely nothing at the time to try and prevent the surgery?"

"I just didn't know what—"

"Miss Austin—"

"I just didn't—"

"Your Honor—"

Judge Dorset rapped his gavel on the dark wood before him and then surprised me—probably surprised us all—by throwing the young woman a life preserver and thereby preventing her from going under a final time. "Counsel," he reminded Stephen, "I asked you to allow the witness the time to answer each question fully. Go ahead, Miss Austin."

She took a deep breath and dabbed her eyes with a tissue. Finally, in a voice that quavered slightly, she said, "I just didn't have the confidence at the time to stop her, I just didn't know enough. Like you said, I hadn't been through anything like that before. But I saw the blood pumping and pumping and I knew something was wrong, and it was only a few hours later that I decided I had a . . . a moral responsibility to tell someone what I'd seen. I didn't want to, I really didn't want to. But I had to. That's the thing: I had to do it."

Perhaps because of the phone call I'd overheard one night between my mother and Stephen—a conversation that seemed steeped to me in flirtatious innuendo—I made a point of being home when he came by our house one afternoon in the week before the trial began. I hovered in the kitchen, pretending to do homework while they met in her office. When he finally left, as my mother walked him to his car, I went to an open window to watch them through the screen. They assumed I had stayed in the kitchen.

Instead of strolling to the car, however, they wandered to my mother's flower garden, stopping somewhere amidst the sunflowers— taller than they by far that date in September, but just about ready to die—in a spot I couldn't see. And so I went back to the kitchen and then out into our backyard through the sliding glass doors. Pressed flat against the side wall of our house, I still couldn't see them, but I could hear parts of their exchange.

I don't know if Stephen had actually tried to kiss my mother before I got outside: In my mind, I can see him taking her hands in his the way he once had by his car, and lowering his lips to hers. But I never saw him do such a thing.

Nevertheless, I've always understood why a lawyer has faith in logical inference, the idea that one doesn't need to hear or see it rain overnight to know in the morning that it did rain if the cars and the ground and the trees are all wet.

And so I believe Stephen may have tried to kiss my mother by the way I heard her saying to him, "No, it's not just the place. It's everything. If I sent you those signals, I'm sorry. I'm really and truly sorry."

◆ ◆ ◆

Before I became a doctor, I couldn't imagine why anyone would become a coroner. I assumed that anyone willing to spend that much time around corpses was inordinately fixated on death or—at best—had never outgrown a nine-year-old boy's interest in vampires and mummies and ghouls. Only after I'd started medical school did the fascinations of that job become apparent to me, and the reasons why so many profoundly—at least outwardly—normal people choose it as their life's work. It's like being a detective. And once you're past your first cadaver, human tissue loses its ability to shock, and organs and bones become routine.

When I was fourteen, however, I imagined a coroner had to be a very sick person. And so I was unprepared for the medical examiner for the state of Vermont when a bailiff escorted him between the two rows of packed benches in the courtroom mid-Friday afternoon, and led him to the witness stand. Terry Tierney looked like any one of the fathers I knew in Reddington who coached Little League baseball in the spring and Pop Warner football in the fall: energetic but patient in carriage, and downright unexceptional in appearance. He was a good decade older than my parents, with a black beard that was graying and eyeglasses very much like Stephen's.

He smiled when Bill Tanner greeted him, and—at Tanner's prodding—explained for the jury his litany of degrees and accomplishments. The two were so chummy that for a few moments I almost expected them to start discussing the deer hunting they could expect later that fall.

When they finally got around to the scene that had greeted Tierney when he walked into the Bedfords' bedroom back in March, however, all of that changed, and Tierney grew serious. He described the way my mother had stitched the exterior incision she'd made and then pulled the woman's nightgown back down over her torso.

"Did Mrs. Danforth tell you how Charlotte Bedford had died?" Bill Tanner asked.

"She said the lady had had a stroke."

"What did you think?"

"I thought it was possible. Anything's possible in a home birth."

"Objection!" Stephen said, shooting up from his seat, and the judge sustained it.

"When did you conduct the autopsy?" Tanner continued, as if there had never been an interruption.

"Later that morning."

"Did you find any indication that the woman had had a stroke?"

"No."

"If Charlotte Bedford had had a stroke, would you have been able to determine that from an autopsy?"

"Definitely. Absolutely."

"Why?"

Dr. Tierney sighed and gathered his thoughts. Looking back, I believe he was merely pausing to frame his answer in a way that would convey the details of postmortem dissection without sickening the jury. But at the time I thought his hesitation was driven by sadness.

"When I examined the brain, I would have found significant changes. I would have seen hemorrhaging—bleeding. The tissue would have softened; it would have gotten almost spongy."

"And you saw none of that—no bleeding, no softening—when you were examining Charlotte Bedford's brain?"

"No, I did not."

Tanner returned to his table, and his deputy handed him what I assumed were his notes.

"Did you examine Charlotte Bedford's abdominal area?"

"Yes."

"Beginning with the incision?"

"That's right."

"Including her reproductive organs?"

"Of course."

"You mentioned Mrs. Danforth had sewn up the skin where she had cut Charlotte open. Did she sew up her internal organs as well?"

"No."

"She didn't sew up the uterus?"

"No."

"Why not?"

"Objection," Stephen said. "Calls for speculation."

"Sustained."

"So you found the uterus had not been repaired," Tanner continued.

"No, it had not."

"Could you tell where in the birth canal the baby had been when Mrs. Danforth pulled him from his mother?"

"No."

"Could you tell if the baby had descended at all in all those hours Mrs. Danforth forced Charlotte to push?"

"Objection, no one forced anyone to do anything."

"Sustained."

Tanner smiled for the jury's benefit, a grin more mischievous than chastened. "Could you tell if the baby had descended at all in all those hours Charlotte was pushing?"

"No, I could not tell."

"Could you tell if there had been a placental abruption?"

"Yes, definitely. There were areas of hemorrhage."

"Was that the cause of death?"

"No. As it occasionally does, it had clotted over. Started to heal itself."

"Was it a factor in Charlotte Bedford's death?"

"It would become one indirectly."

Tanner glanced at his notes and grew quiet. Finally: "How so?"

"The woman had lost some blood during that event. Given the cesarean that would be performed a few hours later, it's impossible to gauge how much. But it was probably a significant amount."

"Meaning?"

"Her body was weaker. She wasn't as strong."

"Why might that matter?"

"As any mother knows, labor's hard work. Incredibly hard work. A woman needs all the strength she can muster, especially if something . . . something unforeseen occurs."

"Did something unforeseen occur in this case?"

"I assume you mean other than the poor woman dying."

"Right."

"Then yes, clearly something unforeseen happened."

"Based on the autopsy you performed, and all of the subsequent laboratory work, what do you think that something was?"

As if he were recalling an event as common as a drive home on slick roads in a blizzard—hazardous, perhaps, but an endeavor everyone in that courtroom had endured and could discuss comfortably at a dinner table—he said, "Well, although there was no medical evidence of a stroke, there were eyewitnesses who saw what apparently looked like a stroke to someone who wasn't a doctor. The woman twitched or spasmed, and then blacked out. The father saw it, the young lady—the apprentice—saw it, and of course Mrs. Danforth saw it. But I don't believe it was an aneurysm that caused the spasm."

"Do you have an opinion as to its cause?"

"Yes."

"Would you tell us what that is?"

"To use Dr. Lang's expression, I think the woman 'vagaled.' "

"Would you elaborate?"

"Right here, in the small of the back of our heads," Tierney said, motioning to the spot on his own head with his hand, "there is a pair of cranial nerves filled with motor and sensory fibers. Those are the vagus nerves. They innervate a variety of organs and muscles—the larynx, for example, and many thoracic and abdominal viscera."

"What does that mean in layman's terms?"

Tierney offered the jury a small, self-deprecating smile. "They communicate between the brain and the heart. They help to carry the information from the brain to the heart about how fast or slow it's supposed to beat. Now, like everything else in the body, the brain needs oxygen. And oxygen is carried to the brain in the blood—blood pumped, of course, by the heart. If the brain isn't getting enough oxygen—if it becomes what we call hypoxic—it doesn't function properly. Or at all. Obviously, there are lots of things that can cause a brain to become hypoxic, including even a planned medical event like general anesthesia. But another cause may be labor, and the way a woman has to push. You take in these very deep breaths, work very hard, and then you exhale at once. And you do this for hours. Suddenly, before you know it, your brain is going hypoxic."

"Is this dangerous?"

"Absolutely. If you strain enough and become sufficiently hypoxic, your heart can slow down or even stop. It's a sort of reflex mediated by the vagus nerve. Your heart stops and you pass out. As some doctors say, you vagal out."

"Can you die?"

"Oh yes, indeed one can. But women in labor almost never do, because a delivery room nurse or an ob-gyn knows exactly what the early symptoms look like, exactly what the first signs are. And it's very easy to treat: You simply have the laboring woman relax for a bit or—in an extreme case—you administer oxygen."

"What makes you think Charlotte vagaled?"

"First of all, she evidenced the symptoms of a person going hypoxic: She had a seizure, lost consciousness, and her heart stopped. That's what the eyewitnesses may have seen. Then, when we were looking for injuries to brain cells in the hippocampus, we saw significant evidence of hypoxia."

"What does that look like?"

"The nucleus of the cell becomes pycnotic—shrunken and dark and really rather unattractive. Meanwhile the cytoplasm of the cell body becomes a deep red, and looks almost glassy."

"So you're saying Charlotte Bedford was forced . . . you're saying Charlotte Bedford pushed for so long she went hypoxic. She vagaled."

"Yes."

"In your opinion, was that the cause of death?"

"Well, that's the thing, I don't think so."

"Why not?"

"This is going to sound pretty ironic, given the reason we've all assembled here, but I believe Mrs. Danforth saved her life after she vagaled. I'm convinced that the CPR Mrs. Danforth performed—all those cycles—actually brought the woman back."

Dr. Tierney's opinion was not a surprise to our family, and my mother barely moved when he spoke. But it was a revelation to most of the crowd, and one of the mothers in the back row must have moved with such suddenness or gasped just loud enough that she woke her infant. We all heard a moment of crying, followed by the rustling we'd all become used to, as the infant's mother worked her way down the thin space between benches and then out of the courtroom.

"What makes you think so?" Tanner asked when the room had settled.

"The amount of blood in the peritoneal cavity—the abdomen. I mean, there were close to seven hundred and fifty milliliters in there."

"Over two pints?"

"Roughly. Plus there was all the blood outside of the wound: Around the incision. On the bedding. And, of course, on that pillow Mrs. Danforth had used to soak some up so she could see what she was doing. Find the uterus, I guess. In my opinion, there would not have been that much blood in the deceased's abdomen and around the bedding if the woman had been dead when Mrs. Danforth tried to perform a cesarean section."

"And so you believe Charlotte Bedford was alive when Mrs. Danforth performed the cesarean?"

"That's correct."

"In that case, what was the cause of death? How did Charlotte Bedford die?"

Dr. Tierney sighed and then looked right at the jury. "As I myself typed on the death certificate—the final one—she died of hemorrhagic shock caused by the cesarean section. In my opinion, it was Mrs. Danforth's C-section that killed her."

NINETEEN

I don't toss and turn, it's not like that. Sometimes I don't even remember listening to Rand's breathing for hours, feeling the heat from his body under the blanket. But in the morning, it's often like I haven't slept. I'm cranky and tired and I go to rooms that are empty and cry.

Stephen says Charlotte's sister doesn't hate me. But he's not a woman, he's never been through labor. He's never seen life surge into a room at birth.

On this one he's wrong.

—*from the notebooks of* SIBYL DANFORTH, MIDWIFE

I WANTED STEPHEN TO TEAR TIERNEY APART. I KNEW THE MEDICAL EXAMINER had been a devastating witness; I understood how powerful his testimony had been: He sounded intelligent and authoritative; he seemed unassailably reasonable. He looked good on the witness stand.

But I also understood that if Tierney's damage could be undone, most of the repair work would have to wait until the following week, when Stephen would put our own "experts" on the stand. Then, I hoped, everyone in the courtroom would see that Dr. Tierney was merely the Vermont coroner. He wasn't from Boston or New York City or Washington, D.C. Tierney's opinion was only one among many, and his was most certainly mistaken: Eventually the jury would be convinced that Charlotte Bedford had been dead beyond question when my mother decided to rescue little Veil.

Stephen, of course, would curry no favor with an Orleans County jury by undermining Tierney simply because he was from Vermont. And so most of his strategy during his cross-examination of the medical examiner late Friday afternoon was simply to lay the groundwork for his own forensic pathologists, and to suggest that there was going to be wide room for disagreement.

"You testified that Mrs. Bedford had about seven hundred and fifty milliliters of blood in her abdomen. Am I correct?" he asked at one point.

"About that, yes."

"If someone approached you and said a woman had died as a result of a cesarean section done under . . . under these circumstances, wouldn't you have expected more blood?"

Tanner stood to object, arguing that it was ridiculous to ask the coroner to conjecture about a hypothetical situation when there was an actual cesarean to discuss, but the judge allowed Stephen to proceed.

"Seven hundred and fifty milliliters is a good amount of blood," Tierney answered.

"But . . . but . . . if someone told you a woman had died from a C-section . . . wouldn't you have expected to find more than that?"

Tierney thought for a long moment. Finally: "I might have."

"Thank you. If you wanted categorical . . . indisputable . . . irrefutable proof that a cesarean section had been the cause of death, how many milliliters of blood would you want to discover in the abdominal cavity?"

Tierney nodded his head slightly as he pondered his response. "Perhaps one thousand," he said.

"Was there that much blood in Charlotte Bedford's abdominal cavity?"

"No."

"Thank you," Stephen said, and he started back to his table. "No further questions." For a brief second I thought this would mark the end of the day—and, therefore, the week—and I grew excited. This seemed to be a wonderful note on which to send the jurors home for the weekend.

But before Stephen had even retaken his chair, Tanner was on his feet for the prosecution's redirection.

"Two quick questions, Dr. Tierney, if I may," he began. "Given everything else you learned from the autopsy, and given the huge amounts of blood that were found outside of the abdominal cavity—such as all that blood Mrs. Danforth soaked up with the pillow—was seven hundred and fifty milliliters enough to convince you that the cesarean had been the cause of death?"

"Yes, most certainly."

"Given all of your experience, and all of the time you have spent on this particular case, do you believe the cause of death was the cesarean section performed by the defendant?"

"Yes, I do."

"Thank you," Tanner said, and Judge Dorset looked up at the clock on the far wall. It was well after five, and the first week of my mother's trial was about to be gaveled to a close.

Before we all left the courthouse and went our separate ways Friday evening, Stephen tried to reassure my parents that this would be the low point of the trial for us—literally, in terms of what my mother's prospects for acquittal appeared to be, as well as emotionally. After all, the State had presented virtually its entire case—the only remaining witness was the widower himself—while we hadn't even begun our defense.

Stephen warned us that during the weekend we could find ourselves preoccupied with what the jury was thinking, and we could become alarmed.

"Remember, there's still a long way to go," he said, and although I wanted to believe him, his reassurance was in conflict with another point I'd heard him make at least a half-dozen times: Our defense would take considerably less time than the prosecution's version. All we needed to do was plant reasonable doubt, and while—to use his metaphor—he wanted to be sure the roots were healthy and secure, he said doubt in this instance was one tough and sturdy little shrub.

The last thing he said before he climbed into his car was that he'd see us on Sunday, when he and Peter were going to come by and help my mother rehearse her testimony and prepare for the cross-examination.

As we drove back to Reddington, my mother asked me how I was doing, and I lied and said fine. Actually, I was fighting back tears. But my parents accepted my response at face value, and that was the extent of our conversation the whole ride home. A combination of fear and exhaustion prevented them from dissecting the testimony we'd heard that day or exploring the quiver that had crept into my voice.

As we approached our house, we saw in our headlights a conga line of parked cars just to the side of our driveway. The bumper sticker on the back of the last vehicle, a rusting pickup truck, signaled to all of us who had descended upon our home: MIDWIVES DO IT ANYWHERE!

The Vermont midwives, some of whom must have left the courthouse before Dr. Tierney finished his particularly lethal interpretation of events, had brought us dinner. Cheryl and Molly and Donelle and Megan and Tracy—names that will always conjure for me effusive women who hugged on sight, and could love without question or reservation or inhibition—had come to rally around my mother. Our stereo was blasting an eclectic dance tape that had Abba following the Shirelles, and Joni Mitchell beside Janis Joplin. The dining-room table was draped in a sky-blue tablecloth, and covered with candles, casseroles, and baskets of freshly baked bread.

Even Cheryl Visco, whose frequent presence at our house throughout the summer had come to annoy my father and me, was a welcome sight. She was as beautiful and powerful as ever, despite a week slouched in a bench in a courtroom: Her massive gray hair managed at once to sparkle like new metal, yet look as soft to the touch as cashmere, and her eyes went wide with joy when she saw us.

She wrapped her arms around me first, before even greeting my mother, as if performing an emotional triage by instinct.

"You are just too thin, even for a track star," she whispered into my ear.

"You're one to talk," I said.

When the other midwives saw we'd arrived, along with their partners and husbands and—in some cases—children, they started to clap for my mother. Cheryl put an arm around her shoulder and led her into the dining room as my father and I trailed a step behind them. Suddenly someone had stopped applauding long enough to give my mother a glass of wine and my father a scotch, and someone else was handing me a cold soda. I looked up to thank whoever had offered me the glass, and I saw it was Tom Corts.

"Want a beer instead? No one would care, you know," he said, and patted my shoulder in a way that was as sweet as it was awkward.

"How did you know about this?" I asked.

"Your mom's friend Cheryl called and got a hold of my mom," he answered, and motioned toward the older midwife.

I looked at the way she had begun cradling my mother in both of her arms, and at the smile she had somehow elicited from her—the sort of broad grin we rarely saw from my mother those days—and the tears I'd been fighting since we left the courthouse began streaming down my cheeks. My sobs were absolutely silent then, and in the chaos and joy that were filling our house no one but Tom was even aware that I was crying.

"Hey, you're home," he said nervously, unsure why I was crying and what he should do. "Everything's going to be okay now."

I shook my head, sure that nothing would ever be okay again. And then I took him by the hand and led him upstairs to my room, where I cried in his arms until all of my mother's friends finally left our house for the night, and the floor below us grew still.

I hadn't seen Asa Bedford since before his son was born and his wife died. There were always rumors floating through the northern part of the county in the summer and early fall that he was visiting Lawson for one reason or another, and whenever someone saw a balding, redheaded father with a baby and a boy, they were likely to suspect for a moment that the poor fellow was back in the state. But aside from when he gave his deposition that summer, I doubt he had ever actually returned: His family and Charlotte's family were all in Alabama, and a single parent with two children to raise can use all the help he can get.

When I saw him Monday morning, he looked like hell. Although he had never been a handsome man in my mind, he had always been so kind with Foogie and Charlotte—and so thoughtful of Rollie and me— that there was something attractive about him. It wasn't so much the pastoral serenity I've come across in other ministers in my life, as it was a profound sensitivity: I've no idea whether it was because of his apocalyptic leanings or in spite of them, but most of the time he was a very sweet man.

The Asa Bedford who was about to testify, however, looked tired and beaten and unendurably sad. There were deep black bags beneath his eyes, and his face had grown lines. There were streaks of white amidst the frizzy red halo that rolled partway around his head like a horseshoe, and his pale skin was tinged by gray. He'd aged, and he'd aged badly.

At the time I didn't know that the name Asa was the Hebrew word for physician, and I'm glad. Given the litany of doctors lined up against my mother, I probably would have taken the idea that Asa was one, too, as an extremely bad omen.

Early into his testimony, Tanner elicited select details about the pastor's life since his wife had died: The daily logistics—the difficulties—of being a widower with children. His inability to sleep. The fact that he was still not emotionally ready to return to the pulpit. He spoke in a soft, halting voice that betrayed no animosity toward my mother, but Asa was as human as the rest of us, and there had to have been a sizable reservoir of rancor inside him.

Then, as he had with Anne Austin, Tanner had the father recall step-by-step what he had witnessed the night and morning his son was born, building to key points he wanted to drive home for the jury.

"And so you asked Mrs. Danforth to try again?" Tanner asked.

"I just couldn't believe Charlotte had really . . . passed away. I just couldn't believe it. So yes, I asked her to try and revive Charlotte again. I think I said something like 'Can't you do more CPR?' "

Tanner nodded gently. As the morning had grown late and they had finally reached the moment in the story when Charlotte had died, Tanner had begun to speak very quietly, as if he wanted to make sure the jury understood that in addition to being a thorough and uncompromising protector of the People, he was also a gentle man who understood this was painful testimony for Asa Bedford. "What did Mrs. Danforth tell you?" he asked.

"She said she—Charlotte—was gone. She said she wasn't coming back." Bedford's voice never broke, but some moments he sounded as if he was still in shock.

"Did you believe her then?"

"Yes, sir, I did. But it was still like I'd been hit hard in the stomach and had had all the wind knocked out of me. Right out of me. I could barely breathe, and I . . . I remember I sort of sagged onto the floor and landed on my knees. I laid my head on Charlotte's chest, and I just stared up into her face. I just stared. I told her how much I loved her. Very much. Very, very much. And I told her how much I wanted her back."

"Did you stay that way with your wife a long while?"

"Oh, no. Not long enough. Not long at all. Mrs. Danforth said something like 'Let's move!' or 'Let's go!' At first I had no idea what she meant by that. I had no idea what she wanted to do. She sounded hysterical, and—"

"Objection."

"Sustained."

"Reverend Bedford," Tanner said, "What did Mrs. Danforth do next? What did she say?"

"Well, she was wiping her eyes and . . . and flailing her arms. She kept saying, 'We don't have any time, we don't have any time!' "

"What did you say?"

"I asked her what she meant."

"And she said?"

"She said . . . she said the baby only had a few minutes, and we had . . . used them . . . used most of them . . . on Charlotte."

"Did you understand then what Mrs. Danforth was planning?"

"No. It just hadn't hit me. I think I even asked her, 'What are you going to do?' "

"Did she tell you?"

"Sort of. She said she was going to save the baby. I think her exact words were 'Save your baby.' But my Charlotte had just died, and the idea of saving my baby and . . . cutting open Charlotte's stomach still weren't . . . linked in my mind. When I finally made that link a couple seconds later—when it dawned on me why she wanted that knife—I asked her again if Charlotte was definitely . . . dead."

With his southern accent he drew two syllables out of the word *dead,* and I found myself wondering how many of the jurors were hearing a southern accent in person for the first time. After all, the first time I'd heard a southern accent was in the Bedfords' house.

"And what did Mrs. Danforth tell you?"

"She said 'Of course.' "

"Meaning 'Of course she was dead.' "

"That's right."

"Did she ask you if you wanted her to try and save the baby?"

"No, sir."

"Did she ask you for your permission to perform a cesarean section on your wife?"

"No, sir, she did not."

"Before she began the cesarean, did you see Mrs. Danforth check to see if Charlotte had a pulse?"

"No."

"Did you see her check to see if there was a . . . a heartbeat?"

"No."

"Did you see her do anything to confirm that Charlotte had indeed . . . passed away?"

"No."

Tanner glanced briefly at my mother, shaking his head in disbelief. She turned away from him and gazed at the lake, while her mother—my grandmother—glared back at the state's attorney. My grandmother had grown angry that week, furious with anyone who would malign her daughter.

"What about the baby?" Tanner then asked the pastor. "Did she check to see if there was a fetal heartbeat?"

"You mean with the . . ."

"The Fetalscope."

"No, sir, I did not see her do that."

"So: You never saw her bother to confirm—"

"Objection."

"Sustained."

"You never saw her confirm that Charlotte was dead or that the baby was alive before she began the C-section."

"No."

"She just plowed ahead."

"Yes."

"What did you do during the operation?"

"I still thought Charlotte was . . . had . . . I still thought Charlotte had passed away, and I went to the window." He motioned toward the easel between his seat and the end of the jury box, which held an overhead drawing of the Bedfords' bedroom.

"Did you watch?"

"I watched some."

"Did you see the first incision?"

"Yes, sir."

"What do you remember about it—that first incision?"

"I remember the blood spurting," Bedford said, his voice rising for the first time during his testimony. "I remember seeing my Charlotte bleed."

I had gotten used to seeing Charlotte's family in the courtroom by the second Monday of the trial. I wasn't ready to wave and say with a sympathetic southern accent, "Hey, how ya doing?" but I no longer shied away from all eye contact. And as I glanced over there as their brother-in-law told his version of what had occurred, I could see in their eyes the fact that we—Sibyl Danforth and her family—were going to lose.

Certainly there were times during Stephen's cross-examination when my spirits would lift: when, for example, with painstaking detail Stephen enumerated all of the reasons why Asa Bedford could not have seen blood spurt or *his* Charlotte "bleed." But when Stephen was done, I still knew we were finished. Asa, after all, was a minister. As powerful as I thought the medical examiner's testimony had been on Friday, even a coroner's credibility pales before a pastor's.

The cross-examination lasted most of the afternoon, and when it was complete Tanner had a brief redirect. Bedford reiterated what he had seen, steadfastly insisting upon the existence and power of one small geyser of blood. And then it was over, and the State rested.

TWENTY

Lawyers have a language as cold as doctors'. But it's not the legal terms themselves that are so icy, it's the way they're used. It's the way those people speak when they're in the courtroom, the way they use even common words and names. Especially names.

Every time Stephen talks about me, he calls me "Sibyl." Every time he talks about Charlotte, she's "Mrs. Bedford" or "Charlotte Bedford." Or, simply, "the wife."

At the same time, Tanner is doing exactly the opposite: When he opens his mouth, I'm always "Mrs. Danforth" or "the midwife." Never, ever "Sibyl." And Charlotte, of course, is always . . . "Charlotte."

Stephen hasn't mentioned it, but it's a strategy both guys are using. Each lawyer is pitting Charlotte and me against each other, and trying to make one of us seem friendly and likable, and the other sort of aloof and formal and distant.

The thing is, I think at one time we were both pretty friendly. If Charlotte didn't have a lot of friends, it wasn't because she was aloof.

I'm supposed to testify Wednesday. Not on Wednesday. Wednesday. The difference, it sounds to me, is one of duration. Between all of the questions I'll have to answer for the two

279

lawyers, I have a feeling I'm going to have to be "Sibyl" and
then "Mrs. Danforth" for a long, long time.

—*from the notebooks of* SIBYL DANFORTH, MIDWIFE

STEPHEN NEVER DOUBTED MY MOTHER WOULD BE AN ATTRACTIVE AND COM-
pelling witness. But he did not want her to be the final witness; he did
not want to end with her the way Tanner had chosen to conclude with
Asa Bedford. He wanted her sandwiched in the middle, between the
road crew members and character witnesses who filled Tuesday's dance
card, and the medical and forensic experts—our medical and forensic
experts, the ones who either believed in their hearts my mother did the
right thing, or were at least willing to say so for the right fee—lined up
for Thursday.

Stephen said he wanted my mother to occupy the middle third of
our defense so she would be an "accessible presence, a woman with a
voice" for the jurors during most of it—especially the critical conclusion
when our expert testimony was being presented. In his opinion, in the
end this would still boil down to a battle of the experts, and so he wanted
to wind up with people who had lots of degrees and dignified suits.

He hoped to complete his defense in three days, but he said it
wouldn't be the end of the world if it lasted four. His principal objective
when he looked at the calendar was to be done by the end of the week,
so the jury wouldn't go home for the weekend with the fear that the trial
was going to drag on forever.

I don't know exactly what Judge Dorset was expecting from my
mother's midwife and client friends as Stephen prepared to present our
version, but Tuesday morning before the jury was brought into the
courtroom, he requested that all of the mothers who had babies wanting
to nurse take their little ones outside the room when they grew hungry.
Stephen objected, contending that changing the rules midstream sent a
signal to the jury that somehow cast a negative light upon midwifery,
home birth, and—of course—my mother. He also implied that the judge
was risking a mistrial.

Judge Dorset smiled: "Unless there is a mother or an infant present
who wants to make an issue of this, I doubt the jury will even notice."

And so we began. Graham Tuttle, Lawson plow driver, told everyone how impassable the roads were on March 14. The phone com-

pany's Lois Gaylord confirmed the hours the phones were down. Our accident reconstructionist reassured the jury that my mother had indeed spun out on the ice in the Bedfords' driveway, and a physician used photos to explain the cuts and bruises my mother had sustained on the slick surface. By lunchtime Stephen had done what he could to convey that my mother was trapped with the Bedfords, and there was absolutely no way they could leave for the hospital.

What Stephen could not do with this particular group of witnesses, of course, was undermine Tanner's contention that she should never have been trapped with the Bedfords in the first place—that a capable and trustworthy midwife would have checked the weather and learned of the oncoming storm, and then chosen to transfer Charlotte Bedford to the hospital the moment her labor commenced. In theory, that responsibility would fall upon the character witnesses planned for that afternoon: It would be up to them to refute any suggestion that my mother was not supremely competent and incontrovertibly reliable.

And most of them did a pretty good job, especially B.P. Hewitt, my mother's backup physician. Hewitt endured a cross-examination that would have withered most people.

"If Sibyl believed the woman was dead, then I believe the woman was dead," he told Tanner at one point.

"Were you present at the autopsy?"

"No."

"Did you examine Charlotte's medical records after she died?"

"No."

"Had you even examined her at any point in her pregnancy?"

"Nope."

"You really have no idea, then, what you're talking about, do you?"

"Objection!"

"Sustained."

"You really have no . . . detailed understanding of this case, then. Do you?"

"Oh, I think I do. I think I understand how a labor develops and—"

"*This* labor. Not any labor. *This* labor."

"I understood your question. You asked me if I had a detailed understanding of this case. Well, I do. And I don't believe it's Sibyl's fault."

"Your Honor, would you please instruct the witness to answer the question?"

"In my judgment, he did."

Tanner was flustered for a moment, but the moment was brief. He stared at his notes, caught his breath, and quickly regrouped.

"Okay," he continued, finally. "You never met Charlotte. You never saw her body after her death. You never saw her records. Why do you feel you understand her death so well?"

B.P. shook his head in astonishment. "Come on, I'm Sibyl's backup doctor. I don't think I've had a conversation with an ob-gyn in the last six months where this case hasn't come up."

"But you know nothing firsthand, do you?"

"I have known Sibyl Danforth for close to a decade. And I know what she has told me about this incident. If Sibyl tells me the woman was dead when she did the C-section, then in my mind the case is closed."

It would not be accurate to write that, the night before she was scheduled to testify, my mother feared she was going to be convicted. The word *fear* suggests that the prospect frightened her, and I think by Tuesday night her fear—and her notebooks indicate that there were moments earlier when she had been very scared indeed—had been replaced by numbness and shock. Rather, the night before my mother would take the witness stand, she simply expected that she was going to be convicted.

My father, on the other hand, was frightened. After one of those cold-cut dinners during which no one eats or says very much, I went upstairs to look at the books I was supposed to be reading for school. I didn't expect to accomplish anything, though, and I figured by nine o'clock I'd be on the telephone with Rollie or Tom, telling them what I thought had occurred that day in the courthouse, and what I thought it meant.

I was sitting on my bed about eight-thirty when my father knocked on my door (a knock that had always been louder than my mother's), and I told him to come in.

"Your mom just went to bed," he said, putting his coffee mug down on my desk. "She wants to get a good night's sleep for tomorrow."

"She tired?" I asked. Over the last few weeks, I'd noticed, he had gone from an occasional scotch after dinner to coffee, and I was glad.

"I guess. I know I am." He turned my desk chair so it faced the bed, and then collapsed into the small wooden seat as if it were a plush little couch. "How about you? Tired?"

"Yup."

"You've been a dream through this, you know."

I rolled my eyes, trying to downplay the compliment. "A dream? Corny, Dad. Very corny."

"I'm getting old."

"Yeah, right. You and Mom had me when you were about seven. If I get pregnant when Mom did, you'll both kill me."

He nodded. "Probably." He reached for his mug and took a swallow so long it surprised me. "Anyway, I just wanted you to know that your mom and I are proud of you. We're proud to have you with us through this whole . . . thing."

"What do you think will happen?"

"Tomorrow? Or when it's all over?"

"When it's all over."

He sighed. "Oh, we'll just go back to leading a normal, incredibly boring life. And we'll love it."

"So you think they'll find Mom innocent?"

"Oh, yes. And if they don't, we'll appeal."

"Have you and Stephen talked about that?"

"It's come up, yes."

He left a few minutes later. When he was gone, I tried not to read anything more into his visit than his desire to offer his daughter praise, but I did. Before I even thought about what I was telling Tom, I heard myself portraying my brief exchange with my father as further proof that my mother was going to be convicted, telling my boyfriend that the very idea of a family life in the coming years that was normal and incredibly boring had become my father's idea of a fairy tale.

"Why don't I go with you to the trial tomorrow?" Tom said.

"You shouldn't miss school. And you probably couldn't sit with me, anyway," I told him. But I liked the idea of Tom in the courtroom, knowing I could turn around and see him there—a sixteen-year-old in a dark turtleneck, surrounded in a back row by little babies and midwives—and I hoped he'd ignore me and skip school.

◆ ◆ ◆

Everything had become for me a dramatic portent of evil, and not just because I was a fourteen-year-old girl with teenage judgment and adolescent hormones. To this day, I believe my take on the trial was accurate, and my actions the next day explicable—if not wholly justifiable.

Later that night when I was finally going to sleep myself, I heard my parents making love in their room, and even that seemed to me a sign that the end was nearing. I put my pillow over my head so I wouldn't hear their bed in the distance and so the pillowcase could absorb my tears. And as soon as the white cotton grew damp and I felt the wetness on my cheek, I was reminded of how my mother had used a pillow to soak up the blood inside Charlotte Bedford.

And then my tears became sobs.

My mother wore the green kilt she had worn the day the trial began, and she put back her hair in the same cornflower-blue hair clip. Her blouse was white, but it had a rounded collar and so much ornate stitching it did not look at all austere. As she sat on the stand, she looked to me like a professional and a mother at once—a mother, these days, too young to have a teenage daughter.

Moreover, because a witness stand tends to exaggerate both a person's aesthetic strengths and weaknesses, my mother's exhaustion gave her an almost heroic-looking stature: The combination of increased height and a waist-level barrier made her look like one of those saintly Red Cross volunteers I'd seen recently on the TV news who had stayed up all night giving coffee and blankets to hurricane victims in the Mississippi bayou.

To the jurors, of course, she might simply have looked guilty. She might simply have looked like a tired woman who couldn't sleep because of the blood on her hands.

But at least in the first two hours of her testimony, she spoke well. She was eloquent when Stephen asked her to explain why she had become a midwife, and why helping women to have their babies at home was important to her. She sounded like the most reasonable person in the world when Stephen asked her about the role hospitals usually played in her practice.

"If I see a danger, I will never let a mother's desire to have her baby at home—even if it's a really powerful desire—cloud my judgment. If there are any indications at all that the baby is in distress, I will always transfer the woman to the hospital."

"What about the mother?"

"Same thing. If there's a problem developing, we'll go to the hospital. A lot of people think midwives are anti-hospital or anti-doctor. We're not. I'm not. I have a great relationship with B.P.—Dr. Hewitt. I do what I do—I help ladies have their babies at home—because I know that I can depend on hospitals and doctors if a medical emergency develops."

And as reasonable as my mother sounded when she discussed hospitals, she was every bit as confident and unwavering when she offered her version of what had transpired on the morning of March 14.

"Did you check one last time to see if the woman had a pulse?" Stephen asked.

"Yes."

"Did you hear one?"

"No."

"Did you check one last time to see if she had a heartbeat?"

"Yes, absolutely."

"And did you hear one?"

"No, I did not."

"You did everything possible to make sure the woman was dead?"

"Oh, yes."

"What about the baby? Did you check to see if the baby was alive?"

"Yes, I did. I listened for a heartbeat with the Fetalscope. And I heard one," she answered, looking directly at Stephen as she spoke. She never allowed her gaze to wander toward my father and me, or toward the other side of the courtroom, where she might risk eye contact with Charlotte's family.

"I did everything I could before I began to try and be sure that Char—the mother—had died, but the baby was still alive," she answered.

"Where were the father and your apprentice when you checked? Were they with you?"

"No, they weren't in the room. I think they were still in the kitchen."

"Getting the knife?"

"That's right."

"So they never saw you check the woman or the baby?"

"No."

"But you did?"

"Yes. For sure."

Midmorning Tom Corts arrived in the courtroom, and I was both surprised and glad. With the exception of the small space beside the Fugetts, there were no seats left, and so he stood beside one of the court officers near the door, with his back flat against the rear wall.

It was sometime near eleven o'clock that my mother's answers started sounding less precise and some of her responses began to grow slightly fuzzy. She had been on the stand for close to two hours, answering questions for Stephen that ranged from such generalities as the sorts of words she might use to convey risk to parents at a first trimester meeting, to the specifics of why she had ruptured the membranes that dammed Charlotte Bedford's amniotic fluid.

"I didn't ask Asa in so many words, 'May I save the baby?' and maybe I should have, but at the time I was just focused on the baby—the baby and the mother—and that conversation seemed unnecessary," she said at one point, fumbling a bit as the adrenaline that had gotten her through most of the morning began to dissipate.

"Am I correct in saying that conversation was unnecessary because in your opinion Asa understood exactly what you were planning to do, and had therefore given his consent?" Stephen asked, trying to bail my mother out.

"Objection. Leading the witness, Your Honor."

"Sustained."

"Did you believe Asa had given his consent?"

"Yes," my mother said.

And then, a few moments later, when Stephen asked, "Did the father try and stop you?" she volunteered an answer that I know wasn't part of the script: "Asa was a husband as well as a father, and no husband in that situation would be in any condition to make any kind of decision."

"But in your judgment he made a . . . conscious decision not to stop you, correct?"

"Correct."

Before the day began, I had worried about the cross-examination, but never about my mother's direct testimony. I did now: I did not believe my mother wanted to be convicted, but as the morning drew to a close, some of her responses almost made it sound as if she no longer cared. Unfortunately, Stephen didn't dare end her testimony at that moment, because then the cross-examination would begin before lunch. I think Stephen thought it was paramount to keep her on the stand until close to noon so the cross-examination would not start until after lunch and he could use the noon recess to buck up her spirits and get her refocused.

Just before eleven-thirty, while still in the midst of her direct testimony, she slipped into one of her answers a sentence that none of us expected, and for which Stephen himself wasn't prepared. If it wasn't the single most damaging thing she could have said from our perspective, it was among the most surprising. It changed everything, and everyone in the courtroom knew it changed everything the moment she said it:

> HASTINGS: And the father was still beside the window?
> DANFORTH: Yes, he was sitting in the chair there, holding his
> baby in his arms. He was looking down at him, and Anne was
> right beside him—kneeling on the floor. From where they were
> they could see there was a body on the bed, but I know they
> couldn't see the . . . the incision, and I was glad. I thought it
> would have been too painful for them to have seen it. I don't
> recall actually turning out the light by the bed when I was
> through, but I looked at my notebooks the other day and I saw
> that I had.

Stephen immediately tried to clarify what she meant, asking, "You mean your medical notebooks, correct?" but it was too late.

"No," my mother answered slowly, her voice meek with shock. She knew instantly what she had done, and she knew what would happen. "My personal notebooks. My diary."

There was no dramatic rumble or murmur in the courtroom, because we were all too stunned to speak. All except Bill Tanner.

With a voice that sounded almost ebullient, he asked the judge if he could approach the bench, and then he and his deputy and Stephen and Peter all congregated before Judge Dorset. In my row, my father, my grandmother, Patty, and the two law clerks stared straight ahead in silence, trying to keep their emotions inside them. But I knew what they were feeling. Everyone in the courtroom knew what they were feeling, because everyone in the courtroom knew what this meant. Even if, like me, they didn't know exactly what the law was or what exactly would happen next, they all knew that my mother had just announced to the prosecution that there existed notebooks they had never seen that might have a direct—and devastating—bearing on her case.

This is the law: In the discovery process in the state of Vermont, Stephen Hastings was under no obligation to inform Bill Tanner that my mother's personal notebooks existed, or to turn them over to the prosecution.

This is the fact: My mother had told Stephen soon after they met that the notebooks existed, and he had read some of them—at least some of them, maybe whole years' worth. When he saw that some of the entries from mid-March could be construed as incriminating, he told her to stop keeping what was in essence a personal diary, and to never speak of the diary again until after the trial. She said she would abide by both requests, and then ignored both—one by design, and one by accident. My mother was simply incapable of not keeping a diary. She had kept one throughout her entire adult life, and it was probably unrealistic to expect her to stop chronicling her actions and emotions in the midst of the worst stress she would ever experience.

And so the State had seen the medical records and charts my mother kept on her patients—the prenatal forms, patient histories, obstetric examination reports—but not what she referred to as her notebooks.

The four attorneys and the court reporter huddled around Judge Dorset in a bench conference that lasted eighteen minutes. The clock in the courtroom read eleven twenty-nine when Bill Tanner stood and eleven forty-seven when the four men returned to their tables and the court reporter sat back down at her desk.

When it had become clear to the judge that the discussion would last more than a few moments, he had had the jury escorted from the room for the duration of the debate. But no one thought to offer my mother the chance to return to her own seat, and so she was forced to sit alone in the witness box the whole time as if she were cornered in a classroom in a dunce cap. Usually she stared into the courtroom or up at the chandelier without expression, her chin cupped in her hand, but she did glance once at our family and offer us a hint of a smile. *This sure smarts, doesn't it?* that hint of a smile said, and in my head I heard her voice saying exactly those words to me, recalling the time years earlier when I'd been standing on one of the picnic table benches in our backyard and slipped off, and banged my elbow on the table itself.

"This sure smarts, doesn't it?" she had murmured, rubbing the skin that would soon bruise with two fingers.

When Stephen returned to his table, he looked glum. It was a short walk from the bench to his seat, but in even those few steps it was clear he had lost for the moment his one-click-above swagger.

The judge scribbled a note to himself before informing us of his decision, and then spoke in a combination of legalese for the lawyers' benefit and layman's terms for the rest of us. Apparently during the conference Tanner had demanded that my mother produce her notebooks so the State could see what was in them. Stephen had argued that they weren't relevant to the event itself, and there was no medical detail in them that mattered. But Tanner insisted that it was, after all, my mother who had brought them up, and she had brought them up to corroborate her own testimony. And so Judge Dorset ruled that he wanted all of the notebooks from March forward in his hands by the end of the lunch break. The trial would be recessed until he had inspected them himself *in camera*—in his chambers.

"I will decide what, if anything, is relevant," he concluded.

He then told us all that the jury would be brought back into the courtroom and that my mother would complete her direct testimony; when she was finished, we would adjourn until he had reviewed the notebooks.

"Your Honor, a moment, please," Stephen said, and the judge nodded. Stephen then motioned for Patty to join Peter Grinnell and him at their table. The three of them whispered briefly together, and then Stephen asked to approach my mother. Again the judge nodded, and Stephen walked quickly to my mother and asked her a question none of us could hear.

But we all heard her response, and I began to realize what would happen next.

"They're right behind my desk," my mother said. "They're on a bookcase, on the lowest shelf."

Did I know exactly at that moment what I would do? I don't

believe so; the idea was only beginning to form. But with merely a vague notion, I still knew what the first step had to be.

My father, my grandmother, and I were separated from the defense table by a link of black velvet rope—the sort of barrier that often cordons off bedrooms in historic homes. For the first and only time during that trial I leaned forward off my seat on the bench, half-squatting, and I tapped Peter Grinnell on the back of his shoulder.

When he turned to me I whispered, "Look, if you need any help, I'll go with you. I know right where they are."

Stephen still had to finish eliciting from my mother her direct testimony, and so Peter stayed with him in the courtroom. It was Patty Dunlevy who was sent to Reddington to get the notebooks.

I went with the investigator, on some level astonished that I was sitting in the front passenger seat of her sleek little car. I told myself that I had not yet committed to anything, I was not yet a criminal; I was still, in the eyes of everyone around me, merely going to my house with Patty Dunlevy to show her where my mother's notebooks were kept so we could bring them back to the courthouse as the judge had requested.

Yet there I was, trying to disregard the way my head was filled with the sound of my beating heart, focusing solely on what I had read late into the night the Wednesday before. I tried to remember which dates were the most incriminating, which entries were most likely to be—as the lawyers and the judge euphemistically phrased it—relevant.

The trees along the road were growing bare by then, a small sign to me of the way the world went about its business while we were squirreled away in a courtroom.

I thought of the far worse captivity that loomed before my mother.

"How are you holding up?" Patty asked, her voice suggesting a maternal inclination I hadn't imagined existed in her.

"Fine," I told her, practicing in my head what I would say when we arrived at my house: *Why don't you wait here, and I'll run inside and get them.*

"What just happened happens all the time. Try not to worry. A trial like this always has some chaos," she went on.

"Uh-huh." As I recalled, there were probably three loose-leaf binders that would matter to Judge Dorset: The March entries were toward the end of one notebook; early April through August were in a second;

and August through September formed the beginning of a third. Those were the notebooks I would need to bring back to the courthouse.

"In the end, this will just be a . . . a little footnote to this whole affair," she said.

I nodded. *Why don't you wait here, and I'll go find them. Don't worry, I can carry them.*

She asked, "You hungry?"

"Nope." I figured I would have at least five minutes before Patty would begin to wonder what I was doing. I couldn't tell if she was the sort who would follow me into the house to help if I didn't return quickly.

"I am. Isn't that unbelievable?"

Fortunately, when my mother had begun keeping her notebooks years earlier, she had chosen to use three-ring binders and loose-leaf paper. Moreover, at some point she had gotten into the habit of beginning each entry on a separate sheet.

"I don't think I could eat anything," I told her. I would definitely remove the March 15 entry, because I knew there was another one on the sixteenth that also talked about Charlotte Bedford's death. I'd have to check to be sure, but I thought there was a chance it was on the sixteenth that my mother wrote about where Asa had been holding the baby and where Anne had been sitting. And there were those entries further on in the summer, the ones in late July and August and even September, where the doubts in her mind had become so pronounced that they were no longer doubts: She was almost certain she had killed Charlotte Bedford.

Those entries would have to go, too.

"Well, after we've given Dorset the notebooks, I'm going to have to steal away and get something to eat."

I nodded.

"Any idea what sort of things your mom wrote in her diaries?"

"She's never shown them to me," I told her.

I think initially Patty was going to keep her car running while I ran inside our house, but I heard her turn off the engine while I fumbled with my key in the front door.

I had to go to the bathroom, but I didn't dare take the time then. I went straight to my mother's office and found the three notebooks the judge would expect, and laid them out upon my mother's desk in a row. I would move chronologically forward from March.

For a second I considered flipping through the pages with my fingertips wrapped in Kleenex, but then I remembered the pages were already covered with my fingerprints from the week before. And so I decided I would only bother with tissue when I pressed down hard on the metal tabs at the top and the bottom of the binder that would release the key pages.

Tom had offered to go with us, but I was glad I'd said no. I felt bad enough about what I was doing; I wouldn't have wanted to involve anyone else.

I was shaking as I worked, a precursor of sorts to the trembling I'd experience while we awaited the verdict. I wasn't sure what law I was breaking, but I knew what I was doing was illegal. And I knew what I was doing was wrong.

When I returned to Patty's car I was still shuddering. I dropped the three notebooks onto the floor below the glove compartment and pushed them to the side with my feet as I climbed in. Five loose sheets of paper, folded down to the size of a paperback book, were pressed flat against my stomach, hidden under my blouse and my sweater and my jacket.

"Is that everything?" Patty asked, glancing down at the notebooks on the floor mat.

"That's everything," I said, the first of at least three times I can recall that I told that particular lie.

By the time we returned, my mother had completed her testimony and the court had recessed. Before taking the binders with him into his chambers, the judge told us he would let us know by one-thirty or two whether we could all go home for the day or whether the trial would resume midafternoon. If we were told to go home, it meant he was probably going to allow some or all of the notebooks, and Stephen and Bill Tanner would be granted a day to examine the entries; if we were asked to remain, it meant the judge had decided nothing in the note-books was relevant and the State would not be allowed to see them.

Stephen was prepared to lose: He was prepared to lose both on the specific issue of the notebooks, and I think he was prepared to lose the case. He knew what my mother had written in March and—perhaps—early April: He probably knew that it only got worse.

And I think my mother was ready for defeat as well. I didn't believe at the time that my mother had slipped on the stand with the conscious hope that it would ensure a conviction—and even today I don't think she hoped for one on an unconscious level—but I think she had become resigned to that inevitability. Given the guilt in her own mind, she must have viewed her notebooks as all the evidence the State needed to convince the jury she had killed a woman in labor.

The difference in my mother's and Stephen's attitudes, if there really was one, is that Stephen still had some fight left in him. He was prepared to appeal a decision that allowed any part of the notebooks as evidence, and he was already modifying his strategy for his expert witnesses: It didn't matter whether Sibyl Danforth thought Charlotte Bedford was dead or alive, because Sibyl was merely a midwife. Our obstetric experts and forensic pathologists were positive, based on their years and years of medical experience, that the woman was dead by the time my mother made her first cut.

The principal issue he would have to overcome was my mother's testimony itself. Carefully he had elicited from her the idea that she had done everything she could to see whether Charlotte Bedford was dead, without ever having her say categorically that she was sure beyond doubt that the woman had died. That part of the transcript has become for me a small study in legal ethics:

> HASTINGS: Did you check one last time to see if the woman had a pulse?
> DANFORTH: Yes.
> HASTINGS: Did you hear one?
> DANFORTH: No.
> HASTINGS: Did you check one last time to see if she had a heartbeat?
> DANFORTH: Yes, absolutely.
> HASTINGS: And did you hear one?
> DANFORTH: No, I did not.
> HASTINGS: You did everything possible to make sure the woman was dead?
> DANFORTH: Oh, yes.

My mother hadn't lied, but if the notebooks were allowed, it would look to the jury as if she had, and not even Stephen Hastings's experts would be able to restore her credibility.

Consequently, our lunch was an extremely quiet affair, and even Patty Dunlevy was subdued while we awaited Judge Dorset's ruling. Occasionally my father or Stephen would try and bolster my mother's spirits as they had in the days immediately before the trial started, and once or twice Peter Grinnell tried to include Tom—who, despite every- thing else on her mind, my mother had somehow remembered to invite to lunch—in the conversation by asking him about school. But most of the time everyone sat around the wooden restaurant table in silence.

While the fears of the adults around me began and ended with the issue of whether Judge Dorset would allow the notebooks to be admitted as evidence, I had an additional worry as we ascended the stairs to the third-story courtroom to hear the judge's ruling. I was afraid he had discovered that pages were missing, and in a voice filled with fury and disgust he would ask Stephen or me what we had done with them. Throughout lunch and as we walked back to the courthouse, I had been sure that everyone around me heard the papers rustling beneath my clothes every time that I moved, and I was convinced the moment the judge saw me that he would be able to tell I was responsible.

When I'd gone to the bathroom at the restaurant, I'd considered ripping the pages to shreds and flushing them down the toilet, but I was afraid: If the judge discovered they were missing and insisted that they be presented, their continued existence might be my only hope for clem- ency. But as we wandered near the ladies' room at the courthouse, the idea crossed my mind once more to destroy them, and I told my parents I had to go to the bathroom and I would catch up with them in the courtroom in a minute.

Tom asked me if I was feeling okay, and I told him I was fine.

In the courthouse bathroom, however, I was again unable to bring myself to dispose of the notebook pages, although this time it was not merely a fear of the judge that prevented me. At some point, I assumed, my mother would get her notebooks back: Although it was unlikely I could ever press the folds from the pages and replace them in the diaries before she noticed they were missing, at the very least I could still return them to her. Someday, I imagined, she would forgive me for reading them—especially, I reasoned, if by some miracle she was acquitted.

But I did read the pages once more in that bathroom, and as I did

I reassured myself that I was making the correct decision: I had to do everything I could to protect my mother and preserve our family.

Besides, my mother's conviction would not bring back Charlotte Bedford. It would merely destroy a second woman.

The jury was not present when Judge Dorset issued his ruling, but most of the spectators had reassembled.

None of us, of course, could see Stephen's or my mother's expressions when he spoke, but I assume if the spectators envisioned anything at all on their faces, they envisioned only relief: The judge ruled that there was nothing in the diaries that was relevant to my mother's testimony specifically, or to the case in general. The notebooks were a personal account of her life but had little relevance to the issues under examination and would therefore not be shared with the State.

Did Judge Dorset—who could stare directly into Stephen's and my mother's faces—see that in addition to relief there had to be surprise? He was an intelligent man, so I'm sure he did. I'm sure he saw disbelief in their eyes: My mother knew exactly what she had written at different points over the last seven months, and they both knew what she had written on March 15.

My mother and Stephen must have thought they had been given— inexplicably, and without reason—an astonishing gift from the judge, a gift that grew tangible when a court officer carried the three blue binders to the defense table and handed them over to my mother. A moment later the jury was brought back into the courtroom, my mother was returned to the stand, and Bill Tanner began his cross-examination.

TWENTY-ONE

I cannot undo what I've done, or what I might have done. I don't think there's anything left for me to set right.

—*from the notebooks of* SIBYL DANFORTH, MIDWIFE

TANNER'S CROSS-EXAMINATION WAS OFTEN BRUTAL AND OCCASIONALLY MEAN-spirited. He was angry that the notebooks had not been shared with the State, and his fury was fresh.

Yet my mother endured and even snapped back at Tanner a number of times. At one point she reminded him that when it came to neonatal mortality, her track record was as good as any ob-gyn's; a few moments later she noted that her mothers' babies were less likely to have a low birth weight. She was even able to reiterate how hard she had worked to try and save Charlotte, and how she had only performed the C-section because there didn't seem to be any other choice.

"I had completed at least eight or nine cycles by then," she told Tanner, referring to the CPR she had performed on Charlotte, "and I still wasn't hearing a heartbeat in the woman—but I was getting one from the baby. What was I supposed to do, let them both die?"

I wouldn't categorize all of her testimony as spunky, but there were some particularly spirited exchanges, and she had regained the clarity of mind she had demonstrated early that morning.

And Tanner never asked the one question I dreaded—and, in all likelihood, the one my mother and Stephen feared most: Is there absolutely no doubt in your mind that Charlotte Bedford was dead when you performed the cesarean? But Tanner had no idea what my mother had written in her diary, and so he assumed there was none. Asking her that question in front of the jury would only hurt the State's case by giving her yet one more opportunity to say Charlotte had already passed away when she chose to save the infant's life.

Although there were occasional sparks that afternoon, my mother's cross-examination and the remainder of the trial seemed anticlimactic to me.

Wednesday night I carried my mother's notebooks into the house from the car for her and offered to return them to her bookcase.

"That would be lovely," she said. "Thank you."

I flattened the pages that I'd removed as best I could before I returned them to the binders, but it would always be clear that someone at some point had removed some entries. Apparently she did not add anything to her notebook that night, and she was so tired she never even looked at the books before going to bed.

The next day, Thursday, our obstetricians and our forensic pathologists all said in one way or another that in their opinion my mother had not killed Charlotte Bedford. But Bill Tanner also made sure each witness acknowledged that he had received a fee for his opinion, and that those opinions were not based on having done—or even having seen— the autopsy. Nevertheless, they were impressive figures, especially the elderly fellow from Texas who had had the misfortune of having to perform autopsies four times on women who had died in botched cesareans, some in desperately poor hospitals near the border with Mexico. In all his years and in all those tragic autopsies, he had never once seen less than eleven hundred milliliters of blood in the peritoneal cavity—a full pint more than Vermont's Dr. Tierney had found inside Charlotte Bedford.

And then on Friday, the attorneys gave their closing arguments, and while they were eloquent, it was clear that both the fly fisherman and the Vietnam veteran were exhausted. I had expected the arguments to last all day—or at least all morning—and I was wrong. The arguments were over by quarter to eleven, and the jury had their instructions from the judge by eleven-thirty. They began their deliberations before lunch.

◆ ◆ ◆

We expected a long deliberation, and so we went home. Stephen had offered to take us to lunch, but my mother said she wasn't hungry.

And so we—the Danforths and their lawyers—left the courthouse, expecting we would separate in the parking lot across the street. Just before my family climbed into our station wagon, as Patty was telling my grandmother and me something about her years on a high-school track team when she was roughly my age, I overheard my father ask Stephen what it would mean if the deliberations went into the weekend.

"This whole business has a lot of great myths," he said to my parents. "Usually, a long deliberation doesn't bode well for a defendant. If a jury's going to send someone away for a long time, they like to make absolutely sure they don't have any doubt about his guilt. And that can take time. But I've also seen cases, even first-degree murder cases, in which it was all pretty cut-and-dried, and the jury came back with a conviction in two or three hours."

"And this one?" my father asked.

"I haven't a clue. But there was a lot of so-called expert testimony they have to wrestle with, and to me that suggests they'll take their time."

"The weekend?"

"There's a chance. But for all we know, the minute you get home you'll get a phone call from me saying to turn around and come right back."

"Are you going back to Burlington?"

"Nope."

"You're staying in Newport?"

"I am."

"So in your opinion, there's a good chance they'll reach a verdict this afternoon."

He shrugged. "I'd hate to get all the way back to Burlington and have them reach their verdict around four o'clock. That wouldn't be fair to you."

"To us?"

"Judge Dorset won't allow the verdict to be read unless I'm present. And you don't want it read unless I'm present. If I couldn't be back here by five o'clock—five-fifteen, at the latest—he'd have to wait until Monday morning to have the verdict announced. And that just wouldn't be fair to you, Sibyl. To any of you."

"No, I guess it wouldn't," my father agreed.

"Nope, not at all."

"Those 'great myths,' " my father said. "Are there more?"

Stephen smiled. "Well, some lawyers think you can tell how the jury has ruled the moment they reenter the courtroom after their deliberations. If they look at the defendant, he's going to be acquitted. If they refuse to look at him—if they're unwilling or unable to look at him—he's going to be convicted."

"In your experience?"

"In my experience? Don't believe it, it's just a myth."

That was the only day during the trial that we had driven my grandmother to the courthouse, and so before we left Newport there was some brief discussion about whether we should go to her home to wait or ours. My mother wanted to go home, and so we decided we would go to Reddington.

"Do you want to join us, Stephen?" my mother asked. "Do you all want to join us? It'll only be sandwiches, but . . ."

Stephen thought for a moment, looked at his team—Patty and Peter and the law clerks—and then at my father. I'm sure my father wasn't happy about my mother's lawyer and entourage descending upon his house once more, but the invitation had come from his wife and so he offered Stephen a small smile.

"Sure," Stephen said, "that would be nice."

My grandmother sat in the backseat of our car and asked me innocuous questions about horses and Tom Corts before figuring out I was uninterested—perhaps incapable—of conversation. All I could think about were the ostensible myths Stephen had shared with my father, especially the idea that some lawyers believed you could tell the verdict the moment the jury returned. It made complete sense to me, it reflected what I imagined was the way I would behave if I were on a jury someday: I knew I would be unable to look at a defendant if I was about to send him to prison.

And so the myth grew real in my mind. It hardened into fact a little later as I drove with Cheryl Visco to the supermarket to get cold cuts and salads and breads for the group of lawyers and midwives that had gathered at our house; it became gospel as I watched the law clerk named Laurel and the midwife Donelle Folino find small reasons to laugh. When my mother was not within earshot, I would hear different groups of adults discussing my mother's future, and I would hear words like *appeal* and *wrongful death,* and I would cringe.

I wished Tom were there, but he had gone to school that day. Besides, I wouldn't have dared call him because that would have meant using the telephone, and the last thing any of us wanted was to be on the telephone if the jury came back with a verdict. ·

And of course the phone rang constantly that afternoon, which was an enormous source of frustration. The calls were always from reporters or my mother's friends, and by two-thirty my father was snapping at them all without discrimination—and no one who heard him could blame him.

Sometimes I heard people talking about the notebooks, but my mother never went to her office to look at them and I was relieved. As far as I knew, she had not opened them on Thursday night either, and so she still hadn't discovered what I'd done.

Would I have broken down as I did if the verdict had come in the following week, would my howls have been quite so loud if the jury had deliberated throughout the weekend? Would waiting the weekend— and therefore having to endure the myth that a long deliberation meant conviction—have caused the same sort of emotional explosion?

Perhaps, but we'll never know, because we were called at three-twenty with the news that we should return to the courthouse.

No one would venture a guess in my mother's presence what a four-hour deliberation actually meant, but I know I was feeling for the first time in well over a week that there was a chance my mother would be vindicated. I could tell Patty Dunlevy felt the same way, and it almost seemed that Stephen had regained his swagger.

But no one would speak of such things to my mother. In one of the strangest exchanges I heard in all of the months before the trial began and the two weeks of the trial itself, my grandmother asked my mother as we drove back to the courthouse, "Have you ever considered putting in another window in your examining room? I think the extra light would make the room much more cheerful."

"I haven't," my mother answered, apparently contemplating a future somewhat different from our fantasies. "But maybe someday when those prenatal posters are gone I'll hang some nice flowered wallpaper. Wallpaper with irises, maybe. Lots and lots of blue irises."

Looking back, I think it was the sheer speed of the deliberations that led to my cries in the courtroom.

By the time we had returned to Newport and climbed the stairs in the courthouse, by the time the judge had told the spectators that he would tolerate "no theatrics, disturbances, or dramatic reactions to the verdict" when it was read, by the time he had asked one of the bailiffs to escort the jury back into their long box and the rest of us were rising in our seats, I had concluded that my mother would be found not guilty on the one charge that mattered: involuntary manslaughter.

I don't think I really cared whether she was found guilty of the misdemeanor, of practicing medicine without a license.

Yet as the jury was being led in, that changed. That changed completely. None of the twelve jurors would look at my mother. They looked straight ahead of them as they walked, they looked at their shoes as they sat. They looked at the clock on the wall, they looked at the lake.

"Please be seated," the judge told us when the jury was back. "Good afternoon," he said to the group, and then turned to one of the court officers.

"Miss Rivers, do you have the envelope with the sealed verdict forms?"

"Yes, Your Honor."

"Would you please return that envelope to the foreman?"

My mother sat unmoving between Stephen and Peter, her hands clasped before her on the table. Beside me I saw my grandmother's hands were trembling.

"Mr. Foreman, would you review the envelope with the forms?"

The foreman had one good hand, and one with only a thumb. But over the years he had apparently become fairly dexterous with his six fingers: With the disfigured hand he used his thumb and palm to hold the envelope, and with the other he flipped through the papers.

"Are they the forms you signed? Are they in order?" Judge Dorset asked.

The foreman looked at the judge and nodded. And still none of the jurors would offer my mother a glance. Not one brief glance. They wouldn't even look at my father or me.

Please, I prayed to myself, *please, look at me, look at my mother. Look at us, look here, look here, look here.* But none would, none did. And then one, the elderly Lipponcott woman, looked toward Bill Tanner, and I knew it was over and we had lost. My mother would be found guilty, my mother would go to jail. My theft of pages from my mother's notebooks had merely been one more meaningless gesture in a meaningless tragedy. Charlotte Bedford was dead, and my mother's life was essentially over. She would go to jail, she would never catch babies again.

And that's when I started to cry. It wasn't simply the pressure that caused me to scream and sob, it wasn't the waiting or the tension or the stress. It was the idea that the roller-coaster ride was finally coming to an end, and it was coming to an end with a long chain of cars—some holding Bedfords and some holding Danforths—smashed on the stanchions that were supposed to carry us all high above the craggy horrors of the earth.

I was not present when the verdict was read, I was with my grandmother and Cheryl Visco and Patty Dunlevy in a small conference room far down the hall. I have been told that when the judge asked my mother to stand and face the jury, Stephen helped her to her feet. Some of those present tell me that he held her elbow as the verdict became public, but others aren't so sure. With my father right behind him, I don't believe that Stephen would have done such a thing.

But I was wrong about so much; he may have.

If my mother believed the myth about juries Stephen had told us earlier that day in the parking lot, and if she had noticed that none of the jurors would look at her, then she may have been surprised by the verdict. I am told she nodded her head a tiny bit and sighed, and my family's relief was manifested much more visibly by my father: He murmured a "Thank you" so loud that people in the rows far behind him could hear it, and looked up toward the ceiling in gratitude and relief.

A long second later, when everyone in the courtroom had absorbed the verdict, there was the sort of spontaneous reaction that the judge chose not to stifle: Charlotte's sister and mother and the midwives started to cry. The midwives cried with joy, while the Fugetts sobbed for their dead sister and daughter and friend.

Some of the witnesses who had been kept from the courtroom through the largest part of the trial, people like Asa Bedford and Anne Austin and B.P. Hewitt, were in the room when the verdicts were announced, but none of them showed much reaction. Not even Asa. He hugged Charlotte's mother and rocked her, but his face remained impassive.

Later Bill Tanner would try and suggest that although my mother had been acquitted on the charge of involuntary manslaughter, the jury had still sent an important message to midwives about home birth: They had found her guilty of practicing medicine without a license, a signal that he said meant Vermont juries were not at all enamored with the idea of home birth.

That evening, however, neither the midwives nor my father cared that my mother had been found guilty of the misdemeanor. A two-hundred-dollar fine was absolutely nothing compared to a manslaughter conviction, and once more the adults played loud party tapes at our house, while I curled up on the couch in their midst and sipped herbal tea till close to midnight.

Even seven years after my mother's trial, many of her midwife friends feared that my decision to go to medical school would be seen by many people as an indictment of home birth. It was not. I became an ob-gyn at least in part because a woman's right to choose to have her baby at home was important to me, and I wanted to be sure there were always doctors on call who would support that decision.

I know there were other reasons as well, but those reasons are more difficult for me to articulate: They begin, on some level, with a desire to be around babies that is so strong it may be genetic, but they go deeper still. A need to know without reservation exactly when someone is alive and when someone is dead. Atonement. A desperate distaste for the whole idea of a C-section, combined with an occupation that will demand I perform the operation with regularity. Reparation. Compensation. Justice.

Some of my mother's midwife friends are aware that I have been writing this book, and they fear now that my recollections will be tinged by my profession. In their eyes, I am not the one who should tell my mother's story, and they want me to leave it alone.

If they knew what I know, if they had seen the notebooks and knew that I had stolen key entries, they would be more than fearful: They would be furious. They would most certainly not want this tale told.

But on the second Wednesday of the trial, my mother's story became my story, too. I know now my mother would want our stories told.

She discovered that someone had folded pages from her notebooks the Monday after the trial was over, just after I had left for school and my father had left for his office. Apparently her first thought was that Judge Dorset had removed them from the binder to read them carefully, and he was the one who had creased them. But the idea that the judge had spent any time at all with those entries and then ruled the notebooks were irrelevant didn't make any sense, it didn't make any sense at all. And so the idea crossed her mind that someone else was responsible, and that someone probably was me.

Midmorning she went to the general store for a newspaper, and her suspicions about me grew more pronounced. Toward the end of a news analysis of the trial, one of the jurors brought up the notebooks.

"We all knew the judge was reading her diary during the recess— that was pretty clear," the juror said. "And so we expected we'd get to hear what she'd written. But then the judge read it and didn't see anything incriminating in it. I can't speak for everyone else, but that mattered a lot to me."

When I returned home from school, my mother confronted me. She said she honestly didn't know whether she should be disappointed in me or proud beyond words. On the one hand, she saw in her daughter a teenage girl who would read someone else's private diaries and then have the audacity to break the law and obstruct justice. On the other hand, she was astonished by my courage and the risk I was willing to take on her behalf. She said she loved me either way, but then asked me a question that revealed yet one more emotion churning inside her:

"What do you think now of what I did?"

I told her I was glad she had saved the baby, but my answer was meaningless. We both understood it was the question that mattered, it was the inquiry that made clear the way our lives as mother and daughter were forever changed: I was fourteen years old, and I knew my mother's worst fear.

Before my father came home, my mother actually suggested that I should go forward and confess what I had done. I was a minor; the penalty couldn't be too severe, she said. Reform school, perhaps. She wasn't serious—just as I did everything I could to protect her, as my mother she would do everything she could to protect me—but for a few hours I hid in my room like a scared kitten, convinced that my mother was willing to destroy us both in a policy of familial scorched earth.

And yet she never even told my father what I had done. When she came to get me for dinner, she told me we would never again speak of what had become our crime.

And until she was diagnosed with lung cancer two years ago, we never did. It wasn't until her third afternoon of chemotherapy—one of the days that I drove her to the oncologist in Hanover, New Hampshire, and kept her company while the poisons were dripped intravenously into her arm—that she brought up the name of Charlotte Bedford.

"Is she why you're becoming a doctor?" my mother asked. "Or am I?"

"Both, I guess."

She nodded, and watched the clear tube where it merged with a needle and then her skin.

"I haven't opened my notebooks in years. I boxed them up when you went away to college. You probably knew that, didn't you?"

I rolled my eyes. "I guess I did."

Not long after she paid her fine, my mother returned to midwifery. She lasted almost a year, and for a time her life was filled with activity, if not exactly joy. There were the prenatals and the consultations, the women—sometimes women and men—coming and going at our house. It was clear to us all that she would be able to rebuild her practice.

But then her new clients started coming to term, and she had to start catching babies again. She discovered during her first delivery that the almost bewitching pleasure that birth had once held for her had been replaced by fear. Every time she encouraged a woman to push, she thought of Charlotte; every time she placed a warm hand on a laboring woman's belly, she was reminded of the imaginary line she'd once drawn with her fingernail from Charlotte's navel to her pubic bone.

And so she stopped. She delivered her last baby on a sunny afternoon in early November, after a labor that was intense but short, and largely uneventful. She was home in time for supper, and my father, my mother, and I ate dinner together. We knew it was the last birth, and my father toasted my mother and all of the beauty she'd brought into the world.

For a short while a rumor circulated in Vermont that my mother had left the profession she loved because of some agreement with Asa Bedford. The rumor implied that neither he nor the Fugetts would press a wrongful death civil suit against my mother if she agreed to give up midwifery, but there was no such agreement.

Asa decided against a civil suit almost immediately because—as he was quoted as saying in one article—he was "not interested in knowing the monetary value of my Charlotte's life." Besides, Asa was a good man and he was a minister: He knew as well as anyone to whom revenge really belongs.

Nevertheless, my mother never did catch another baby after that final November birth. Exactly as she had told her own mother she would, she pulled down those prenatal posters and covered the walls of what had once been her office with blue iris paper. She then read in that room and she quilted in that room, and I'm sure when the house was quiet she sat alone in that room and stared at the mountains in the distance. For a few more years she kept writing in her diary in that room.

And then, suddenly, she boxed up the binders and carried them up to the attic. I came home from college the Christmas of my freshman year, and I looked in on her study and saw the notebooks were gone, the shelves filled now with gardening books and decorating magazines.

"Do you know where I put the notebooks?" my mother asked me as the toxins dripped into her arm.

"The attic, right?"

"Right. They're yours if you want them. When the time comes."

I tried to laugh: "Mother, don't be morbid." But as a doctor and an emeritus midwife, we had both done our homework on her cancer, and while we had never verbalized the statistics aloud, we knew the prognosis was bleak. Her particular form of lung cancer was deadly. She had some chance for a brief remission, but virtually no chance of recovery.

"I didn't say the time is coming tomorrow. But I want you to know they're yours. Do with them as you will."

She was told she was in remission a mere four and a half months after her diagnosis, but the remission lasted barely a season, and she died five months after the cancer returned.

Of the men in my life the year I turned fourteen, it is only my father I continue to see regularly. And I have always been blessed to see him a great deal. He still lives in Reddington, and I've joined a practice in central Vermont, and so we've been able to have lunch or dinner at least once a week since my mother died. He no longer works: When my mother was diagnosed with cancer, he sold his part of what had become a fifteen-person firm.

Tom Corts did escape his family's automotive garage. He left for one of the state colleges while I was in high school, and we broke up soon after that. But our paths cross periodically as adults, because he works for a company that designs software for the medical community. He also attended my mother's funeral, a gesture that moved both my father and me.

Tom is married, I am not. Someday I hope I will be, too.

Until recently, I continued to see Stephen Hastings's name in the newspapers and his one-click-above strut on television. No more. Apparently as he has gotten older, he has chosen to do less criminal law.

For a long time my family received holiday cards from his firm every December, and for a few years they included notes that Stephen himself wrote. But then the notes diminished to a salutation, a wish, and a signature, and then the cards themselves stopped coming.

I don't believe my father missed them, but I am sure on some level my mother did.

I have never spoken to the Fugetts, but I did speak once with Asa Bedford. I went to see Mobile and the towns around it like Blood Brook, and I learned that Asa had eventually remarried and returned to the pulpit in an Alabama coastal town called Point Clear. I hadn't gone to Alabama planning to visit Asa, at least not consciously, but when I got there the desire to see him was almost overwhelming, and so I called him from a pay phone at a convenience store.

He said he was in the midst of packing for a ministerial conference upstate, but he certainly had a half hour for someone who'd come all the way from Vermont. He said he and his wife would be hurt if I didn't come by the parsonage. And so I did, and the three of us had iced coffee, and Asa and I spoke of our lives in the years since the trial.

Foogie, I learned, had recently moved to Texas so that he and his wife could be closer to her family. He was about to become a school-teacher. And Veil, the little baby whose life my mother saved, had grown into a handsome young man, who, if he didn't exude such health and vigor and strength, would be the spitting image of his mother.

When Asa walked me to the door of the modest little house, we stood at the screen for a long moment and then he hugged me, patted my back, and wished me peace.

TWENTY-TWO

—from the notebooks of SIBYL DANFORTH, MIDWIFE
March 15, 1981

*The room was really quiet, it was like even the ice and snow
had stopped banging against the window. For a second I was
aware of this chattering and I looked around figuring that Asa
and Anne must have heard it, too. But they didn't, because it
was in my head. It was my teeth.*

*My teeth were actually chattering. The room was per-
fectly warm, but my teeth were still chattering. I looked down
at my hands, and they were trembling so badly the knife was
shaking.*

*And so I inhaled really slowly and then exhaled. When I
cut into Charlotte, I didn't want to be shaking so much I
couldn't control the knife and accidentally hurt the baby. I
then made a line with my fingernail from Charlotte's navel to
her pubic bone, and reminded myself that doctors did these
things all the time without hurting the baby. I've seen lots of
C-sections in my life, because most of the mothers who I transfer to hospitals end up having them, and never once have I
seen a doctor nick the fetus. So I told myself I just had to be
incredibly careful, and then I went ahead.*

*I just did it, I pushed the tip of the knife firmly into the
skin.*

I don't think anyone but me saw the body flinch. At the

time I just thought it was one of those horrible postmortem reflexes that you hear about in some animals, and so I went on. I thought the same thing when there was all that blood, and it just kept flowing.

After all, I'd checked for a pulse and I'd checked for a heartbeat, and there hadn't been one. So how could she have been alive? The fact is she couldn't, I thought to myself, and she wasn't. That's what I thought as I drew the knife down, and I know I was absolutely sure of that then.

But looking back on it now—a day later, after I've gotten some sleep—I just don't know. Whenever I think of that flinch, I just don't know . . .

ACKNOWLEDGMENTS

I AM ENORMOUSLY GRATEFUL TO AN ASTONISHING WOMAN WITH APPARENTLY limitless patience: Carol Gibson Warnock, a midwife who was willing to invite me into her life, share with me the joys that mark her profession, and read this novel in at least a half-dozen stages.

I also want to thank four other experts—now friends—for enduring my questions and inquiries, taking my calls day and night, and also reviewing successive drafts of the story: Lauren Bowerman, chief deputy state's attorney for Vermont's Chittenden County; Kerry DeWolfe, a criminal defense attorney in Vermont's Washington County; Dr. Nancy Fisher, ob-gyn; and (once more) Dr. Paul Morrow, Chief Medical Examiner for the state of Vermont. This is the second story I've told in which Paul's wisdom was a tremendous help.

A variety of books was important to me in my research, but two stand out. Ina May Gaskin's *Spiritual Midwifery* was a beautiful introduction to midwifery and a constant reminder that birth is a sacrament. Likewise, Laurel Thatcher Ulrich's portrait of an eighteenth-century midwife and healer, *A Midwife's Tale,* reminded me of the long tradition of which modern midwives are a small part.

Sibyl Danforth, I am sure, would have read both books and cherished them.

Nine people offered additional literary counsel, medical advice, or both: Dr. Eleanor L. Capeless, Stanley Carroll, Dr. J. Matthew Fisher, Ellen Levine, Russell Luke, Ken Neisser, Nancy Stevens, Dr. Ivan K. Strausz, and Dana Yeaton. And while Lexie Dickerson—now a big girl in elementary school—has not read a word of *Midwives,* the book would have been quite different had she not come home from day care one day entranced by the word *vulva*.

Finally, two women served as midwives for this story from its conception—or inception—and made my labors a dream: Anne Dubuisson and Shaye Areheart, one an agent and one an editor, each the sort of miraculous friend the soul needs.

I thank you all.